RAVE REVIEWS FOR MANDALYN KAYE!

For *BEYOND ALL MEASURE* . . .

"This is the finest and funniest romp of the season . . . Mandalyn Kaye's witty and sometimes uproarious sense of humor adds glitter to this charming romance."

—*Romantic Times*

"A clever witty tale . . . that will delight and entertain."

—*Rendezvous*

For *FOREVER AFTER* . . .

"A glorious Regency romp! Passion, adventure, and romance fill the pages of *FOREVER AFTER.*"

—Susan Wiggs, author of *Miranda*

"Kaye weaves a tale of British intrigue with wonderful flair . . . *FOREVER AFTER* is a wonderful romantic adventure."

—*Affaire de Coeur*

For *THE PROMISE* . . .

"Mandalyn Kaye makes a remarkable debut with this sensual, funny adventurous romance that is a delicious treat for those craving a delightful night's read."

—*Romantic Times*

"A fast-paced, action-packed historical romance that will grab and maintain readers' attention from the very first page . . . Mandalyn Kaye deserves all the accolades she is bound to receive for this entertaining first novel that is nothing short of brilliant."

—*Affaire de Coeur*

ROMANCE FROM HANNAH HOWELL

MY VALIANT KNIGHT   (0-8217-5186-7, $5.50)

ONLY FOR YOU   (0-8217-4993-5, $4.99)

UNCONQUERED   (0-8217-5417-3, $5.99)

WILD ROSES   (0-8217-5677-X, $5.99)

Scandal's Captive

Mandalyn Kaye

Zebra Books
Kensington Publishing Corp.
http://www.zebrabooks.com

ZEBRA BOOKS are published by

Kensington Publishing Corp.
850 Third Avenue
New York, NY 10022

Zebra and the Z logo Reg. U.S. Pat. & TM Off.

First Printing: January, 1998
10 9 8 7 6 5 4 3 2 1

Printed in the United States of America

One

London, September 1818

"Come back to bed, Brandt, or you'll make me pout."

The Earl of Brandtwood continued deftly retying his cravat and raised his eyes in the mirror to watch the nude woman in his bed. Her luxurious pale gold hair was spread over the pillows in tangled disarray, and her voluptuously opulent figure was displayed at its most tempting with his sheets draped just so across her most prominently alluring features. The embroidered Brandtwood crest on his sheets barely covered the rosy tip of one perfectly round nipple. She bent one elegant knee and tipped forward enough to afford him an enticing view of her ample bosom in a manner he suddenly found too practiced and too predictable. He cast an irritated glance at the gold clock on his dressing table, aware that he would be late for his scheduled rendezvous. "Nonsense, darling," he drawled, flipping the end of his cravat through the perfect knot, "you know how I detest pouting women."

Lady Isabelle Rotherton flopped back against the pillows, raising her arms above her head in a lazy gesture meant to seduce and watched him put the finishing touches on his cravat. "I think that's dreadfully ungrateful of you, Brandt. You know how much I risked by coming here tonight."

He reached for his elegantly tailored evening jacket and shrugged into it, straightening his cuffs with a casual precision that betrayed his considerable expertise in redressing himself after countless such occasions in the past. "Then perhaps you should have resisted the temptation and stayed by your husband's side this evening. I'm certain his Lordship would have been delighted to share your bed."

She leaned forward once again. Her breasts swelled from the provocative position as she studied his arrogant profile. His dark hair lay in a silken wave to just below his collar. The starched whiteness of his cravat and evening shirt displayed the handsome bronze skin of his hard-planed face. Even his cynically drooped eyelids couldn't hide his legendary jungle-green eyes, and Isabelle Rotherton fought the urge to shiver under the cool, predatory look he gave her. She was used to lovers who succumbed to her every whim, but from the beginning, the Earl of Brandtwood had been a challenge. Even tonight, she'd risked her reputation by coming alone to his residence in London's fashionable west end. Calling upon years of experience in bringing her paramours in line, Isabelle delicately wet her lips with the tip of her tongue and leaned a bit closer to the edge of the bed. From this position, she knew her figure, the same one men had written sonnets and poems to immortality, fought duels over, and risked their fortunes to see in its current nakedness, was displayed to perfection. He would have to be inhuman to resist her. "The question isn't whether or not Robert would have been delighted, Brandt," she drawled, her voice a sultry whisper in the heavy air. "Were *you* delighted?"

Marcus Brandton raised one eyebrow at her artless question and made a rapid decision. He had enjoyed Isabelle's company for the last four weeks since his return to London for the start of the Season, but she had become too reckless with her affections. He had returned to his residence that evening to replace a cuff link he'd lost earlier and found Isabelle naked in his bed, awaiting his arrival. At the time, his libido had had a great deal to do with his capitulation to her open invitation, but he'd found her behavior to be somewhat presumptuous. While he had been only too willing to take advantage of the pleasure she had offered him, he had no intention of allowing her any proprietary notions.

He suddenly found that the woman who had been flame-hot in his arms only minutes before now failed to stir his blood as she so evidently expected. Perhaps it was that very expectation that smothered whatever passion had previously existed, but in any case, he had no intention of pleasuring himself with Isabelle's voluptuous body again. His lips twisted in a half smile and he watched with some perverse pleasure as her confidence slipped slightly beneath his cold gaze.

"You haven't answered my question, Brandt. Were you delighted when I surprised you tonight?"

She had begun to sound petulant. He noticed for the first time how her heavy perfume clung to the darkness of his room, its suffocating scent invading the privacy of his own sanctum. He lost what little remained of his patience. A second glance at the clock verified that he would indeed be late for his appointment, adding to his growing irritation with Isabelle Rotherton. He despised being late. "Surely I gave you evidence of that a few minutes ago, Isabelle. Now I think you should consider returning to your own bed before your husband comes looking for you."

There was a cold note of warning in his voice that those who knew him well would not have ignored, but Isabelle Rotherton was used to having her way. She tipped her head provocatively and lowered her lashes over her blue eyes. "How can you be so cruel as to turn me out? You know how much I need you, Brandt. I always need you."

The passionate note in her voice, used with that very same inflection, had been known to bring men to their knees for her. She clearly didn't know that Marcus Brandton kneeled for no one. His eyes narrowed. Something dangerous sparked in their green depths. He was well aware that women like Isabelle Rotherton considered taming him a challenge for their feminine prowess. There had been more than enough women in more than enough beds to convince him long ago that his open disregard for the conventions of society, his rakish reputation, his arrogant—almost dangerous—self-possession, and his experienced lover's hand drew women almost irresistibly to his bed. Even had he not possessed an immense fortune, there would have been a steady stream of society's most cultured ladies ready to offer him their charms.

And Marcus Brandton despised the entire lot of them. While he was more than willing to indulge himself in the ample, and ofttimes exotic pleasures they provided, he had not a modicum of affection for any of them. He had a reputation for being brutal, almost cruel in his casual dismissal of his lovers, and while he was unusually generous in the farewell gifts he bestowed upon them, he knew full well they were attracted more to his reputation and the aura that accompanied it than to the man few knew intimately and none fully understood. There was a certain raw, untamed power that lurked slightly below his civilized veneer, and women found the urge to expose that power irresistible.

Yet had Lady Isabelle Rotherton recognized the steel glint in his green eyes—eyes that could reportedly ignite passions so intense and desires so hot that women had been known to abandon more rational behavior in pursuit of their heated look—she might have exercised more caution. But the time for caution was long past, and Marcus was in no mood for feminine theatrics. Isabelle's heated statement still hung in the air, and he leaned back against the dresser, his eyelids drooping cynically, his lips twisted in their familiar laconic slant. "I take it this need you profess to so virulently is the reason for your abandoned behavior this evening."

"Of course, Brandt. You know what Robert would do if he found me here."

Marcus turned slightly and opened a small door in his dressing table. He sifted absently through the contents, his fingers settling on a small black velvet box. He turned back to Isabelle, and found her still propped against the pillows, her blue eyes studying him warily. Marcus tossed the black box casually to the bed and watched it land delicately between Isabelle's ample breasts. "I certainly wouldn't want to be responsible for the interruption of your marital bliss, Isabelle. I've enjoyed our time together, though."

Isabelle's face flushed slightly, and she snatched the box away from her bosom. "Brandt, you can't possibly mean . . ."

"I do mean, Isabelle. Please accept that as my thanks for your generosity."

"You cannot mean this, Brandt. You cannot mean to simply dismiss me with a . . . a token of your affection? I love you."

Marcus nearly laughed. The "token" in that black box had cost almost two hundred pounds. "Don't be trite, Isabelle. I detest trite women nearly as much as I detest pouting ones. You're no more in love with me than I am with you. Now I suggest you get dressed and return to your husband before your precious reputation is spoilt."

Isabelle threw back the sheets and stepped from the bed, her glorious blond hair spilling over her naked shoulders. Few men she knew could remain unmoved by the sight. The Earl of Brandtwood proved to be the exception. She sniffed delicately, fighting an imaginary burst of tears, and reached for his brocade dressing gown that lay casually slung over the arm of the long velvet sofa. "You've hurt me dreadfully, you know? I do love you, Brandt. I can't believe you've done this to me."

His eyes narrowed dangerously and he watched her slip into the long robe and drop the black box into the pocket. His lips twisted cynically. Isabelle was evidently not so grieved as to turn down an extremely valuable parting gift. "I can only hope, Isabelle, that my generosity will assuage some of your grief."

His voice dripped with unmistakable sarcasm. She sniffed again and looked at him closely. "I don't know how you can be so cruel, Brandt."

Marcus's lip curled slightly, his cool gaze sweeping over her insolently as he strode to the door. "I'll expect you to be gone when I return, Isabelle."

He slammed the door behind him and exhaled a heavy sigh.

As a rule, he detested emotional scenes. It had been a mistake, he realized now, to have become involved with a woman like Isabelle Rotherton. She was far too impulsive to be practical about such things, and while he didn't care one whit about his own reputation, knowing full well it could hardly be any worse than it already was, he also didn't relish the thought of some hotheaded husband like Robert Rotherton calling him out to defend his besmirched honor.

Marcus paused briefly to check the time and muttered a silent curse. The unexpected encounter with Isabelle had thrown his schedule awry, and he was a good seven minutes late for his appointed rendezvous with Lady Worthingham. A footman appeared from the shadows of the large foyer and swung open the heavy wooden door. Marcus noted with absent satisfaction that his carriage was exactly where it was supposed to be, the door perfectly aligned with the door of his house. In three strides, he was up the small step and settled inside the comfortable interior of his lacquered carriage. The well-sprung wheels began turning almost immediately, and Marcus reached up to rap sharply on the small hatch with his silver-handled walking stick. The hatch slid open and Marcus saw the fading stars as the sun began to chase away the darkness. He cursed silently, abhorring to be late, and snapped up at his driver, "We're seven minutes behind schedule." He heard his coachman's short answer and felt the carriage accelerate even as the small hatch slid silently shut.

In the quiet darkness of his carriage, Marcus leaned back against the velvet cushions and considered the note he had received from Thacea Worthingham, dismissing his lingering irritation over the incident with Isabelle.

It had been two years since he'd last seen Lady Worthingham. He hadn't known, in fact, that her husband's assignment as a British foreign officer in India had ended until he had received her note that afternoon requesting that he meet her before dawn. The brief request explained that she had something of great importance to discuss with him. There had been no explanation, however, for the odd hour, but he remembered Lady Worthingham had always been somewhat mysterious. When he had first met her, Marcus had immediately decided he would very much like to have an affair with Thacea Worthingham. There had not been time, however, to pursue the notion before she departed with her husband for India. It occurred to Marcus now, with some growing sense of anticipation, that perhaps Lady Worthingham was prepared to start where they'd left off. If she were even half the woman he remembered, the idea was promising indeed.

Marcus leaned forward and jerked back the curtain, increasingly irritated now that he was truly late. He would have Isabelle Rotherton's head if Thacea Worthingham had disappeared once more, having given up hope that he would keep their appointment.

She nearly had, and she sighed in relief when she saw Marcus's carriage round the corner. She pulled her thin wool cloak tighter around her shoulders and sagged back against the garden wall, watching the approach of his carriage. Her slender fingers curled around the hilt of the golden dagger she held and she cast an anxious look over her shoulder for the source of an imagined sound. Only shadows lurked there, and she drew a deep, calming breath, thinking briefly of her brother, Raman.

He would severely disapprove of the business she was about to conduct with the Earl of Brandtwood. She was certain of that. For that matter, she wasn't particularly thrilled about it herself, but as long as Raman remained protected, then even she could dismiss any regrets she might have. She had a few lingering doubts about the wisdom of her decision to solicit the Earl's help. He was, after all, only a passing acquaintance, but desperate circumstances required desperate measures, and in her present predicament, she had seen no other solution. Nevertheless, her fingers curled more tightly on the hilt of the dagger, and she wondered a bit hysterically if his eyes were still that unsettling, impaling shade of green.

When the carriage finally rolled to a stop directly in front of her, she took a deep breath and stepped away from the wall. A footman was already pulling open the carriage door, and Marcus stepped from the dark interior onto the pavement. When his eyes met hers, she forgot to breathe. Even at a distance, the heat of his molten gaze made the color rise in her face.

Yes, Marcus decided, Thacea Worthingham was no less spectacular than he remembered. Her note had been a stroke of exceedingly good fortune. He found he was already looking forward to the rather pleasurable prospect of deepening their acquaintance. She was standing alone, her deep blue cloak pulled about her shoulders, the hood shielding her head from the fine mist that had begun to fall. Marcus stepped forward and extended his hand, a rare smile on his lips. "My Lady, I am delighted to see you again."

Thacea slipped her gloved fingers into his, hoping he would not notice the way they trembled slightly. "Thank you for coming on such short notice, your Lordship. I'm sorry to have disturbed you at this hour of the morning."

Marcus took her small, elegant hand in his and lifted it to his lips. He was pleasantly surprised to find that his memory had not exaggerated the color of her eyes. They had taken him by surprise the very first time he'd met their intelligent, inquisitive gaze. He had expected her eyes to be dark, in keeping with the almost blue-blackness of her hair, but they were the deep, stormy blue of a winter sea. He was absurdly pleased that his memory had served him so well. He hadn't missed the slight tremble in her fingers when he'd taken them into his larger hand, and pressed his lips to her glove, his eyes never leaving hers. He raised his head, but did not relinquish his hold on her hand. "Are you in the habit of meeting your male acquaintances on abandoned street corners?"

She didn't miss the cynical tone in his voice. She pulled ineffectually on her fingers. He tightened his grip. "I am in the habit of doing whatever is necessary," she said shortly, casting a hurried glance over her shoulder. "And if it would not inconvenience you unduly, I think perhaps we should continue our discussion inside your carriage."

Marcus barely resisted the urge to smile at the haughty tone in her voice. She had changed very little indeed since he'd last seen her. The aristocratic lift of her chin, the line of her nose, her proud carriage and the almost arrogant inclining tilt of her head were all still in evidence. But his shrewd eye, well accustomed to monitoring the moods of women, did not miss the nervous way she chewed on her full lower lip. Her eyes still held the tiny spark of fear he remembered. He silently vowed that this time, he would learn its source.

His eyes crinkled in amusement at her near command and the agitated way she tapped her dainty foot on the pavement, clearly expecting him to have played the gentleman and offered his carriage long before now. He inclined his head in a slight nod. "Of course," he said smoothly, turning to let her pass. The black folds of his fur-lined evening cloak swirled about his elegant trousers and boots, and he pressed a hand to the small of her back, gently urging her forward toward the open door of his carriage. "Forgive me for not having thought of it. I, too, will find the privacy useful."

Thacea wasn't entirely certain how to interpret the cryptic comment, and she nearly refused to enter the carriage. Discretion seemed the wisest course of action at the moment, however, so she stepped into the comforting security of the carriage, exhaling a small sigh. At least she was safe within the confining walls. Now, if only the Earl would agree to help her, she might still have enough time to return to George's lodgings in London before her absence was noted.

Marcus settled across the seat from her, and rapped sharply on the hatch. "Drive the block," he said quietly to his driver. When the well-sprung wheels began to turn, he settled back against his seat and crossed his long legs in front of him, wondering just how long he should wait before he pulled her across the carriage and covered her lips with his own. He found he had a growing preoccupation with just how exotic she would taste. Forcing a casual note into his voice, he said, "I cannot believe it has been over two years since I last saw you."

Thacea smiled at him. "Lord Worthingham and I have only just returned to London. George received a duty assignment in India shortly before we left Bath that summer. I regret I was unable to say good-bye to you before our departure."

Marcus leaned back and thoughtfully stroked his chin. He had regretted it as well, but the timing had not been right. Lord George Worthingham had brought Thacea to Bath for their honeymoon, if he recalled, and even Marcus was not so crass as to initiate an affair with a new bride. He much preferred to have them after they were properly settled in with their husbands. "The Indian provinces are rather prestigious within the Foreign Office, I believe," he said. "Your husband must be distinguishing himself rather quickly to have earned such an important location after his first assignment was completed."

Thacea didn't miss the sarcasm in his voice. Marcus had learned in Bath, as had nearly everyone else George occasioned upon, that her husband was fresh off his first Foreign Office Post in Ardahan, a small, independent sheikdom strategically located on the Black Sea. Thacea was a member of the royal family in Ardahan, and George had managed to assure his rapid rise to the top of the embassy echelon by marrying her. He had boasted of the fact rather virulently on their honeymoon, and Thacea had not forgotten the disdainful look Marcus had bestowed on her new husband. "George would like to ascend in the ranks a bit faster, I believe. He has his eye on Paris."

Marcus raised an eyebrow in surprise. "Indeed," he said cynically. "I'm aware of several top-level officials who would like just such an appointment themselves."

Thacea nodded. "Paris seems to be the great plum to them all."

"But not to you?"

She smiled at him. "Contrary to what you might believe, no. Not to me. I have little desire to be trapped beneath the artificial lights of Paris."

Marcus leaned forward, his elbows resting on his knees. "I

can imagine the notion of being 'trapped' anywhere is not one you find appealing, your Ladyship."

She sucked in a deep breath and decided she didn't like the inflection in his voice. In the darkened light of the carriage, Thacea saw the hard planes of his face and wondered again about the wisdom of her choice. Marcus Brandton was a difficult man to know. She had been almost magnetically attracted to him from the very first, and the very madness of that attraction frightened her. Yet, she knew instinctively, that he would not betray her trust. She drew a deep breath and met his gaze. At the unmistakably heated look in his eyes, she felt her skin grow warm. She sent up a silent prayer that the flush in her cheeks would not be visible in the dim light. "I come from a country vast and untamed, your Lordship. The confines of English propriety have presented a somewhat difficult adjustment for me."

Marcus could not help but wonder precisely how untamed she herself was. He felt a growing heaviness in his loins at the thought of exploring that notion. "I can only imagine."

The carriage had begun to grow warm, so she loosened the clasp of her cloak, pushing the hood back from her hair. Marcus's eyes followed her every move, and Thacea felt suddenly transparent. He was deliberately baiting her. She searched in vain for a way to steer the conversation back to more comfortable footing. The moment she felt her sanity returning, Marcus reached up and brushed a stray tendril of her hair away from her cheek. She started under his touch. "Now, Lady Worthingham," he said, his tone maddeningly calm. "I don't believe you requested my presence this morning to discuss the nature of your husband's career or your adjustment to the English world. You said in your note that you needed my assistance. You know I will help you if I can."

His voice startled her back to the moment at hand. Her fingers clasped tightly around the hilt of the golden dagger. How could she have been so foolish as to have forgotten the matter? "I hope you will be able to help me," she rushed out. "I have something I need to sell, and I do not know where to find an appropriate buyer."

Marcus raised an eyebrow. "This is something you thought would interest me?"

She shook her head. "I do not think so, but I did think you would be able to help me fetch a fair price."

His interest was piqued now. "It is something of value?"

She nodded, and produced the dagger from beneath her cloak. "It belonged to my father. I remembered that you and I discussed Eastern Medieval art one evening in Bath, and I had hoped you would know where I could find a purchaser."

Marcus leaned forward and took the dagger, holding it up to the light of the carriage lamp. He remembered that discussion with vivid clarity. Through a great deal of maneuvering, no small amount of which had been spent satisfying Sibyl Heldly's rather insatiable sexual appetite, he had convinced Sibyl to invite George and Thacea Worthingham to her dinner party. A deft change of the seating cards before dinner had ensured that Lady Worthingham would be seated on his right. Despite Sibyl's hostile eye, he had managed to converse with Thacea quite easily that evening, and had found, to his surprised delight, that she had an extensive knowledge on a wide range of topics he found exceedingly interesting. To be entertained, rather than bored, by one's dinner companions, was a rare treat indeed, and it had caused the incident to remain firm in Marcus's mind.

He smiled at the pleasant memory and continued to weigh the dagger carefully in his hand. Its bejeweled handle glistened in the dim glow. "It is early thirteenth century, I believe," he said.

She nodded. "Or late twelfth. I'm unsure. My father swore it belonged to Genghis Khan and was stolen from him during one of his raids." She paused and smiled at him. "Although I suspect that is little more than an Ardani legend created to impress children."

Marcus looked at her and laughed. "And did it make an impression on you?"

"Of course. Had my father told me he had taken it from the Mongol himself, I likely would have believed him."

Marcus weighed the golden dagger in his hand once more and mentally estimated its worth. The gold and jewels alone were probably worth three or four hundred pounds, but Thacea was right in assuming that the weapon's historical value, Genghis Khan's or not, was considerably larger. It was certainly worth at least a thousand pounds, perhaps even more if it were a particularly rare item. She would, however, have considerable difficulty finding a buyer who would give her its worth on such short notice. "Do you truly wish to sell this?"

She shook her head. "I have no wish to sell it at all. It's one of the few possessions I have left from Ardahan." She paused to look at him. She had to swallow hard past the unexpected knot in her throat. "I have no choice."

Marcus studied her carefully. He was aware that the ladies of the ton often gambled among themselves, occasionally running up considerable debts, but he wouldn't have suspected it from Thacea. He found the notion oddly disappointing. "Have you gotten yourself in trouble with the duns, your Ladyship?" he asked cynically. "Under the hatches, so to speak?"

She shot him an offended glance. "No. It's nothing like that. I simply need the money to make a purchase. I had hoped you'd be willing to assist me, but if you aren't, I will . . ."

He raised his hand. "Forgive me. The matter is certainly none of my affair."

Thacea shot him a dry look. "No, your Lordship, it is not."

His eyes glinted with amusement. The royal princess was back in full show. He inclined his head in a slight gesture of defeat. "I will spare you the trouble of pointing out that, in light of my reputation, I don't suppose I've much of a right to stand in judgment. I will, however, be delighted to help you find a buyer. How much will you need for it?"

She accepted his half apology without comment and looked at the object a bit wistfully. "Its value is above price for me. I cannot accept less than five hundred pounds."

Marcus nodded and pocketed the dagger in his cloak. "That should be no trouble at all. I will see to it first thing this morning."

Thacea smiled at him sadly. A hint of moisture stung her eyes. It had all happened much more quickly than she'd imagined. She felt the pain of parting with the family object acutely. There really was no other way around George's requirement for the money. "It already is first thing this morning, my Lord."

He pulled back the curtain, allowing a slender filigree of light to seep into the carriage. Thacea mopped at the tears in her eyes with the back of her hand in a decidedly unfeminine gesture he found strangely endearing. "So it is," he said. "I will see to it, then, as soon as I return home."

She felt strangely relieved to have the matter resolved. She lay her hand on his forearm. "I cannot thank you enough for this, my Lord. I didn't know where else to turn."

Marcus looked at her in surprise as he gave her fingers a gentle squeeze. "I'm pleased you thought of me."

Something odd passed between them at the brief contact. Thacea abruptly dropped her fingers from his arm and reached for her small reticule. "I will give you the address where I can be reached." She studiously avoided his gaze. "I would appreciate it if you would let me know as soon as you have found a buyer."

He accepted the small piece of vellum paper she handed him. "Are you certain there is nothing else I can do for you?"

Had she merely imagined the innuendo in the question? She looked up, drawing in a sharp breath when his green gaze locked with hers. "No, I . . ." she trailed off, unsure what he expected.

"Thacea." His voice felt like warm silk against her taut nerves. "I want very much to . . ." Marcus bit back a curse when the carriage rolled to an abrupt halt, pitching her slightly toward him.

Instinctively, she reached out her hands and planted them on his strong thighs to prevent herself from falling. Even through the warm, fur-lined leather of her gloves, she felt the hard heat of him. She lifted her startled gaze to his, unprepared for the molten look he gave her. She drew in a sharp breath and yanked her hands away, fumbling awkwardly for her reticule. "We must have completed our turn around the block," she said at the same instant he pulled back the curtain to reveal the corner where they'd met earlier. "I must be going. I cannot thank you enough for attending to this matter for me."

One of his footmen swung open the carriage door. Thacea turned to alight. Marcus leaned forward and grasped her hand just before she stepped away from the carriage. Turning it over, he kissed the pulse at her wrist. "I will see you again," he said.

There was no question implied in the simple statement. "Yes. I'm sure you will."

Marcus gave her fingers a brief squeeze before he released them. She stepped away from the carriage, turning to make her way back down the narrow street. She glanced back only briefly when she heard the soft *click* of the carriage door and the snap of the reins. Marcus's elegant carriage disappeared into the fog.

Two

Thacea barely resisted the urge to run after him. With visible effort, she turned and hastened down the street, anxious to slip back into the house before she was missed. George had been out all night. She expected his return shortly after dawn. He would be enraged if she were missing when he arrived at their small lodgings.

She was less than a block from the town house George had borrowed from one of his many London contacts. Thacea hastened across the courtyard, relieved to find the door she'd used that morning still unlatched. If any of the servants had been stirring about, they'd have locked the door. With a little luck, she could return to her room undetected.

She didn't breathe again until she slipped inside the confines of her bedchamber and shut the door silently behind her. The clock on the mantel chimed six o'clock. She'd been terribly fortunate not to have been spotted. Quickly, she removed her clothes and slipped back into her nightgown and dressing gown, carefully placing her clothes back in the heavy wardrobe where they'd been just hours before. With a deep sigh of relief, she crossed the room to push open the heavy wooden casement.

In truth, her encounter with Marcus Brandton had gone even better than she'd expected. She'd been a bit surprised that she was still as attracted to him as she had been at Bath, but if he could truly find a buyer for the dagger, it would solve a great many of her problems.

A sudden memory of the heated look in his eyes forced another sigh from her lips, and she leaned a bit farther out the window and propped her elbows on the sill, resolutely dismissing the image from her mind as she watched the bustle of the awakening city with avid curiosity. The sun had finished its morning ascent only minutes before, but London was already teeming with activity. Handsome carriages, much like the one Marcus used, clipped along the cobbled streets, returning their owners to their London residences after a night of endless parties, gaming, and frivolity. But even as the sunrise signaled the end of a day for the British ton, it was the beginning of a day for the working class.

Market vendors tugged at their colorful carts, piled high with fresh produce and dairy products, while ragged-looking children dashed about between the rolling carriage wheels, searching for dropped shillings and pence among the uneven cobbles. The steady cadence of horses' hooves sounded beneath the quiet din of the street noise, and Thacea laughed delightedly at a small young farmer directly beneath her window. He was pulling on the harness of a very determined-looking mule. She watched him for several minutes, unaware that the connecting door between her room and her husband's had swung open.

"Thacea. Come away from the window. You look like a common street whore gaping out the window like that."

She started visibly at the sound of George's voice and jumped away from the window, pulling the casement shut. "I'm sorry, George. I wasn't thinking." In truth, she'd been thinking rather intently about a pair of jungle-green eyes and the effect they'd had on her. She noticed, belatedly, that George was fully dressed. Perhaps he would be spending the day at the Foreign Office. "Are you going out, my Lord?"

He cast her a disapproving look. "You know I've got meetings at the Foreign Office. I have yet to file my report on my success in India, and I have reason to believe the Regent himself has expressed an interest."

Thacea nodded automatically. Silently, she marveled at

George's arrogance. She very much doubted that the Prince Regent had even the slightest interest in the Under Deputy Adjutant Ambassador's report on the Bangalore Province. "You look wonderfully handsome this morning. I'm sure you'll be a great success."

George's thin lips twisted in what could almost be deemed a smile. He crossed the room to stand next to her. Reaching down, he tugged aside her brocade dressing gown and ran his finger along the lace neckline of her nightgown. Thacea suppressed a shudder at his touch. George's eyes narrowed. He shifted his hand, roughly grabbing her breast in his palm. She gasped at the small spasm of pain, and noticed with some revulsion the desire that sparked in her husband's eyes at the sound. "My bride," he whispered, his hot breath fanning across her cheek. "Did you miss me in your bed last night?"

She had answered this question too many times in the past not to know what the proper lie was. "Of course, George. You know I did."

His lips twisted again. He squeezed her breast harder. "I was with a whore last night," he said casually as his heavy lips slid across her cheek in a wet caress. "She was very lush in her appreciation of me."

"I'm sure she was, my Lord."

His other hand twisted in her hair to pull her head back. He stared down at her, his hand still flexing against her breast. Thacea barely resisted the urge to pull away from the cruel pressure of his hand. This was a new game for George, one he'd begun before they'd left India. George had always been . . . she hesitated before admitting the word . . . perverse in his sexual preferences, but he had only recently begun recounting details of his extramarital activities to her.

Thacea watched him carefully now, uncertain how to read his mood. George had always been unpredictable, and while they were isolated in India, he had grown even more difficult. Thacea remained constantly on her guard with him, never certain what he would demand of her. As long as Raman was in potential danger she couldn't afford to . . . the sound of tearing fabric arrested her attention. She jerked her thoughts back to the present. George had torn the neckline of her nightgown open to force both his hands inside, to knead her breasts. She shuddered, hoping he would misinterpret the involuntary action for passion.

He must have, she decided when he smiled as he dropped his hands. "I will not allow you to tempt me now, my darling," he said, pulling her brocade robe closed over her exposed breasts. "But perhaps I'll make it up to you tonight if you behave yourself at Regina Hawthorne's."

Thacea groaned inwardly. She had completely forgotten that they were expected at the Dowager Duchess of Hawthorne's town house that evening. She managed a slight smile instead and raised her eyes to his. "You know I only want to please you, George. When you are happy, I am happy."

He kissed her briefly, his hard lips moving over hers in a wet, passionless caress. "Make certain you are ready promptly at eight. I do not wish to be late."

"Yes, George." She had to stifle a sigh of relief when he stepped away from her.

"I'll see you later this afternoon then." He made his way to the door. He paused, his long slender fingers on the handle. "And Thacea?"

"Yes George?"

"You have not forgotten the four hundred pounds I require?"

"Of course not. I will have it converted to English pounds by the end of the week."

"Excellent. I hope to have a commission for Paris soon. It will be very expensive while we are here in London."

"I know, my Lord."

"If you have a letter you would like me to post to Raman, perhaps you should give it to me as soon as possible."

Thacea didn't miss the veiled threat in George's tone. "Thank you, my Lord. I will finish it this afternoon."

"Send him my love," George said drily, and pulled the door shut behind him.

She crossed the room to give the bell pull a mighty tug. There was nothing in the world she wanted more at that moment than a hot bath with plenty of soap to wash away the memory of George's touch, but as long as he held Raman's fate in his hands, she had no choice but to surrender.

Three

Marcus pulled his gold watch from his pocket and confirmed he would not be late for his abhorrent duty of taking tea with his mother at four o'clock that afternoon. It was now ten minutes until four, and he leaned back in his carriage, his mind turning for the hundredth time to his earlier meeting with Thacea Worthingham. She had affected him no less acutely than she had two years prior in Bath. And this time, he was determined not to let her slip away. He had returned immediately to his town house, where he'd placed the dagger in his safe, and considered carefully what he should do.

Thacea had made it clear she was loath to part with the item. He was equally loath to make her do so. He knew instinctively, however, that she would not simply accept money from him, nor would she fail to suspect his motives if she knew he planned to purchase the dagger himself. The best course of action, he decided, was to have one of his solicitors notify her that an anonymous buyer had been found, and that the sale price had been one thousand pounds. He would then have the money transferred to her in cash, thereby solving her problem, his problem, and salvaging her pride in the meantime. Satisfied with the plan, Marcus sent word to his London solicitor that he wished the matter to be taken care of that afternoon if at all possible.

That done, he should have been able to dismiss her from his mind, but he found his thoughts haunted by her for the rest of the afternoon. The circumstances surrounding their meeting were strange at best. Her obvious anxiety perplexed him considerably. She had said she needed five hundred pounds for the dagger, and while not really a fortune, it was a rather large sum. He supposed her husband might have gotten himself into debt, but still, it didn't explain why George Worthingham hadn't sold the dagger himself. Nor did it explain why Thacea had clearly been so concerned over the possibility of being caught making the transaction with him. In all, he was deeply disturbed by the entire situation, and determined to unravel its mystery before many more days had past.

Marcus was so lost in his reverie, he was startled when the door of his carriage swung open in front of his mother's house. One of his footmen was watching him expectantly. He stepped down from the carriage, resolutely mounting the stairs to the town house he supplied as his mother's London residence. She had demanded his presence for tea this afternoon, and he dearly hoped he could determine what she wanted as quickly as possible and be done with the entire matter.

The enormous wooden door opened before he reached the top step. Marcus stepped inside. The soft *thud* of his boot heel on the marble floor echoed in the spacious foyer. He looked casually at the butler, and noted absently that he'd never seen the man before. His mother had a great deal of difficulty maintaining servants, and given her disposition, Marcus found it entirely understandable. "I believe her Ladyship is expecting me," he said, handing his hat and gloves to the butler.

"Yes, your Lordship. She's in the drawing room."

Marcus removed his cape with a sweep of his hand, gracefully tossing it to the butler. "Leave those nearby. I won't be here long." He strode purposefully toward the door, his mood darkening with each step.

When he entered the plush room, Marcus's eyes swept over his mother's reclining form, taking in her nearly transparent tea gown. He smiled a bit cynically and wondered what unfortunate young buck was scheduled to follow him in the drawing room.

"Had I known you were dressed for tea, Harriet, I would have carried my hat and cape to the drawing room and placed them inside the door as etiquette dictates."

She looked up from her position on the sofa and shot him a waspish glance. "A custom with which you are clearly familiar. Tell me, Marcus, how many times has the habit saved you from an uncomfortable encounter with a jealous husband?"

"Countless," he answered, crossing the room to settle in one of the leather armchairs. "It allows for a hasty retreat, as you know."

"Really, Marcus," she sniffed. "I didn't invite you here to argue with you. Why must you insist on irritating me?"

With some effort Marcus squelched an insolent retort. He lifted her hand for a perfunctory kiss. "Quite right. It was most ungrateful on my part after you've taken all the trouble to have me in for tea. How have you been, Harriet?"

She looked at him disapprovingly as she handed him a cup of tea. He laced it liberally with brandy from one of the crystal decanters on the beverage cart then leaned back in the chair. She continued to glare at him. "It's most improper for you to call me by my first name, Brandt. I don't know why you can't simply call me *Mama,* as other children do."

He raised one eyebrow. "I was always under the impression you had no wish for Society to know you were old enough to be anyone's mother. Least of all mine."

With a sigh, she plunked her cup down on the low table in front of her. "Really, Brandt, can't you let what's behind us stay behind us? When did you become so hard-hearted?"

"I've always been hard-hearted. You simply hadn't noticed it before."

She pouted delicately and took a sip of her tea. Her eyes carefully watched him over the rim of her cup. "I'm concerned about you, Brandt."

His lips twisted slightly. "That is certainly an unexpected turn of events. You've never been concerned about my welfare before, Harriet. Why begin now?"

"You haven't been yourself, Brandt. Not for the past three or four months anyway. Ever since you brought that street urchin into your house. . . ."

Marcus's eyes narrowed dangerously. "I've told you before, Harriet, Madelyne is none of your concern. I have no wish to discuss the matter with you."

"You're making a fool of yourself. You don't really believe that ridiculous notion that she's your father's daughter?"

"If his sexual exploits were half what yours are, Harriet, I'm prepared to believe he may have a dozen or so other progeny running about. They simply haven't had the good fortune to find me yet."

She exhaled sharply and glared at him. "She's using you, Brandt. Mark my words. She knows you'll support her and that's why she's feigning illness."

Marcus lifted an eyebrow. "I thought that's what relatives were for. They exist to use one another. I have simply accepted my role as the one most often used by nature of my position as the holder of the family purse strings."

"Brandt, be reasonable. If she truly is ill, then she belongs in an asylum. She hasn't spoken since the day you picked her up in that filthy workhouse."

Marcus slammed down his teacup with such force he nearly snapped the fragile handle in two. "I will make that decision. Madelyne is in my charge, and she will remain there until I see fit to do otherwise."

Harriet muttered an exasperated oath. "Why must you be this way? You've always been so difficult to get along with."

"One reaps what one sows." He settled back in his chair, crossing his long legs in front of him. He draped one hand casually over his knee. "Now why have you called me here? Surely it wasn't to express your maternal concern after thirty-two years. Do you need money?"

She flushed somewhat. "No, of course not. You're very generous to me."

"I'm delighted you realize that."

"I need you to escort me this evening. I've been invited to the Dowager Duchess of Hawthorne's conversational soiree this evening. I want to go, and I need you to take me."

"Good God! Is Regina Hawthorne still alive? I would have thought that old harridan had died years ago."

"Brandt! Regina Hawthorne is one of the most respected ladies in the Beau Monde. It would serve you well to remember that."

He leaned back in his chair and studied his mother. She was aging, it was true, but still a uniquely beautiful woman. He knew from experience there were half a dozen or so young bucks more than willing to help her recapture her youth in exchange for the generous lifestyle she afforded them—a lifestyle he paid for by giving her nearly unlimited access to the family fortune he'd managed to triple in the ten years he'd held the title. "Why on earth would you need my escort this evening? Surely one of the young dandies who frequent your boudoir would be delighted to take you."

Her eyes flashed angrily at him. "The Duchess of Hawthorne had a great deal to do with my successful entrée into Society. Had it not been for Regina, I would never have secured a marriage proposal from your father. I would not insult her by bringing scandal into her home."

"I shall have to remember to extend my deepest gratitude for her matchmaking."

"Then you'll take me this evening?"

He sighed heavily, seeing no real reason not to honor her request. He was also aware that Regina Hawthorne's parties were always well attended by the more respected members of the ton, and while he was seldom, if ever, included in that particular circle, he hoped the evening would give him a chance to talk to several of his acquaintances within the Foreign Office and perhaps glean some information about George Worthingham. "I will," he finally answered. "Though God knows what I'll do to prevent myself from dying of boredom."

The Dowager Countess of Brandtwood leaned back on her sofa with a delicate sigh. "Thank you, Brandt. It's very kind of you to agree. Now if you don't mind terribly, I'd like to get some rest before this evening."

Marcus shot her a knowing glance. He set his saucer and cup down on the small table beside his chair with a decisive *clink*. He knew his mother well enough to realize her desire to rest was due to the impending call of her most current lover—a gentleman half her age, no doubt. "Of course, Harriet, I wouldn't want to disrupt your *rest* this afternoon."

She frowned at the insolent comment, but let it pass. "What time will you collect me?"

He pulled out his watch. "I need to call on a certain ballerina I fear is feeling somewhat neglected these days. Will eight o'clock suit your plans for the evening?"

"That will be fine. Thank you."

"Enjoy your afternoon. I'll see you this evening." He let himself out of the drawing room, and strode through the marble foyer, resisting the urge to scowl at the young fop seated outside the library. Harriet's tastes were evidently running younger these days. While he didn't care a whit who availed themselves of his mother's charms, he couldn't help wondering a bit cynically how much the young man's elegantly tailored jacket and breeches had drained the Brandtwood fortune.

He collected his cape and hat from the butler, then stepped outside, drawing a deep breath of the afternoon air. With any luck, the Hawthorne affair would give him some answers about Thacea Worthingham. He stepped into his carriage and decided he must make plans to see her again as quickly as possible. Marcus hesitated only briefly before giving an address to his driver. He would first travel to his house in Chelsea. Odette, the French ballerina who'd been under his protection for the last several months, was proving to be a nuisance. He had neither the time or patience for another of her tantrums. Having already dispensed with Isabelle Rotherton, he was almost free to pursue Thacea Worthingham with a clear conscience. Only Odette stood in his way.

The decision made, Marcus settled back in his carriage and smiled. It was turning out to be a most productive afternoon.

Four

Marcus leaned back idly against the mantel and fought the urge to yawn. The heat was stifling in the crowded salon. The dull ache that had developed at his temple did little to lighten his sour mood. Marcus surveyed the occupants of Regina Hawthorne's salon with something akin to distaste. His gaze swept scornfully over the collection of Society's finest. The very air reeked with a certain stuffy convention that made him yearn to be free of the room. His reputation for decadent parties and scandalous behavior generally excluded him from these types of events. He was beginning to be grateful for the slight offense. It was well known that the shocking nature of his usual associations, and his open disregard for convention of any sort made his presence there a startling contrast to the usual places he frequented; it was nearly laughable. Though he found the startled glances he received, and the dark whispers that hovered around him vaguely amusing, in all, he was bored beyond reason.

He shifted again on his feet, silently cursing the pain in his head. His glance strayed to the clock on the wall. Another two hours, at least, he knew, and then perhaps. . . . His thoughts ended abruptly when the door of the salon opened and Lord George Worthingham stepped inside the room. His wife's delicate hand rested on his forearm.

From his vantage point across the room, Marcus received his first glimpse of Thacea in clear light. The carriage had been so dimly lit that morning, it had been difficult for him to make out her features. It struck him now that she appeared tamer, more subdued than when he'd seen her in Bath, and the notion disquieted him somewhat. Resolutely, he pushed away from the mantel and began to weave his way through the crowd, intent on a closer inspection.

Thacea looked around the room wearily and resisted the urge to groan. Instead, she reached down to brush an imaginary piece of lint off the deep blue fabric of her gown. Her gaze met the sheen of a pair of highly polished boots. "What an unexpected pleasure, your Ladyship," a low voice said.

Thacea recognized Marcus's voice immediately. She hadn't expressly warned him about the secrecy their early-morning meeting required, although she imagined the circumstances must have made it rather obvious. The Earl was an intelligent man, well-versed in societal intrigue. She could only hope that he wouldn't betray her. When she met his warm gaze, she felt reassured by the look in his green eyes. "Your Lordship. How delightful to see you again."

Lord Worthingham abruptly turned around and Marcus smiled briefly at Thacea before turning to look at her husband. "Welcome home, Worthingham. I understand you and your wife have just returned from India."

George Worthingham seemed to fidget a bit under Marcus's disarming stare. He pulled Thacea's hand more securely through his arm. "Yes that's quite right. We have. It's good to see you again, Brandtwood."

Marcus raised an eyebrow at Worthingham's familiar use of his name, thinking that the bastard's arrogance had risen proportionally to his career. "The feeling is mutual, I'm sure."

Thacea looked up at her husband a bit anxiously. "My Lord, do you see the men you wished to speak with?"

He shot her a brief glance. "Yes, I do." He turned his gaze back to Marcus. "I'll see you about town, I'm sure, Brandt-wood."

Marcus felt the corner of his mouth twitch. He stepped for-

ward, lifting Thacea's free hand and pulling it through the crook
of his arm. "Surely you don't intend to steal your wife away so
soon? I'll be delighted to see to her comfort for you."

Lord Worthingham's eyes narrowed and he looked down at
Thacea. An unmistakable hint of malice tainted his gaze. Marcus hadn't missed the way the young diplomat's face had grown
more angular, his eyes almost imperceptibly harder, and the
lines around his mouth more pronounced. His face had a certain
debauched slant that Marcus recognized immediately, having
seen it countless times before. "I wouldn't want to burden you,
Brandtwood. We won't be staying long."

George gave Thacea's hand a brief tug and she started away,
giving Marcus only a wistful glance. His eyes narrowed, but he
conceded the slight battle of wills and settled back against the
wall, watching their progress around the room. He stood, content for the moment, to study her from afar.

It was nearly an hour later when he saw her slip through the
terrace door and make her way into the gardens alone. With a
satisfied smile, he shouldered his way as unobtrusively as possible through the dense crowd.

Thacea pulled the terrace door silently shut behind her. The
crush inside the salon had become too oppressive for her. The
cool evening air was a welcome relief from the heat of the room.
The silver glow of the moon cast delicate shadows among the
trees and arbors of the gardens. She inhaled a deep breath of
the flower-scented air. Gently, she wended her way along the
brick path through the elegant gardens of Hawthorne House.
She was careful to avoid hidden corners and dimly lit passages
as she walked, for it was here in the gardens that dozens of
romantic trysts and forbidden rendezvous took place. She tipped
her head and listened carefully, mindful of the whispered affections riding gently on the breeze. The air was heavy with the
feel of intrigue. It would not have shocked her to come upon
two embracing lovers at any turn in the path. Finally, she found
an arbor not yet claimed for an amorous reunion and slipped
inside its comforting shelter. She leaned back against a tree,

turning her face to the stars, and allowed her thoughts to drift to her brother, Raman.

He had been just fourteen when she'd married George, and in the three years since she'd seen him, she wondered how much he'd changed. Raman was a young man now, nearly ready to fulfill his birthright as the Sultan of Ardahan. She knew, though, that her uncle would go to any lengths to retain the throne he now controlled, and Raman must be protected until he was old enough and strong enough to claim his due. Thacea studied the stars more carefully. Raman slept under those stars every night, safe, she prayed, within the confines of a nomad camp. Only George knew where Raman was hiding, and until her uncle posed no threat to her brother's life, she had no choice but to give George what he wanted. She closed her eyes, her thoughts drifting aimlessly in the cold evening air.

"I had nearly given up hope of finding you," Marcus said, stepping into the arbor.

Thacea started. "You frightened me, my Lord. I didn't hear you approach."

"I saw you slip through the terrace door a few minutes ago and followed you outside. I didn't mean to startle you."

She looked at him anxiously, and cast a brief glance beyond his shoulder. "Did anyone see you?"

"Your husband, you mean?" He waited patiently for her brief nod. "Let me reassure you, I am rather skilled at this particular type of meeting. No one will know I am here with you."

Thacea shifted a bit uncomfortably beneath his unwavering stare. "I have yet to thank you for the matter you handled for me earlier," she said. "Your solicitor contacted me this afternoon with a very generous offer."

Marcus casually removed a thin cheroot from his jacket pocket and lit it. The orange glow of the match flared briefly in the darkened arbor. "He found a buyer already?" he asked casually. "How fortunate. I assume the sum was sufficient."

"Oh, yes. I was delighted. He has promised to transfer the money to me in pounds tomorrow afternoon." Marcus nodded briefly as he exhaled a long plume of smoke. Thacea took a deep breath, enjoying the pungent fragrance of his eastern tobacco. It reminded her of Ardahan.

"I'm pleased I could be of assistance," he said. "I was honored, if somewhat surprised, that you chose to take me into your confidence."

Thacea laughed delicately at the cynical tone in his voice. "You may have fooled the ton, my Lord, but you haven't fooled me at all."

Marcus leaned his shoulder against the tree. "What precisely does that mean?"

She studied him thoughtfully, then reached up impulsively to push a lock of his heavy dark hair off his forehead. "You're not so cold as you would have us believe, Lord Brandton," she said, lowering her hand.

"I can produce any number of witnesses to attest to the notion that I'm not cold at all."

Thacea felt a warm flush steal up her cheeks. How she wished he wouldn't insist on trying to embarrass her. "You're likely to offend my sensibilities if you continue on in that vein of conversation. That isn't what I mean at all, and you know it."

He took another long draw on his cheroot. "You don't believe I'm cold?"

She cleared her throat. "I believe that despite your efforts to convince those around you to the contrary, you're not such a hard-hearted person. If you were, you would never have taken the time to know me in Bath."

"Has it not occurred to you that my motivation may have been entirely self-serving?"

Thacea felt her stomach flutter. She cast another nervous glance beyond his shoulder. "I think, Lord Brandton, that perhaps I should thank you now for assisting me with my problem, and then return to the salon before we continue this conversation any further."

Marcus put out his hand and touched her forearm. "What are you afraid of?"

She had to stifle a nearly hysterical giggle. *You, of course. I'm damn near terrified to death of you.* "Nothing. Nothing at all."

His fingers stroked her arm slightly in a warm caress. "Then you won't find it at all disturbing if I tell you the truth about why I pursued your acquaintance in Bath?"

She swallowed a thick knot in her throat and shook her head. "Of course not."

"And it won't disturb you now to learn that my motives are the same?"

She shook her head again, unable to answer him a second time.

His green eyes glittered in the darkened arbor. "I have every intention of making love to you."

Thacea's eyes widened. She felt the inside of her mouth grow dry. She hadn't expected him to be so blunt. She should have known better. She tugged at her arm, relieved when his fingers released their grip. She took several steps back. She had a sudden need to place some distance—even a small amount—between them. She was uncertain whether to be offended at his suggestion, or relieved that he, too, was aware of the attraction between them. She couldn't think at all, though, when he was that close to her.

"Was this to be a onetime venture, or a long-standing agreement?" She heard the breathless tone in her voice and wished she were slightly more experienced at this type of thing. He must think her an idiot.

He was regarding her with an amused glint in his eye that did nothing to lessen her embarrassment. "I had thought perhaps I would ask you to be my mistress as long as we both found the arrangement mutually agreeable."

Thacea shifted uncomfortably. *Why must he be so damned calm about the whole thing?* "And if I refuse? What then?"

"Would you refuse?" he asked, his voice a dark seductive whisper.

Thacea drew a deep breath. "I'm not certain I would find the offer appealing. Especially in light of your reputation."

"But would you refuse?" he pressed.

"If I did, you would doubtless find someone else to fill my place. Probably," she added pointedly, "some other man's wife."

He felt a smile tug at the corner of his mouth at her entirely accurate, if exceedingly impertinent assessment. "Perhaps. Perhaps not. What makes you so certain?"

She leaned forward, her fingers brushing his shoulder. She removed a long, incriminating strand of decidedly pale blond hair and held it up for his inspection. "I used the evidence available, along with a healthy knowledge of your . . . colorful reputation. In any case, strange though it may seem to you, I find the notion of cheating on my husband rather distasteful."

He leaned back against the tree once more and studied her. "Ah yes. George. I'd nearly forgotten." He dropped his cheroot to the ground, crushing the ember beneath his heel. "Can it be that you are so smitten by your husband, that you haven't the need to look elsewhere for . . . companionship?"

Thacea took a deep breath and looked at him frankly. "I'm not prepared to explain myself to you. I hardly think that my relationship with Lord Worthingham can be of any interest to you."

"On the contrary. I find the subject quite fascinating."

Thacea studied him carefully. "You confuse me, my Lord."

"In what way?"

"You are so . . . open about your intentions, and yet, I cannot help but feel you have other motives. There is something else you want from me."

"Aren't most people like that? They tell you one thing and mean quite another."

She managed a slight laugh at that. "But you've got it all backwards. You're supposed to *tell* me you're interested in my knowledge of medieval weaponry, or some such notion, and *mean* you want to make me your mistress."

Marcus laughed softly. "I assure you, my Lady, if I've hidden motives, they haven't anything to do with your knowledge or possession of medieval weaponry."

"Well, that's certainly a relief. I'm afraid we'd exhaust the subject rather quickly." She felt more comfortable with the light banter between them.

The look in his eyes was no less intense. "There is something I do want from you, however."

"Your Lordship, please don't ask me. You've been a good friend to me, and I . . ."

He raised his hand to interrupt her. "You have already indicated to me that your answer to that particular question would be no—at least for the moment. I will therefore refrain from asking it."

"For the moment?" she asked.

He smiled. "For the moment. No, there is something else. Something rather awkward."

Thacea looked at him curiously. *Awkward* was not a word she would have associated with Marcus Brandton. "You have already said, rather bluntly, that you would like to . . ." she paused, too embarrassed to continue, and noticed with some irritation that he appeared to be laughing at her. "What could possibly be awkward after that?" she asked indignantly.

He glanced at his boot tops. "It pertains to my sister, Madelyne."

The turn in the conversation took her completely by surprise. "I was under the impression you were an only child."

"She's my half sister, actually. Her mother was a Russian opera singer. My father fell madly in love with her when I was ten years old."

"They had an affair?"

"A lifelong one. He left my mother and me and disappeared. I did not hear from him again."

He was unemotional in the way he delivered the pronouncement, almost as if he were reading a report from the papers. Yet Thacea heard the lonely little boy, abandoned by his father, behind the blunt statement, and had to stifle an almost physical need to offer him comfort she knew he needed but would not want. "Madelyne was their child?" she asked quietly.

"Yes. I didn't know of her existence until four months ago. It's almost a miracle, really."

"That you found her?"

"That she found me. Evidently, her mother died and sent Madelyne to London to find me. There don't seem to be any other living relatives, and she is only eighteen. She couldn't have survived on her own."

Thacea shook her head. "Her mother took a terrible risk. What if you hadn't accepted Madelyne?"

"Any number of things could have happened. She had with her a letter from her mother addressed to me, explaining the situation."

"Are you certain she's really your father's daughter?"

Marcus nodded. "Completely. I knew it the moment I saw her."

"Then you couldn't have turned her out, of course. It wouldn't have been right."

"Perhaps not, but you're right in saying her mother took a great risk. I might have turned her away."

"But you didn't," she said quietly.

"No. I didn't. I brought her to live with me instead."

"Brought her? I thought you said she found you."

"The details are a bit fuzzy. The best I've been able to determine, Madelyne arrived in London eight to ten months ago. My secretary received a communication from a workhouse on the east side of the city that a woman claiming to be my sister had fallen gravely ill. Under normal circumstances they wouldn't have bothered to contact me, but she had papers, they said, supporting her claim."

"The letter," Thacea said.

"The letter. It isn't uncommon for me to receive these types of notices. When someone has money—particularly a great deal of money—a good number of people suddenly find they are close relatives to that individual," he said drily.

"But you believed this one."

"It's my policy to investigate every relational claim. If I prove the claim to be incorrect, it saves a good deal of trouble later, and if the claim is accurate, they are my responsibility anyway. So my secretary, John Samuelson, traveled to the workhouse to see to the matter. He brought her back that day, completely convinced her claim was valid. After I saw her, I agreed."

"Is she well now?"

He turned his gaze to the stars. "Physically, she is well."

"However . . ."

"However, she has not spoken a word since we brought her to Brandtwood House."

Silence fell between them, and Thacea studied his proud profile in the glow of the moonlight. She had been correct in her earlier assessment. Marcus Brandton wasn't hard-hearted at all. She wondered what was wrong with the ton that they had failed to notice the compassionate streak in his nature. "And what is it you wished to ask of me?"

He looked startled, as if he'd forgotten her presence altogether. "Oh . . . I had hoped I could convince you to call on Madelyne. Perhaps to read to her. She doesn't have any companions, obviously, and I certainly can't fill that role for her."

"But you think I can."

He shrugged elegantly. "You are a lady of the Peerage, not much older than she. You have a cultured voice, an extremely well-rounded education, and considerable knowledge in a variety of disciplines."

"And I have good teeth, too."

He laughed at that. "I suppose it did sound rather like an assessment of a thoroughbred. I didn't mean any offense."

"None was taken," she said softly, admiring the way his eyes twinkled when he laughed. His laugh sounded rusty, as if he didn't use it very often. That was rather unfortunate. It was a nice laugh. "I'm curious as to why you'd want me. Surely there are any number of women in your closer circle of acquaintances who would be appropriate."

He shook his head. "In truth, the notion has just now occurred to me. I've been at a loss as to what to do for Madelyne. I have only just this moment thought of this as a possible solution."

"It wouldn't, I suppose, have anything to do with your previous suggestion?"

Marcus smiled unrepentantly. "I won't deny that I find the opportunity of seeing you once or twice a week, even if we are chaperoned by my sister, a pleasant convenience. It will give me better leverage with which to press my advantage."

She looked at him closely. "At least you are honest."

He nodded. "You will find that is almost always the case. I don't believe in hidden motives, and I find nuances acutely irritating."

"I shall have to give this matter . . ."

"Thacea!" It was George's voice that rang out in the darkness from somewhere farther down the path. She froze, her sharp intake of breath betraying her sudden fear. She had completely forgotten the time, and realized only now how long they'd been away from the salon. George would be furious. "Thacea, where are you?"

She swung around abruptly to Marcus. In the fragrant closeness of the arbor, he felt rather than saw her fear. "Please, he mustn't find us here."

Marcus narrowed his gaze momentarily before stepping out of the arbor and onto the path. The footsteps had drawn quite close. He knew there was no hope of their presence going undetected. "Thacea," George called again. "Show yourself. I know you're out here."

Marcus made a rapid decision. Quickly, he reached for the solid gold fob that held his pocket watch and snapped the fragile chain with a sharp tug. The *crunch* of George's boots on the gravel grated his nerves. Marcus reached briefly for Thacea's hand, stuffing the broken chain between her fingers. "Ah! There it is," he exclaimed. "I cannot thank you enough for having helped me find it."

"Thacea, is that you?"

She looked at Marcus briefly, a flash of gratitude in her eyes, before she diverted her attention to the pathway. "I'm here, George."

George Worthingham rounded the corner and came to an abrupt halt when he saw the two of them together just outside the arbor. "What the bloody hell is going on here?"

Marcus brushed an imaginary spot of dirt off his shoulder. "I stepped out into the gardens for a breath of fresh air and somewhere along the path, the clasp of my watch fob broke. The chain fell to the ground, and your wife generously agreed to help me find it." He extended his hand to Thacea. She dropped the gold chain onto his palm. "I cannot thank you enough for your help, Lady Worthingham. I hope I haven't inconvenienced you."

She stepped forward, linking her arm through George's. "It was no trouble at all, Lord Brandton. I was glad to be of assistance."

Marcus looked at George. "I would have hated to have lost it. It has great sentimental value to me, but unfortunately, I do not see well in the darkness."

George appeared to be somewhat flustered by the logical explanation and the evidence of the obviously broken fob. He turned to look at Thacea. Marcus watched with some irritation as his eyes narrowed on her in a gaze that was somehow menacing. "You shouldn't have been out here alone, my love. You know how I worry about you."

"I know, George. Of course I know. It was just so hot in the salon, and I needed some air. You know how unused I am to large crowds."

"Well, you should not have been gone so long," George said, petulantly.

"That's entirely my fault, Worthingham," Marcus interjected. "I believe your wife was on her way back to the salon when she found me looking about for my fob. I deeply regret if I've caused you any concern."

George looked at Marcus. Thacea watched nervously as her husband cowered. "Well," he said, visibly flustered, "I suppose there is no real harm done."

Marcus smiled at him. Thacea thought that it looked very much like the smile a lion gave his prey before he devoured it. He turned to lift her hand to his lips for a perfunctory kiss. "Thank you again, my Lady, and I hope you will give careful consideration to my suggestion."

She nodded. "I will do that, my Lord. I'm glad we were able to find your fob."

"As am I." He looked at George once more. "Thank you again, Worthingham. I'm sure I'll be seeing you about. You are in London for a while before your next assignment? I believe someone told me you were to be stationed in Egypt?"

His voice was so polite, Thacea had to stifle a laugh. George would be incensed with the suggestion that he might receive a duty station as unprestigious as the Near East. "It hasn't been decided," he snapped. "I am under consideration for Paris, and I have it on good authority that I am near the top of the Regent's list of candidates."

Marcus let out a low whistle. "Paris? Well, that is something. But if you are only near the top, and not at the top, don't you fear losing the assignment?"

George glared at him. "I haven't made my case to the Foreign Office yet. I have every confidence I will procure the position once I do."

Marcus regarded him with a sly smile. "Perhaps I will put in a good word for you with my contacts at the Foreign Office. I'm sure it couldn't hurt."

Thacea coughed, aware that George was seething at the condescending tone in Marcus's voice. She felt his arm tense beneath her hand. "Thank you for the offer," George bit out. "It's very generous of you."

"It was the least I could do after your wife was so kind to me this evening." He turned his gaze to Thacea, and she felt its heat all the way down to her toes. "Good night, Lady Worthingham."

"Good night, your Lordship."

Marcus disappeared down the brick path. "We're leaving," George said through clenched teeth. Thacea followed him resolutely back to the salon.

George did not speak to her again until they were settled inside his carriage. He sat across from her, and lit a wide cigar, his eyes glittering angrily. "Did you have an enjoyable evening, my love?"

Thacea knew he was angry. Mentally, she braced herself for the confrontation. She leaned back in the carriage to study her husband's features. He had been drinking heavily throughout the long evening, and she knew that was contributing considerably to his dark mood. "I thought the evening went very well. Didn't you, George?"

He shrugged and took another long draw on his cigar, the brief flare of amber flame casting his angular profile into prominence in the darkened carriage. "I suppose. It would have been much more productive if I hadn't needed to waste time searching for you in the gardens."

"I'm sorry. I lost track of time."

"You should not have been out there alone with Brandtwood. You know better."

"Yes, George."

George exhaled a heavy breath. Thacea smelled the whiskey all the way across the carriage. "I don't like that bastard. He's an arrogant son of a bitch."

"I don't know him as well as you do," Thacea said. "I've only met him a few times. The first time was while we were at Bath, and then again tonight."

George shook his head. "He was too accommodating when we were at Bath. Almost too friendly. I think perhaps he wants something from me."

"Perhaps."

George seemed to consider the matter thoughtfully. "That

would explain his offer to speak to his contacts at the Foreign Office about my Paris appointment."

"Do you think perhaps he can help you?"

He shot her a quelling glance. "I don't need any help—especially not from the likes of Marcus Brandton."

"Of course not, George. I'm sorry."

"At any rate," he continued, "Brandtwood's an unpredictable fellow at best. I'd certainly like to know what game he's about." He leaned back against the seat and shut his eyes, clearly through with the conversation.

Thacea continued to study him, uncomfortable in the prolonged silence, until a sudden thought occurred to her. "George?"

He opened his eyes and cast her an irritated look. "What?"

"Something . . . something just occurred to me."

"I've developed a monstrous headache, Thacea. Is it important?"

"It may be," she said cautiously. "Do you remember what the Earl said to me when you arrived?"

"I'm through with this discussion."

"I know, but you said you were interested in his motives. I thought this might help."

George regarded her frankly. "What might help?"

"Do you remember he asked me to carefully consider his suggestion?"

"Yes. Yes, I do remember now. What the hell did he mean by that?"

"He has a sister—a half sister really—who is quite ill. He asked me if I would be willing to call on her and read to her twice a week."

George looked at her suspiciously. "Why on earth would he want you of all people? You hardly know the man."

She shrugged. "I don't know. Perhaps he thinks it will enable him to get what he wants from you."

She watched George closely, silently hoping his arrogance would override his suspicious nature and he would agree to the suggestion. It would be a welcome respite from George's oppressive household to call on Madelyne Brandtwood. She was certain her nervousness was in anticipation of George's response; that the dampness of her palms and the flutter in her stomach had nothing whatsoever to do with the thought of seeing Marcus Brandton again.

The silence seemed to drag on eternally before George spoke again. "Yes," he said thoughtfully, drawing once more on his cigar. "Yes, I believe you're right."

Thacea took a deep breath and smoothed her palms on the soft wool of her cloak. "Then would you like me to notify him that I would be willing to call on his sister?"

George nodded briefly. "Yes. I want you to do that first thing in the morning."

She stifled a contented smile. "I will do it, George—first thing tomorrow."

He dropped his cigar to the floor of the carriage, ground it out with his heel, then reached across the darkness and laid his hand against her face. He caressed the high bone of her cheek with the pad of his thumb. "It's been a successful evening thus far, Darling. Thank you for not angering me."

"You know I try not to."

His fingers tightened momentarily against her face. She resisted the urge to pull away from the bruising grip. She felt the hot, whiskey-laden caress of his breath fan across her face. George leaned forward to press his lips to hers in a hard kiss as the carriage rolled to a stop in front of their London residence. He dropped his hand and leaned back as the door was swung open by a footman. "I won't be coming in with you," he said, reaching into his jacket pocket for another cigar. "I have a liaison with Claudette Castlebury this evening."

Thacea turned to smile at him as she alighted to the pavement. He was right. It was turning out to be an enjoyable evening after all. She was ecstatic beyond words that anyone other than she would be the recipient of George's amorous affections. "I shall miss you, George," she said with practiced precision, and wondered why he still believed the words after so many times.

His lips curled in a slight smile. "Perhaps I can make it up to you later in the week."

"Perhaps," she said, and turned to walk up the stairs.

When she was finally settled in her room for the evening, she went to her desk to write a long letter to Raman. It felt wonderful, she told him, to have a friend—someone she trusted as much as she trusted Marcus Brandton. The letter rambled on for several pages about London news and gossip, and then she concluded it with her usual promise:

> *As usual, I will go to sleep dreaming of you and Ardahan, anxiously awaiting the day when we can be together again.*
>
> *Your loving,*
> *Thacea*

Her dreams that night, though, were not of Ardahan or of Raman. Instead, they were dominated by a pair of jungle-green eyes and a voice as smooth and warm as heated silk.

Five

Thacea awoke the next morning with a smile on her lips. She couldn't remember the last time she'd felt so content. She rolled over and stretched her arms above her head, luxuriating in the warm rays of sunlight that stretched across her bedcovers. This morning she would call on Lady Madelyne. If all went well, it would be the beginning of a new adventure. The thought of having something to look forward to, of being free of George's ever-watchful eye and the speculative looks she received from his servants, was exhilarating.

It took her nearly twice as long as usual to dress. She wasn't certain what to expect from Marcus's sister. She changed gowns three times before she decided on one in pale blue with navy insets at the shoulders and skirt. It was a relatively new gown she'd had made just before she and George had left India. She especially liked the way the color heightened the deep blue of her eyes. Her eyes had never been blue enough to suit her—always looking more like charcoal grey in her opinion.

She struggled for a while with her hair, finally managing to twist the heavy black waves into a plait of passable neatness. She had never had a lady's maid—not trusting George's servants any more than she trusted George.

It was nearly ten o'clock when she left the house. She knew George would sleep for at least another two hours—even more if he'd continued drinking once he'd left her the previous evening. There was nothing to stand in the way of her morning. She scooped up her letter, on the way out the door, pausing only briefly in the library at George's desk. She wrote him a short note telling him she'd gone to call on Marcus Brandton and asking him to post her letter to Raman, then called for the carriage and gave George's driver the address for Brandtwood House.

Marcus's house was as impressive as its owner. Thacea stepped inside the enormous wooden door. Her eyes widened slightly at the size of the immense foyer. It was lavishly appointed with rich tapestries and paintings, completely tiled in black marble. It was so overwhelming, it took her several long seconds to focus on Marcus's butler. She gave him an embarrassed smile and handed him her card. "I am Lady Thacea Worthingham. I'm here to call on Lady Madelyne."

The butler looked at her curiously before he accepted her cloak. "His Lordship is in the library," he said. "I will let him know you are here." He hurried off before she had the chance to thank him. Thacea stood rather nervously, smoothing an invisible wrinkle from her gown. It occurred to her for the first time that she should have arranged a time with Marcus before she simply turned up on his doorstep. He likely wouldn't appreciate her unannounced arrival. She had no way of knowing if his sister was even well enough to receive guests in the mornings. After all, Marcus had said that . . .

"His Lordship will see you, Lady Worthingham."

Thacea started at the butler's voice. "Thank you," she said, wondering why it was suddenly difficult to catch her breath.

She knew when she entered the library. Marcus was standing in front of his desk, a broad, welcoming smile on his handsome face. His skin looked even more bronzed than she remembered against the starched whiteness of his intricate cravat. The deep green of his whipcord jacket set off the breadth of his shoulders. His burgundy waistcoat tapered neatly at his waist. Fawn-colored trousers were tucked into perfectly polished Hessians. The moment she saw him, she stopped breathing altogether. The entire morning snapping into sudden, startling focus. She quit pretending she'd spent so much time with her hair and her gown for any other reason than the appreciative look in those heated green eyes that had haunted her dreams for the better part of the night.

The butler left them alone and the door clicked silently shut. Marcus walked forward to lift her gloved hand. His lips moved against the sensitive strip of exposed skin between the cuff of her glove and the hem of her sleeve. He looked up at her, his eyes glittering in the sunlight flooding in through the windows. "Good morning." His voice had the same seductive tone she remembered from the arbor.

She released the breath she'd been holding. "Good morning."

Marcus slowly released her hand. "I'm very glad you're here."

She took a hasty step backward to place some distance between them. "I only just now thought of the notion that I should have contacted you before I arrived unexpected on your doorstep. You may have other plans for the morning." She knew she was rambling, but wasn't entirely certain what to do about it. The look in his eyes unnerved her. She barely resisted the urge to glance down and check her appearance.

Marcus shook his head. "I couldn't be more delighted. I thought of you all night."

Thacea felt her mouth go dry. She simply couldn't tell him she'd thought of him all night as well. She must make it clear that she wasn't any more open to his advances now than she had been the night before. "I dreamed of you," she blurted out, horrified the moment the words escaped.

Marcus laughed delightedly as a delicate blush swept over her face. "Well, that is certainly a step in the right direction." He indicated one of the chairs. "Please make yourself comfortable. Would you like something to drink?" He retrieved his cup and saucer from his desk and set them on the low table in front of her.

Thacea settled into the chair, grateful for the turn in the conversation. "Coffee would be lovely. Thank you." While he poured, she studied the room. The library was as impressive as the foyer had been. She noticed several priceless paintings before he reclaimed her attention and pressed the saucer into her hand. She set it on the table, then carefully removed her gloves. "Are you quite certain the time is convenient for you?" She slipped her gloves into her reticule. "It wouldn't be any trouble for me to return later in the day."

Marcus settled on the long sofa across from her. "It's no trouble at all. I had just finished going over some correspondence with my secretary, and was on my way up to see Madelyne. I generally try to visit with her in the morning, before there are too many demands on my time."

Thacea felt a smile tug at the corner of her mouth. She wondered if perhaps she should remind him that coldhearted men didn't make time in their busy schedules to visit with ill relatives. She took a sip of her coffee instead. "Will this normally be the best time then?"

He shrugged. "It's hard to say. Madelyne is . . . unpredictable. Some mornings she is alert and in good humor, and other mornings, she barely seems to recognize me. I'm not entirely certain what you are expecting."

Thacea smiled. "My father used to say, 'it is unwise to enter a camel dealer's tent expecting to find anything other than a Persian carpet.' "

Marcus blinked. "I beg your pardon?"

She laughed at his baffled expression. "It's an Ardani proverb. I suppose it loses something in the translation."

"It must," he said drily.

"What I mean to say is, Lady Madelyne is your sister. Therefore, I expect to find her to be much like you. In Ardahan, as in most of the Near East, camel traders are very wealthy, and very shrewd. Persian carpets are made of the finest weaves and finest dyes available. While most camel dealers will wear ragged clothes and live in ragged tents to convince their customers that they are hardworking merchants, they will settle for no less than Persian carpets in their homes. Even if the carpet appears to be of lesser quality, if you flip the corner and look at the underside, you will find it is Persian after all. So where your sister is concerned, I suspect I will find she is really as finely crafted as you are, no matter what her appearance."

Marcus studied her, his expression pure astonishment. Abruptly he rose to his feet, extending his hand to assist her. "My Lady, I believe that is one of the nicest compliments I have ever received."

She slipped her hand into his, allowing him to pull her to her feet. "Now you are flattering me."

"I most certainly am not." He pulled her hand through his arm. "Though if you'll promise me I can advance my cause by doing so, I will begin the practice immediately."

"You are indeed hopeless, Lord Brandton. I am beginning to understand why you have developed such an extensive reputation."

His eyes met hers. "Could we not forget," he said quietly, "about my past, and concentrate, for the moment at least, on the focus of my future attentions?"

Thacea drew a deep breath and ran her tongue nervously over her upper lip. "I . . . I think perhaps it would be best if we visited your sister now."

Her eyes pleaded silently with his. He hesitated for a moment before he raised her hand for a brief kiss. "Your wish is my command, my Lady."

They walked in silence through the foyer and up the long wooden staircase. Thacea's fingers tingled where they rested on the green whipcord of his jacket sleeve. When they reached Madelyne's door, he paused to knock twice before he turned the latch. The room was brightly lit, completely dominated on its far side by three enormous windows extending from ceiling to floor. Madelyne was seated next to them, staring silently out the window. She did not look up until they reached her side, and Marcus laid his hand on her shoulder. "Madelyne, I have brought someone to see you."

Madelyne turned her head. Thacea nearly gasped at the almost startling resemblance between sister and brother. Her hair was cut short, and it lay in crisp dark waves to her shoulders.

Her face was classically carved, just like Marcus's, and her eyes were the same, unmistakable shade of green. Marcus had been right. There was no doubt whatsoever that she was his sister.

"The resemblance is rather unsettling, isn't it?" Marcus said quietly.

Thacea slipped her hand from his sleeve. "Definitely Persian," she said, seeing his smile from the corner of her eye. Madelyne was regarding her curiously. Thacea took one of her hands. "Good morning, Madelyne. I'm Thacea Worthingham. I'm delighted to meet you."

Madelyne studied her for several long seconds before she turned her anxious gaze to Marcus. He smiled at his sister, then settled down in the chair next to her. "Madelyne, Thacea is my friend. I've asked her to come here twice a week or so to keep you company." She grabbed his arm, a worried expression in her eyes. He shook his head. "No, of course I won't stop coming myself. I simply thought you might like someone else to talk to."

Thacea noticed that Madelyne's fingers seemed to relax a little on Marcus's sleeve. She sat down in the remaining chair and studied the girl carefully while Marcus continued to talk to her. She was unquestionably beautiful, her classic features and strong coloring a match for Society's finest. There was something disturbing about her appearance, though, and it took Thacea several minutes to put her finger on it. It was her gown. It was white muslin, spotlessly clean, and hopelessly out of fashion. Surely Marcus hadn't . . . Thacea's eyes widened with the realization that evidently he had. Marcus had brought Madelyne to live with him and failed to buy her a wardrobe. She suspected the dress had been purchased from one of the maid servants in the household and was likely one of only two or three that Madelyne owned.

"Madelyne," Thacea said abruptly. Both Marcus and Madelyne looked up in surprise. She smiled reassuringly at Madelyne. "Would you like some new gowns?"

Madelyne's eyes widened. Marcus cast Thacea a puzzled look. "What are you talking about?" he asked.

"My Lord, surely you haven't brought your sister here to Brandtwood House and not supplied her with a wardrobe?"

"She has clothes."

Thacea snorted. "She has muslin dresses, and not more than three at the most, I'll wager. Good Lord, Marcus. What were you thinking?"

A hint of a smile tugged at the corner of his mouth. "I was thinking that Madelyne hasn't been well enough to go anywhere, and wouldn't need anything other than what she has."

"That's a ridiculous notion. She wouldn't want to go anywhere dressed like that." Her gaze turned back to Madelyne's. Thacea had to stifle a laugh. She looked completely appalled that anyone would speak to her brother in that tone. "Isn't that so, Madelyne?"

Madelyne blinked several times. Marcus's expression turned contemplative. "I must admit, the thought never occurred to me."

"Well it certainly should have. I shall have to see to the problem right away." Madelyne's fingers closed tightly on Marcus's sleeve. Thacea saw the action and pressed, "It isn't, after all, a matter of expense is it?"

"Good God, no!" He shot her an offended look. Madelyne's grip relaxed.

Thacea pulled her gloves from her reticule, then slipped them on with practiced precision. "Well, in that case, we can't waste any more time. Madelyne and I will be going out for the remainder of the afternoon. I'd be grateful if you would provide us with two maids to accompany us."

With an amused glint in his eye, he rose to his feet. "I shall see to it directly."

"Thank you," she said, with a brief nod in his direction before she gave Madelyne a satisfied smile.

"I have a feeling I will regret this immensely," he said.

"Oh, I think not," she shot back, linking her hand through Madelyne's arm. "I don't think you'll regret it at all."

Six

Thacea couldn't remember the last time she'd enjoyed herself as much as she did that afternoon. For four glorious hours, her mind was taken completely off her own worries and focused on the pleasant task of spending an unlimited budget dressing someone as lovely as Madelyne. Occasionally, her fingers would curl enviously into a piece of heavy silk or crushed velvet, but she dismissed the notion as quickly as it occurred to her. She hadn't been able to afford any but the least-expensive clothes since she'd left Ardahan, and there was no sense in brooding over it.

Under Thacea's direction, Madelyne was fitted for day dresses, tea gowns, evening gowns, riding habits, and outfitted with endless pelisses, reticules, gloves, parasols, bonnets, cloaks of every shape and description, and an extensive collection of undergarments. When they were finished, her wardrobe consisted of every imaginable garment a young debutante could possibly need, and a good many more besides. Thacea smiled in open appreciation when one of Madame Drussard's seamstresses put the final touches on the gown Madelyne was to wear home. The rest of the wardrobe would be delivered later, of course, but Thacea had insisted that her young charge must have a gown to wear back to Brandtwood House. At the mention of the Earl's name, a gown had miraculously appeared. The seamstress had altered it to fit Madelyne that very afternoon. An intricate gown, it was, perhaps, a bit fancier than Thacea would have chosen, but she couldn't deny that Madelyne looked radiant in it. It was white, befitting her status as a debutante, but the shoulders were trimmed in emerald green velvet ribbons that brought out the color of her eyes. The matching bonnet framed her dark hair and oval face, and even the seamstress appeared somewhat amazed at the obvious transformation. Madelyne was beautiful.

Thacea gave her hand a reassuring squeeze as she left final instructions with Madame Drussard. When they climbed back into Marcus's carriage, Madelyne sat across from Thacea, who was nervously twisting the handle of her reticule. Thacea stilled the action with a brief pat of her hand. "You look beautiful, Madelyne. Marcus will be very proud of you."

A dubious expression danced across her face. Thacea nodded. "He will. You'll see." Madelyne clearly didn't believe Marcus would be pleased at all, but Thacea leaned back in the carriage to watch Madelyne contentedly. From what Marcus had told her, the girl had shown more personality and interest today than she had since she'd been at Brandtwood House. By the time the carriage rolled to a stop in front of Marcus's home, Thacea was feeling immensely pleased with herself.

Inside, she handed her cloak to the butler and waited for Madelyne to do the same. She felt a smile of satisfaction tug at the corner of her mouth when she saw his eyebrows lift slightly over his otherwise expressionless face. "Is his Lordship about?"

"Yes, my Lady. He's in the library with Mr. Drake. He asked to see you as soon as you returned."

"Thank you." She linked her arm through Madelyne's. "Now, Madelyne." She tugged the reluctant girl along as she followed the butler to Marcus's library. "Stop frowning. You've nothing to worry about."

The butler pushed open the door and announced them. Thacea and Madelyne stepped inside the well-lit library. There was a long moment of silence, when Thacea nearly lost her nerve. Then she heard Marcus's low, irreverent whistle. "Well,

I'll be damned." He set his brandy down on the mantel, then crossed the room. "I believe you've worked a miracle."

Thacea released her hold on Madelyne's arm. "Don't be ridiculous. The ingredients were there all along. You just don't recognize a Persian carpet when you see it."

"Where on earth have you been hiding this treasure, Brandt?"

Thacea noticed the other young man in the room. The butler had told her Marcus was with a guest. "If this is a bad time . . ." she began.

"Certainly not," the young man said. "Brandt's been keeping secrets from me, and I don't intend to be left in the dark any longer."

Marcus gave Thacea a grateful look before he turned his attention to the other man. "All right, Peter, I suppose I can't keep this from you. Peter Drake, this is Lady Thacea Worthingham." Peter stepped forward and lifted Thacea's hand for a brief kiss. "And this," Marcus continued, "is my sister, Madelyne."

Peter Drake's surprise registered on his handsome features. "Brandt, I thought you said . . ."

Marcus cut him off smoothly. "Now, you know why I've been keeping this so private. I didn't want every buck and dandy in London beating my door down."

Peter lifted Madelyne's hand and held it considerably longer than was conventionally acceptable. Thacea noted with some pleasure the delicate flush that covered Madelyne's face, and the frown that marred Marcus's. She stepped forward to touch Madelyne's elbow. "Madelyne?"

The girl seemed to reluctantly turn her attention from Peter to look at Thacea. "Are you tired?" Madelyne hesitated only briefly, then nodded. "Then perhaps you'd like to rest before dinner." Madelyne nodded again and turned toward the door, only then realizing that Peter Drake hadn't let go of her hand. Marcus's frown deepened to a scowl. Thacea had to bite back a delighted laugh. Peter released his hold, and Madelyne smiled at him shyly before she walked over to kiss Marcus on the cheek. With a final shy glance at Thacea, she slipped from the room, pulling the door silently shut behind her.

Marcus exhaled a deep breath and looked at Thacea. "I cannot thank you enough. She looks better than she has in weeks."

Peter Drake shot Marcus an exasperated look. "Good God, Brandt! What were you thinking keeping that girl under lock and key? She'll set Society on its ear."

Marcus glared at him. "It isn't as if I've been holding her prisoner, Peter. She's been quite ill."

"She doesn't look ill to me," Peter muttered, earning himself another dark scowl from Marcus.

"And I'll be damned," Marcus continued evenly, "if I'll have some fop like you pawing all over my sister."

"Well, that's a fine way to talk to your best friend."

Thacea laughed delightedly. The soft sound captured the full attention of both men. "Gentlemen, I believe it's a bit early in the game for this conversation. The Earl is absolutely correct. Madelyne has been quite ill, and it will be some time before she's well enough to make a debut. Don't you agree, my Lord?"

Marcus nodded. "Absolutely."

Peter glared at him. "Well, Society or not, I've met her now, and you're not going to keep me from seeing her again. It suits me just fine if she doesn't debut. I won't have to fight my way through a crowd to see her when I want to."

"Only through me," Marcus bit out.

Peter laughed as he walked toward the door. "I'm not afraid of you, Brandt. I've known you too long to believe you'd actually do anything to me."

"I'm not bluffing, Peter."

"No, of course you aren't," he conceded, shooting Thacea a knowing look. "It was a pleasure meeting you, Lady Worthingham. I trust I will be seeing you again?"

"As I am to be Lady Madelyne's chaperon and companion for the time being, I trust you will. I warn you, though, Lord Brandtwood isn't the only one who stands between you and Madelyne."

Peter rolled his eyes and tugged open the door. "That *truly* frightens me." He looked at Marcus. "Are we set for tonight? Eight o'clock?"

Marcus nodded briefly. "That will be fine."

"All right then. I'll see you this evening." He paused once more to nod at Thacea. "Good day, Lady Worthingham."

"Good day, Mr. Drake."

When Peter Drake left the library, Thacea heard Marcus grunt when the door clicked shut. "Insolent fop," he grumbled.

Thacea smiled at him. "He seems quite taken with her."

"It will last only until he sees the next beautiful woman."

Thacea tipped her head to one side. "She is beautiful. Isn't she?"

Marcus walked forward to take her hand in his. "She is. The outing seemed to do her a world of good. I can't tell you how grateful I am."

"I can't remember the last time I enjoyed myself more. I'm afraid we put a rather large dent in your pocketbook."

His thumb lazily caressed her hand. She wondered if he had any idea what he was doing to her. "I assure you, if the rest of the wardrobe is comparable to what I've just seen, I won't regret a cent of it."

She tugged ineffectually at her hand. He increased the pressure of his fingers. "I'm glad you're pleased."

"I'd be more pleased if you'd agree to ride with me tomorrow morning."

She looked at him in surprise. "I can't."

"You can't, or you won't?"

"I can't. I can't be seen with you. Surely you know that."

"We don't have to be seen. I have a private green that's only a seven-minute carriage ride from here, where I exercise my horses. You could meet me there tomorrow morning. No one will know we've been together."

"And how am I supposed to arrive there? Do I simply wish myself into your presence?"

"Do you?"

She blinked. "Do I what?"

"Wish it." She had no answer for that. Marcus let her off the hook. "Don't you have a servant you trust to bring you? Tell your husband you've gone to your dressmaker."

She shook her head. "They are George's servants. All of them. If I used a carriage, he'd know by tomorrow afternoon I'd been with you. I won't risk that."

Marcus finally released her hand and looked at her intently. "If I can arrange it so he won't know, will you ride with me then?"

"Even *you* can't do that, my Lord."

"Will you?" he pressed.

She looked at him skeptically. "You can't, you know?"

"But will you?"

She paused as she considered it. It was impossible, she knew, but it was a very pleasant daydream. "All right. If I know I won't be betrayed, then yes, I'll ride with you." His eyes sparked triumphantly. She shook her head. "I'm warning you, my Lord, I won't risk it if I have even the slightest doubt."

Once more, he raised her hand to his lips and lingered on the soft skin. "My Lady." He lifted his head. His gaze locked with hers. "You will soon learn not to give me a challenge. I'm very used to having my own way."

Thacea looked at him a bit dubiously as she tugged her fingers free from his grasp. "Then you are about to be disappointed, your Lordship."

Seven

It was well after four o'clock when Thacea arrived home. She was more than a little relieved to find that George had been gone since before noon and not returned to the house. She passed a pleasant afternoon in her room writing a long letter to Raman and reading a book she'd been saving for just such a day. When the clock on her mantel chimed eight, she looked at the fading sunlight in surprise. She hadn't realized the hour had grown so late.

In truth, her mind hadn't been on the book. She'd only turned four or five pages since she'd begun. Her thoughts continued to stray to the forbidden prospect of riding one of Marcus's horses. He would own superior horseflesh. She had no doubts on that count. It had been years since she'd ridden a spirited mount. George didn't believe it was ladylike for women to ride fiery mounts. He'd restricted her to dull-witted mares with little more than a trot in their temperaments.

Her eyes strayed to the window. She stared out into the fading light, remembering the lost joy of galloping across the open desert of Ardahan. Resolutely, she snapped the book shut. It wouldn't do to daydream about something that simply couldn't be. There was no possible way she could meet Marcus in the morning and that was that. She'd survived her marriage to George by refusing to dwell on the "might-have-beens." She rose from her chair to cross to her wardrobe, wondering if

George would be home for dinner or if she could look forward to an evening alone.

The knock on the door startled her. She didn't have a lady's maid. It was highly unusual for any of the servants to come to her chamber. She looked at the door a bit curiously, thinking perhaps she'd imagined it. The knock sounded again with more persistence.

"Come in?"

The door opened. Thacea had the sincere impression of a tornado turned loose in the room. A tornado with blond curls and more energy than an Ardani dervish.

"Good evening, your Ladyship. I'm here to help you dress for dinner. Will you be requiring me to do your hair? Because I don't think I'm very good with hair, but I'm willing to try of course. You just have to tell me what you want, and then be patient until I get it right. I've never had to do much hair, but I've dressed plenty of ladies before. Will you want to wear a gown this evening or just your wrapper? Cook says his Lordship won't be home until after midnight, so you'll be eating alone. I thought you might want to just eat here in your room rather than in that big dining room all by yourself." The young woman paused in front of the wardrobe and looked back at Thacea. "Your Ladyship? Is something wrong?"

Thacea blinked several times and stared at her. She had absolutely no idea who the girl was, certain she'd never seen her before, and equally sure she wouldn't have forgotten if she had. She was short, not more than five feet tall at best, a bit on the plump side, with a mop of blond curls that looked like they were perpetually mussed. Her uniform was immaculate. Her face far too pleasant and friendly to be a servant in George's employ. In the short space that she'd been in the room, the young woman had tidied the bed, straightened the cushions on the sofa, hung Thacea's brocade wrapper on the back of the wardrobe door, poured her bath, and put away her nightgown from that morning. She wondered vaguely when the girl found time to breathe amid all those sentences.

"Your Ladyship?"

"Who are you?" Thacea said, still a bit dazed.

The girl blushed furiously. Her hands flew to her flushed cheeks. "Oh, your Ladyship, you must think I'm daft. I completely forgot to introduce myself." She paused, a rarity as far as Thacea could tell, and dropped a quick curtsy. "I'm Molly Hale. I'm your maid."

Thacea shook her head. "I haven't got a maid."

"Oh, you have now, your Ladyship. Will you be wanting a bath? Well, I'll go ahead and heat the water just in case. His Lordship's secretary expressly told me I was to be your personal maid. I wouldn't have taken this job if that hadn't been so. It would have been a step down, you know. After having served her Ladyship for so many years before."

Harold Pinkerton was George's secretary. He was an extremely disagreeable man. Thacea found it rather difficult to believe that he was suddenly so concerned with her welfare that he took it upon himself to provide her with a maid. "Mr. Pinkerton sent you to me?"

"Mr. Pinkerton? Oh no, ma'am. I don't know who Mr. Pinkerton is. It was his Lordship's secretary who hired me."

"His Lordship's secretary is Harold Pinkerton."

"No ma'am. He said his name was Mr. Blake. Or perhaps it was Drake. I'm not so good with names. I'm sure it wasn't Mr. Pinkerton, though. It didn't sound anything like that."

Thacea stared at her. "Drake? *Peter* Drake."

"Well, I don't know his first name, ma'am. He didn't tell me. Did you decide if you wanted a gown tonight? I'm sure it was Drake, now that you mention it."

"What happened to Mr. Pinkerton?"

"I don't rightly know, your Ladyship. Mr. Drake didn't say anything about Mr. Pinkerton. He seemed rather nice, though. His Lordship told me he would be."

"Lord Worthingham told you that?"

"No, ma'am," Molly said, looking a bit flustered by Thacea's inability to follow the conversation. "It was the Earl of Brandtwood who sent me here. I'd been working for his mother before."

Thacea's eyebrows lifted slightly at the mention of Marcus's name. He certainly was used to getting what he wanted. "Lord Brandton sent you?"

"Yes, ma'am. Me and Jake."

Thacea blinked again. "Who on earth is Jake?"

Molly blushed as she stuck her hand in the bathwater to test it. She seemed satisfied that it was warm enough, and walked around to undo the buttons at the back of Thacea's gown. "Jake's my sweetheart, ma'am. He's down working in the stables now."

Thacea looked at Molly in surprise. "Mr. Drake hired Jake as well?"

"Oh, yes, ma'am. His Lordship made it clear it was to be a job for both of us."

With a brief shake of her head, Thacea stepped out of her gown. "I'm sure he did." She sank down gratefully in the heated bathwater and tipped her head back with a contented sigh. "Go ahead and prepare my gown, Molly. It doesn't matter which one. Something simple is fine."

"Yes, ma'am. Will you be wanting me to do your hair as well? I'll do my best, but I can't guarantee . . ."

Thacea opened her eyes. "Molly," she interrupted.

Molly didn't seem to notice she'd been cut off in midsentence. "Yes, ma'am?"

"Please send someone to Mr. Drake, and tell him I'd like him to join me in the dining room for dinner this evening."

"Mr. Drake, ma'am?"

"Yes. Mr. Drake."

Molly shrugged and pulled open the wardrobe doors. "Yes, ma'am, I'll do that as soon as I've prepared your gown. Do you want the blue one, or the green one?" Molly pulled out the two gowns and held them up for Thacea's inspection. Thacea opened her mouth to say it didn't particularly matter, but Molly put the green one back and pulled out a white one. "Or the white one? I think the white one. It will look nice with your hair."

Thacea thought that was rather like saying the hem would go nicely with her feet, but she refrained from saying so. Instead, she nodded her approval and noticed absently that Molly had already replaced the blue gown in the wardrobe, evidently deciding she didn't need Thacea's consent. She leaned back in the tub, absently watching Molly fuss about the room, listening inattentively to the constant stream of chatter. She was still silently marveling at the revelation that within one afternoon, Marcus had replaced George's secretary and hired two additional servants for the household. He certainly couldn't be accused of wasting time.

Molly finished with the gown and laid it out on the bed, before she looked at Thacea. "I'll be back to help you dress in a minute, your Ladyship. I just need to tell Mr. Drake you'd like him to join you and alert Cook the two of you will be dining together downstairs." Molly raced out of the room like a ship in full sail. Thacea leaned back, a slight smile tugging at the corner of her mouth. Molly was indeed colorful, and she found she rather enjoyed her ceaseless chatter after so many months of silent solitude.

It was nearly an hour later when she walked downstairs and found Peter Drake waiting for her in the dining room. He rose from his chair, crossing to her side to lift her hand for a perfunctory kiss. "Your Ladyship. May I say what a pleasure it is to see you again."

Thacea looked at him skeptically. "An unexpected surprise, I'm sure."

With a devilish smile, Peter pulled out her chair, waiting for her to be seated. "This is the most amazing coincidence. . . . Don't you agree?"

He seated himself across from her. Thacea flipped her napkin onto her lap, and watched him in amusement. "Is that so?"

He nodded. "Yes. This very afternoon, I arrived home and found a note from my cousin, Harold Pinkerton."

She took a sip of her wine. "Harold Pinkerton is your cousin?" she said skeptically.

He nodded again. "That's right. And Harold's mother was taken gravely ill with a very sudden disease of a rather complicated nature."

"That sounds tragic."

"It is, I assure you. Harold felt duty-bound, you see, to go to his mother in Kent, but he didn't feel comfortable about leaving his Lordship without proper notice."

"So he notified you. The two of you are obviously quite close." She was beginning to admire Peter's ability to tell the story with a straight face.

"Oh yes, very. He knew I was at odds these days. My former employer passed away just a few months ago, you see."

She waited expectantly while the servants laid out the first course. Peter fell silent until they were alone once again. "So Harold contacted me and asked me if I would be willing to stand in for him until his mother recovers."

"And you gallantly agreed."

"Well, I was at loose ends, after all, and I didn't want to let him down."

"And how does Lord Worthingham feel about this?"

Peter swallowed a spoonful of his soup and grinned at her. "He was rather relieved, of course. He didn't want to bother with the mess of finding a new secretary in the midst of his negotiations over a new post."

"No, of course not."

"So he hired me this very afternoon."

"And what about Jake and Molly?"

Peter swallowed another spoonful of his soup. "That was a pleasant stroke of good fortune. One of his Lordship's maids and one of the grooms happened to quit today. They up and left with no notice. I was fortunate to find Molly and Jake so quickly."

Thacea could stand it no more. She dropped her spoon on the table and burst out laughing. "Peter Drake, you are hopeless."

With a broad grin, he leaned back in his chair. "I must admit, it's a relief to have something to do for a change. I've been at odds since I left my regiment. I was pleased when Brandt contacted me this afternoon and asked for my help." He paused and checked over his shoulder to ensure they were alone. He leaned forward and said in a conspiratorial whisper, "Worthingham's a bit of a bastard anyway, and I can't deny I enjoy knowing we're getting the better of him."

Thacea shook her head at him. "You do know what all this is about, don't you?"

Peter grinned again. "I haven't known Brandt for twenty years without learning some things about him. He's quite taken with you."

Thacea felt the color rise in her cheeks. She took another sip of her wine. "How did you meet his Lordship?"

Peter looked at her knowingly and settled back in his chair once more. "His mother hired me to play with him." Thacea looked up in surprise, and Peter nodded. "His father left when he was ten years old. Brandt was a surly bastard, even when we were children. His mother, not being the most charming woman herself, wanted to keep him occupied and out of her hair. She was more interested in pursuing matters of the heart than she was in raising Brandt."

"But she *hired* you. She paid you money?"

"Um-hmm. My father was Sir Reginald Drake. We're descendants of Sir Francis Drake. That, by the way, is my only claim to nobility. My father used to say that the Drakes were nobility only by the whiskers."

Thacea smiled at him. "In my experience, being noble has very little to do with bloodlines."

"Well, in my case, it's got very little to do with them indeed. At any rate, my father may not have had the most esteemed title in London, but he had one of the best business minds about. He made a fortune by investing in Indian shipping when no one else believed the markets would open."

Thacea nodded. "George and I saw a good bit of that when we were in India. Men like your father made enormous fortunes if they entered the market early."

"My father was one of the first to invest in India. It paid off handsomely, and women like Harriet Brandton didn't fail to notice."

"How did you fit into this equation?"

"Harriet complained about Brandt a good deal to my father. My mother had died when I was born, and you might say I didn't have the most sheltered upbringing. My father was rather open with me about most things. He told me about Harriet's aggravation."

"You and Marcus are the same age?"

"He's two years older. Do you know, no one calls him Marcus but you. I think he likes it." Thacea looked at him in surprise, but Peter continued. "I suppose I inherited a good deal of my father's business sense. I would have squandered his business by now if I hadn't. I immediately saw the Countess's frustration as an opportunity. I convinced my father one day to take me with him when he called on her, and through a good bit of weaseling on my part, I needled Harriet into paying me to spend the day with Brandt."

"Does he know that?"

Peter nodded. "Well, of course he knows. Like I said, he was a mean little bastard—even then. As soon as I met him he made it abundantly clear he wanted nothing to do with the likes of me. In truth, he scared me to death, but his mother was paying me handsomely, and I wasn't nearly prepared to turn down that much money. 'Look here,' I said. 'Your mother paid me four pounds to keep you busy for the day. I'm not going to give away four pounds just because you don't want to be kept busy.' "

"What did he say?"

"He hit me."

"He *hit* you?"

"Square on the jaw. So I punched him back. We had a nasty fistfight over the entire matter, and once we were both good and bloodied, we agreed that I'd give him two of my four pounds for every day his mother paid me to spend time with him." Peter paused, a slight reminiscent smile on his face. "I bought my very first horse with money I won by betting the money I'd earned from Brandt's mother."

Thacea was appalled. There was something deeply disturbing about the thought of Marcus's mother paying Peter to entertain her son. Even if the two boys had become good friends as a result, the situation must have taken its toll on Marcus. "Peter," she said tentatively.

He shook his head. "I don't know," he answered, reading her thoughts. "He was already like that when I met him. I like to think I helped—not made the situation worse."

Thacea nodded. "Yes, I'm sure you did. Marcus is obviously quite fond of you."

Peter grinned, the gravity gone from his expression. *"Fond* isn't a word many people credit to Brandt. He's not particularly fond of anything, except causing scandal."

She made a disgusted little sound. "People misread Marcus. He simply enjoys giving that impression. Wouldn't you, if you knew your mother had to pay other children to play with you?"

He looked momentarily startled, then his expression softened. "I'm pleased to say, Lady Worthingham, that you have just met with my approval. I've seen Brandt go through a lot of women, and I've never approved of a single one until just this moment."

Thacea tried to ignore the slight stab of jealousy at Peter's casual comment. She knew, of course, about Marcus's extensive experience with women. Everyone knew. It didn't mean it irritated her any less, though, to think she was only one in a line of conquests—nothing more than another slit in his tent, as her father would say. She resolutely pushed the notion aside, arguing that she had no interest in his love life, as she had no intention of being a part of it. "Well, I'm quite glad you approve, Mr. Drake, because it seems I've ruined your plans for the evening, and you're stuck with me now."

"It will be a pleasure, I assure you. In truth, I've grown rather tired of Brandt's style of entertainment. This has been a welcome respite."

They passed the remainder of the evening in companionable

conversation. Thacea ascended the stairs later that night content in the notion that, for the first time since her marriage to George, she had someone she could trust in the household. She decided against adding that bit of information in her letter to Raman, however, not wishing to burden him with the unhappy details of her marriage. She had always been careful to avoid references to George's behavior, and much as she'd like to share her good news with her brother, it didn't seem prudent. She let Molly dress her for bed and was alone in her room, sealing the letter, when the connecting door opened and George walked in.

She looked up in surprise. He must have just arrived. He was still wearing his evening cloak. He looked irritated. Her stomach clenched. It had been a long day. She didn't have the energy for a fight with George. "Good evening, my Lord," she said cautiously.

He glared at her. "There's nothing good about it. I've had a hellish day, and when I returned here this afternoon to collect my money from you, you weren't here. Where have you been?"

"Didn't you get my note, George? I was with Madelyne Brandton."

He muttered something beneath his breath as he stalked across the room. "All day?"

She nodded. "Yes. All day. I'm sorry your day has been difficult. Is there anything I can do?"

"Give me the money."

Thacea quickly opened the small chest where she'd put the currency. Carefully, she removed the four hundred pounds, shielding the chest from George's view with her body. It wouldn't do for him to know there was a thousand pounds in the box. He would demand all of it. She snapped the lock shut on the chest, then extended the money to him. He snatched it from her hand and counted it.

He looked up, his expression still menacing, and stuffed the money in his waistcoat pocket. "I needed it this afternoon."

"I'm sorry, George."

He took two steps closer. "Why do you insist on making me angry? You know how much I hate to be angry with you."

She refused to step away from him. "I know, my Lord. It slipped my mind. You have it now, though."

"Yes, I have it now. But only after I had to make excuses to my tailor this afternoon." His hand shot out to coil in her hair, jerking her head back. "I have an appointment tonight, but I think you should spend the evening thinking how you will make this up to me. I don't want to punish you."

She winced slightly when he tightened his hold on her hair. "I will, George."

George finally let go of her hair, but his presence was no less menacing. "When I married you, your uncle assured me you were well-versed in the customs of the East. That you were raised in the harem and knew the erotic arts." Thacea swallowed hard and watched him. They'd had this discussion before. "But you don't, do you?" She shook her head, and George grunted with disgust. "The Ice Princess! That's the title he should have given you."

She didn't have an answer to that, so she continued to watch him warily. George had been heavily drinking. She could smell the liquor on his breath now that he stood so close to her. His moods were always unpredictable when he was drunk. His eyes glittered in the dim light of her room. She chewed apprehensively on her lip, all the while willing him to leave. Suddenly, he stepped closer to her. His hand closed on the nape of her neck. She stifled a gasp when he pulled her up against him, forcing her head back so her eyes met his. "But I'm your master, am I not?" His voice was dangerously low.

She swallowed again and nodded.

"Say it," he demanded. "Tell me I'm your Lord."

Thacea's eyes widened. She pushed ineffectually at his chest. "George, please. Let me go."

As suddenly as she said it, he thrust her away from him so forcefully that she nearly fell. "I hate you," he muttered. "How dare you make me come to you and ask for money. You enjoy that, don't you?"

Thacea took a deep breath, glad to finally know the source of George's temper. It was easier to diffuse if she knew what had caused the tantrum. "No, of course not, George. You know it's only because it takes time for me to have the money converted into pounds. You don't have to ask. Everything I have is yours." He seemed to calm a bit at the soothing tone in her voice. She tentatively lay a hand on his sleeve. "I'm sorry I inconvenienced you today, my Lord. I lost track of the time."

He looked at her. She felt the muscles in his arm bunch beneath her fingers when, with no warning at all, he lifted his other hand and hit her square across the face with the back of his knuckles. Thacea gasped. Her hand flew to her stinging face. "Next time," he growled beneath his breath, "you'll have a reason to remember the time." He abruptly left the room, slamming the door behind him.

Thacea stood still a very long time, her fingers gingerly caressing the side of her face. She had completely misread his mood this time, and made a disastrous miscalculation in the process. Try as she might, she wasn't certain where she'd missed his intent. Finally, she crawled into bed, wincing when her face touched the pillow. She remembered a little sadly that George had said he'd be back later that night. That meant, she knew, that she would be unable to ride with Marcus in the morning after all. It seemed that Peter Drake's hard work had been for naught.

She awoke to the pleasant aroma of fresh coffee and to the realization that someone was talking to her—nonstop. Thacea's eyes popped open. Molly puttered about her room, talking in a steady stream of nearly incomprehensible sentences. "Molly," she said.

Molly turned around and smiled at her. "Your Ladyship! You're awake finally. That's your coffee there by the bed. His

Lordship—Lord Brandton that is—said you liked it with nothing at all in it. Just the coffee."

It seemed an odd thing for him to recall. She was so busy pondering the information that she missed the next four of Molly's sentences. "I'm sorry, Molly. What did you say?"

"I asked which habit you'd be wearing this morning. His Lordship—Lord Worthingham—said you were going riding this morning."

Thacea raised her eyebrows. "George said that?"

"Oh yes, ma'am. Mr. Drake said yesterday afternoon when he was talking to his Lordship—Lord Worthingham, not Lord Brandton—the first time, that he asked his Lordship if there were special arrangements to be made about your schedule."

"My schedule?"

"Well, yes. You know. Things like when do you take tea, when do you go to your dressmaker's, or does she come here, when do you entertain, who is on your usual guest list? Do you want the burgundy habit or the grey one? Burgundy I think, the grey won't look as nice on the horse." Molly pulled out the burgundy habit and shook out the wrinkles with an efficient flick of her wrist. "And his Lordship said you didn't have a schedule. None at all. Well, Mr. Drake said that surely you went riding each morning as did the other ladies of the ton. It's quite the fashionable thing, you know. And if you don't ride every day then you certainly must look rather peaked, and that won't do at all."

Thacea took a long sip of her coffee. "No that certainly will not do."

"And his Lordship agreed and said even if you didn't want to, you were to go riding this morning. Well, Mr. Drake said he knew just the place and told his Lordship he'd take care of the horses."

Despite herself, Thacea laughed. "And where is his Lordship this morning?"

Molly paused and looked at Thacea in surprise. "Well, didn't he tell you? He got called away to a meeting at the Foreign Office early this morning. Said he'd be gone all day. Mr. Drake assured him there was nothing to worry about, he'd take care of everything."

Thacea set her cup down on the small table by her bed and threw back the covers. "Yes, I'm quite sure he did." She looked at Molly. "All right, Molly. Let's have a go at my hair."

By the time Thacea was dressed and ready, she was a jumble of nerves. She couldn't deny she was intrigued at the thought of seeing Marcus again, but neither could she deny she rather resented his presumptive handling of it all. He seemed determined to take over her life. She and Molly had struggled with her hair a good long while before they'd managed to bind it in a queue of questionable stability. Thacea was concerned that the bruise on her face was too noticeable, but since Molly had not even mentioned it, she relaxed somewhat. Molly had been right about the habit, however. The burgundy habit was her best one. She made a mental note to tell Marcus she'd picked it because it would go best with the horse.

She met Jake for the first time, and was completely unsurprised to find he was the groom on duty who would drive her to meet Marcus. He was a pleasant young man, as tall as Molly was short, and as quiet as she was talkative. Thacea would never have pictured the two of them together until she saw the adoring light in Jake's eyes when Molly handed Thacea into the carriage. Jake glowed at Molly and Molly at Jake. Thacea stepped hurriedly into the carriage, to give them a moment of privacy.

She arrived at the green before Marcus. Three of his grooms awaited her with a saddled chestnut mare. At her first glimpse of the horse, she drew a deep breath of admiration. It exceeded even her greatest expectations. She mounted it with an eager anticipation she hadn't felt in years. The groom holding the reins appeared to be the oldest of the three. "She's a beautiful horse," she told him.

He nodded. "She's one o' his Lordship's favorites. Just gave him a foal last year. She ain't lost none o' her fire, though."

The horse was prancing about nervously, unaccustomed to

standing still with a rider on her back. "May I give her her head?"

"Aye, yer Ladyship. His Lordship'll be along shortly. I'll send him after ye, if that's what ye want."

A thrill of anticipation tripped up her spine as she considered the joy of an uninhibited ride. "That's exactly what I want," she said, sinking her heels into the mare. She inhaled a great breath of the cool morning air as the horse bolted forward across the green.

It was one of those rare fall mornings when the weather was just warm enough to encourage truly vigorous exercise from the horses. Marcus was galloping well into his second mile when he finally caught up with her. He reined in his mount to sit watching her for several minutes, intrigued by her display of horsemanship.

He noticed with appreciation the way her hair glistened with blue highlights against her ivory skin in the early morning sunlight. Several unruly strands had worked their way loose from her queue to curl riotously around the oval of her face. Her burgundy riding habit was cut to perfection. Marcus's masculine eye traveled the length of her generous curves with an appreciative gleam, ending where her dark, wine-colored skirt flared over the flanks of her chestnut mare. The horse was high-spirited—he'd chosen it for her deliberately. He couldn't help but admire the ease with which she guided it. She was quite at home in the saddle, and her love for both the exhilaration and the animal were evident.

It was several long minutes before she noticed him watching her. She seemed to falter slightly before she reined in her horse and began riding toward him at a more sedate pace. He nudged his mount forward, meeting her in the center of the clearing.

"Good morning, my Lady. I'm pleased you decided you could join me."

An amused glint appeared in her deep blue eyes. "I don't think I had much choice."

He felt a smile tug at the corner of his mouth. "I warned you about the consequences of giving me a challenge."

"In this case, I will admit they are rather pleasant consequences."

He slowly raised her hand to his lips. "I'm glad you find it agreeable."

She swept a stray tendril of her black hair off her forehead. When he noticed the dark bruise at her temple, his smile faded into a frown and he released her hand. "That's rather a nasty bruise you have there. Did you fall?"

She looked startled, and touched the bruise with her fingers. "Yes . . . yes, I fell this morning. It was dreadfully clumsy of me."

Marcus frowned again, unconvinced. He didn't miss the delicate flush in her cheeks from her vigorous ride, nor the noticeable sparkle in the depths of her eyes. At that moment, the amusement in them helped ease his bad temper. The morning's exercise had been good for her. "It does nothing at all to detract from your appearance. You look lovely this morning."

She tipped back her head and laughed. Marcus decided that he liked the soft sound. It was a far cry from the brittle affected laughter of the Society beauties. It had a certain genuine lilt that refreshed his soul like a cool breeze on a warm summer day. "And now I can say my experience with you is complete, your Lordship," she said, her voice laced with amusement. "I have been graced with the consummate Brandtwood charm."

"It isn't an honor every woman can attest to."

"So I have heard. It makes the compliment so much more the better then, doesn't it?"

"You should know by now that a good deal of my reputation is enhanced by societal gossip."

Thacea patted the neck of her prancing horse. "We have a saying in my country that goes something like this: 'A good reputation sits still, but a poor one runs about.' "

He silently marveled at the woman who could lighten his spirit so thoroughly within a mere half hour. "Mine is halfway to France, no doubt."

"Then perhaps I shall catch up with it. George seems to feel he is close to earning his Paris appointment."

Their horses were anxiously prancing about. He stroked the neck of his black gelding with a soothing touch. "Will you be happy in Paris, Thacea?" he asked earnestly.

"I don't believe it really matters whether I will be or not."

"I believe the proper answer is that you'll be happy wherever your husband is." He couldn't resist the cynical taunt. It didn't set well with him that she'd rejected his advances on behalf of her spineless bastard of a husband.

"I cannot fight the feeling, my Lord, that you're much more interested in the truth than you are in propriety. Now if you don't mind, my mount is growing restless, and I'd like to finish my ride."

He raised an eyebrow at her abrupt change of subject, but decided to let it pass. "There's a lake at the far end of the green." He swept his hand in the general direction. "I'll give you a ten-pace lead if you think you can beat me."

She looked at him, a hint of a smile on her lips. "Very well, my Lord. I trust you can keep up." She spurred her mount into a full gallop.

He enjoyed the next quarter hour immensely, easily keeping pace with her vigorous gallop. They had ridden another three miles out before she began to slow the pace. She finally reigned in her tired horse at the edge of the small pool, where she dismounted and dropped the reins, allowing the large animal to slake his thirst. She sank to the warm earth, her skirts billowing out around her, and looked up at Marcus as he approached. "You did rather well, my Lord. I suspect I could have outpaced you, however, had I not been hampered by the saddle."

He led his horse to the pool before seating himself beside her. "You are used to riding without a saddle?" There were extensive gaps in his knowledge of her, and he found the notion both disconcerting and intriguing. He was unused to women with more than a surface level of experience. He rarely took the time to know them. In truth, he didn't find them interesting enough to bother. But instinct told him that Thacea Worthingham would be a difficult woman to understand. The idea enchanted him.

She flopped back on the grass and stretched her arms above her head, turning her face to the sun. "In my country, women ride astride, like the men, and we generally use blankets instead of saddles."

There was something primitive about the picture of her galloping across an open field astride a massive animal, her hair flying free behind her. He couldn't resist the urge to allow his eyes to roam restlessly over her exquisite curves. "Tell me about Ardahan," he said quietly.

She looked at him in surprise. "Are you truly interested?"

He nodded. "Everything about you interests me. You seem to be quite in love with your homeland."

A breath, a wistful, sighing kind of breath, passed between her lips. "One cannot help but fall in love with Ardahan. You told me at Bath you had traveled in the East."

He nodded. "Quite extensively, and while I've never been to Ardahan itself, I have seen a number of the countries along the Black Sea. They are magnificent in their vastness."

"Yes, that's it exactly. The desert goes on for miles in every direction. The mountains are among the highest in the world. It is the starkness and the immensity that I love." She looked at him with a faraway look in the depths of her eyes. "The most beautiful spot on earth is in Ardahan."

"And have you seen so much of the earth that you're such a qualified judge?"

She smiled back at him. "Now, you are mocking me. I have traveled a good bit, as it happens, though seldom beyond the confines of the Black Sea, and to India with George, of course, but it doesn't matter. I don't need to compare it with anything to know I am right."

"It must be a spectacular spot."

"From that spot, one can see all the beauties of Ardahan. The mountains rise out of the hot desert and touch the sky. Our legends say their snow-capped peaks hold the canopy of the world in place. Along the rock faces, icy waterfalls of melting snow plummet to the earth, landing amidst the dense evergreens that grow only at the base of the mountains. And there, where the black mountains disappear into the sea, on a ledge high enough for eagles to roost and spirits to soar, where the tops of the trees tower amid tumbling water and unforgiving rocks, where the hot breezes from the desert turn cool as they skim the surface of the ice, one's soul becomes a part of the divine creation, and you know without a doubt that it is the most beautiful spot on earth."

Marcus exhaled a long breath. He realized he had stopped breathing during her discourse. The passionate note in her voice had seized his attention. At the moment, he was quite prepared to agree with her, despite never having been to Ardahan himself. "I would very much like to see it." The truth of the admission surprised him.

She looked at him. "I would like to show it to you. I believe you would understand."

Something passed between them. He reached over to smooth a lock of her hair away from her forehead. His voice was barely above a whisper when he spoke. "Your name," he said, "what does it mean?"

She didn't seem surprised that he knew the customs of her country well enough to know her name would have a translation. "My full name is Thacea Kamal Hamid. It means *Wing of the Raven.*"

"Because of your hair?" he asked.

She shook her head. "Because of my strength." He looked at her curiously, and she smiled. "My mother was an English diplomat's daughter, as you know. She met my father when her father was on assignment in Ardahan. My father, Aladar Hamid, was the oldest son of my grandfather, the Sultan. Her family was scandalized when she told them she was in love with my father. And the Sultan forbade my father, as the Crown Prince, to marry an Englishwoman. So they escaped together into the desert, where they were married according to the customs of Ardahan."

"Everyone was furious, I imagine."

"It caused an international incident. The English didn't recognize the marriage, of course, and my grandfather was enraged when King George claimed that my mother had been abducted. Her family was expelled from Ardahan. It wasn't until years later that the Sultan accepted my father and mother back at the palace. Mother never contacted her family again, and we lived there until my parents' death in a boating accident twelve years ago."

"And your name," he prompted.

"Oh. My name. Yes, well, as I said, my mother was English. It was very difficult for her to adjust to desert life, and while my father did all he could to make her comfortable, I don't believe she ever really felt healthy. She was happy, though, and that more than compensated. I was born a year after my parents disappeared from the civilized part of Ardahan. My father had to deliver me into the world, as there were no midwives in the desert, and he told me later it was the first and only thing he'd ever feared in his life. My mother had a terrible time with me. We both nearly died, but Baba told me that when I fought myself into the world, I opened my mouth and my cry sounded exactly like a raven's cry, and it was the most beautiful sound he'd ever heard. When he named me, he called me Wing of the Raven, because the wing is the strongest and most intricate part of the bird, and I made the raven's cry my own."

It fit perfectly, he decided. The woman before him was indeed an intricate one. The more he knew of her, the more he was drawn to her in a way that was different from anything he'd ever experienced. It wasn't merely the physical attraction he felt for her, which he admitted was intense, but something deeper and more potent. So potent, in fact, he found it disturbing. Some instinct told him he would be exceedingly wise not to examine

it further. The exhilaration of the ride, coupled with the satisfaction he had found in having gotten his way, had clearly
caused his feelings to get jumbled. That decided, he felt better
about it. He rose to his feet suddenly, extending his hand to her.
"I believe your father was right. It suits you."

She looked at him curiously, and slipped her hand into his,
allowing him to pull her to her feet. "Do you think so?"

He nodded. "You are one of the strongest women I have ever
known—inner strength, I mean."

She flushed slightly, as if somewhat embarrassed by the
strange turn in the conversation. "And what of you, Marcus
Brandton? Do all the names they've given you suit you as well?"

He knew she was referring to the fact that the ton called him
everything from *The Wicked Earl* to *Satan Incarnate*. He leveled
his gaze at her. "Every one of them is completely appropriate."

"Are they all true? The stories, I mean?"

"Which stories in particular?"

"I was especially intrigued by the report that you once had
a party where all the women were naked."

"That particular story escaped my attention. Do you believe
it is true?"

She studied him for a long moment, and then shook her head.
"I don't think so. Scantily clad, perhaps, but not naked. I think
you would find that degrading."

He turned and walked to the horses, grabbing the reins and
bringing them around. "I think perhaps you've given me a good
deal more credit than I deserve. That particular incident may
be exaggerated, but I assure you a good number of those stories
are true. I have no great love for convention. That's how I've
earned all those names."

She allowed him to help her mount. "But they don't suit you
at all. They are nothing more than the trite labels of a society
too immersed in false convention."

He swung into his saddle and narrowed his gaze at her. "And
what name would you have chosen had you been given the
option?"

"Talal a Zalan—Heart of a Lion," she said quietly. He raised an eyebrow in expectation, and she continued, "Because you are like a lion in many ways. Feared. Powerful. Arrogant. Proud. Even your eyes are a lion's eyes. But your heart is a lion's heart. You would give your life to protect what you love."

"You are mistaken there," he answered. "There is nothing and no one I love enough to sacrifice my life for."

She nudged her mount forward with her knees. "I think perhaps Madelyne would disagree with you."

He frowned and watched her goad her horse into a gallop before he set off after her. The entire conversation disquieted him. He studied her silently as she rode at a brisk pace in front of him. The morning hadn't gone at all as he'd intended, yet he'd enjoyed himself immensely, feeling more refreshed than he had in years. Resolutely, he increased his pace and rode alongside her, reaching out a hand to take hold of her reins.

He reined in both horses. Thacea turned to look at him curiously. On impulse, he bent to kiss her. It was the barest whisper of a kiss, feather-light in its caress, soul-shattering in its intensity. When he raised his head, several heartbeats passed before she opened her eyes. "Thacea, I'm sorry. I didn't ask you here simply to . . ." he trailed off, uncertain what he meant.

Something flashed in her eyes. She pulled away from him. "To ask me again to be your mistress?" she finished helpfully.

He shrugged, uncomfortable with the shallow sound of it. "I suppose."

Thacea tipped her head. "I've nearly decided I don't think I want to be your mistress, my Lord." He looked so shocked by her direct statement that she laughed out loud. "I don't mean to shock you. It's simply that I suspect you'd be much more loyal to your friends than to the women who share your bed."

He pulled in an irritated breath. "Perhaps. I've never considered the matter before."

She continued to regard him frankly. He was distinctly uncomfortable under her direct inspection. "You don't have many friends, do you, my Lord?"

"No, I don't suppose I do."

"Is Peter Drake the only one?"

"It depends on what you mean by friends."

"Is he the only one you're close to?"

"I'm not close to Peter. Not in the sense you mean. I've known him a very long time."

"And are you paying him to entertain me as your mother paid him?"

He looked at her carefully. "Peter is rich as Croesus. He doesn't need money from me."

"He's working for George on your behalf for nothing more than the money George is paying him?"

"That's right."

"Then he must be your friend. What other motivation would he have?"

"Boredom," he said bluntly.

She pushed herself up in her saddle to kiss his cheek. "You've a very low estimation of yourself, Marcus. I think perhaps I'll have to change that." She smiled at his stunned expression and patted his arm. "Now, that I've quite shocked you with my brazen behavior, it is really time we rode in. I can't monopolize your entire day, and I'm sure Madelyne is expecting me. I promised her I'd be there when her new wardrobe arrived."

"I haven't been shocked in longer than I can remember. You certainly haven't done it now."

"We have a saying in Ardahan I would like you to remember. My own language is closest to Arabic, and it is difficult to translate into English, but . . ."

He interrupted her by raising his hand. "I speak classic Arabic fluently."

She smiled at him. "Strangely, that doesn't surprise me at all. Very well, my Lord," she answered, switching to the lilting cadence of her native language, her eyes growing suddenly serious, "in Ardahan we say that when true friends are born, their souls are linked until the mountains slip into the sea, the rain pools in the desert, and the stars fall from the heavens."

She turned abruptly and galloped toward the stables before he could think of an adequate response.

Eight

The next few weeks passed in a haze of contentment for Thacea. George spent most of his days, and a good many nights, away from the house. Thacea rode with Marcus every morning, and where time allowed, spent her afternoons with Madelyne. Although Madelyne still hadn't broken her silence, Thacea felt she was certainly more alert. Peter Drake called on Madelyne at least once a week. Thacea found it vastly amusing to watch Marcus glower over the pair like a frustrated mother hen.

She was standing in the library one afternoon with Marcus, who was anxiously watching Peter and Madelyne seated in a small arbor fifty feet away. She laid her hand on his arm to capture his attention. "If you continue to frown like that, your face will freeze in that position."

Marcus looked at her in surprise. "I'm not frowning."

Thacea laughed. "For heaven's sake, Marcus. If you glared at Peter any harder, you'd burn a hole clear through him."

He turned away from the window. "You have turned me into a scheming mama. I find myself wondering if Peter is the best match for Madelyne. I can't believe I've resorted to thinking of something so trite."

"I think it's rather nice."

"Then I suppose it has some redeeming qualities after all."

Thacea turned away, idly toying with a gold letter opener on his desk as if it had suddenly become the most fascinating item in the world. With each passing day, she found more and more of her thoughts occupied with Marcus. He was becoming very important to her. She was beginning to fear the consequences less than she enjoyed the few hours of stolen pleasure in his company. Over the past few weeks, Marcus had almost stopped making comments to her that insinuated any desire to deepen their relationship. She suspected he had probably lost interest, and had dismissed the notion after she had rejected him. At some level, she knew she was vastly relieved.

Marcus now seemed much more detached to her. While they enjoyed long hours of conversation on any number of subjects, he appeared to have dismissed his earlier objective of a more intimate relationship. Occasionally, however, he would allude to it, and she was never entirely certain how to respond. She decided this time to ignore it altogether. "Did I tell you George is traveling to Paris next week?"

Marcus settled himself in one of the large leather chairs, staring absently into the fire. "You mentioned it, yes. He's going to tout the Foreign Office personnel, I imagine."

"I suppose so."

As strained silence fell between them, Thacea fidgeted before she sat down on the long sofa across from Marcus. "Marcus?"

He turned his head to look at her. She nearly gasped at the intense look in his green eyes. "Yes?"

Thacea ran the tip of her tongue across her upper lip, determined to pursue the conversation she'd been avoiding for days. Her mouth had gone suddenly dry. "Marcus, I've been thinking." His eyes narrowed. He waited in silence for her to continue. She took another deep breath. "I think it would be best if I not see you again. George seems to feel he's very close to obtaining his appointment in Paris. We will no doubt be leaving for the continent as soon as the Season ends in London. I think it will be easier on both of us this way."

Marcus leaned back in his chair and crossed his long legs in front of him. "When you finally leave for Paris, there won't be any emotional ties here in London. Is that it?"

She nodded warily. "Well, yes. That seems to be the best thing for both of us."

"For both of us? Do you think you're in a position to comment on what's best for me?"

She looked at him carefully. "Marcus, I don't know what to say. I simply thought . . ."

"And what of Madelyne?" he interrupted quietly. "She's become very fond of you."

"I will still visit Madelyne, of course. Until I actually leave for Paris."

"I see. I am the only one you cannot be emotionally tied to."

She sighed in exasperation. "Yes, all right. I cannot be tied to you. Is there some satisfaction in that for you?"

He lifted an eyebrow. "In truth, there hasn't been any satisfaction at all. There are any number of women more than willing to be emotionally tied to me."

Thacea gave him an angry look. "And that's been it all along, hasn't it? You pursued me because I was a challenge to you. You warned me not to challenge you, Marcus. I should have listened."

"Perhaps you should have," he bit out.

"How can you not understand this? Surely it doesn't surprise you that I have no desire to be one in a long stream of your conquests."

"I had no idea my reputation bothered you so much. I was under the impression it was your devotion to your husband that kept us apart."

She flushed. "Don't you dare make this my fault, Marcus. You seem to find endless pleasure in flaunting your exploits in front of me, while you scorn me for my standards."

"I haven't scorned you. I simply find it incomprehensible that you are so loyal to your bastard husband—particularly when he makes you so miserable."

"I'm not willing to sink to George's level of degradation. If I do, then I am no better than he."

Marcus shook his head. His green eyes glittered with barely

disguised anger. "What power does he hold over you, Thacea? I know you aren't afraid of him. Not really. Why do you let him control you?"

She swallowed past a knot in her throat and contemplated for the thousandth time telling Marcus about Raman. She trusted him implicitly, of course, but Raman's life hung in the balance. It didn't seem wise to burden Marcus with that. She longed to tell him, though, to finally confide in someone she trusted about the terrible strain of guarding Raman's secret. She looked at him for several long seconds, then decided against it. Raman was her responsibility and hers alone. "He doesn't control me," she evaded. "I choose."

"And you choose to let him manipulate you through fear and force." She looked at him in surprise and he waved his hand in her direction in exasperation. "Do not think me a fool, Thacea. I've seen the bruises. I've heard the fear in your voice when you speak of him. I'm not an imbecile."

Her eyes pleaded with him. "There is more than you know about the situation."

"Then tell me. For God's sake, let me help you."

She shook her head. "How? How will you help me? Will you make me your mistress—offer me your protection until you tire of me? Then am I truly better off with you than I am with George?"

His eyes flashed angrily. "Do not dare argue with me that what I proposed to you puts me in the same class as your husband."

"Why not, Marcus? An affair. A casual liaison. Isn't that what you wanted? Would that really be any different?"

"It isn't the same."

"Isn't it? What would happen when you grew bored with me—as you no doubt would after the challenge was met? Would you simply discard me with an expensive bauble as a token of your respect?"

"You are angering me," he bit out.

"Why? Because I'm too close to the truth? Look me in the

eye and deny it. I would be nothing more than another slit in your tent when you finished with me."

He blinked. "A what?"

"In Ardahan, men cut tiny slits in their tent for each woman they've had amid their cushions." She saw a smile tugging at the corner of his mouth and she glared at him. "It isn't funny."

He sobered suddenly. "No, it isn't. And I resent your insinuation. Have you no more respect for me than that? Have you really believed every story you've heard about me rather than the evidence before your eyes? I thought you were above all that," he said bitterly.

Her control snapped. She leaned forward in her chair, feeling perilously close to hysteria. "Marcus, why are you doing this to me?" She heard the desperate note in her voice and took a deep breath. "I thought it would be easier this way."

"Easier for whom?"

Thacea felt the tears well up in her throat and eyes. She squared her chin, resolutely fighting the urge to weep. "For me. It will be easier for me." Despite herself, the last word wavered. A sudden tear stung the corner of her eye before it spilled down her cheek.

Marcus was instantly alert. He levered out of his chair and sank down on one knee in front of her, gently catching the tear with his thumb. "I've made you cry. It was not my intent. I only wanted to make you see that . . ." He caught another tear with his thumb. His green eyes filled with regret. "My only excuse is weeks of frustration."

She managed a weak smile. "I made myself cry. It seems I've been rather foolish and unsophisticated about all this."

Marcus exhaled a deep breath as he pulled her head to his shoulder. "No, I am the one who has been foolish. I believed if I gave you time you would . . ." he trailed off again. Thacea thought it odd for a man who was seldom at a loss for words. He continued to look at her earnestly as his hand lazily stroked the back of her head. "I misjudged you. I'm sorry."

She sniffled against his coat, then raised her head. "You must think I've gone daft. It isn't like me to be so overwrought."

Marcus's eyes had taken on a new intensity. His hand still rested casually at the nape of her neck. He seemed ready to speak when, without warning, he groaned and leaned forward. His lips met hers in a soul-wrenching kiss. Thacea gasped in surprise. The cool pressure of his lips rocked against hers, sending a bevy of sensations swirling about her insides. Marcus shifted slightly to deepen the kiss. An exultant sound escaped from the back of his throat when she sighed and parted her lips. His tongue swept inside, demanding possession.

Before she was fully aware of what she was doing, Thacea leaned against him. Her arms twined around his neck. She buried her fingers in the crisp hair at his nape and surrendered to the exquisite feel of his lips. She moaned softly when his hand came up to cup her breast, and without thinking, she leaned into the caress, seeking the greater pressure of his palm through the confines of her gown. She wondered if he had any idea what he was doing to her.

She was driving him mad. Marcus moved his hand restlessly over the soft swell of her breast. He groaned deep in his chest. Her fingers moved restlessly over the sensitive skin of his nape. He was vividly aware of the growing heaviness in his loins. When the soft pad of her thumb found the curve of his ear, he sucked in a ragged breath and forgot to release it. Marcus wrenched his lips from hers to trail a hot line of kisses along the graceful curve of her cheek and over her throat.

She tipped her head back. A soft whimper escaped from between her lips. She clung to his head. The heat of him was consuming her, absorbing her. When his mouth found the sensitive hollow at the base of her throat, she gasped and tugged on his hair. Marcus raised his head in answer to her silent command, and his eyes met hers. The smoldering heat in their green depths scorched her. His hand still cupped her breast. The slow caressing motion caused heat to flow through her blood. She briefly considered that her sanity had fled before her eyes fluttered shut. She pulled his head to hers once more.

Marcus slanted his lips over hers in a possessive kiss, demanding nothing less than total surrender. When he felt her tongue duel restlessly with his, he groaned and gave her her way. She explored his mouth tentatively at first, then with more urgency. All the frustration of the last few weeks poured into the intensity of the kiss.

Marcus heard the muffled cough from the terrace door. He was so lost in the exquisite sensation, he entertained the notion of ignoring it completely. When it sounded again, a bit louder, and certainly more persistent, he raised his head. Thacea, he noticed with no little amount of satisfaction, looked stunned.

She blinked twice before he snapped into focus. She was on the verge of an embarrassed apology when she noticed Marcus was looking, not at her, but at the terrace door. She turned her head with a sinking feeling of dread and found Peter and Madelyne standing in the doorway watching them intently. Peter was grinning unabashedly. As for Madelyne, she looked shocked. Thacea felt a tide of crimson sweep up her face and into the roots of her hair. She buried her head on Marcus's shoulder with a tiny exclamation, willing the floor to open up and swallow them whole.

Marcus set her gently away from him. He smiled at her reassuringly before he turned to look at Peter once more. "You have lousy timing, Drake."

Peter raised an eyebrow. "It appears to me that my timing is grand. To think that you glower at me when I suggest I'd like to walk alone with your sister."

Marcus glared at him. "And don't think it's escaped my attention how long you've been out there."

"I could have stayed a good while longer, evidently."

Thacea was horribly embarrassed. Their light banter was doing little to comfort her. She coughed delicately and rose to her feet, managing to smile slightly at Madelyne. "Peter, I would like you to take me home, now," she said. "I'm sure George will not appreciate your having been gone such a long time."

Peter shrugged. "He's gone himself. As far as he's concerned, I'm with his solicitors discussing his financial matters."

Marcus raised an eyebrow and looked at Thacea. He had long since determined that she had sold the dagger to meet George Worthingham's demand for money. He made a mental note to discuss the matter more intimately with Peter. His estimation of Thacea's husband slipped another notch. "Peter, will you wait for Lady Worthingham outside, please."

Thacea looked up in surprise. "Oh, no. I don't think . . ."

Marcus interrupted smoothly. "We haven't finished our conversation."

She fell silent, unwilling to discuss the matter in front of Peter and Madelyne. Peter cast her an inquisitive look. She nodded silently. He pulled Madelyne's hand through the bend of his arm once more and led her to the door. "Brandt," he called over his shoulder, "make sure you give me fair warning next time. I could have benefitted from an additional ten minutes or so in the arbor."

Marcus glared at him when the door clicked shut. Thacea stood in the center of the room, uncertain what to do. She rubbed more vigorously than was necessary at an invisible spot on her gown, simply to avoid looking at him.

"You'll wear a hole in that if you aren't careful."

She gave him a guilty look. "There's a spot." A smile tugged at the corner of his mouth. She thought a little wildly how wonderful those finely chiseled lips had felt against hers. She dropped her hands, smoothing her damp palms on her skirt, and looked at him nervously. "I don't think this is wise."

He crossed the room, lifting one of her hands in his. "You cannot simply walk away from me. Not now," he said quietly.

She shook her head, refusing to be intimidated by his heated gaze. "I must. Especially now."

"Why must you insist on fighting me?"

"You saw what just happened, Marcus. I'm not strong enough to fight that when I'm with you."

"How long will George be gone?"

The sudden question surprised her, and she blinked. "What?"

"George. How long will he be in Paris?"

She looked at him warily. "He's leaving in four days and he'll be gone for over a fortnight."

"Then give me that time. Give me two weeks."

"No, Marcus. I can't."

His hands grasped her shoulders, and he shook her gently. "Look at me." He took her hand and laid it against his heart. "Don't you know what you do to me?"

Beneath her palm, she could feel the steady beat of his heart and knew it matched her own. She raised her eyes to his. "It will be best for both of us this way."

Marcus's fingers closed over hers, holding her palm flat against his chest. "If I can arrange it, if you know there will be no scandal, will you agree?"

"Marcus, I . . ."

"I swear I won't do anything you don't ask me to. I swear it. Just give me two weeks to convince you we belong together."

"And how do you propose to accomplish this scandal-free, gossip-free miracle?" she asked skeptically.

His gaze narrowed. "Give me your word you will agree if I can do it."

"Marcus . . ."

"Your word. Please."

Thacea briefly closed her eyes. When she opened them again, his gaze was no less intense. She was lost. "All right."

He raised her hand to kiss the palm. His lips lingered on the soft skin before he released it. "I promise you will not regret this."

She stepped away from him, finding it was much easier to breathe when he was not so close. "I hope you are right, Marcus. I cannot avoid the feeling that I have just sealed my fate."

He shook his head and walked with her to the door. "I am right. I know I am. If after a fortnight I have failed to convince you, I will do whatever you wish."

She looked up at him, her fingers on the door latch. "I cannot let you break my heart, Marcus. I will have nothing left if you do."

He dropped a quick kiss on her forehead. "I'll take care of your heart. It's all I ever wanted to do."

Nine

Marcus leaned back in his chair and watched his secretary, Colonel John Samuelson, sort through the enormous stack of mail on the desk. Marcus had finally given in to the older man's request and agreed to work through the correspondence that had accrued in the last few weeks. Not for the first time that morning, Marcus's eyes strayed to the window of his library, as he allowed his thoughts to drift to Thacea.

It had been three days since he'd last seen her. To his annoyance, he had been unable to find a solution to the problem. He had considered dozens of possibilities, even entertained the notion of taking her to his country estate, but nothing provided the environment he wanted. He drummed his fingers on the arm of his chair in a distracted manner, and replayed his last conversation with her in his mind.

Irritated, Marcus rose abruptly from his chair. He walked to the window, ignoring Colonel Samuelson's startled glance. It was raining. The streets were crowded with carriages and merchants hurrying about in the early hours of the morning. The grey sky mirrored his mood, and he laid his palm on the window, his eyebrows drawing together in a deep frown. He was so lost in thought, several minutes passed before he realized his secretary had spoken. Marcus turned from the window. "I'm sorry, John, what did you say?"

Colonel Samuelson studied his young employer. He had been engaged as secretary by the Earl of Brandtwood shortly after his commission in Wellington's army had expired. In the six years he'd been in Marcus's employ, he'd never seen the young man so pensive. Bouts of rage, irascible behavior, scandalous activity, all were normal in the Brandtwood household, but the Earl's current mood was unreadable. John Samuelson was uncertain how best to approach it. "I believe we've completed the correspondence for this morning. Was there anything else you needed?" he repeated.

Marcus opened his mouth to dismiss the older man, then paused abruptly as a sudden thought occurred to him. "Have there been any invitations?"

Colonel Samuelson looked at him in surprise. "The usual assortment. Three balls, six dinner parties, two conversationals, and a house party in Sussex. I didn't recognize any of the names as your usual circle, so I took the liberty of declining them all. I'm sure that's reversible, however, if . . ."

Marcus raised his hand to interrupt him. "No. That's not what I need."

John Samuelson raised his eyebrows. "Are you looking for something in particular, your Lordship?"

"No. Yes." Marcus frowned. "It's rather complicated, Colonel. I'm in search of a completely respectable, utterly dull, scandal-free environment." He shot John Samuelson a dry look. "It isn't the type of event I'm generally invited to attend."

Colonel Samuelson nodded. He suspected Marcus's strange mood had something to do with the notable absence of Lady Thacea Worthingham, but he knew better than to say so. "Are you thinking along the lines of one evening, or an extended affair?"

The irony of the comment echoed in Marcus's soul. "Extended. Definitely extended."

"Then I believe a house party is in order."

Marcus stroked his chin thoughtfully. "I've thought of that. I can't host it, though. My name alone will taint the matter."

"Perhaps you can manage to obtain an invitation."

"Not just anyone will have me in their home, John, no matter how respectable my intentions may be. I'd have to either motivate them by their fear of vexing me, or by their curiosity. The latter would certainly make for a more interesting experience."

"I quite agree, sir. Your usual social circle seems . . ." Colonel Samuelson hesitated.

"Unsuitable?" Marcus supplied helpfully. At his secretary's stricken expression, Marcus added, "Don't fret over it. I'm well aware my acquaintances aren't . . . the right sort. I need something of a different matter entirely."

John Samuelson nodded carefully. "Something does come to mind. I only know of it by accident, really. I'm not entirely certain, however . . ." he trailed off.

Marcus narrowed his gaze. "What is it, John?"

He cleared his throat. "Well, as you know, my brother is secretary to Lord Philip Thomason. I spoke with my brother yesterday afternoon, and he mentioned in passing he would have the next fortnight or so free. Lord and Lady Thomason will be attending a house party at the country estate of the Marquess and Marchioness of Ridgefield. It may be what you are looking for."

Marcus leaned against the mantel and studied the older man. Jace and Caroline Erridge, the Marquess and Marchioness of Ridgefield, were among the most esteemed members of the Peerage. The Marchioness was an American, however, and had a reputation for being somewhat impulsive. Her parties were renowned for their respectability. She had distinguished herself among the ton as an hospitable hostess. Her salons were famous for their intellectual and cultural level. Under any other circumstances, John Samuelson's suggestion would have been an excellent one.

Few were unaware, however, that the feud between the Marchioness of Ridgefield and the Earl of Brandtwood ran deep, harkening back to her first days in London, when Marcus had given her a direct cut at the Earl of Helsley's spring ball. Caroline Erridge wouldn't likely be enticed into entertaining Marcus Brandton, no matter how great her curiosity.

The idea suited his purposes too nicely to allow it to pass

without proper consideration, however. Marcus tapped his finger idly on the mantel, a speculative look in his eye. "John, I need you to procure a book for me."

"Your Lordship?"

"This afternoon, if possible," Marcus continued. "It's a new volume by the American novelist Susanna Haswell Rowson. I believe it's considered a somewhat scandalous work, and you may have trouble finding it."

"I'll see to it immediately, your Lordship."

Less than three hours later, Marcus was silently marveling at John Samuelson's efficiency and considering the need to significantly augment his compensation. He leaned back in his carriage, patting his coat pocket, where he'd slipped the small volume. He wouldn't be at all surprised if Caroline Erridge refused to see him. He had, after all, paid her a nearly unforgivable insult when she'd first arrived in London. He couldn't quite remember what it was now, but he was certain she'd have no difficulty reciting it back to him verbatim.

He did remember that her casual disregard for his importance within Society had annoyed him. Bastard that he was, he'd gone out of his way to make her miserable. If she hadn't already managed to catch Jace Erridge's eye, Marcus would most likely have scared her back to America, where he had once believed she belonged.

But Caroline had proved him wrong. To say she was beloved by the ton was an understatement at best. She was charming, compassionate, witty, and had a certain air about her that attracted men and women alike. She had proven to be one of London's most successful hostesses, her husband's important social position notwithstanding.

Now, he mentally chastised himself. He should have apologized to the Marchioness of Ridgefield many years ago. He hoped that Caroline would see past their former disagreements and that her somewhat renowned curiosity would get the better of her. After all, he thought, as his carriage rolled to a stop, most members of the ton would all but die to enjoy as much speculation as she would if she included him in her house party.

Marcus alighted onto the pavement and straightened his jacket with a sharp tug. Patting the book in the pocket of his greatcoat, he walked purposefully up the stairs. There was an unusually long delay before the large wooden door swung open. A short, stout butler with a bad wig and an ill-fitting black jacket and waistcoat regarded Marcus with a surprised look. Marcus stepped inside the foyer and handed a small card to the butler, who appeared to be somewhat stunned by his presence. "Good afternoon," Marcus said. "I am the Earl of Brandtwood. I would like an audience with her Ladyship, if she's available."

The butler stared at the card for several long seconds before he turned on his heel and marched in the direction of the drawing room, mumbling something beneath his breath. The older man's stockings slipped loose from their garters and wrinkled about his ankles. His wig tilted slightly to the side. The staff at Brandtwood House were flawless. They were flawlessly polite. Flawlessly discreet. Flawlessly groomed. And flawlessly dull. He should have known that Caroline Erridge would surround herself with an eccentric staff.

Several minutes passed before the butler returned. He barely paused in front of Marcus when he announced, "Her Ladyship will see you in the drawing room," and continued shuffling in the opposite direction, tugging on one of his stockings as he walked. Marcus straightened the points of his waistcoat once more before striding toward Caroline Erridge.

He opened the heavy door and had to scan the room for several seconds before he identified the Marchioness. Caroline was seated on one of the long leather sofas, her blond head bent in intense conversation with an older gentleman Marcus didn't recognize. Neither seemed particularly disturbed by his presence, so he paused and removed his coat, laying it carefully on the small chair by the door. He retrieved the book from his pocket, then turned about to study his surroundings.

Even to Marcus, who found very little shocking, Caroline Erridge's drawing room was a bit startling. An enormous American-style leather saddle hung on one wall, surrounded by a magnificent display of handwoven horse blankets. He had traveled a good deal in the Americas and recognized several objets d'art that were distinctly Native American. The burgundy leather furniture and heavy oak paneling was accented with intricate Indian beadwork. Marcus immediately noted the effective mix of Ojibwa, Apache, and Shoshone handcrafts surrounding the impressive Blackfoot warbonnet centered on the east wall, between the two large windows. He felt the corner of his mouth twitch when he mentally identified the flamboyant painting over the mantel. American artist John Trumbull's depiction of the Battle of Bunker Hill was particularly suited to Caroline's personality. The English were still none too fond of the Americans, and memories of the American Revolution did little to foster good will. Yet the British had won the Battle at Bunker Hill, and Marcus suspected the painting had been a compromise between Lady Caroline and her husband. In truth, he suspected the entire room, of which he had heard a number of awed observations by members of the ton, was likely Caroline's way of poking fun at the often stuffy English Peerage. Once more, he mentally berated himself. He'd been wrong. It was *definitely* her way of poking fun.

Marcus realized, belatedly, that Caroline and her guest were looking at him expectantly. He advanced into the room. "Thank you for seeing me, my Lady. I'm sorry if I've disturbed you."

Caroline gave him a suspicious look. "Not at all, my Lord, Mr. Clark has been staying with us for a few weeks. He was just relating to me several stories about his explorations in the western territories of the United States. Won't you sit down?" She waved a graceful hand in the direction of a large leather chair with carved bone legs. Marcus casually settled himself into it before turning his attention to the other man.

"You wouldn't perchance be George Clark, would you?" he asked.

The man nodded delightedly. "Why, yes. I am."

Marcus slanted a look at Caroline, gratified by the surprised look on her face. "I've read a good number of the reports you and Meriwether Lewis filed after your expedition. I find them quite fascinating."

George Clark smiled abashedly. "I had no idea our work had been circulated to any extent in England. It's amazing country. Vastly untamed, you know."

Marcus nodded. "I have actually considered purchasing a good deal of land in America as an investment. Your Congress is making it rather difficult, however."

"They don't look kindly on foreign ownership. We've lost some of our most treasured possessions that way." George Clark cast an enamored look in Caroline's direction. Marcus suppressed a teasing smile.

"Your loss has most certainly been our gain, Mr. Clark."

The older man seemed embarrassed by the turn in the conversation. He cleared his throat, standing abruptly. "Well, I've several more letters to write, yet." He awkwardly kissed Caroline's hand. "I hope we can continue our conversation at a later date?"

"Of course, Mr. Clark. I'm counting on it."

As George Clark hurried from the room, Caroline chided Marcus. "You've intimidated the poor man, you know?"

"From what I've observed, Lady Caroline, you've no shortage of admirers to take his place."

Caroline laughed. "The only thing George Clark admires about me is my money. He's trying to finance another expedition, and hopes I'll agree to underwrite some of the cost. Beyond that, he thinks I'm a terrible traitor."

Marcus didn't miss the slight bitter tinge in her voice. "If you are, may I say on behalf of England that we are delighted to have you on our side."

She looked surprised. "I recall you had a distinctly different opinion when I first arrived in London."

Marcus opened his mouth to retort when the door crashed open. The same harried-looking butler shuffled into the room with a heavy-laden silver tray precariously perched in his arms. He plunked the tray down with an unceremonious clatter on the low wooden table in front of Caroline, then paused to adjust his sagging stockings. "Will there be anything else, my Lady?"

Caroline seemed to struggle against an amused smiled. "No, Mr. Coggins. That's quite enough."

The old butler pursed his lips sourly at Marcus as he marched out of the room, slamming the door behind him. Caroline cleared her throat. "May I offer you some tea, Lord Brandton?"

"May I be assured that it isn't tainted with arsenic?"

Caroline lost what remained of her composure and burst out laughing. "Mr. Coggins is not . . . well trained," she managed to say. Marcus raised an eyebrow at the understatement. She went on, "But he's very loyal to me. And I can overlook his eccentricities in light of the fact that he genuinely cares for me and my husband. Do you take sugar?" she looked up from the teapot.

He shook his head and accepted the cup from her. "Have you had difficulty finding good staff?"

She settled back on the sofa, her teacup balanced delicately in her hand. "I did when I first came here. Jace released a good number of his existing staff because of their attitudes toward me. It was difficult to replace them."

Marcus felt unaccustomedly guilty. The feeling was beginning to gnaw at his insides. It was becoming painfully clear that Caroline's adjustment to England had not been easy. His own behavior had certainly not helped. "How did you find the loyal Mr. Coggins?"

"I became so frustrated one day, I stormed over to the referral service and demanded they provide me with qualified applicants. They fidgeted a good bit, trying to claim they'd done their best for me. I was on the edge of a genuine tantrum when Mr. Coggins entered the office. He was there seeking employment, and was nearly as agitated as I over the lack of response he'd received to his applications." She lowered her voice to a conspiratorial whisper. "In truth, I think he lied on his references. He doesn't seem to have any training at all."

Marcus took another sip of his tea as he watched Caroline's animated features. "But you hired him without verifying his references?"

"That would have taken the longest time. His previous employers lived nowhere near the city, and I didn't have time to wait for responses to letters. And besides," she paused and looked at him sheepishly, "I hired him primarily to spite the referral agency."

Marcus laughed. "And now you've a butler with a bad wig, sagging stockings, and a surly disposition."

"But loyal. And that counts above all else."

"I imagine it does." He set his cup on the table beside him. "It wasn't easy for you when you arrived in London, was it?"

She shrugged nonchalantly. "No, I suppose not. I had Jace, though. That was enough."

"But it would have been much more pleasant if you'd been readily accepted by the ton?"

Her eyes narrowed. "Perhaps."

Marcus shook his head. "Without a doubt." He paused to carefully choose his next words. "I owe you an apology, Caroline."

"Good heavens. It's a little late in the day for that, don't you think?"

"I owe it to you all the same. My behavior was inexcusable. And I hope you'll forgive my actions as those of a callow youth with little of importance to do with his time."

She raised delicately arched eyebrows. "If I didn't know better, I'd think perhaps you were having fits of conscience, my Lord."

"I don't think I'd recognize my conscience if it knocked me square on the head. I do know, however, that I was unforgivably rude to you, and I regret any undue pain my callous behavior may have caused."

"For your edification, what you are experiencing is precisely what it feels like when your conscience knocks you square on the head."

Marcus laughed. "Then I am forced to admit I'm none too fond of the occasion."

"And may I be so bold as to ask what has brought about this monumental event?"

Marcus reached into his pocket and pulled out the book. "I am in need of a favor—a rather large one. And I have brought a peace offering in hopes that you would soften to my request."

Caroline accepted the parcel. She tore the brown paper back and exclaimed delightedly, "It's *Charlotte, Tale of a Lady!* I've been looking for this volume all over London. How ever did you find it?"

"I've an extremely efficient secretary."

"Lord Brandton, this is truly delightful. I cannot tell you how much I appreciate it."

Marcus silently added *gracious charm* to his growing list of Caroline's endearing qualities. "I hope it has the desired effect."

Caroline set the book on the table, then looked at him intently. "I must admit, I'm immensely curious. What on earth could you possibly need from me?"

He shifted in his chair. "It's awkward—unforgivably rude, really. But my time is short, and I am in need of a solution." Caroline waited for him to continue. Marcus leaned forward in his chair, his gaze meeting hers. "I need an invitation for Lady Thacea Worthingham and me to your house party at Sedgewood next week."

Caroline looked at him in surprise. "Begging your pardon, my Lord, but my house parties are hardly the type of affair you generally frequent."

Marcus winced. He had no doubt Jace Erridge would be horrified at the thought of entertaining him at his country home. He also had no doubt that Lady Caroline Erridge could entice her husband to capitulate. "You shouldn't necessarily credit everything you hear as accurate, my Lady. However, I will admit a good deal of what they say about me is true, and I can understand your hesitation. You have my promise, though, that this is an extremely delicate matter of an entirely different nature, and there will be nothing whatsoever to offend your sensibilities."

"Are you suggesting that my sensibilities are unreasonable?"

He shook his head. "Not at all. I am merely saying that this particular occasion will obey all the dictates of propriety. You have my word, I will not bring scandal into your home."

"I wasn't entirely sure you knew the meaning of the word *propriety,*" she said with a slight smile.

"I've a rather healthy understanding of *impropriety,* however, and in this instance, I am more than willing to avoid it. I am finding, as of late, there is a whole side of myself I had thought long since gone. That's the gentleman who knows the meaning of propriety and who listens to his conscience."

"And could this great awakening have anything to do with Lady Thacea Worthingham?"

Marcus reached for his teacup and handed it to her to refill. "As a matter of fact, yes it does, but not in the sense you mean."

"Now, Lord Brandton, how on earth would you know what I mean?"

He accepted his tea. "I am assuming, of course, that certain aspects of my reputation have not escaped your ear. And I mean, simply, that where my reputation may have preceded me, my relationship with Lady Worthingham is not at all in the same class."

Caroline cast him a dubious look. "You seem certain of that."

"Without trying to offend you, my Lady, I consider myself somewhat of an expert in scandalous behavior. This does not qualify to even the most sensitive observer."

Caroline still looked unconvinced. "Yet this woman with whom you are not involved is your reason for your rather re-markable behavior this afternoon."

His brows knit together in a slight frown. "She is Lord George Worthingham's wife. I befriended her Ladyship," he paused and looked closely at Caroline, "and I mean that in the purest form of the word, at Bath two years ago. Her marriage is . . . less than ideal. Lord Worthingham will be in Paris for at least the next fortnight, if not longer, and I felt that your party would be a welcome respite to what is otherwise a rather tedious existence."

"And you believe the oppressive Lord Worthingham will allow his wife to attend my house party unescorted?"

"I know your husband's prestige with the Foreign Office will be enticing to Lord Worthingham, and I'd hoped by procuring an invitation from you, I could provide Lady Worthingham with a two-week holiday while her husband is on the continent."

Caroline watched him speculatively. "You seem determined. Wouldn't it be much simpler to find a woman whose husband or, preferably, lack thereof, would be more inclined toward your usual diversions?"

"No doubt," he agreed. "But I seem unable to control this situation entirely, and I know only that I have a nearly overwhelming desire to do what I can to help Lady Worthingham."

"Do you believe Lady Worthingham needs assistance?"

"I'm certain of it." He leaned forward, his hands on his knees. "Caroline, I am completely convinced that George Worthingham mistreats her. I'd be willing to bet bad odds that he's abusive. I know he's mean-spirited at the very least. I've witnessed that myself. I suspect there is something else he threatens her with, though I have no evidence. I'm almost positive however, that his behavior doesn't stop with verbal attacks."

Caroline looked appalled. "Do you believe he beats her?"

"I believe he does."

"And you say this man is a high-ranking official in the Foreign Office?"

"He's currently seeking a post in Paris."

"I don't think it's in the King's best interest to have a man like that representing him in foreign lands."

"I tend to agree, my Lady. And that's primarily why I'd like your husband to meet her Ladyship."

Caroline drummed her fingers thoughtfully on the back of her other hand. "Jace won't like this, you know. He'll be incensed that I even agreed to see you this afternoon."

"I'm aware of that. But I was willing to chance that your

curiosity and your sense of adventure would win over your commitment to propriety."

Caroline smiled at him. "You know me rather well for a man who doesn't know me at all, Lord Brandton."

He indicated the eclectic room with a sweep of his hand. "I saw all I needed to when I entered this room."

Caroline laughed delightedly. "You know, you're the very first Englishman I know, outside my husband's family, to recognize that you're being made fun of."

"It's a very tasteful jest."

"And that's a very diplomatic concession." She tipped her head and looked at him, once more turning the topic back to the house party. "So am I correct in assuming that at least part of your purpose is to bring about the demise of Lord George Worthingham's distinguished career?"

"At least part. I would be lying, though, if I didn't admit to you that I find Lady Worthingham extremely attractive."

"You know I will not tolerate that type of behavior in my home. I've worked very hard to build a respected reputation. I won't allow you to jeopardize it."

He shook his head. "You have my word. Nothing will pass between her Ladyship and me that will cause scandal."

"And if, in the process, we can ensure that her husband's behavior prevents his ascension in the Foreign Office, you will meet at least one of your objectives."

"Yes, I will."

Caroline leaned back against the cushions of the sofa and smiled at him mischievously. "You know, Lord Brandton, I think perhaps it's best that you and I started off on such a bad foot."

Marcus felt his spirits lift. "Why do you say that?"

"Because had you and I become friends, we would have likely gotten into a great deal of trouble."

Ten

Thacea looked at the invitation skeptically and dropped it on the low table in the drawing room. That afternoon, a uniformed footman had arrived with an invitation from the Marquess of Ridgefield. The very idea that Jace and Caroline Erridge would invite George to bring his wife to one of their house parties was nearly laughable. She didn't doubt for an instant that Marcus was behind it.

George was scheduled to leave for Paris in the morning. Thacea nervously considered what she should do. It wouldn't be wise, she knew, to give Marcus his way in the matter. In the years since she'd married George, she'd managed to learn his ways and adjust to the solitude of her life with him. The last few weeks she'd spent with Marcus had sharpened her focus. Every hour of stolen pleasure had made the reality of her life with George starker and more difficult to bear. It was no longer a matter of happiness. It had become a question of survival. As long as Raman's life was in danger, she could not risk inciting George's anger. Yes, her head told her she'd made the right decision.

But her heart was not so sure. The temptation of two weeks in the country with Marcus Brandton was a powerful one. Her eyes strayed to the window as she imagined what it would be like to be away from the oppressive nature of George's house. She could take Molly, of course, and Jake would drive them. From the moment they left London, she would be free. Even the thought of it made her heart beat a bit faster. She wouldn't be able to wait too much longer before she responded to the Marchioness's invitation. There was the packing to be done, of course, and . . . Her thoughts trailed off when she considered the notion of packing for one of Caroline Erridge's parties. The Marquess of Ridgefield was one of the richest men in England, and while Thacea's wardrobe was certainly adequate for the circles she and George frequented, she couldn't hope to compete among Caroline Erridge's elegant friends.

No sooner did the thought pop into her head than she chided herself over the vanity of it. She caught a glimpse of herself in the mirror over the mantel and stared at her reflection. Her emerald-green gown was several years old, but it showed only slight signs of wear. If she replaced the lace at the décolletage, and retrimmed the cuffs, she might make do. She grimaced and shook her head. A new blanket on an old camel didn't make the camel any more attractive. Resolutely, she turned away from the mirror and picked up the invitation. She would send Caroline Erridge a note with her regrets and let her know she couldn't attend the house party.

She was halfway to the door when it flew open and Molly came rushing into the room. "Oh, ma'am, I'm so sorry. I was talking to Jake, and we were discussing what we were going to do with the extra money his Lordship gave us, and I completely forgot about the note. I know I should have given it to you earlier, but I lost track of time and I . . ."

"Molly," Thacea said patiently, an amused light in her eyes, "what note?"

Molly blushed and pulled a slightly crumpled piece of paper from her pocket. "Why this one, ma'am. It came with the money and I was so excited, I had to tell Jake. It slipped my mind and I . . ."

Thacea took the note as she idly listened to the girl's constant stream of chatter. She looked at the masculine scrawl on the elegant crested vellum paper and felt her heart leap. It could only belong to Marcus. She ran her tongue nervously across the curve of her upper lip and opened the paper.

Your Ladyship,

My sister seems somewhat at odds in light of your recent absence. There are several trunks full of new garments she cannot determine how to wear without your able assistance. I would very much appreciate it if you would call on her this afternoon and restore some semblance of order to my household.

Respectfully yours,
Brandtwood

Thacea felt a smile tug at the corner of her mouth. She had completely forgotten about Madelyne's wardrobe. The first of her gowns had arrived weeks ago, but many of the fabrics and materials Thacea had selected had to be imported from France. A few of the more exotic items were being shipped in from India. She doubted Marcus would find the task of helping Madelyne sort through the trunks of colored silks and brocades anything less than a deadly bore.

". . . but I told Jake, ma'am, that you wouldn't be too upset." Molly paused and looked at Thacea nervously. "You aren't, are you? I mean, was it terribly important?"

Thacea looked up in surprise. She had been so lost in thought, she'd completely missed the last few minutes of Molly's explanation. "No, Molly, it's all right."

"I told Jake it would be. It was just the money, ma'am. It was so generous and all."

Thacea tipped her head. "What money?"

"Why the thirty pounds the Earl sent us. He said he'd give us twice that if we helped you prepare for your house party and if Jake got you there safe by the day after tomorrow. You are going, aren't you ma'am? I mean, I don't want to pry, but you would have a good holiday, I think. You don't get out much if you don't mind my saying so, and I thought it would be good if . . ."

"Molly!" Thacea laughed. "I haven't decided yet whether I'll go or not, but you are right. That's very generous of his Lordship. I'll be certain to tell him you and Jake did your best to convince me. I'm sure he'll make good on his offer whether I attend the party or not."

Molly shook her head. "Oh no, ma'am. It isn't the money. It's not that at all. I think it would do you good to get out of the city for a while is all. Jake agrees, ma'am. He says you never look as happy as you do after your rides."

"Jake may be right. I haven't decided yet." She waved the vellum paper she still held in her hand. "Before I do, though, I need to call on Madelyne Brandton. Will you ask Jake to bring the carriage 'round?"

Molly dropped a curtsy. "Yes ma'am. I'll fetch your cloak and send word to Jake. He'll be around front with the carriage in just a moment, your Ladyship. I'm sure he won't take long at all . . ."

"Molly! Why don't you see to it?"

Molly blushed and dropped a second curtsy. "Yes, ma'am. I'm sorry, I do get a bit carried away."

Thacea watched Molly retreat from the room. As soon as she returned from Brandtwood House, she would send her regrets to Caroline Erridge.

When Thacea arrived, Marcus was not in evidence. She did her best to feel relieved, but didn't quite accomplish it. Madelyne was seated by the window and looked up in delight when Thacea was announced. Thacea hurried forward to take her hand. "I'm so glad to see you again Madelyne. I'm sorry I've been too busy to call on you in the last few days."

Madelyne looked at her dubiously and indicated the chair across from her. Thacea sank into it with a soft sigh. "I can see you don't believe me. It is true though. George will be leaving London tomorrow afternoon, and I've had a great deal to do."

Madelyne nodded, a knowing look in her eyes. Thacea laughed. "All right, I confess. I haven't been 'round because I was too embarrassed after what you witnessed in the library." Madelyne's smile was her undoing, and Thacea continued. "It seems rather foolish now, I'm sorry."

Madelyne reached out to squeeze Thacea's hand. "You're

right. It isn't worth fretting over. I understand from your brother we have a number of trunks to go through." Madelyne rolled her eyes and rose from the chair, indicating the enormous pile of trunks in the corner. Thacea groaned. "I think we'd better get started. It will likely take the rest of the afternoon."

They spent the next several hours delving into the trunks. Yards and yards of silks and velvets and brocades spilled out. With the help of two maids, Thacea and Madelyne sorted riding habits, day gowns, pelisses, ball gowns, reticules, bonnets, and undergarments until the light in Madelyne's room began to fade. Thacea was seated on the floor next to one of the large trunks when she pulled the last reticule from the bottom and looked at Madelyne. "This appears to be it. I had no idea this could be so exhausting."

Madelyne shook her head and pointed to the corner. Thacea turned her head. There was still another trunk. "Oh, Madelyne, how can there still be another trunk? We can't possibly have ordered this many gowns."

One of the maids tugged the trunk to the center of the floor. "They all came together, your Ladyship," she said. "Are you sure you want to do them today?"

Thacea nodded. "We'll never get through them if we don't finish this evening." She levered herself off the floor and walked to the trunk. Leaning over, she grasped the latch and snapped it open with an efficient flick of her wrist. When the trunk lid fell back, Thacea gasped in surprise. The wardrobe she'd ordered for Madelyne was composed of pale colors, entirely suitable for a debutante. This trunk was different, however. The splash of color inside was rich in depth, filled with blues and purples and greens. "I don't understand." She reached down to finger the soft velvet of an indigo riding habit.

"Is something wrong?" Marcus's voice sounded from the doorway.

Thacea snapped her head around to look at him. She cursed the flush that spread over her cheeks. "Your Lordship! I didn't realize you were there."

He looked at her carefully and walked into the room. "When I returned this afternoon, Colonel Samuelson informed me you had arrived." He looked at the trunk. "Is something wrong with the gowns?"

She shook her head. "The gowns are beautiful. They simply aren't what I ordered."

He removed a ball gown in deep violet. "Are you certain?"

Enviously, she fingered the rich silk skirt. "Of course I'm certain. I ordered a debutante's wardrobe—basically white, nothing wilder than pale blue."

He handed her the dress. "My Lady, I have seen *wild*. That most certainly does not qualify."

"Wild or not, they are not what I ordered." She looked at the gowns in consternation. "I took Madelyne to Madame Drussard. She's supposed to be the best in London. She must have included gowns from another lady's order. I'm not sure what to do. We will have to send them back, of course. They are entirely inappropriate."

Marcus gave the trunk a thoughtful look. "Perhaps . . ." he paused and redirected his gaze to her. "Perhaps you should try them on."

She raised her eyebrows. "Try them on? Marcus, that's ridiculous. I couldn't wear those."

He crouched down by the trunk and idly riffled through the gowns. "I don't see why not. I think the colors would suit you very well."

"It isn't that. I didn't pay for these gowns." She paused and looked at him closely. "I *can't* pay for them."

"I don't see why that should be a problem. Madame Drussard wouldn't have sent them unless they'd already been charged to my account. If I remember correctly, Colonel Samuelson informed me that bill has already been paid."

Thacea's eyes narrowed. "Marcus, did you . . ." she trailed off.

"Did I what?"

She felt the color rise in her face. "I'd like to speak with you alone, please."

He rose to his feet and nodded briefly at the two maids. "Leave us." They hastened nervously from the room. Marcus swiveled his gaze toward Madelyne, a cool smile on his lips. "Darling, Peter Drake returned with me this afternoon. He's downstairs waiting for you in the library. Would you mind giving us a few minutes of privacy?"

Madelyne smiled, a delighted light in her eyes, and all but rushed from the room. Marcus turned to Thacea. "I'd say that had the desired effect."

Thacea frowned. "Marcus, I want to know where these gowns came from."

"They came from Madame Drussard, of course."

"They are not part of the wardrobe I ordered for your sister." He shook his head. "No. They aren't."

Thacea fought a wave of apprehension. "You ordered them for me, didn't you?"

"I think perhaps we should sit down."

"I don't want to sit down. Marcus, this is inexcusable. I cannot accept such an extravagant gift from you."

"I believe you are misreading my intent."

Exasperated, she tapped her foot. "And what was your intent? Haven't you ordered gowns for your mistresses before? Isn't it merely a standard token of your affection?"

He shook his head. "In truth, no, I haven't. I've paid for plenty of jewels, I'll concede, but I've never ordered gowns. I understand some men do, however."

"Then why should I think this is any different?"

"You aren't my mistress. A fact of which I am rather painfully aware."

His voice was clipped. She winced slightly beneath his intense stare. "I might as well be from the looks of this. I am not so addlepated as to believe this is merely an extravagantly generous gesture on your part."

He raked a hand through his thick hair in frustration. "Despite what you may believe, I did not intend to offend you."

"Then what did you intend?"

"To help."

She walked toward the window and stared out at the setting sun. She was perilously close to tears. She took several deep breaths before she was able to speak again. "It isn't fair, you know?"

He walked up behind her and settled his hands on her shoulders. "What isn't fair?"

"My father used to say the sun plays no crueler trick than when it casts mirages in the desert." His fingers slowly caressed her shoulders and she turned her head to look at him. "It's rather trivial, actually. I mean, I shouldn't want them so much, should I?"

Gently, he turned her to face him. "There is no vice in desiring them. I'm exceedingly gratified you approve of my taste."

She tipped her head onto his shoulder. "I don't know what to do, Marcus. Propriety demands that I refuse them."

"But your heart demands that you don't?"

"It seems to be a consistent problem for me recently."

"Is there something else you are having trouble deciding?"

She smiled against his lapel. No one could accuse Marcus of not being direct. "I received the Marchioness's invitation this afternoon."

"Ah."

"I imagine that is of your doing as well."

He set her away from him. "That is the reason I ordered the gowns. I was afraid you would refuse to go if you felt you would be out of place." She opened her mouth to speak, but he pressed his index finger to her lips. "That's not meant to be insulting. It's merely an insight into the feminine mind."

Her eyes strayed to the trunk. "A rather astute insight, I concede." He waited for her to continue, and she finally looked into his eyes. The silent plea in their vivid depths proved to be her undoing. "I don't suppose," she said cautiously, "there would be any harm in trying them on."

His eyes twinkled. "None at all." He leaned forward to kiss her forehead. "Thank you."

She cast him a disparaging look. "All right. Send me a maid."

"Shall I also send word to Lady Erridge that she may count on your presence next week?"

She hesitated, frowning disapprovingly at the satisfied smile on his lips. "Marcus, I don't know. It doesn't seem wise."

"Two weeks is all I've asked of you. I've given you my word."

Thacea ignored her mind's warning that she was being exceedingly foolish. "You'd best get to it right away. I'm sure the Marchioness would like to know how many guests will be attending her party."

Eleven

The clock on the mantel chimed midnight and Thacea turned nervously away from the window, twisting the tie of her brocade dressing gown. It had been well after seven o'clock when she'd left Brandtwood House. She hadn't realized how late the hour was until she'd finished repacking the gowns in the trunk. Peter Drake had come looking for her in Madelyne's chambers. Thacea remembered with a start that George had planned a small dinner party for the evening. When she arrived home, George's guests were already with him in the dining room. Rather than enter late, she'd gone to her room and sent word that she felt too ill to come down.

She'd spent the next five hours in her room, pacing anxiously, worrying over George's reaction to her absence. In the chilled quiet of her room, she cast a worried glance at the clock. George was leaving for Paris in the morning. She was already beginning to regret her decision to attend the house party. Angering George this evening had been foolish. He would never give his permission for her to attend the party in his absence if he was in the fit of rage she suspected. Yet to attend without his consent would almost certainly spell disaster when he returned.

The room was silent except for the relentless ticking of the mantel clock, and she tightened the lapels of her dressing gown. A shiver of fear raced up her spine when she heard movement in George's room. She contemplated the wisdom of locking the connecting door, but thought better of it, knowing it would only serve to enrage him further. Long, tense seconds passed. Thacea wiped her damp palms on her dressing gown and turned from the door, walking resolutely toward the window. If she stood in the center of the room, thinking of nothing but the inevitable confrontation, she would drive herself insane with anxiety. Instead, she leaned her forehead against the cool window and stared at the moon, thinking of Raman.

At the sudden crash of the connecting door, she started. Her stomach churned into knots. Clenching her nails into the soft skin of her palms, she turned from the window to face George. In the flickering firelight, his eyes bored into her, glittering dangerously. His shirt was unbuttoned to the waist, and she could see the rapid rise and fall of his chest as he drew short, angry breaths. She forced her eyes to meet his, determined not to flinch beneath his impaling gaze. His lips twisted in an ugly sneer as he stalked across the room with long, determined strides. "I trust you are feeling better," he said, his voice deceptively low.

She clutched the lapels of her dressing gown with one hand. "Yes. I had a terrible headache earlier."

George's hand shot out. He grabbed her wrist, wrenching her fingers from her lapel and twisting her arm behind her back. She toppled against him, thrown off balance by the awkward position. He curled his other hand into her unbound hair, forcing her head back with a sharp yank. "Isn't it fortunate that you are well now?"

She inhaled a quick breath, gasping when his hand tightened in her hair. "Please, George. You're hurting me."

"I am beginning to believe you enjoy being hurt, Princess. Why else would you insist on making me angry?"

"I didn't mean to, George. I swear, I . . ." She stifled a cry of pain when he jerked her arm harder behind her back.

"Where were you?" he bit out.

She hesitated until he gave her arm another painful twist. "I was with Madelyne Brandton." George cursed beneath his breath and thrust her away from him so quickly her hip slammed into the window ledge. She winced, righting her balance. "I lost track of time, George, and by the time I returned, my head was aching so much, it didn't seem prudent for me to go downstairs. Surely your friends didn't miss me?"

"Don't be ridiculous. I was forced to make excuses for your absence."

"Couldn't you simply tell them I was unwell?"

"It was painfully apparent to me and to my colleagues that I am unable to control my wife."

Thacea swallowed past a lump in her throat. "That isn't true, George. It isn't true at all."

He took a step closer. "Isn't it? For three weeks you've spent nearly every day at Brandtwood House. To date, you have reported nothing of value to me."

She leaned back against the window and looked at him nervously. "I have learned nothing. You know I would have told you if I had."

He took another step closer. "Then what is it at that house that lures you to completely forget I am expecting you to play hostess to my colleagues?"

"Nothing, George."

He traced a line along her collarbone with his finger. "Nothing? Nothing at all?"

She shook her head. George grabbed the lapels of her dressing gown and tore them open, pulling her back against his body. "Come now, Princess. Do you expect me to believe that you haven't given your body to Brandtwood?"

"No, George. I swear that's not true!"

He stared down at her angrily before he released her robe. She stepped away, tugging it closed around her. His lips curled in an unpleasant smile. "Remove it," he clipped.

"What?"

"Remove your robe. The nightgown, too."

"George, I . . ."

"Do it."

His voice was low with suppressed rage. Thacea clenched

her fingers into the soft folds of her robe. "No, please, George. It isn't what you think."

He hit her across the cheek with his knuckles. "Remove it," he said, his teeth clenched.

She slowly dropped the dressing gown to the floor, her eyes silently pleading with him.

He stared at her figure silhouetted against the moonlight. Lust flared briefly in his eyes. "Now, the gown."

"George, please . . ."

He smiled unpleasantly. "That won't be the first time tonight you'll say that. Remove your gown, or I'll tear it off."

Thacea pulled her cotton nightgown over her head. When she stood naked before him, she fought the urge to cross her arms over her breasts. His gaze seared her. She shivered, more from fear than from cold. George stepped forward and wrapped a hand around her nape. His other hand menacingly caressed her cheek, where it still burned from his fist. "I'm sorry I hurt you," he said softly. She nodded, unable to meet his gaze. "I was angry," he continued, his fingers moving along the delicate line of her jaw. "Why do you insist on making me angry?"

"I don't mean to, George."

He dropped his hand to her breast. Thacea closed her eyes, fighting an almost uncontrollable urge to pull away from him. George stood so close, she could feel his hardness pushing against her belly. He had been aroused by his anger. She sank her teeth into her lower lip until she tasted the coppery flavor of blood on her tongue. His hand cupped her breast, roughly pushing against her nipple. "You make me so angry," he whispered. "You know I don't want to hurt you."

"Yes, George," she whispered.

"I was going to punish you for this." His fingers continued to flex. Thacea's stomach knotted at the thick tone of desire in his voice. "But then I realized the cause of your behavior."

She raised her eyes reluctantly to his. A shiver of revulsion raced down her spine at the heated look in his eyes. "You did?"

He bent his head, his lips settling on hers in a wet kiss. He ran his tongue along the line of her jaw, while his fingers tightly squeezed her nipple. When his lips reached her ear he whispered hotly, "I've neglected you too long." Thacea twisted her head to stare at him uncertainly. George's eyes burned into hers. "You need a lesson in who your master is, Princess. It's been too long since I've had you in my bed."

His hot breath caused a flutter of panic to race along her limbs until her knees felt weak. "I . . . I know how busy you've been, George."

His hand tightened on her breast. "I've been pleasuring myself with whores when I should have been concentrating on taming my wife."

She shook her head. "George, please don't do this. Not now."

Her voice wavered on the last word. Something flared in the depths of his eyes. "That's most appropriate, Princess. You look like a doe caught in the hunter's snare."

"Please, George."

He ran his fingers along the line of her throat, pulling her closer so she could feel his hardness. He rubbed against her belly with a deliberate motion and smiled when she shivered. "Didn't you learn in your uncle's harem that your body exists only to serve your husband's desires?" She closed her eyes and George laughed softly. "Tonight you will give me my rights as your husband." He yanked on her hair until her eyes flew open. "Remove my trousers, Princess. When I've finished using you, you'll have no thought for Marcus Brandton again."

When she hesitated, he gave her hair another tug. "Or would you like for me to send word to your uncle that your brother is alive and well with his nomadic relatives?"

Thacea felt a tear slip from the corner of her eye. Resolutely, she moved her hands to the buttons of his trousers.

She awoke in the early hours of the morning, just as the sun began to chase away the dark shadows in her room. George still lay beside her, one arm thrown possessively over her waist. She shut her eyes, shivering slightly at the memories of the previous night. George had been brutal in his demands of her. She was certain she would find a host of bruises on her skin when she dressed later.

George stirred and mumbled something in his sleep, and Thacea turned her head away, sickened by his presence. He was scheduled to leave shortly after dawn. His valet would be calling for him soon. The darkness in her room had faded to a pale rose glow. She stared at the dying embers of the fire and thought of Marcus. She had promised to meet him at his riding green outside London so they could travel together to the Marquess of Ridgefield's estate. No one would see them leave the green together, and there would be no gossip if Jake brought the carriage back to George's lodgings later that morning. She had left the trunk containing her new gowns at Brandtwood House, knowing she could find no decent excuse for its presence if George were to find it. Marcus would bring the trunk with him, and she and Molly would only have to pack her personal items and undergarments.

Still, she couldn't simply disappear from George's house for two full weeks without being missed. Jake would be questioned when he returned with the carriage, and Molly's absence would be noted as well. Peter Drake was her only hope. Peter would run the household in George's absence. If he gave the staff no reason to think there was anything odd about her disappearance, they would not be likely to comment. George was not expected back from Paris for well over a fortnight. If she returned after two weeks, surely she and Peter could find a plausible explanation for her absence.

It seemed risky, but she was certain Peter wouldn't betray her. She drew a deep breath and stared at her dressing gown, which still lay in a heap on the floor. For two weeks she would be free of George, free of his threats, and free of her fear. She had protected Raman from George for nearly three and a half years, now. Surely the fates wouldn't begrudge her two weeks of stolen pleasure.

A sharp knock sounded at the door and George groaned against her neck. Thacea pushed at his arm, determined to do whatever was necessary for him to leave on time. "George. George, you must wake up. You don't wish to be late."

He grumbled and tightened his hold on her waist. "Are you in a hurry to toss me from your bed, Princess?"

"No, of course not, George. It's just that . . ." She was interrupted by another knock on the door. George swore beneath his breath. "It's just that I know you wanted to leave by seven," she rushed out. "I don't wish to be responsible for making you late."

He raised up on his elbows to stare at her. "Don't you want to warm my cock once more before I leave?" He rubbed himself against her.

She drew a deep breath and forced herself to lie still. "There isn't time for you to humor me, George. The sun's already up." He briefly looked at the window. "You see," she added. "It's already dawn. You'll have to hurry."

He moved against her once more. Lust flared in his eyes. "I can hurry," he said suggestively.

The knock sounded again with more persistence. She ran her tongue nervously over her lips. "George, please. I'll . . . I'll miss you, of course, but I'll be all right. I don't want you to be angry with me for making you late."

He sighed heavily when the knock sounded for the fourth time. Finally, he rolled away from her. "I'll have to satisfy myself with a ship's whore," he said. "Claudette Castlebury will be aboard, but she's become entirely too possessive." He looked over his shoulder at Thacea again. His lips twisted into a semblance of a smile. "What will you do without me in your bed, Princess?"

She swallowed. "I'll be all right, George."

He tugged the sheet down to her waist, settling his palm on her breast. "I've left my mark on you." He ran his fingers over a dark bruise on her breast. "Make sure you're in my bed, waiting for me, when I return."

She nodded, stifling a relieved sigh when the knock sounded again. George bit out a curse and rose from the bed. "I'm coming," he barked, and strode from the room, slamming the connecting door behind him.

Thacea shivered and threw back the covers. She reached for the bellpull, fervently hoping Molly had already heated the water for her bath. It would take most, if not all, of a cake of soap to erase the lingering feel of George's hands on her body.

Twelve

The moment he saw her step from the carriage, Marcus drew a deep breath of relief. He'd convinced himself she wouldn't meet him at the green that day. He had been certain something would prevent her from coming. Until the very last moment, when her carriage door swung open and she alighted onto the green, he'd prepared himself for her refusal. His relief was palpable. He stepped down from his own carriage, his gaze never leaving her face.

Thacea had changed her mind a half dozen times since George had left that morning. Even now, she was fighting a frantic urge to leap back into her carriage. Peter Drake stepped down from behind her and settled his hand on her elbow. She cast an anxious glance over her shoulder at him. The now customary frown that had settled between his eyebrows was firmly in place. Peter's disapproval had been evident since early that morning. It had done little to lighten her own mood.

Marcus's warm voice, on the other hand, thawed a good bit of the cold knot of anxiety in her stomach. "Good morning, my Lady. I'm delighted to see you."

His voice slipped across her frayed nerves like warm silk. She turned her gaze from Peter to smile at him. "Good morning, your Lordship."

Her breath formed a gentle plume of mist in the frosty air, and Marcus lifted her hand to his lips. Thacea fought the urge to fidget beneath his penetrating stare. She'd asked Molly to arrange her plaited hair on the side that morning to cover the bruise at her temple, but Marcus's eyes seemed to see right through her. Marcus kissed her hand through the soft leather of her glove before he pulled her arm through the bend of his elbow and turned his attention to Peter Drake. "Thank you for escorting her here this morning, Peter. I trust everything is in order?"

Peter nodded abruptly. He signaled Jake to move the small trunk to Marcus's traveling carriage, where Molly would ride with Marcus's valet. Thacea looked at Marcus, a worried look in her eyes, but he gave her hand a reassuring squeeze. "I cannot tell you how much it means to me that you are here," he said. "You aren't worried, are you?"

She shook her head. "It's Peter. He's been in a temper all day. I think perhaps he disapproves."

Marcus looked at his friend thoughtfully. "No, I don't think so."

Thacea frowned. She genuinely cared for Peter. It disturbed her that he was so obviously out of sorts. "Something must be wrong, Marcus. I think perhaps he believes that you and I . . ." she trailed off, an embarrassed flush staining her cheeks.

"If you will wait for me in the carriage, I will speak to him. I'm sure you've imagined it."

Her brows knitted together as she looked once more at Peter. "I hope so. I like Peter, Marcus. I don't want him to think I'm behaving improperly."

Marcus shook his head. "I'll see to it. I promise."

Thacea hesitated, then walked to Marcus's carriage. She tried to ignore the tiny aches and pains she still felt from the previous night. Her discomfort would make the carriage ride seem longer than necessary, she knew, but she resolutely put the thought out of her mind, determined not to let it spoil her day.

Marcus stood watching Peter oversee the transfer of Thacea's trunk. She was right in her assessment of his mood. Peter was certainly in a temper. "Drake," he said quietly, waiting for Peter to acknowledge him. "I'd like to speak to you."

Peter looked at him sharply and gave a curt order to Jake before walking over to Marcus. "Did you want something, Brandt?"

At his clipped tone, Marcus raised an eyebrow. "Not especially. I think perhaps you do, however."

Peter stared at him for several seconds. "I've known you for over twenty years, Brandt. I've never interfered in your personal life before. I don't see any reason to begin now."

"I see every reason. I've always counted on your honesty, Peter."

Peter's eyes narrowed. "What do you hope to accomplish?"

Marcus looked at him in surprise. "What do you mean?"

"I mean, what do you want out of this escapade? You take her off for two weeks to a house party, talk her into falling in love with you—a rather short drop I believe—and then what? Turn her back over to her bastard husband because you've grown bored?"

Marcus's eyes flared angrily. "You know nothing at all about this situation, Drake."

"I know a good deal more than you give me credit for. I know you better than anyone else on this earth. And I live in that house, for God's sake. Don't you think I know what goes on?"

"What are you talking about?"

"I'm talking about how she's going to recover when you're done with her. Thacea Worthingham is different from the rest, Brandt. You can't simply throw her back in the sea with an expensive brooch for her troubles and hope she'll learn to swim again."

"That's not my intent."

"Isn't it? I know you. You've only stayed interested in her this long because she's held you at arm's length. Hasn't it occurred to you that that may be her only way to survive?"

Marcus looked at him cynically. "And why this sudden burst of conscience? You certainly haven't lacked for a constant stream of women in your life."

Peter shrugged. "I'm not sure. Perhaps because I genuinely care for this one. Perhaps because I care more for Madelyne than I want to admit, and I know how much your sister cares for Thacea Worthingham. I don't know. But I do know this. She won't survive if you show her a taste of freedom and then send her back to that prison she lives in."

Marcus felt a sliver of dread work its way into his blood. "How bad is it, Peter?"

"I know she's got a bruise the size of a goose egg on her temple this morning—and I'd wager a good many more that aren't visible. I hear things and see things that make my stomach churn, and I know that George Worthingham is a genuine bastard. You'd kill him if you saw even a tenth of what I have."

Anger flared in Marcus's soul. He cast a quick glance over his shoulder to where Thacea was speaking with Molly. "I'll take care of her. I promise. I won't let her get hurt."

"You can't guarantee that. What do you think it will be like for her after you're gone? There won't be any more holidays, and you will have tainted her contentment with her current situation."

"I've done everything I can to bring her happiness. You cannot fault me for that."

"Can't I? You've been too selfish to see what you're doing to her. You're tearing the poor woman apart."

Marcus sighed in frustration. "What do you want from me, Drake?"

"Walk away. Do it right now, before it's too late."

Marcus looked back at Thacea for several long seconds before he met Peter's gaze once more. "I can't," he said.

Peter looked at him angrily. "Then God help you, Brandt-wood, because I'll personally see to it that the consequences are yours if she comes to any harm." Peter turned and swung up into the carriage, slamming the door shut behind him. Marcus hesitated only briefly before signaling Jake to drive home.

Thacea had been watching the entire encounter from the corner of her eye while only half listening to Molly's chatter. When she saw Marcus striding toward her, she looked apologetically at Marcus's valet, who would have the task of riding with Molly all the way to the Marquess of Ridgefield's estate. "Molly," she said, cutting off the girl in mid sentence. "Perhaps you should climb in now. I believe his Lordship is ready to leave."

"Oh, yes ma'am. And here I am going on like a magpie. Jake tells me I talk too much, but he says he doesn't mind. It's just that I . . ."

"Molly!"

Molly blushed. "Yes, ma'am," she said, and climbed into the carriage, happily introducing herself to Marcus's valet. The footman shut the door and Thacea could still hear Molly's chatter when Marcus walked up beside her. "Are you ready?" he asked.

She glanced at him sharply when she heard his dark tone. "Is everything all right? With Peter, I mean?"

Silently, he handed her into the carriage. He stepped up behind her and settled onto the comfortable leather cushion, his eyes watching her intently.

The instant the carriage door clicked shut and the wheels began to move, he levered down on one knee in front of her, lifting the plait at the side of her face. When he saw the dark bruise at her temple, he bit off a curse, his green eyes flaring angrily. "Damn it!" She started at the angry tone in his voice. He traced the bruise gently with the tip of his finger and she shivered. "George did this."

There was no question in his tone. Thacea decided no confirmation was needed. She wrapped her fingers around his wrist instead. "It isn't painful." His eyes met hers and he stared at her for long seconds. "Not anymore," she added weakly.

Marcus moved to sit beside her, pulling her head onto his shoulder. "Are there others?" he asked quietly. She started to say no, but he squeezed her shoulder. "Do not lie to me."

"Yes. There are others."

"Did he do this last night?"

"Yes," she said again.

Marcus's body tensed. "Did he . . . touch you?"

She heard the angry tone in his voice and moved her head back to look at him. His jaw was clenched. A muscle twitched in his cheek. His eyes glittered with barely suppressed rage.

Gently, she laid her fingers on the tight line of his jawbone. At the touch of her hand, he turned his head to stare at her. "Marcus," she said quietly, "you have promised me a two-week holiday. I do not wish to spend it talking about George."

He hesitated briefly before he kissed her palm. Taking her slender fingers in his hand, he gently removed her glove and laid her palm against his heart. "I'm sorry."

"Can we not simply put it all behind us?"

With a heavy exhalation of breath, Marcus reached over to pull her onto his lap, ignoring her startled protest. "Today we can do whatever you wish. I will not press you on the matter again."

She stopped trying to squirm off of his lap, discovering the position was significantly more comfortable than the hard leather seat had been. Her body didn't ache nearly as much when he held her like this. "Thank you, Marcus," she said, stifling a slight yawn. The gentle motion of the carriage, coupled with the heat of the sun pouring through the window and her sudden contentment, were making her sleepy. She rarely slept well at night, never feeling completely safe in George's house, but here, protected by Marcus, isolated from the outside, she felt cocooned in a haven of warmth. She yawned again and looked at him apologetically. "Would you mind terribly if I slept for a few minutes? I'm very tired suddenly."

He stretched out his long legs across the carriage so she would be more comfortable. "You may sleep to your heart's content, my Lady. I have no greater desire, for the moment, than to hold you."

She traced a lazy pattern on his shoulder with her fingers. "Thank you, Marcus. I'm . . ." she yawned again, "so tired, I can barely keep my eyes open."

Her voice trailed off on the last word. Marcus briefly tightened his arms, vowing that he would not let any more harm come to her. Peter had been right. He could not simply return her to the world she'd left. He would have to keep her in his.

Thirteen

Marcus nestled his fingers in her black hair and groaned when she shifted against him. Thacea had been asleep for nearly an hour. He'd done everything he could think of to distract himself. Despite his efforts, he was growing increasingly aware of how well she fit against him, and the pleasant sensation of her soft bottom wedged against his thigh. Her hair smelled of roses. He inhaled a deep breath, burning the scent into his memory. The soft clatter of the horses' hooves and the jingle of the harnesses did little to take his mind off the exquisite feel of her. One wheel of the carriage dropped into a shallow rut and Thacea jostled a bit, sliding into a more advantageous position.

Marcus closed his eyes and tipped his head back against the wall of the carriage. This, he supposed, was his punishment for a life lived in careless disregard for propriety. The hem of her gown had ridden up her ankle. The enticing view of her rounded calf and her delicate striped stockings proved to be his undoing. He wondered how long she would sleep if he moved his fingers beneath the hem and explored the softness of her stockinged legs. By shifting only slightly, he would have better access. He would be able to move his palm over her flesh all the way to her thigh, where he could untie her garters and slide her stockings away.

He wondered a bit madly what color her garters were. While he suspected they were a functional white, he suspected she would have preferred something more scandalous. For the sake of his sanity, he dismissed the notion of scarlet garters and forced his thoughts back to white ones. They would be tied around her silken thighs, and when he tugged loose the bows, he could pull them away and watch the soft ribbons glide over her skin like a lover's caress. He imagined she would moan when he did that.

She moved against him once more, and when her breasts pressed against his chest, he felt his loins tighten. His masculine eye hadn't failed to appreciate the graceful proportions of her figure. If he peeled away her bodice and lowered his lips to her breast, he was certain he could have her clutching at him in minutes. The thought of tugging the turgid peak of her nipples between his lips and suckling wrenched a groan from his chest. He felt a trickle of perspiration slide down his spine.

Her hair was so dark, it occurred to him that her nipples might well be the soft exotic brown of eastern women instead of the pinkish hue he was accustomed to. The irreverent thought snapped what remained of his control. He shifted her gingerly to the seat beside him. He had taken all of the exquisite torture he could endure.

Free of her weight, he pulled back the curtain, struggling to rein in his unruly thoughts. He cast another glance at her and promised himself he would do all he had imagined and more before very much longer. At the rate he was going, his sanity depended on it.

The sun had risen high in the sky, burning away the morning's frost. The Marquess's country estate was just two and a half hours northwest of London. They were making excellent time, and barring any mishaps, they would easily arrive in time for luncheon. Marcus checked his pocket watch just to be sure, then leaned back against the carriage seat, his eyes returning to Thacea's peaceful profile.

He was obsessed with her. He'd been denying it for days, but there was simply no other explanation for his recent behavior. The very idea of accompanying her to this house party was insane. There was simply no plausible reason for his continued pursuit. That she excited him physically was certainly undeniable. He grimaced ruefully and shifted in his seat, the tightness in his loins an uncomfortable reminder of his earlier train of thought. But he had been physically attracted to thousands of women, many of whom he'd made love to and plenty of others whom he had not. That alone didn't explain his all but overwhelming desire to own her. It ran deeper, he knew, than merely protecting her from her husband, or anything else for that matter. He wanted to possess her.

He had told her before that he was used to getting precisely what he wanted. That he had been thwarted in his efforts so far did not sit well with him. Thacea had made it quite clear she wasn't interested in the only arrangement open to the two of them. She would not be his mistress no matter what manner of promise he made her. Had he been thinking rationally, he should have dismissed the matter weeks ago and moved on to more fertile territory.

She stirred slightly in her sleep, pillowing her head against his shoulder. He exhaled a slow breath. In truth, he hadn't been interested in another woman since the morning she'd given him the dagger to sell. It was odd—almost ludicrous really. Given his past associations, sexual abstinence was not something he was overly familiar with. He found the entire matter vastly unsettling, and the more he thought about it, the more he began to doubt the wisdom of the plans he'd made for the next two weeks.

Thacea awoke abruptly, her sharp intake of breath piercing the stillness of the carriage. She sat up and stared at Marcus, her stormy blue eyes slightly disoriented. She reached up a hand to straighten her hair, and managed a crooked smile. "How long have I been asleep?" she asked, struggling with one of her hairpins.

He watched her, an unreadable expression in the depths of his eyes. Thacea's hand stilled. She shifted uncomfortably beneath his heated gaze. He reached over to secure the pin for her. "Only slightly over an hour."

A delicate flush swept over her face. "You shouldn't have let me sleep so long. I must have made you uncomfortable."

Marcus nearly laughed at the accuracy of the innocent statement. Instead, he dropped his hand, pausing to tuck a stray tendril behind her ear. "Not at all. I use this carriage for traveling because of its added space." He didn't bother to tell her he'd spent the last hour fantasizing about what he'd like to do to her in that space.

Thacea turned to look out the window. A slightly tense silence fell between them, and Marcus studied her profile, his eyes moving leisurely over her features. Yes, she was driving him mad. He was certain they would have to reach some clear decision about the future of their association in the next two weeks, or he'd end up in Bedlam.

Thacea stared at the passing countryside and silently agonized over the wisdom of her decision to attend the party with Marcus. She had realized earlier that morning that somewhere between start and finish, she'd allowed herself to fall in love with him. She really felt rather stupid for not having recognized it before. She'd been old enough when her mother died to have seen all the symptoms. She remembered the way her mother's eyes had gone soft when her father entered the room. She remembered the whispered exchanges, the veiled glances, the way her mother overlooked her father's more obvious flaws while focusing on the obscure ones. Thacea had been no different with Marcus.

In the past three weeks, she had noticed how much brighter the room seemed when he entered. She had deliberately ignored the gossip she heard about his behavior, dismissing it as trite and inconsequential. She had begun to notice tiny details of his person, like the way the corner of his mouth crinkled almost imperceptibly when he teased her. Or the somewhat predatory glint in the depths of his gaze when his temper was riled. He was generous to a fault, yet she found the meticulous precision with which he ran his household annoying.

She looked at him from the corner of her eye. It had been a dreadful mistake to fall in love with Marcus Brandton. The knowledge of leaving England with George—no matter what their destination—had suddenly become intolerable. She could no longer bear the thought of the loneliness. Yet she could not betray Raman. Were the circumstances different, it would be precisely the type of problem she would take to Marcus, but to confide in him about Raman would risk her brother's life. No one else but George knew Raman was still alive. For her brother's sake, it must remain that way. She could not afford to trust anyone with the information, much as she wanted to.

Her spirits lifted slightly with the knowledge that she had two weeks of uninhibited freedom. Two weeks to forget her problems. She stole another sideways glance at Marcus. He looked remarkably handsome in his black greatcoat. His curls lay in their customary unruly waves—the perfect foil for his personality—and his starched white cravat lay in an intricate knot beneath the strong angle of his chin. She allowed her eyes to move downward slightly, admiring the charcoal grey of his jacket, the emerald-green brocade of his waistcoat. His fawn-colored breeches disappeared into mirror-polished Hessians, accentuating the length of his muscular legs.

The carriage had grown suddenly warmer. She shifted in her seat, tearing her glance away from him. For two weeks, she would live in another world. The new gowns, the elegance of the Marquess's estate, and above all, the luxury of Marcus's undivided attention, all lent an aura of unreality to the experience. She thought of Raman again, and pictured him astride a horse, sitting alone in the desert. In the distance, she imagined, he could see the Sultan's palace—the palace that was his by birthright. Whenever she thought of him, she always pictured him against that backdrop. Surely her own circumstances were not so very different.

Her life with George was much like living alone in the desert. She was isolated from her family. She lived among harsh, unforgiving conditions where the loneliness and emptiness threatened to overwhelm her. Now, however, she was standing on the edge of an oasis—a tiny piece of paradise within the dry barren expanse of the desert. Inside, there would be comforts she had nearly forgotten, but the two weeks would end. She would have to return to the heat of the desert.

Anxiously, she stared out the window. Uncertainty gnawed at her until she nearly decided to ask Marcus to turn the carriage around and return her to London. And then she saw him.

Beside the road, a small boy was floating tiny sticks in a mud puddle, watching in avid fascination as they swirled in the dirty brown water. She had a sudden memory of crouching by an oasis pool with her father while he launched broken bark from the date palms into the clear water to amuse her. It was nearly dark, and the heat of the desert had passed. They had stopped at the oasis early that afternoon. Her mother had fallen asleep under one of the tall palms. She remembered smiling up at her father and eating the sweet dates he handed her before he released the slips into the pool. "Baba," she had said, "are we leaving the oasis now?"

He nodded. "Yes. The heat has passed. It's time to move on."

She had been disappointed, preferring the cool comfort of the oasis to the more unforgiving desert. "I like it better here."

He rubbed her head with his hand. "It is more comfortable in the oasis, isn't it, Ayat?"

Thacea smiled in memory at her father's name for her. It translated loosely into *cub* in English. "Yes, Baba. It makes it hard to return to the desert once you've been here."

He shook his head. "No. Once you've been in an oasis, you have only to close your eyes in the heat of the desert. Then remember the feel of the cool sand between your toes, and the taste of the water from the pool."

"Is that what you do, Baba?"

He nodded. "Yes. My memories of the oasis make the desert heat less scalding and my throat less parched." She remembered the way he'd reached out his hand to tap her forehead. "Not even the cleverest thief can rob what you treasure in here, Ayat. Remember the oasis and the desert will not seem so harsh."

Thacea smiled at the memory and silently thanked her father for the advice. It was still sound. Marcus leaned forward and touched her knee, breaking her reverie. "We will be stopping soon. Is there anything you need from your trunks before we arrive at the Marquess's estate?"

She looked at him in surprise. "Why are we stopping?"

"I think it would be best if we did not arrive in the same carriage. I do not wish to cause unnecessary gossip."

Thacea's eyes twinkled in amusement. "You have never been shy of gossip before, my Lord."

He laughed. "I will admit it's a new experience for me. I have made arrangements at an inn, however, for an unmarked carriage to convey you and your trunks on ahead. I will wait an hour or so before I follow."

She nodded thoughtfully. "I should take Molly too, I suppose. I imagine your valet's nearly gone daft after an hour alone with her."

"Either way. It wouldn't be untoward for me to arrive with both servants."

"I believe your valet would argue the point. Molly is rather . . . outspoken."

Marcus raised an eyebrow. "Do you find her irritating? I will replace her if you do."

"Oh no," she rushed out. "I think she's charming. I'll admit she found me a bit off guard when I first met her, but now I'm quite used to it." She tipped her head and looked at him thoughtfully. "Besides, I wouldn't replace a servant over something so trivial. You wouldn't replace Mr. . . . ." she paused, aware that she didn't know the name of his valet. "What is your valet's name?"

"I don't know."

Her eyes widened. "You don't know?" she said in amazement.

"My secretary hires my staff. I don't need to know their names. If they are unsatisfactory, I discharge them."

"But you know Colonel Samuelson rather well."

"That's of a different nature of course. I know John personally because his son was under my command on the continent. It isn't at all the same as my valet."

She was aware she was virtually gaping at him and didn't seem to be able to do anything about it. "Marcus, how can you not know the people around you? You see your valet several times a day, for heaven's sake. Do you mean to say you don't know anything about him?"

"There is no need for me to know anything about him. He serves me. What he does beyond the doors of my household is none of my affair."

"I see," she said quietly.

His gaze narrowed. "Do you disapprove?"

"No, of course not. You are free to run your household however you see fit."

"I'm pleased you understand that. Now, can we not turn our attention to something more interesting than my household staff?"

She exhaled a deep breath. "I have actually made a decision I think you will find rather to your liking."

"This could prove rather interesting."

"Not that much to your liking," she scolded.

"One can always hope."

"One always can, but in this case, I think you will find this quite agreeable."

"You have my undivided attention."

"It has occurred to me that two weeks is really quite a long time. It would be different if this were merely an extended weekend."

He nodded. "That's true."

"Therefore, I have decided that I shall live each day of these two weeks with no thought whatsoever to the next. If I spend my time anxious about what I'll do when I return to London, it will mar the entire fortnight."

His gaze narrowed on her. "And what is it about this momentous decision that I am supposed to find agreeable?"

"I have decided to entirely dismiss from my mind the rather unpleasant notion that we will return to London in two weeks, where you will return to your world and I will return to mine.

Instead, I want to spend what time we have storing memories for when I return to the desert."

Marcus felt a smile tug at the corner of his mouth. It disconcerted him that he was beginning to understand her funny little riddles. He lifted her hand to his lips. He lingered longer than was necessary, his eyes locking with hers in a heated gaze filled with seductive promise. "I shall do my very best to make them fond memories."

His voice slid over her in a now familiar warm rush. She felt a blush steal over her skin. Nervously, she withdrew her hand from his and diverted her attention to the window once more. The carriage was turning in at the courtyard of a small inn and she sighed, more than a little relieved. "If it isn't too much trouble," she said, "I would like to change my gown before I leave here."

He nodded. "Of course. I will have your trunks carried upstairs. Would you like refreshment as well?"

"No. I don't want to delay too long. Is the Marchioness expecting us for luncheon?"

"Yes. I responded for both of us and told her you would arrive before me, but that we would both be in time for luncheon this afternoon."

The carriage rolled to a stop and the door opened instantly, bright sunlight flooding the inside. Thacea accepted the footman's hand and stepped down. Marcus followed her. She noticed he never even glanced at the footman. When she turned to thank the young man for his assistance, the carriage door was already shut. He had already stepped back onto his box at the rear.

After the discussion she'd had with Marcus about his valet, she was noticing for the first time how that strange level of detachment and precision was evident at every level of his staff. She had a brief memory of her father sitting on horseback, laughing uproariously with his personal servant Saban, and an amused smile twitched at her lips. Perhaps Marcus was trapped in a desert as well. It wouldn't harm him any to step into the oasis for a fortnight.

Marcus finished relaying his orders to one of his outriders then returned to her side. He pressed his palm to the small of her back. "I'm sorry. I was giving instructions for your trunks."

She smiled at him, a knowing glint in her eyes. "No matter. I was making decisions."

He moved with her toward the entrance of the inn. "For what you will wear?" he asked, more for conversation than for interest.

"No," she said, stifling a tiny bubble of laughter. "For what I will change."

Fourteen

Thacea slipped her arms into the sleeves of her traveling gown as she remembered Marcus's expression. She hadn't given him the chance to ask what changes she planned. The door to the inn had swung open and the portly innkeeper had gushed over them, waxing with delight over the enormous sum of money Marcus handed him to provide her with a room. Molly had followed her upstairs, and they'd made quick work opening the trunk and selecting a gown.

"There, ma'am," Molly said, pausing for the first time in her usual chatter. "I think that looks lovely."

Thacea turned to survey her expression in the mirror. The gown was a periwinkle-blue brocade with white velvet ribbons and insets along the sleeves and skirt. She suppressed a twinge of guilt when she considered the cost of the gown. It fit her perfectly, as had all the clothes Marcus had purchased for her. He'd spent a small fortune. Resolute, she thrust the notion aside. She'd already accepted the extravagant gesture, and couldn't change that now. "I think we must do something with my hair, Molly. I fell asleep in the carriage. My plait is untidy."

Molly delved into the trunk for Thacea's combs and brushes. "You know, ma'am, I think that gown is ever so much nicer than your old one. The color suits you perfectly. Do you want your plait on the side again?" Molly's head popped out of the trunk. "Or do you want it down the back? I rather like it on the side. It covers that . . ." Molly trailed off, an embarrassed expression on her face.

"It covers the bruise, you mean?"

Molly nodded. "I didn't mean any disrespect. It's just that I thought you might want to . . ."

"I know you didn't. And you're right. I think we should plait it on the side. At least for today. Perhaps it will have faded enough by tomorrow that we can just use some powder."

Molly raced forward with the brushes in her hand and began pulling at Thacea's hairpins. "I think so too, ma'am. This is so exciting, you know. I've never been to a house party before. Jake is terribly jealous. He says I'll probably meet some groom in the Marquess's stables and forget all about him, but I told him that wasn't nearly likely." Molly tugged the dark strands of Thacea's hair into an intricate plait. For all her protestations that she wasn't very good with hair, Molly had turned out to be something of an artist when it came to coiffure. Thacea was convinced Molly could make a fortune if she set her mind to it. She would need a French name—Madame somebody or other—but beyond that, she could set up shop in London and charge outrageous fortunes to do original coiffures during the season.

Thacea watched in the mirror as Molly completed the intricate plait and secured it with a twist, just for flourish. The girl was still chattering on about Jake and his thoughts on the house party when she said something that arrested Thacea's attention. "It was then, ma'am, that Mr. Langford told me . . ."

Thacea's eyes met Molly's in the mirror. "Mr. Langford?"

"Why yes, ma'am. That's his Lordship's valet. I've known him for the longest time. He worked for his Lordship's father before he disappeared. Anyway, Mr. Langford said that I wouldn't likely meet any of the men servants at this party, but I would be able to talk with the other maids. I think I'll enjoy that, to compare gowns and hair and such. Not that I would gossip, ma'am. I would never do that. But I . . ."

"Molly," Thacea said thoughtfully.

"Yes, ma'am." Molly didn't seem to notice she'd been interrupted.

"How much do you know about his Lordship's father?"

"Oh, not much, ma'am. The Earl left before I went to work for her Ladyship—that being the Dowager Countess."

"But you know a great deal about her Ladyship?"

"Well, yes, ma'am. I worked there for six years, you know."

"You'll be riding the rest of the way with me in a separate carriage, Molly. I'd like you to tell me everything you can remember about the Countess while we travel."

Molly looked at her a bit dubiously. "We aren't allowed to gossip, your Ladyship. It's his Lordship who employs us, not her Ladyship. And he makes it quite clear we'll be dismissed without references if we gossiped."

Thacea smiled at her reassuringly. "And that's a very good policy. What his Lordship means is that he doesn't want you repeating below stairs what you've heard or seen above. This is different, though. I promise you can trust me."

"Oh, I know that, ma'am. I just don't want anyone to get in any trouble is all. It's a good job, you know. I wouldn't want to lose it."

"I assure you that you are in no danger of losing your job. I don't want you to tell me if you're uncomfortable about it, Molly. I'd never ask you—or order you—to do anything that made you uncomfortable." She looked thoughtfully at Molly. "It's simply that I know little about his Lordship, and I thought perhaps I would understand him better if I knew more about his past."

Molly glanced cautiously at the door before she bent down and whispered in Thacea's ear. "She's a harridan, that woman. I'll tell you all about her in the carriage, but there's a footman outside the door none of us trusts very much. If Henry hears me say anything, he'll report it directly to Colonel Samuelson."

They shared a conspiratorial glance. "Thank you, Molly," she said more loudly than was necessary. "I'm glad to know I'll be able to trust you once we reach the Marquess of Ridgefield's estate." Molly looked at her in surprise. Thacea lifted a finger to her lips, signaling her to be quiet. "I was concerned you might be tempted to gossip."

Molly's gaze turned knowing. "No, ma'am. You won't have to worry about me any. I'll not say a word to anyone."

In silence, they hurriedly repacked the trunks, then waited while Henry carried the luggage downstairs.

Five minutes later, Thacea walked back downstairs, her traveling cloak slung over her arm. Marcus had rented a private salon—although the term was loosely applied to the small room connecting to the main dining room. Henry escorted her past the curious gazes of the dining room's inhabitants. He knocked briefly on the door of the salon then swung the door open at Marcus's curt command.

Marcus stood alone in the room, staring out the window, his back to the door. Thacea silently admired the breadth of his shoulders as the door shut behind her. "I am ready, my Lord."

He swung around in surprise. "I was expecting my brandy. You are through more quickly than . . ." His voice trailed off. An appreciative gleam entered his eyes as he surveyed her appearance.

Marcus had not yet seen her in any of the gowns he had purchased. She shifted, nervous beneath his inspection. His breath came out in a low whistle. "An hour's wait would have been worth the bother. You are beautiful."

His voice was low and warm, and Thacea walked slowly across the room. "Oh, Marcus, no I'm not." She raised up on her toes to kiss his cheek. "But it doesn't mean I'm any less glad that you think so."

He captured her about the waist with one strong arm and held her close against him. "I am going to say something that is arrogant in its presumption," he warned.

"I wouldn't recognize you without your arrogance."

With one hand, he gently caressed the side of her face. "I do not like the thought of you wearing gowns—or anything else for that matter—purchased by your husband."

She tapped him on the chest. "Did you know a male camel will charge over an embankment if he thinks it will impress a female?"

Marcus raised his eyebrows. "Madam, are you comparing me to a camel?"

"Most certainly not. You would never spit on me, and you would certainly never bite me." At the heated look he gave her, she blushed. "But male arrogance is universal. And you needn't worry about my gowns," she continued, in a more serious tone. "George never purchased any of them."

Marcus bit back a silent curse. He had not missed the worn appearance of Thacea's wardrobe. It was fashionable enough, but then, fashion had changed very little in the years since the war. He suspected that skillful use of a needle had more to do with her presentable appearance than George's generosity with the household budget. The thousand pounds he'd paid for the dagger should have amply augmented her wardrobe, but the money had evidently gone to other pursuits. Marcus felt a seething knot of anger settle in his gut. He should just kill the bastard and be done with it. He released a quick breath and kissed her forehead. "I am glad," he said, meaning it thoroughly. He had deliberately refrained from purchasing undergarments for her, more for the sake of his sanity than the sake of her pride. It relieved him more than he cared to acknowledge that the garments next to her skin had not been purchased with Worthingham's money. He smiled ruefully at the barbaric notion. "I did not think you would have allowed me to purchase your undergarments."

She pushed ineffectually against his chest. "No, of course not."

He pulled her closer, his other arm wrapping around her shoulders. "It would have driven me mad, you know."

She ran her tongue nervously over her lips. "What would have?"

"Sitting across from you at the supper table wondering whether you were wearing the scarlet garters or the blue ones."

Her mouth dropped open in surprise. Marcus took full advantage. He bent his head and crushed his lips to hers in a kiss of blatant possession.

Thacea gasped in surprise, caught off guard by the potent sensuality of the kiss. Marcus's lips moved across hers in a heated caress, while his tongue explored the inside of her mouth in open invitation. When she heard herself moan, she tipped her head back, to give him better access.

Marcus made a tiny exultant sound as he brought one strong hand around to hold her face. He plundered the interior of her mouth, his other arm still holding her locked against him. She made the most wonderful sounds at the back of her throat. He released a heated breath when her fingers delved into his hair to pull his head closer to her own. Her tongue dueled restlessly with his and he relented, allowing her access to his mouth.

She explored the curve of his lips with the delicate tip of her tongue, driving him daft when she sucked his lower lip between her teeth. Her fingers moved restlessly in his hair. She slid her tongue over his teeth. Marcus ran his fingers along the sensitive curve of her throat. She blindly continued the tender assault on his sanity. When he could bear it no more, he slipped one finger into the bodice of her gown, and nestled it snugly between her breasts, tugging her closer.

Like a man starved, Marcus drank in her softness. In another minute or two, he would have her on the floor if he didn't pull away. The sharp knock at the door demanded his attention, and he tore his mouth away from hers, nearly losing his resolve when he saw the flushed passion on her face. He drew a ragged breath as he set her gently away from him, waiting patiently for her eyes to focus. The knock sounded again. Thacea looked at him in surprise. He dropped a soft kiss on her forehead before he stepped away from her. "Enter," he barked.

The innkeeper rushed into the room with a bottle of brandy and two glasses. Thacea leaned a little weakly against the window. Marcus always had the same overwhelming effect on her. He had only to touch her and she forgot everything else but the feel of his hands and the taste of his mouth. She drew a ragged breath and lifted a hand to her heated face. She began to fear that she'd never find a way to withstand the temptation.

Marcus dismissed the innkeeper with a short nod. "Would you like a glass of brandy before you go?" He seemed unaffected. The idea both disturbed and irritated her.

"No," she said, more forcibly than she'd intended. Her only motive at the moment was to put distance between them. "I think I should leave now. I do not wish to be late."

He studied her intently. "Your carriage is ready. Your trunks should be loaded by now. We have a few moments."

She ran her tongue over her lips. "Marcus—"

His cool gaze met hers. "Yes?"

"I . . ." she trailed off, unsure of what to say to him. "Thank you."

He scooped her cloak from the arm of the sofa. Without comment, he turned her to face him so he could deftly secure the silver clasps and pull the hood over her head. "It is only the beginning, Thacea," he said. His voice fanned across her face in a warm caress. "I will see you in an hour or so."

Not sure how to interpret the cryptic comment, she decided to ignore it. "I'll tell the Marchioness to expect you."

Thacea left the salon without so much as a backward glance in his direction. Marcus took a long sip of his brandy, marveling at the way his hand shook. He'd nearly rattled the crystal decanter when he'd poured the fiery liquid. His blood was still racing, but he hoped Thacea had not noticed the slight flush of his skin or the unsteadiness of his fingers when he'd fastened her cloak. If he controlled his desires long enough to make her burn for him as he did for her, she would not resist him any longer. He was certain of it.

He tipped back his head and swallowed the contents of his glass, thankful for the way the cheap brandy burned his throat. It was a sound plan, he knew. The trick would be maintaining his sanity in the process.

Fifteen

Thacea handed her blue and white cloak to the butler and looked around the massive foyer in pleasant surprise. In her experience, the English preferred cold, uninviting interiors in their houses, but the Marquess and Marchioness of Ridgefield proved to be the exception. Everywhere, there were flowers and plants of different shapes and descriptions. The walls were decorated with distinctly American tapestries. The enormous Abusson carpet muffled her footsteps on the vast marble floor. A fireplace at one end of the foyer, offered a bright, welcoming blaze.

The butler seemed a bit young to hold such an esteemed place in the household staff. He couldn't be a day over thirty-five, she was sure. He was handsome too, now that she thought about it. He had opened the door when she arrived, and smiled at her with perhaps more friendliness than was absolutely necessary, but the Marquess's staff, and how he trained them was really none of her business. "I am Lady Thacea Worthingham." The butler smiled at her in a manner that was almost impudent. She studied him curiously. "I believe her Ladyship is expecting me."

He cleared his throat. "Of course, your Ladyship. I will show you to the salon." He pivoted, her cloak still draped casually over his arm. A tiny frown creased her forehead as she followed him. His black trousers and grey jacket were certainly well tailored, but then, she imagined the Marquess of Ridgefield could well afford to uniform his staff any way he saw fit.

The butler pushed open the large salon door and stepped inside with a dramatic flourish. "Thacea, Lady Worthingham."

Thacea stepped tentatively past him into the salon. He really was a rather odd fellow. Thacea had met the Marchioness of Ridgefield once before and recognized her immediately when she rose from the long sofa. Caroline Erridge walked across the room, a welcoming smile on her face. "Tryon, really," she said to the butler. "You shouldn't tease Lady Worthingham. She's only just arrived." She took Thacea's hand in hers. "I'm delighted you are here, your Ladyship. Was your journey comfortable?"

Thacea opened her mouth to reply when she noticed the man at the window. His back had been to the room when she'd entered. When he turned to greet her, the glare from the sun blocked her view of his features. He stepped up behind the Marchioness, and Thacea immediately noticed the almost startling resemblance he bore to the butler. She looked back at the butler in obvious confusion. Except for a long scar along the other man's jaw, the two were identical.

The butler laughed at her startled expression. "I'm sorry, my Lady," he said, lifting her hand in his. "My sister-in-law is quite correct. I should not have tricked you."

Thacea felt the blush creep over her face. She struggled in vain to control her embarrassment. "I . . . you must be Lord Ridgefield." Belatedly, she remembered that the Marquess and his younger brother were twins.

He nodded, his smile warm. "I am. And I'm sorry I embarrassed you. It was a logical conclusion on your part. I was on my way out for a walk. When I opened the door, you assumed the obvious."

The Marquess frowned at his brother before turning his attention to Thacea. "You must accept my apologies, Lady Worthingham. My brother is fond of mischief. I am Jace Erridge. It is a pleasure to have you in my home."

She curtsied briefly, her gaze meeting his. "I cannot thank

you enough for your hospitality, your Lordship. It is very gracious of you."

Beside her, the younger Lord Ridgefield snorted. "It isn't you he's being gracious to," he muttered.

Caroline shot him a quelling glance. "Tryon. Stop playing the brag-about to my guest." She linked her arm through Thacea's and pulled her toward the long sofa. "I must beg your forgiveness. You must be exhausted from your trip. Please sit down."

The door flew open and a man who was clearly the legitimate butler of the household came doddering in. At first glance, Thacea estimated his age to be somewhere between eighty and undeterminable. Caroline looked up and smiled. "Ah. Here you are, Mr. Huddings. Lord Ridgefield has been doing a most unscrupulous impersonation of you."

The butler teetered forward unsteadily, his feet shuffling on the thick carpet as he walked. "What's that?" he shouted.

Caroline opened her mouth to retort, then seemed to change her mind. Instead she said, "Lady Worthingham has just arrived. Send in tea, please."

"It's after three?" he shouted, pulling out his watch to check the time.

Caroline shouted back. "No. *Tea,* Mr. Huddings. Send in tea."

The old butler grumbled something. He looked at Thacea, seemingly aware for the first time that there was a guest in the room. He looked back at the Marchioness. "One of your guests has arrived. Do you want tea?"

Tryon Erridge smirked as he flopped down in the high leather chair across from Thacea. "He's deaf as a doorpost," he said, earning a quelling glance from his sister-in-law.

"Yes." Caroline nodded. "I want tea."

"For three?" the butler asked.

Caroline sighed and held up four fingers. "For four, Mr. Huddings. And please take Lady Worthingham's pelisse when you go."

His expression registered his surprise. "You want the tea served with beets, your Ladyship?"

Caroline shook her head as she pointed to Thacea's cloak where Tryon had draped it over the arm of the chair. "No, Huddings. Her cloak. I want you to take her cloak."

He walked from the room, ignoring the cloak as he left. Jace Erridge groaned and lowered his large frame onto the sofa next to his wife. "There's no earthly way of knowing what he thought you said. Darling, when are you going to let me retire that man?"

"You can't simply put him to pasture," Caroline scolded. "He's worked here for nearly seventy years."

"He's deaf." The Marquess shot his wife a disgruntled look.

"He's not deaf. He's only hard of hearing."

Tryon laughed. "If he brings beets in with the tea, I'll wager you've lost that point to Jace."

Caroline rolled her eyes and looked back at Thacea. "Pay them no mind," she said. "They aren't worth the bother. Now," she settled back against her husband's arm. "I want to know all about your trip. How long were you traveling?"

Thacea leaned against the comfortable sofa. "Just under three hours, I think. It's very pleasant countryside."

Caroline nodded. "Jace purchased Sedgewood from the Comté de Verchieux. The Comté was strapped for cash, so he sold us his London town house and Sedgewood a little over a year ago. I've always enjoyed the drive from town."

"I understand your ancestral home is south of London, your Lordship," Thacea said to the Marquess.

Jace's face lit up. "That's right. Ridgefield is an hour south of London. My parents live there now."

"And I live whereever any of them will have me," Tryon interjected.

The Marquess frowned at his brother. Thacea laughed. "You have forgotten, Lord Ridgefield, that I spent two years in India. I know your name rather well. If memory serves correctly, you made enough money from your shipping interests in the East, that you could afford to live anywhere in the world."

Tryon smiled at her unabashedly. "As long as my relatives continue to house me free of charge, however, I have no incentive to spend my hard-earned reserves."

With a laugh, Caroline patted Thacea's hand. "Don't let him fool you. For all his talk of the poor, outcast relation, Tryon owns four different properties, including a scandalous château in the south of France."

Thacea nodded. "I know that as well. My husband is embassy personnel. We are afforded an extensive knowledge of the holdings of the British Peerage."

The Marquess looked at her speculatively. "I understand your husband is in France, pursuing a new post."

Thacea opened her mouth to respond when the door opened once again. Caroline exclaimed in delight at the couple who appeared. She leapt from the couch, racing across the room. "Sarah. I'm so glad to see you."

The young woman embraced the Marchioness. "It's delightful to see you too, Caroline. It's only been a month, however. I'd have been here sooner but we dropped the children with Mama and Papa."

Caroline kissed her on the cheek, then turned to embrace the gentleman. "Nevertheless, it's been too long since we've talked. How are you, Aiden?"

The man kissed her forehead. "I am well, Caroline. Thank you." He turned to assist his wife with her cloak. "Where is Mr. Huddings?" he asked, shrugging his own greatcoat from his shoulders.

"Looking for beets," Tryon called out.

Caroline frowned at him. "Stop that!" She turned her attention back to Sarah. "I want you to meet Lady Worthingham."

Sarah looked at Thacea, a warm light in her eyes. Her eyes were the most unusual shade of purple. Nervously, Thacea wished Marcus would appear. She was beginning to feel uncomfortable. The woman walked across the room and took her hand. "I'm Sarah Brickston. It's wonderful to meet you."

Thacea nearly choked. Sarah Brickston was the Duchess of

Albrick. Her husband, the Duke, was one of the highest ranking officials in the British War Department. George had an intense dislike for the man, complaining often of his arrogance and highhandedness. Based on George's descriptions, she had expected the Duke to be considerably older. She managed to drop a polite curtsy. "I'm honored, your Grace."

Reprovingly, Sarah looked at Caroline. "You evidently haven't informed Lady Worthingham of the house rules," she said.

Caroline laughed. "She's only just arrived, and I've been too busy apologizing for your brother's caddish behavior."

Sarah shot Tryon a knowing look. "Have you been causing mischief?"

He looked offended. "Now, brat, you know better than to accuse me of that."

With a delicate snort, she turned back to Thacea. "They are uncontrollable. The entire lot of them are. You mustn't let him tease you."

Thacea looked curiously from one man to the next. Finally, Caroline intervened on her behalf. "Lady Worthingham, I see we've completely baffled you. Sarah is Jace's sister. The other couple we are expecting are Lord and Lady Thomason. Anabelle Thomason is my cousin from America."

Sarah removed her gloves. "And I, for one, refuse to be *your-graced* for the next two weeks. If we are to have a holiday, then I want a holiday from titles."

"Actually," Aiden Brickston said, laying the cloaks over the end of the sofa and walking to his wife's side, "you aren't in a position to make that decision, Love. You're outranked at this affair." He smiled at Thacea and lifted her hand for a perfunctory kiss.

Sarah looked at him in surprise. "What do you mean?"

He looked at her in amusement. "Your duchess status is secondary in the household. Lady Worthingham is actually a member of the royal household in Ardahan." He turned to look at Thacea once more, a warm glint in his eyes. "Isn't that so, your Highness?"

Thacea's eyes widened. She hadn't used her royal title since her marriage to George. It sounded almost foreign to her. She was shocked that the Duke of Albrick should be aware of it. "Well, yes. I suppose it is."

"So you see, Darling," he said to Sarah, "the experience may be a new one for you, but you are most definitely outranked."

Sarah wrinkled her nose. "I don't care a whit about being outranked, but we aren't going to have a very enjoyable holiday if we have to be so formal with one another."

Aiden Brickston looked at Thacea. "I don't think Lady Worthingham will mind dropping the formalities."

Thacea warmed to him immediately. He had managed to include her in the intimate circle of friends with his graciousness. "Certainly not," she said. "No one has used my royal title in years. I would probably forget to answer to it."

"There." Caroline smiled in satisfaction. "That has worked rather nicely, I think. Now, when Philip and Anabelle arrive, we won't have to worry with any of it."

Jace Erridge looked at his wife. A frown creased his brow. "When are you expecting Brandtwood?" he said, his voice sharp.

Thacea looked up warily. "His Lordship sent word that he would be here in time for luncheon."

Aiden sank down into one of the leather chairs and pulled his wife onto his lap, despite her protests. "How encouraging," he said drily.

The Duchess poked his shoulder in warning. "Aiden, I warned you."

"You frightened me, too."

"I mean it," she said tightly. Sarah looked back at Thacea apologetically. "You'll have to forgive my husband. He isn't always certain how to conduct himself."

Thacea felt a smile tug at the corner of her mouth. "Then he and Lord Brandtwood should get along famously."

Sarah burst out laughing. "There you are, Caroline. I have

decided I like her immensely. When Anabelle arrives, the four of us shall have a wonderful time together."

The door to the salon crashed open. The butler entered with an enormous silver tray. To Thacea's immense relief, Marcus trailed behind him, a laconic smile on his lips. The butler dropped the tray on the low table with a loud clatter. Purple juice from a small bowl of pickled beets sloshed over the rim. Thacea bit back a smile at the Marquess of Ridgefield's muttered oath. Caroline was on her feet, walking forward to greet Marcus before Thacea lifted her eyes to his. He met her gaze briefly, his green eyes warm with amusement.

The Marchioness reached his side and tugged him farther into the room as the butler exited, slamming the door behind him. Marcus greeted Caroline. "I see your country staff is no less eccentric than your London staff."

Caroline laughed. "I fear boredom above all things, my Lord. I trust your journey was not unpleasant."

His eyes rested briefly on Thacea's face. "No. It was not." He lifted Caroline's hand for a brief kiss. "I must thank you again for including me in your plans."

Thacea noticed that Jace Erridge had surged off the sofa to stand behind his wife and was glowering menacingly at Marcus. Marcus didn't seem to be daunted. He met the Marquess's gaze coolly and extended his hand. "Ridgefield," he acknowledged. "Good to see you again."

Jace Erridge frowned as he shook Marcus's hand. "And you, Brandtwood."

Sarah looked at the two in disgust. She levered off her husband's lap. "The four of you deserve each other," she said, indicating the male inhabitants of the room with a sweep of her hand. "You're like a flock of male peafowl strutting around with your feathers rankled." She glanced at Thacea. "I am going upstairs to settle my things. Would you care to join me?"

Thacea looked nervously at Marcus, unsure what he expected. His gaze remained locked with the Marquess's. She de-

cided a retreat might be advisable. She turned to Sarah and
nodded. "I think perhaps that's an excellent suggestion."

"Caroline?" Sarah said. "Are you coming?"

Caroline frowned at her husband. "Yes, I am. Jace, do try
not to break anything if the four of you decide to pummel one
another. I've only just finished decorating this salon. I have no
desire to begin again."

The Marquess looked at his wife, a thoroughly disgruntled
expression on his face. "For God's sake, Caroline. This isn't
Gentleman Jack's. I have no intention of hitting the man."

"Well, I should hope not. I've told you my thoughts on this
matter, and I won't have you making my guests feel unwel-
come." She ignored his frosty stare and looked back at Sarah
and Thacea. "Shall we go?"

Sarah grasped Thacea's hand, tugging her past the four gentlemen. She paused in front of Marcus. "Good afternoon, Lord
Brandtwood. I can't remember the last time I saw you."

He acknowledged her greeting with a slight bow. "The pleasure is mine as always, Duchess."

She gave her husband a smug look. "You can't fault his manners, at any rate."

Aiden glared at her. "Sarah, don't get any ideas while you're
out. I don't want to catch you overexerting yourself."

"For heaven's sake. I'm going upstairs to my room to make
sure my gowns are unpacked properly." She looked apologetically at Caroline. "And to put on a pair of breeches. The waist
in this gown has already become too tight."

Caroline smiled at her in pleasant surprise. "Sarah, are you
expecting again?"

Sarah nodded. "Yes. I would have told you sooner, but I
wasn't certain until several days ago."

Aiden walked to her side and kissed her lightly on the forehead. "Sarah didn't want any of you to know just yet, but I'm
depending on all of you to help me keep her in line."

Tryon laughed. "You must be jesting, Brick. We've never
been able to do that. Not even when she was a child."

Aiden grinned at his brother-in-law. "If we can manage to keep her off the back of a horse for the next two weeks, I'll be satisfied."

Sarah punched him affectionately in the ribs. "I've already promised you I won't ride."

"Nothing but me that is," he said baldly.

Sarah blushed furiously. "Aiden Brickston!"

He leered at her briefly before he shifted his gaze to Thacea. "I must apologize, your Ladyship. It isn't often I am able to render my wife speechless. You will understand I must seize every opportunity."

Thacea smiled at him. "I would be quite careful, however your Grace. It is probably not wise to push too hard." She shot Marcus a knowing look.

Marcus lifted an eyebrow and waited silently for Thacea to leave the room with Sarah and Caroline. An uneasy silence filled the room when the door clicked shut behind them. Marcus waited. The silence stretched on for long, tense seconds. He hadn't initiated this conflict. He had no intention whatsoever of initiating its resolve.

Finally, the Marquess of Ridgefield cleared his throat and took a long swallow of his brandy. "All right, Brandtwood. I think we'd better come to an understanding. I don't like having you in my house. I only agreed because Caroline insisted."

Marcus nodded. "Given the circumstances, that's perfectly understandable."

Jace studied him carefully. "I will not have my house turned into a backdrop for your scandalous behavior. I would like to know what your intentions are toward Lady Worthingham."

Marcus strolled to the beverage cart, helping himself to a glass of brandy. "I would be lying if I did not tell you I have every intention of making her my mistress." Aiden swore beneath his breath. Jace's expression turned menacing. Marcus savored a swallow of the brandy before he continued. "I have given your wife my word, however, that I will conduct myself with the utmost deportment while under your roof."

Jace's eyes narrowed. "Why the hell should I believe that?"

Marcus squarely met his gaze. "Why shouldn't you? There is no logical reason for my attendance at this affair. My presence is not welcome here—something I was completely prepared for. Had I merely planned an illicit rendezvous, my usual social circle would have been much more accommodating."

Tryon shifted in his chair and studied Marcus closely. "Why are you here, Brandtwood?"

Marcus set his glass down and faced the three men. "I feel I should speak first on behalf of Lady Worthingham. I would not wish you to judge her merely by her association with me. The lady has made it quite clear she has no intention of disgracing herself by accepting my advances."

Aiden raised an eyebrow. "She's clearly a good deal more intelligent than your usual sort."

Marcus let the slight cut pass, knowing it was well deserved. "Her life is not an easy one. I have significant reason to believe her husband mistreats her. As he is currently traveling in Paris seeking a Foreign Office post, it was my desire to provide her Ladyship with a two-week holiday from her troubles."

"That sounds almost noble," Jace Erridge said cynically.

Marcus inclined his head in a slight nod. "I will not deny I have hopes that she will leave here more kindly disposed to my suit. I will do whatever I can, however, to avoid the appearance of any impropriety so long as you are my host."

Jace inhaled a deep breath, his nostrils flaring slightly. "There is no good reason why I should trust you, Brandtwood."

Marcus shook his head. "No. That is true."

"And yet that is what you ask of me."

"I ask only that you observe closely what you will see while we are here. I believe you will note a woman of fine character, well above my level of standard. If at any time you wish me to leave, I will do so immediately."

Aiden lowered himself into a chair. "Worthingham wants a Paris post, did you say?" he asked casually.

Marcus looked at him closely. Aiden Brickston's contacts and prestige within the War Department and the Foreign Office were legendary. It was rumored he had played a direct role in Wellington's defeat of Bonaparte on the continent. "Yes. That is so. Do you know George Worthingham personally?"

"Not personally, no. I do know of his reputation and record, however. Paris seems a bit above his station."

Marcus nodded. "He has had only one other assignment. The Bangalore Province, I believe."

Aiden thoughtfully stroked his chin. "Your charge that he mistreats his wife is a serious one. Do you have evidence?"

Marcus wondered vaguely what he should do. He hesitated to voice his suspicions about George Worthingham until he was more certain of the Duke's motive for wanting to know. It would be unwise to trust too readily too soon. Carefully, he chose his next words. "I would prefer not to betray her Ladyship's confidence to any great degree. If she chooses to confide in you during her time here, I will gladly tell you whatever I know. In the interim, I prefer that the decision rest in her hands."

With a nod, Aiden looked at Jace. "The decision is yours. It is your household."

Jace pursed his lips as he studied Marcus for several long seconds. Finally he drew a deep breath and set his glass down on the table. He extended his hand to Marcus. "Very well, Brandtwood, for the moment I will accept what you have told me. I will not hesitate to act, however, if you should disturb my household in any way."

Marcus clasped Jace's hand. "I understand."

Sixteen

Thacea stood at the window of her bedchamber and watched the sun creep over the horizon. The rest of the previous day had passed peacefully after Marcus's confrontation with the Marquess. Lord and Lady Thomason had finally arrived a few hours after luncheon. Thacea had spent the better part of the afternoon with the three ladies. She had not seen Marcus again until dinner, and while he had been attentive during the meal and later, when the entire party had retired to the salon for conversation and whist, he had made no effort to see her alone.

She'd gone to bed pleasantly exhausted and fallen asleep the moment her head touched the pillow. When she awoke, it was with a deep sense of satisfaction and contentment that she slipped from the large, comfortable bed and walked to her window. She had not enjoyed the warmth of a family since the death of her parents. In the ensuing years in her uncle's palace, and then in her marriage to George, she had nearly forgotten the comfort it provided.

She smiled as the sun gently heated the glass beneath her hand. It promised to be an unusually warm day. She had every intention of spending the greater part of it astride one of the Marquess's horses. She had been seated on the Marquess's left at dinner where he'd turned to her with a warm smile.

"Your Ladyship," he said. "My wife informs me you are an experienced rider."

"Yes. I rode quite extensively before I left Ardahan."

"As it happens," he continued smoothly, "I have just purchased three new horses of Arabian blood. Two stallions and a mare. I would very much like your opinion of them."

"I am not an expert in horseflesh by English standards."

He raised an eyebrow. "How do you mean?"

"In Ardahan, a horse is not valued for his teeth or his coloring. He is valued for his strength and endurance. The curve of his spine, the straightness of his legs, the width of his hooves, are all much more important than his aesthetic appeal." She had become so engrossed in the conversation, she failed to notice the sudden quiet in the room. She twirled her glass thoughtfully between her fingers and continued, "When an Ardani chooses a horse, he looks for intelligence and strength of spirit. A horse is not merely a possession to bring pleasure, but is essential to survival. What is seen on the surface may not be as important as what lies in the heart."

The Marquess's eyes shifted to rest on his wife. "It is rather the way an Englishman chooses his bride."

Thacea laughed, aware for the first time that their conversation had become the focus of attention. "Only the wiser of the breed, your Lordship. I know many Englishmen who give no thought to such matters. I imagine they are disappointed when the markings begin to fade and the mane thins and turns grey." There was a general burst of laughter. Thacea felt rather than saw Marcus's eyes resting on her face.

Jace Erridge raised his glass in silent salute. "I would wager a considerable sum that you are correct in that assumption, my dear."

The conversation in the room resumed and Thacea leaned forward, intent on finishing her discussion with the Marquess. "My point being, your Lordship, that I will be delighted to give you my opinion on your horses. I will have to ride them, however, before I can make a sound determination."

He smiled at her knowingly. "And I imagine a simple trot around the green wouldn't begin to touch the surface."

She shook her head. "A much more extensive workout would be necessary."

"By all means, my Lady," he said. "You must avail yourself of my stable. I am eager for your assessment."

"Thank you, my Lord."

He nodded. "Ask for Noah in the stables. He's one of my head grooms, and he'll assist you with whichever mount you choose."

As the sun continued to rise, Thacea thought back on the conversation with renewed pleasure. The Marquess had been exceedingly gracious in his offer. She was intent on seeking Noah's assistance as early this morning as possible. She turned from the window to consider the problem of what to wear. Propriety demanded that she wear a habit, and Marcus had provided her with two extremely fashionable ones. One was a deep blue velvet, and the other a dark green wool. She looked at the green one for several long seconds, fingering the black silk frogs on the jacket. It was exceedingly fine, and she hesitated to wear it for such vigorous exercise. It was the type of habit ladies wore for gentle gallops through the park when their appearance was considerably more important than their horsemanship.

Today, however, she had every intention of working both herself and the animal into an extremely unladylike, if intensely pleasurable, sweat. She smiled at the notion, thinking briefly that George would have been revolted at the sight of her hair dampened with perspiration, her face flushed from exhilaration. No one was likely to see her, however, until after she returned to the house. If she wore a cloak to the stables, she would be able to disguise her appearance until she reached her room and changed into more suitable clothing. She thought briefly of the Duchess of Albrick running about in breeches the afternoon before and decided then that the risk would be minimal. Her fellow guests didn't seem overly concerned with convention.

Resolutely, she opened her trunk and removed the gauzy white pantaloons and tunic she'd packed on impulse. They were all that remained of her clothing from Ardahan. She'd kept them more for their sentimental value than their practicality. George would never have allowed her to wear them.

She slipped out of her cotton nightdress and quickly donned her undergarments before pulling on the soft pantaloons. The material caressed her skin in soft folds. She sighed in pure pleasure at the comfortable fit. The white tunic hung to her thighs and buttoned at the wrist and throat. Scarlet-dyed leather decorated the shoulders and wrists. She riffled through the trunk until she found the scarlet sash for her waist. A short pair of red suede boots completed the outfit. Wriggling her toes inside the soft, worn leather, she reveled in their comfort. The final touch was a long strip of red leather she used to bind her hair into a queue at the nape of her neck. She studied her reflection with a wicked grin. George was not the only one who would be shocked.

She found her black traveling cloak and pulled it over her shoulders. It fell nearly to her ankles. There was no reason at all for anyone who happened to see her making her way to the stables to suspect she wore anything but a conventional habit beneath the cloak.

Marcus stood at his window and watched Thacea hurry across the lawn toward the stables. His eyes focused on the red boots beneath her cloak. He had risen before dawn, and dressed for his customary morning ride. He had been tugging on his boots when he heard the soft creak of a door hinge down the hall from his room. Immediately, he'd known who it was. Thacea's eyes had been particularly animated the previous evening during her discussion with the Marquess. Marcus never doubted that she would make her way to the stables as soon as she awoke the next morning.

From his vantage point at the window, he watched her steal a glance over her shoulder in the early morning light. God only knew what she had on beneath that cloak. He was willing to wager bad odds it wasn't her green wool habit. There had been a suppressed excitement about her the previous evening that had kept him awake most of the night. She had spoken to the Marquess about his horses with a light in her eyes Marcus had never seen before. He had been unable to tear his gaze from her for the greater part of the evening.

She reached a bend in the path that led to the stables and disappeared from his sight. Marcus turned resolutely from the window, slipping his arms into his chocolate-brown riding jacket. He had only seen Thacea ride according to English conventions. Her skill had always impressed him. He had spent several restless hours, however, imagining the picture of her astride one of the Marquess's horses. He had vowed to himself that he would not miss the opportunity of comparing the actual image with his mental picture. Marcus walked silently down the hall and strode from the house, making a determined path for the stables.

Thacea looked at the magnificent Arabian stallion and released a low breath of admiration. "He's magnificent, Noah," she said to the old groom.

"He is that, yer Ladyship. He's one of the finest we've had in a good while."

The horse's flesh rippled with barely suppressed energy, and he pulled against the reins, his neck arching proudly. He was predominately black, with tiny flecks of white across his nose and forelocks, and even in the darkened stable, Thacea could see the glittering fire in his eyes. His nostrils flared as he took in her scent and she turned to Noah and smiled. "He's very large, isn't he? Fifteen hands, would you say?"

Noah looked at her in admiration. "Fifteen and a quarter." The horse bucked against his rein. Noah concentrated for several seconds on quieting him. "The other one's even larger. Almost sixteen hands, he is."

Thacea nodded. She'd seen the other stallion, and had been equally impressed, but something in this one's spirit had appealed to her. "Has his Lordship named them yet?"

"It's her Ladyship who names them. Always has, as far as I know. She calls the larger one Concord. The mare is Lexington, and this one here's Saratoga. Strange names, they are, but who am I to say?"

Thacea bit back a smile. She wondered what the Marquess thought of having his horseflesh named after American victories in the revolution against Britain. She stroked the stallion's nose. "I don't know. I think *Saratoga* suits him rather nicely." She looked at Noah resolutely. "I wish to ride him, Noah."

The groom hesitated. "His Lordship sent me instructions to give ye whatever horse ye wanted, yer Ladyship, but are ye sure about this one?"

She nodded. "I can handle him."

"He's rather high-spirited this morning. Are you certain I can't talk you into seating Lexington?"

"I spent more of my childhood on a horse than on my own feet. I won't have any problems."

"I don't think ye'll be able to control him with a side saddle, yer Ladyship."

She shook her head. "I don't intend to use one. I want a conventional saddle." To her surprise, Noah looked more relieved than shocked. If he thought it odd she wanted to ride the animal astride, he certainly didn't say so. He seemed more concerned about her safety than her propriety. She gave his arm a reassuring pat. "Don't worry. Saratoga and I will be fine."

"I'll get him saddled for ye, yer Ladyship." Noah reluctantly released the latch on the stall to lead the enormous stallion past Thacea. A shiver of anticipation raced through her as she watched while Noah and two other grooms wrestled with the English saddle. She would have preferred just a blanket, but Noah would have blanched, she was sure, at the mere suggestion. If she wished, she could always remove the horse's saddle after she rode beyond eyesight of the stable.

Noah finished securing Saratoga's saddle and tack, then walked the animal back to her side. The stallion pranced anxiously, unsettled by the weight of the empty saddle. Thacea unclasped her cloak at her neck. She shrugged out of it, not daring to look at the groom's expression, and tossed it casually across the gate of Saratoga's stall. "I'll fetch that when I return," she explained, slipping her toe into the cradle of Noah's fingers. He boosted her onto the stallion's back. Her fingers closed in his mane. Noah handed her the reins with a worried expression. She laughed. "You'll not lose your job over this, Noah. I promise you that."

He shook his head as he walked ahead to swing open the stable doors. "Ye aren't the first young lady to come down here wanting to seat a man's horse. Ye likely won't be the last, either."

Thacea drew a deep breath and released the pressure on Saratoga's reins. His energy was barely in check. The instant she touched her heels to him, he bolted from the stable, his powerful legs pounding at the earth. Thacea leaned against his neck and turned her face to the wind, happier than she had been in years.

Marcus watched the magnificent animal disappear from sight and stepped out of the shadow. He had arrived at the stables only moments after Thacea, but she had been so absorbed in her inspection of the stallion, she'd failed to notice his presence. He had settled back against the wall, virtually hidden from view by the shadow of the stable door, and watched her animated discussion with Noah. When he'd seen her drop her cloak, he'd nearly lost his composure.

The sight of her mounted astride the enormous beast, clothed in the Ardani pantaloons and tunic had sent his pulse racing. She looked almost unreal, with her delicate hands clasped in the mane, her strong, shapely legs fitted against the horse's muscles. Marcus's mouth went dry at the unholy thoughts racing through his mind. It had taken every ounce of self-control he possessed to remain where he was until she left the stable.

As soon as she disappeared, he walked forward to speak with Noah. The groom looked at him in surprise. "I didn't see ye come in yer Lordship. Do ye want a mount?"

Marcus nodded briefly in the direction Saratoga had disappeared. "Something fast enough to catch that horse."

Noah wiped his hands on his shirtfront with a relieved sigh. "I didn't want her Ladyship to go off on that horse alone." Noah cast him a worried expression. "I did warn her."

Marcus nodded. "I heard. Her Ladyship is a bit determined."

Noah grinned. "She sits him well enough, though. I think she'll be all right. I'll feel better knowing ye've gone after her." The groom turned to walk along the stalls. "I've got just the horse for ye, yer Lordship. She won't be able to outpace ye on Revere."

Marcus smiled at the name. The Marchioness's humor was rather appreciable. Paul Revere would have been proud of his namesake, Marcus decided. The chestnut stallion was enormous—at least eighteen hands. Its muscular build and strong frame were dimmed only by the fire of his personality. The horse reared against his rein. His ears lay close to his head. Marcus swung into the saddle, taking the reins firmly from Noah.

Once astride the animal, Marcus felt the energy in the stallion's flanks and legs. He nodded in satisfaction to the groom before he gave the animal his head, knowing Thacea would have gained nearly a mile on him already.

He rode for an hour before he found her. Revere had not yet begun to show signs of fatigue, and Marcus had followed the contours of the land, suspecting Thacea would do the same. He finally saw her when he crested a small rise. He reined in his mount, pausing to watch her in silent admiration. She handled Saratoga with the same ease he had seen so many times when they'd ridden together in London. She had relaxed into a comfortable gallop, her hands barely touching the reins. Both rider and horse seemed to enjoy the freedom.

Marcus followed her at a distance for another several yards. Occasionally, she would throw back her head to inhale a great breath of the morning air, then lean low over her stallion's neck once more. They galloped on until the sun had risen quite high in the sky. Marcus felt a steady stream of perspiration sliding down his spine from the warmth and the exercise.

A warm breeze ruffled Thacea's damp hair. She sighed in

pure contentment. Saratoga was beginning to tire, as was she. She determined she would rein in as soon as she found water. The gentle downward slope of the land indicated water would be nearby. She slowed her pace a bit, not wishing to overexert the animal, and realized for the first time that her own breathing was heavy from the exercise. She had not ridden so vigorously in a good many years. Her muscles were already beginning to feel stiff from the strain of controlling the spirited animal.

The quiet pool that lay ahead was a welcome sight. Thacea dismounted several yards from it in the shade of a large tree. She stroked Saratoga's nose as she slowly removed his bridle. "You'll have to cool down, yet. If you drink that water now, you'll have a tremendous bellyache." The horse flicked his head free of the bridle and pranced nervously. She continued to talk in a soothing voice as she moved to his side to remove the saddle. His flanks were covered with a heavy lather. She rubbed his smooth, damp flesh with her hands. "You've more energy than you have sense, Saratoga. You should have slowed your pace."

The horse tossed his head. Tiny drops of water slung from his mane. She dropped the saddle to the ground, reaching for the sodden blanket. "Just because you're wet doesn't mean I have to be." The horse flared his nostrils at her and she laughed, slapping his rump. "Drink your fill, you great brute. You still have to carry me back, you know."

She watched as the horse trotted to the water. Tossing the blanket to the ground in a patch of sunlight, she unbuttoned the leather cuffs of her tunic and turned the sleeves back, walking slowly to Saratoga's side. She knelt beside the horse to plunge her hands into the cold water. Splashing it onto her face, she shivered when it touched her heated flesh. When she felt a man's boot planted squarely on her backside, she gasped in surprise and whipped her head around, slinging drops of icy water. "Marcus. You frightened me."

He laughed and lowered his foot. "I should think so. I could have easily tossed you into the water."

She wiped her eyes on her sleeve. "How long have you been there?"

He brushed a sodden tendril of her hair off her forehead "I've been riding behind you for nearly an hour."

She shifted uncomfortably beneath the heated look in his eyes. "I didn't see you," she said unnecessarily.

At the disgruntled tone in her voice, Marcus grinned. She wiped her wet face with her sleeve again. Marcus decided he liked the unfeminine gesture. He liked it a lot. "Evidently not Were you always this alert in the desert?"

She noticed for the first time that he'd removed his riding jacket. He held it loosely in his right hand. The snowy whiteness of his shirt made him appear larger than usual. "In the desert the dangers are enemies and wild animals. I had no reason to fear either here."

His grin widened and he dropped his jacket to the ground strolling leisurely to the pool. He lowered himself down on one knee and scooped up a handful of the cool water. "Are you certain of that?" he asked, swallowing the water and scooping up another.

She laughed unsteadily. "As certain as one can be under the circumstances, my Lord." She had been unable to divert her gaze from the damp triangle on his back where his perspiration had soaked through the fine lawn of his shirt. It clung to the strong muscles of his shoulders. She swallowed a knot in her throat when he rolled back the cuffs to expose the bronzed length of his forearms.

Marcus was aware of her eyes on him. He took his time washing the sweat and dirt from his face. He splashed water over his face and neck, tugging loose his cravat, and finally rose from the pool. When he turned to her, he saw her flush. "I recommend we find a place in the sun. It's warmer there."

She tore her gaze from him, walking resolutely away from the shade of the trees. She noticed, belatedly, that he had unsaddled his horse. The large stallion was drinking his fill next to Saratoga. She smiled uncertainly at Marcus, feeling oddly out of sorts. His unexpected arrival had caught her completely unaware. The way he looked at her made her stomach flutter.

Marcus stretched his tall frame out on a wide expanse of grass and linked his hands beneath his head, turning his face to the sun. Thacea hesitated, noticing he took up most of the sunlit space. She would be forced to sit close to him if she wanted to share the sun's warmth. His eyes had drifted shut, and he seemed not to notice her indecision. Gingerly, she sank to the grass in the shade. Only her feet extended into the bright patch of sunlight.

Marcus inhaled a great breath and flexed his shoulders. He wondered briefly how long it would be before she scooted completely into the sunlight. He opened his eyes lazily to smile at her. "Did your mount live up to your expectations?"

She nodded in delight. "Oh, yes. He's a fine horse. It's been a long while since I've ridden this extensively."

He closed his eyes once more as he leaned back on his hands. "London can't begin to provide this type of exercise. That's one of the reasons I prefer the country."

A cool breeze ruffled her damp hair. Thacea felt the gooseflesh raise on her arms. Her feet were pleasantly warm, however, and she cast an anxious glance at Marcus. His eyes were still shut, so she shifted silently to extend them all the way into the warm light. "But you spend most of your time in London," she said.

"Umm." He sounded sleepy. "That's true. The country seldom provides the entertainment I prefer." He bit back a smile when she changed positions again and moved closer to him.

"Female entertainment, you mean?" She couldn't help the slight edge to her voice. "I should think it would be easy enough for you to import." She shivered again when a stronger gust of cool air bit through her damp tunic. He looked so damn comfortable—and warm—it was beginning to irritate her.

Marcus felt her slide closer to him. All but her shoulders and head were in the sunlit patch. He hadn't missed the sharp tone in her voice either. He allowed himself a feeling of satisfaction. Things were proceeding extraordinarily well. He forced a yawn.

"I've tried that a number of times. It's never as convenient as it seems."

With a frown she scooted along the ground until she lay next to him. His warmth blanketed her cooled flesh. He was very nearly asleep, it seemed. She basked in the sun a few minutes, waiting for the tip of her nose to warm. There was no reason on earth why his casual comment should disturb her so much. No reason except that she'd been foolish enough to fall in love with him. The thought of him surrounded by a throng of beautiful women made her so jealous her eyes burned as green as his. "No," she finally said in answer to his blithe comment. "I suppose it isn't."

He reared up on his elbow, suddenly looming over her. All pretense of fatigue had suddenly evaporated. He smiled a slow, knowing smile at her surprised expression. "Are you jealous, love?"

She pushed ineffectually at his chest. "Certainly not."

He traced a finger along the rounded neckline of her tunic. "There's no reason to be, you know. I've never been obsessed with any of them. Until now."

Thacea swallowed hard, her eyes widening slightly. Every nerve in her body was attuned to the featherlight caress of his fingertip. "Marcus . . ."

His eyes burned hotter. He slowed the movement of his finger. "Say it again," he prompted. "I like the sound of my name on your lips." Her mouth went dry. She moved her lips, but no sound came forth. "Close enough," he whispered. His warm breath fanned over her. "Are you still cold?" He tipped his head until his mouth was mere inches from hers. "I suppose I'm obliged to warm you."

The instant his mouth touched hers, Thacea spiked her fingers into his thick, damp hair. There was no point at all in pretending this had not been what she'd wanted since the very moment she'd seen him standing behind her. Her uninhibited ride had unleashed a certain primitive energy in her. She had ached for Marcus's kiss even before she'd realized it.

He moved his mouth over her cool lips and drank in the scent and the taste of her. His hand stilled at her collarbone where he splayed his fingers over her shoulder, continuing the tender pressure of the kiss.

Thacea was having none of it. When he made no move to deepen the kiss, she sucked at his lower lip to gain his attention. Her fingers moved restlessly in his heavy hair and she arched her neck, bringing her mouth into close contact with his. Finally, she nipped his lower lip lightly with her teeth. He growled and bore down on her. His tongue swept into the hot inside of her mouth in a silken stroke. Filled with pleasure, she sank back against the grass, wrapping her free hand around Marcus's waist.

She tasted so damn good. Marcus felt his passion spiral. He plundered the depths of her mouth. He slid his palm along the curve of her arm and over her rib cage until his hand settled on the curve of her breast. She moaned deep in her throat as she moved against him. When he felt her small hand tug his shirt from the waistband of his trousers, he dragged in an essential breath.

She ran her hand restlessly over the smooth plain of his back. Marcus's thumb massaged her tight nipple through the gauze of her tunic. She arched into his hand, seeking to increase the exquisite pressure. He tore his mouth from hers with a ragged groan and slid his lips along the length of her throat. His fingers moved to the buttons of her shirt, and he flicked them open, following the path with tiny damp kisses.

His other hand still rested beside her head. Thacea turned her face against it, rubbing his fingers with the soft skin of her cheek. He flexed his hand, and, in a moment of utter insanity, she drew his index finger between her teeth where she laved it gently with her tongue.

Marcus groaned. "Yes, love. Feel this with me." His voice was a strained whisper. He slipped loose the fifth button on her tunic, then gently pushed the fabric aside. He buried his face in the sensitive hollow between her breasts and nearly died when he felt her fingers dig into his back. The rounded swell of one breast, its taste beneath his lips, made his desire harden almost unbearably. When the fabric fell away and her brown nipple was visible beneath the lawn of her chemise, he sucked in a breath and stared at the diamond-hard tip.

Thacea's eyes flew open in alarm. She had forgotten. . . . She clutched at the edge of her tunic and struggled away from him, pulling anxiously on the buttons. With a visible effort, Marcus reined himself in. His chest rose and fell with his labored breathing. She didn't meet his gaze as she concentrated on the buttons of her tunic. Silently, she cursed the flush that covered her face. "I'm sorry." She slid the last button into place and scooted even farther away from him.

He looked at her, confused, his blood still smoldering. "I'm not. I'm not sorry in the least."

She felt the heat rise in her face. She pulled her knees to her chest, still unable to meet his gaze. "Yes, well, now at least you know. That clears the air between us, doesn't it?"

Marcus stared at her blankly. What the bloody hell was the woman talking about? "Thacea," he started cautiously.

She surged to her feet. "I don't want to talk about it, if you don't mind." She scooped up her horse's blanket and noticed with some dismay that Marcus lay between her and her saddle. She moved to walk around him, but he sat up and clasped her ankle, halting her progress.

"What don't you want to talk about? That I nearly made love to you just now? That a few more minutes and I would have been inside of you?"

Her mouth fell open. "Marcus. Are you always so blunt?"

He stared up at her, his eyes almost predatory. "I don't see any reason not to be. Do you deny it?"

"I told you, I don't wish to discuss it. Why must you insist on insulting me?"

"I am not insulting you."

"Aren't you? Aren't you going to tell me the only reason you stopped was because . . ." she trailed off, unable to finish the sentence.

Marcus released her ankle and rose to his feet, towering over her. His gaze narrowed on her face as he clasped her shoulders, forcing her to look up at him. "The only reason I stopped," he said, his voice low, "was because you pulled away."

Her eyes widened. "You mean you . . ."

She bit off the end of the sentence in embarrassment and Marcus gave her shoulders a gentle shake. "For God's sake, Thacea, finish a damned sentence. If it isn't enough that you speak in riddles half the time, you expect me to read your mind the rest."

She looked at him in surprise, thinking wildly that she loved the way he said her name. She drew a deep, shaky breath and dropped the blanket she'd been holding, burrowing her face into his chest. He clasped her tight against him while she gathered her courage. "I thought you were—" she hesitated, "—shocked—by my coloring." She was sure he could feel the embarrassed heat of her face burning through his shirt.

Marcus bit back an angry oath. He set her away from him so he could see her face. "Did George tell you that?" When she didn't meet his gaze, he shook her once. "Did he?" he demanded.

"Yes." Her voice was so low, he barely heard it. He uttered a colorful streak of expletives, then pulled her back against his chest in a crushing embrace.

"That son of a bitch," he bit out. "I'd like to tear his damned throat out." He stroked her hair, exhaling a deep, angry breath. "I'm sorry." Though iron still laced his tone, his voice was calmer. "Not that I'd like to kill the bastard," he explained with a wry smile, "only that he hurt you."

She looked at him anxiously. "He's right, though. I'm different from English women, aren't I?"

Marcus caressed the curve of her jaw. "You're different from every woman." His voice was a low caress.

She studied him carefully. She suspected Marcus would be horrified if she started to cry. "I . . . George says I look—uncultured."

Marcus's eyes flared. He spit out another stream of expletives, this one more vivid than the last. "Do you know what it does to me when I think of him touching you?"

She thought of how jealous she felt when she thought of the countless women in Marcus's life. She nodded. "I think so."

"You can't possibly."

"I know how I feel when I think of how many women have shared your bed. I know how my stomach knots and my blood heats whenever I imagine you with an endless stream of companions to warm your sheets."

Something flashed in Marcus's eyes. He stroked her face with his large hand. "Is that true?"

Turning her gaze from his, she nodded. There was no sense in denying it. He kissed her forehead. "Then perhaps this encounter has not been a complete loss after all. I have learned that you are jealous, and I have filled in another hole in my fantasies."

Thacea tipped her head and looked at him curiously. "What do you mean?"

"I have two fantasies that plague me at the moment. As I have said, I find I have a continuing obsession with the color of your garters. While I expect they are probably white, the thought that they may be scarlet, or even violet pops into my head at the most inopportune moments."

Her mouth dropped open in surprise. "Marcus."

He seemed undaunted by her embarrassment, and continued, "And I have wondered for days now whether the tips of your breasts were a very common English pink or an exotic Eastern brown." He laughed at the crimson flush that stained her cheeks. "Now I know that only your blush is pink."

Seventeen

After Marcus's outrageous comment, Thacea had been quite sure she would not recover for the rest of the day. Marcus seemed to turn his attention to other, less scandalous matters, however, and had spent the better part of the afternoon riding over the estate with her. He showed her various aspects of English landscaping and estate-planning, explaining in detail the differences demanded by the wet weather of the north and the drier weather of the south.

They discussed any number of things, their conversation ranging from literature to politics. It wasn't until Thacea felt her stomach rumble unpleasantly that she remembered she had skipped breakfast and it was now well past luncheon. She looked at Marcus in alarm. "You must be nearly starved, my Lord. I did not realize the hour was so late."

He shrugged. "I'll admit my hunger has been clawing at me for some time. I was willing to overlook it. Hunger of an entirely different manner occupied my thoughts."

Thacea ignored the leading comment and reined her mount around, intent on returning to the stables. "The former I am prepared to fill, Lord Brandtwood."

She touched her heels to her horse and galloped away from him. He sat for several long seconds, watching her. "The latter is becoming the more urgent, Lady Worthingham," he whispered, nudging his mount into a gallop.

* * *

It was after three o'clock when they returned to the house.
Save for a few curious glances, no one seemed particularly concerned by their extended absence. Thacea murmured an apology
to Caroline and hurried up the long staircase to her bedchamber.
She was tying the belt of her brocade dressing gown when Molly
entered to draw her bath. "Your Ladyship! I was beginning to
wonder if you'd make it back at all today. You left so early this
morning, I didn't know you were gone until after eleven. I
thought you would sleep late, so I didn't check on you until it
seemed nearly impossible." Molly threw open the door that led
to the bathing closet and knelt down to test the water. "These
modern houses are amazing, you know. Imagine having your
bathwater right next to your room. And always hot, too. Do you
know that the Marquess redesigned this house so the heat from
the kitchen would keep the water in the tubs hot? Of course, the
footmen have to empty the bloody thing every day, else you'd
have dirty bathwater. It's convenient all the same, though."

Thacea smiled, thankful for Molly's chatter. It prevented her
from thinking about Marcus. "Molly?"

"Yes, ma'am?"

"What do you know about the ball the Marchioness is hosting
this evening?" Thacea untied her robe and slipped gratefully
into the warm water. Her body was already beginning to ache
from her unaccustomed ride. She welcomed the soothing heat.

"Her Ladyship hostesses a ball every time she comes to the
country for a house party. Patsy, that's her Ladyship's maid, told
me there will be over two hundred guests." Molly loosened the
leather strip binding Thacea's queue and began to work her fingers through her thick hair.

"Two hundred? Aren't we a bit far from London for that size
crowd?"

"Oh, no, ma'am. Patsy says people travel all the way from
the city for one of the Marchioness's balls. She's very exclusive
about her invitations. Not just anyone attends an event in the

Erridge household." The last was delivered with something close to arrogance. Thacea suppressed a smile as Molly continued to extol the virtues of the Marchioness's hospitality. She had evidently been privy to quite an earful below stairs. "It will very likely run into dawn if it's anything like her usual affairs." Molly paused to wring the water from Thacea's hair. "You might want to have a rest this afternoon."

The warm water, coupled with Molly's thorough attention to her hair, was causing Thacea's eyes to grow heavy. "I think perhaps you're right, Molly. Please convey my apologies to the Duchess of Albrick. I was supposed to join her for tea this afternoon. I think I will stay here and rest instead."

"I will, ma'am." Molly held out an enormous towel. Thacea stepped from the bath, tucking it neatly around her breasts. "Will you be needing anything else from me this afternoon?"

Thacea shook her head. "No. Enjoy your day. I'll need you to call for me at six-thirty." She glanced at the clock thoughtfully. "Will that give you enough time to do my hair for dinner?"

Molly picked up Thacea's tunic and pantaloons where they lay across the arm of a chair. "You're braver than I am if you want me to do your hair for a night like this. Are you certain you don't want one of the other maids?"

"Of course not, Molly. No one could do it as well as you."

Molly looked at her skeptically. "Well, do you know which gown you'll be wearing tonight? Because if I can convince the gardener to send me up some flowers of the right color, maybe no one will notice if your hair's a bit crooked."

"Which gown do you like best?"

Molly opened the wardrobe and fingered the delicate silks. "Well, you wore the violet one last night. I like the blue, it nearly matches your eyes. The green one's pretty too, it suits your coloring." Molly paused and looked at her closely. "But this is a grand affair. I'd say his Lordship would like you to stand out a bit." Molly ignored Thacea's startled glance and continued. "So if I was you, I'd wear the white one with the diamonds. It'll look the best when you're dancing."

Thacea looked at the dress. It was a magnificent, extravagant creation. It was a heavy white satin brocade. The décolletage and hem were trimmed with lace. Diamonds and pearls were sewn along the skirt. Thacea had nearly refused to accept it until she'd consoled herself with the knowledge that Madelyne would be able to wear it after they returned to London. Molly was chattering on about the white suede slippers that went with the gown and how comfortable they would be for a night of dancing. Thacea studied the gown, her fingers moving over the elegant material. "Molly?" she said suddenly.

Molly paused in mid sentence. "Yes, ma'am?"

"Do you think his Lordship's gardener will have star orchids?"

Molly looked at her in surprise. "Well, I don't know. It's certainly worth asking. I imagine he might."

Thacea continued to thoughtfully study the dress. "If he has star orchids, I'll wear the gown."

Molly smiled at her. "I'll go and see to it right now, ma'am." She gathered up the rest of Thacea's discarded clothing. "Will you be needing anything else before this evening?"

"That's all, Molly. Go and see about the flowers and be sure to call for me by six-thirty."

Molly left the room muttering something about star orchids and whether or not they were big enough to hide Thacea's hair. Thacea waited for the door to click shut before she carefully closed the wardrobe door and snuggled down among the warm quilts on her bed. Her lack of sleep the night before had taken its toll. She fell asleep almost the moment her head touched the pillow.

Molly's knock finally penetrated her dreams. Thacea rolled to her side and stared at the clock on the mantel. How had she managed to sleep so late? "Come in, Molly," she called, throwing back the heavy quilts.

Molly rushed into the room, a bright smile on her face.

"Look, ma'am. I got the orchids," she said, and held out the small basket for Thacea's inspection.

Thacea lovingly fingered the delicate white flowers. "Thank you, Molly. They are precisely what I wanted."

Molly set the basket down and hurried to the wardrobe. "We'll have to hurry for you to be ready for dinner. I'm not at all sure I'll be able to work those flowers into your hair." She pulled the white gown from the wardrobe and spread it on the bed. "I think it will work all right if I plait it, though. Have you seen the shoes for this dress?"

Thacea sat down at her dressing table. "They are in the trunk, Molly." Molly headed for the trunk and began digging for the shoes. Thacea studied her own reflection in the mirror. "Do you think you could arrange the plait on the side? I thought that was particularly flattering."

Molly's head was buried in the trunk. She tossed one slipper over her shoulder, still digging for the match. "I don't know, ma'am. I'll try of course, but you know I'm not so good with hair. I do think you should have one of the other maids do it for you. She could do anything you wanted. I've never used flowers before. Except in my cousin Jeannie's hair, and that doesn't likely count, as she's my cousin, and all. I found it!" Molly announced, reemerging from the trunk, the suede slipper in her hand. She scooped up the other one and laid the pair by the bed, smoothing an imaginary wrinkle from the gown.

When Thacea surveyed her final appearance in the mirror, her eyes widened. The white gown was deceptively elegant and sophisticated. Molly had plaited her hair on the side and coiled it into a thick knot, linking the flowers in the loops of the braid.

Thacea looked with alarm at the cut of the décolletage and winced. It was much lower than she remembered, and certainly lower than she normally wore. Molly walked up behind her. Their eyes met in the mirror. "It's a lovely gown, your Ladyship."

Thacea drew her eyebrows together in a worried frown. "You do not think it is too . . . sophisticated?"

Molly shook her head. "Oh no, ma'am. All the ladies will have them."

Thacea tugged ineffectually at the low neckline. "I don't remember it being cut so low, but then, I tried the gowns on in a bit of a hurry. I may have overlooked it."

"I wouldn't worry about it at all, ma'am. I'm sure it's just as his Lordship wanted it."

With a frown, Thacea turned to look at Molly. "What do you mean by that, Molly?"

Molly looked at her in alarm. "Well, nothing special, ma'am. I just mean his Lordship must have wanted you to look like this or he wouldn't have given you the gown. I didn't mean to suggest . . ."

"Molly." Thacea interrupted. "This afternoon when you said you thought Lord Brandton would want me to 'stand out,' what were you saying?"

Molly looked flustered. "I didn't mean any harm, ma'am, really I didn't. You know I'd never say anything that might . . ."

"Molly!" Thacea was beginning to lose patience.

"Well, I've known his Lordship for a long time, having worked in his mother's house and all. And I've always noticed, he likes his . . ." she paused noticeably and cast Thacea a worried look.

"His paramours?" Thacea added bluntly.

Molly nodded. "Yes, ma'am. His female companions to look particularly sophisticated. I . . . I assumed that's why he ordered the gowns for you."

Thacea gritted her teeth. "Do the servants below stairs believe that his Lordship and I are . . . romantically involved?"

Molly blinked. "Well yes, ma'am."

Thacea muttered under her breath and reached for the suede slippers, jamming on each one in turn. "All my eye," she grumbled finally. "And what about you, Molly? Do you believe that as well?"

Molly looked at her anxiously. "Not anymore!" she said, her voice a question.

"Well, we aren't—not that I should have to explain that to all and sundry."

Molly shook her head in silent agreement, apparently rendered momentarily speechless. "All right, I'm ready. I certainly hope his Lordship is downstairs." She stalked toward the door and caught Molly's anxious glance from the corner of her eye. She paused, turning to look at the maid with a reassuring smile. "Don't look so gloomy, Molly. I'm not angry—with you," she added meaningfully.

"I didn't gossip, ma'am. Honest I didn't. They all knew below stairs, and I didn't say anything—to anyone."

Thacea exhaled a long sigh and patted Molly's arm. "I know, Molly. It isn't your fault. You aren't to worry about it either. I'll take care of everything."

"Are you going to tell his Lordship?"

"In a manner of speaking." At Molly's anxious glance, Thacea continued, "You have nothing whatsoever to fear. I wouldn't give you up when you've just now learned to do my hair."

Molly smiled at her a bit uncertainly. Thacea swept out of the room, her thoughts focused entirely on Marcus.

Marcus put the finishing touches on his cravat as he studied his reflection in the mirror. The day had been particularly enjoyable. All told, things were going very nicely according to his plan. It was true Thacea had pulled back from him that morning by the pool, but he was willing to lay odds she wouldn't be so inclined after a few more days and afternoons in the lazy atmosphere at Sedgewood. He made a mental note to thank his secretary upon his return to London and straightened his cuffs with a sharp tug.

The clock on the mantel chimed eight. Marcus reached for his emerald cuff links. He was surprised to find he was actually looking forward to the evening ahead. He generally found Society's entertainments deadly boring, but there was a certain anticipation he could not deny. He slipped one cuff link into place and twisted the catch.

He was beginning to wonder if the long weeks of waiting for Thacea Worthingham to come around had not been rather advantageous after all. Marcus had not experienced an extended period of time without female companionship—particularly companionship of a sexual nature—in longer than he cared to recount. As a consequence, he could not remember the last time he'd so readily anticipated a lady's company.

He walked to the door as he looped the cuff link into his sleeve. He nearly smiled at the stunned expression on his valet's face. The man clearly wasn't used to seeing him in such good humor. "I'll be late," Marcus said. "You needn't wait up."

The valet nodded imperceptibly. Marcus excused him from duty only when he anticipated the company of a lady in his bedchamber. The man understood without further comment, that he was to build the fire, lay out Marcus's dressing gown, have a bottle of champagne chilled and ready, and be gone from the room well before Marcus returned with his guest. It was a long-standing custom between the Earl of Brandtwood and his valet. "Yes, sir. Will there be anything else, your Lordship?"

Marcus paused, his fingers on the catch of his cuff link. "No, the usual arrangements will be fine." He strode down the hall, ignoring a slight twinge of guilt. He had long since decided that Thacea Worthingham rated far better than the "usual arrangements," but in truth, he was certain she would not join him in his bedchamber that evening. Not only had he given his word to the Marquess and Marchioness of Ridgefield, but Thacea was not yet ready. Nevertheless, Marcus didn't want his valet to have cause for speculation, as he certainly would if he knew Marcus planned to sleep alone. In any case, it wouldn't hurt to be prepared. It suddenly occurred to him that he had never enjoyed the pleasure of dancing with Thacea. He smiled to himself in anticipation of the opportunity. He knew by the way she moved that she would dance well. There was a certain grace about her that would make waltzing with her a distinctly pleasurable experience. Other activities wouldn't present any hardship either. At the irreverent notion, he thought briefly that he very much hoped she would wear the white gown this evening.

He saw her as soon as he reached the long staircase. He was still struggling with the catch on his cuff link when he paused at the top of the stairs to look down at her. She was standing in the foyer, tapping her fan on the back of her wrist in animated agitation. She had yet to see him above her. Marcus seized his advantage and allowed himself a leisurely perusal of her figure accentuated by the lines of the white gown. His masculine eye moved appreciatively from the lace-trimmed hem where it touched the top of her feet, along the narrow lines of the skirt, over her gently flaring hips and small waist, and on up to . . . he frowned when his eyes settled on the neckline. He was certain he had not ordered it so low.

He grumbled as the catch on his cuff link stubbornly refused to budge and hurried down the stairs, intent on making her return to her bedchamber and change her gown for something more suitable—preferably something that didn't provide such an ample view of her bosom.

Thacea heard his footsteps on the stairs and turned to frown at him. She was still smarting over Molly's remarks, and had every intention of telling Marcus he must do something to correct the situation. The almost predatory look in his green eyes caught her off guard, however, and she momentarily forgot her impassioned speech in light of the imposing figure he cut striding toward her.

She'd seen him in evening clothes before, of course, but tonight, he looked particularly devastating. His black evening jacket accentuated the breadth of his shoulders. His snowy-white cravat and shirt highlighted the strength of his chin and his bronzed face. He wore an emerald-green silk waistcoat, and the tiny emerald buttons that glittered in his shirtfront matched the fiery light in his eyes. Thacea smiled at him a bit uncertainly, not entirely comfortable with the look he gave her. He reached the bottom of the stairs and planted his boot heel on the lowest step, staring at her menacingly. "Did I pay for that gown?" he demanded.

She looked at him in surprise. Without thinking, she reached out to finish attaching his cuff link. "Of course. Don't you remember it?"

His eyes swept over the low curve of the neckline. She was unconsciously adjusting the cuff at the sleeve of his evening jacket. Marcus wavered between feeling absurdly pleased at the small action, and irrationally jealous. "I don't recall ordering anything so . . . fashionable."

Thacea felt her face warm as a blush crept over her skin, but she refused to let him divert her. "Marcus, I have no intention of discussing my gown with you. I . . ."

"Neither have I," he cut in smoothly. "Go upstairs and change it. I'll wait for you here."

She glared at him. "Marcus, I am not changing my gown. I have something of importance to discuss with you and I will not be . . ."

"We will have something of importance to discuss if you don't change that gown. I will not have you flaunting about in front of God knows who with that indecent neckline." He took a step closer and towered over her, doing his best to intimidate her into giving him his way.

She didn't back down. "Do not try to divert my attention. Are you aware of what the servants are saying?"

Two of Caroline's guests walked by on their way to the supper room. Marcus didn't miss the way the gentleman looked at Thacea. He growled something beneath his breath and glared at him ferociously. Curling his fingers beneath Thacea's elbow, he guided her away from the stairs into a more secluded corner of the room, careful to keep her back turned to the foyer and any other inquisitive eyes. "What I'm aware of is that every young fop in that room will be spending the evening staring down your dress. As I have no desire to spend the better part of tomorrow defending your honor, I demand that you go upstairs and change that gown."

"Marcus, you are shouting."

"I am not," he roared. Thacea looked at him in surprise. He spent several long seconds visibly reining in his temper. "Thacea, do not argue with me."

"I am not arguing."

"Excellent. Then I'll wait here while you change."

Thacea glared at him. "My gown is not the issue. You are deliberately trying to distract me."

"It most certainly is the issue."

She sighed in exasperation. "Marcus, are you or are you not aware of what the servants are saying?"

"I do not make it a practice to keep abreast of below-stairs gossip."

"Even when it concerns you?" she asked. His eyes flared angrily and she smiled at him smugly. "At least now I have your attention."

Marcus's eyes narrowed dangerously. "If any of my servants have been gossiping, I will dismiss them immediately. I want their names right now."

She poked him in the chest. "Oh stuff and bother. *Your* servants haven't been gossiping. It's the others."

He blinked. "Does this have some relevance to me?"

"Of course it's relevant. The servants in the household are convinced that you and I are . . ." Thacea paused and leaned closer to Marcus. "They think we're *lovers,* Marcus."

Her voice had dropped to a conspiratorial whisper and Marcus felt a smile tug at the corner of his mouth despite his lingering irritation over the gown. "They don't?" he said in mock horror.

She nodded, completely missing the facetious tone in his voice. "They do. Molly told me so this afternoon."

"You were shocked, of course?"

"Of course. Marcus, what are we going to do?"

He ran an idle finger along the curve of her jaw. "The servants are generally the first to know, but I'd imagine a good number of the ton have the same notion."

Thacea's eyes widened. She pushed his hand away from her face. "Do you think so?"

"Umm. Undoubtedly." Not to be deterred, he moved his fingers over the curve of her collarbone.

She pushed at his chest and backed away several steps. "Marcus, stop! This isn't at all funny."

"No, it isn't."

"What are you going to do?"

"I'm not going to do anything."

"But Marcus, we cannot simply ignore the rumor."

He shrugged. "Of course we can. It's unfortunate, of course, but understandable given the circumstances."

Thacea was stunned. *"Unfortunate?* It's disastrous. You must do something."

"What would you like me to do? Deny it? Don't you believe that would only serve to worsen the situation?"

Her eyebrows knit together. Surely he understood the gravity of the rumor. He could not simply dismiss it with his casual disregard for gossip. "I am serious."

"So am I. Thacea, you must understand how things like this begin. Society thrives on rumors and gossip. Even though we have exercised the utmost discretion, the mere nature of your association with me is certain to have caused a lifted eyebrow or two. Consider our presence here at Sedgewood. Did you think it would pass without notice?"

"I didn't think anyone would find it strange." She glared at his mocking look. "It isn't as if everyone is coupled off. Lord Ridgefield is here without companionship."

Marcus rolled his eyes. "Only in deference to you." She was beginning to look hysterical. Marcus reached out, grasping her shoulders firmly. "I assure you, you needn't worry about it. It's all completely harmless."

She glared at him. "It is also all completely untrue. You cannot expect me to simply ignore it."

"That's precisely what I expect."

"You are being completely unreasonable about this. Why can't you understand why this is so important to me?"

A sudden thought occurred to him and he frowned. "Are you afraid George will hear of this?"

"No, yes, damn it! I don't know. I'm upset, and I want you to be upset, too, damn you."

Marcus lifted an eyebrow, amusement sparkling in his eyes. "I'm surprised at you, Lady Worthingham. Your language seems to have taken the same bad turn as your reputation."

"It's the company I've been keeping," she bit out.

"Undoubtedly." When she glared at him again, his expression sobered. "I wasn't aware this would surprise you. I assure you that you are unnecessarily concerned."

"You promised me, Marcus. You promised you could control the gossip. You cannot understand how much I trusted you. I think it would be best if you and I were not seen together for the rest of the evening."

Before he could stop her, she stalked away from him. Marcus straightened his waistcoat with a sharp tug and followed her with his eyes. He decided it would be unwise to tell her well over two dozen guests had already observed their animated conversation. She might choose to avoid him for the rest of the evening, but she would be unable to avoid the speculative eyes of the ton.

Thacea entered the ballroom. Nervous and upset, she scanned the crowd. She sent up a silent prayer that the gossip would find another target for their attention.

God wasn't listening.

Thacea was suffering through another dance with yet another young man who was extolling her virtues in sickeningly florid language. Her eyes strayed to Marcus across the room. She noticed, somewhat waspishly, that he didn't appear to be the least bit disconcerted by her lack of attention. He was surrounded by a veritable crowd of women, all of them fawning over him with something akin to adoration. There was one in particular,

Thacea noticed, who seemed to have a fixation with his sleeve. She'd been tenaciously clinging to it for the better part of the evening. Thacea glared at her and turned her attention back to her partner.

"As I was saying, Lady Worthingham, I was delighted to hear you enjoy riding. I hope when you return to London you will honor me with a ride one afternoon."

Thacea stifled a groan. It was not the first such invitation she'd received that evening. "That's a very kind invitation, Lord Walshton, but I do not think my husband would approve of the notion."

He looked at her dubiously. "I must admit, your Ladyship, I am a bit surprised."

"Why should you be, my Lord?"

"There are many of us in London who are somewhat . . . concerned about your reputation."

Thacea raised her eyebrows. "It is a matter that also concerns me. Are you suggesting that an afternoon in the park with you would enhance it?"

Lord Walshton flushed. "Forgive me, my Lady, if this seems somewhat impertinent, but your recent—ah—affiliations are somewhat unconventional."

Thacea's lips tightened in silent anger. The arrogant young man was no longer mildly boring, he was beginning to be immensely irritating. "Forgive *me,* Lord Walshton, but your supposition is insulting at best. I resent your insinuation."

The young man nervously cleared his throat. "Well, you must admit, Lady Worthingham, the Earl of Brandtwood does invoke a certain level of, well, concern among the ton." When Thacea merely stared at him, he looked at her anxiously and went on. "You know what they call him, of course?"

"I'm not at all certain what you are talking about, Lord Walshton." Thacea silently dared him to continue.

Walshton seemed not to notice. "Come now, Lady Worthingham, there isn't a soul in London who is unaware of Brandtwood's reputation."

"I do not think it at all proper for you to be discussing this with me, your Lordship."

Walshton laughed unpleasantly. "From what I understand, Brandtwood is seldom concerned with propriety. He hasn't earned his reputation by following the notions of convention."

Thacea's blood ran hot with anger. "And what of you? Are you committed to following the notions of convention?"

"Of course, your Ladyship."

Thacea stopped dancing, ignoring the startled looks of the other couples on the floor. "And that's why you've asked me to ride alone with you in London," she said, considerably louder than necessary.

Lord Walshton looked anxiously around. "Please, Lady Worthingham, I meant no offense."

Thacea glared at him. "You meant no offense? You have asked me to ride alone with you—and certainly insinuated a good deal more, and you say you meant no offense?" Thacea was aware that a number of people were staring at them, but she was too intent on telling Lord Walshton exactly what she thought of his behavior to back down.

He shifted uncomfortably. "Your Ladyship, my apologies of course, if I . . ."

"You are despicable. How dare you insult the Earl, and me, based on your hypocritical notions of propriety." Thacea was aware she was shouting, but she had endured an entire evening of barbed comments and insolent remarks. The unfortunate young man had snapped what remained of her control. Despite the fact that she knew she was causing a scene, she was too trapped in her anger to stop her tirade. "You have not only offended me, you have disgusted me as well," she continued.

"Lady Worthingham . . ."

"In the future," she continued, undaunted, "you will kindly keep your opinion and your insulting comments to yourself. I have no desire to listen to your inane conversation, and even less of a desire to listen to your vapid innuendos." Lord Walshton was staring at her in astonishment, as were the other two hundred guests in the room. Thacea's anger suddenly got the better of her. She gave Walshton's shin a vicious kick and stomped out of the ballroom, slamming the terrace door behind her.

Marcus took a long swallow of his champagne as he fought a satisfied smile. He'd watched the entire scene from across the room, where he'd been afforded a clear view of Thacea's animated features. After her dramatic exit, a bevy of whispers had erupted in the crowded ballroom. Marcus saw Caroline Erridge working her way steadily in his direction. He nearly grinned at the mischievous look in her eye. Lady Ridgefield was evidently enormously pleased with the disruption. Her ball would be the toast of the Beau Monde by the next morning. Caroline was reveling in her success.

"Lord Brandton," she said, reaching his side. "I think perhaps you'd better dance with me. My guests appear to be enjoying themselves so much, they've forgotten that the purpose of a ball is dancing."

He offered her his arm. "I'd be delighted, my Lady." He led her to the center of the room and slipped his arm about her waist. "If I didn't know better, I'd believe you were enjoying this immensely."

Caroline laughed and began waltzing with Marcus. "You don't seem overly put off by the incident yourself, your Lordship."

"Beside the fact that I have every intention of speaking with Walshton about his behavior, I would have to admit I find it rather gratifying that the lady saw fit to defend my honor."

Caroline's eyes sparkled. She waited until she and Marcus were directly in front of the terrace door where Thacea had left the ballroom. The guests had recovered, at least in part, from their earlier astonishment. Caroline smiled up at Marcus. "I think perhaps you'd better go and see to the comfort of your champion."

Marcus kissed Caroline's hand. "Thank you, Caroline. I am in your debt."

"You have made me the most talked-about hostess of the Season, your Lordship. I believe your debt has been paid."

With a smile Marcus slipped through the terrace door, intent on finding Thacea.

He finally found her seated in a secluded arbor, miserably rubbing the toe of her white slipper in the dirt. He stepped beneath the low-hanging ivy. "I had nearly given up hope of finding you at all. I should have remembered to look in the arbors."

She didn't look at him. "Go away, please."

He pulled a cheroot from his jacket pocket and lit it, studying her carefully. "You'll ruin those shoes if you continue to grind them in the dirt."

"As I have been forbidden to wear the gown they accompany, it doesn't seem of much import whether they are spoilt or not."

"I wouldn't have credited you with petulance."

"I am *not* being petulant."

"What would you call it?"

She raised her eyes to his and he saw the tears that threatened to spill down her cheeks. *"Misery.* I'd call it misery."

Marcus crushed out his cheroot beneath his heel. He moved silently to sit beside her on the low bench. "If I were you, I'd be feeling rather pleased with myself. You made an ass of Walshton. I suspect he deserved it."

"I created a scene. I've spoiled the Marchioness's ball by losing my temper."

"I just spoke with Caroline. She's delighted. She'll be the talk of London by tomorrow morning."

Thacea groaned. "Marcus, you cannot understand how this makes me feel. All evening I have listened to spiteful comments and innuendos. Walshton was not the first."

Marcus swore under his breath. "I want a list of their names. I will take care of it."

She moved her hand in a tiny gesture of exasperation. "You don't understand. I don't want you to call them out."

"Would you rather I hold them still while you kick their shins? That seemed to be effective."

She glared at him. "Don't you see, Marcus? They didn't even know they were insulting me. They assumed that I am a prize to be won or stolen away. Because they believe that you have . . . compromised me, I have no honor. If I don't have that, I have nothing."

Marcus studied her profile for several long seconds, wondering how best to handle the situation. He'd never spent longer than a few seconds dwelling on the nature of his reputation. He was having a great deal of difficulty understanding why the issue was so important to Thacea. "Are you certain," he said carefully, "you are not worried that your husband will hear of this rumor?"

"That is not the issue. George will not concern himself with the matter unless he feels it will harm his own reputation. He will be more angry if he learns of what I did tonight than if he hears a rumor that you and I are . . ." she trailed off, unwilling to finish the statement.

Marcus frowned. "Then you are right, I do not understand. Surely you know that rumors of this nature are commonplace. The ton will soon find something considerably more interesting to dither about, I assure you."

"But in the interim, men like Lord Walshton believe it is acceptable to make advances toward me. Clearly, if I will associate with you, I will associate with anyone," she said bitterly.

"Yes, I suppose that's true."

There was a note of cynicism in his voice that Thacea didn't miss, and she met his gaze squarely. "Doesn't that disturb you at all?"

"The fact that Walshton insulted you disturbs me considerably. In fact, I have every intention of speaking with him as soon as . . ."

"No, Marcus," she interrupted in agitation. "Not what he said to me. What he said about you. Don't you find it insulting?"

Marcus looked at her in surprise. "The nature of my reputa-

tion has never concerned me before. I see no reason to begin
bothering with it now."

She swore softly, earning an insolent grin from Marcus.
"They are so far beneath you, my Lord."

"I cannot say I have ever heard anyone put it that way to me
before."

She laid her hand on his arm. "That is why I lost my temper,
Marcus. Not because Walshton insulted me—heaven knows it
isn't the first such invitation I've received. But he has no right
to openly insult you, to insinuate that you are some disreputable
charlatan because of your behavior."

"Thacea, you must understand. I have flaunted Society's conventions for the better part of my life. I have made no pretense
of adhering to the strictures of the ton."

"Yet they condemn you because you do in public what they
do behind their drawing room doors. Consider it, my Lord. Have
you ever beaten a woman, taken her by force?"

He frowned. "How could you ask me that?"

"I knew you had not. Do you believe for an instant that every
man in that ballroom can attest to the same standard? Do you
believe not a one of those well-dressed, impeccably mannered
gentlemen has ever beaten his wife before turning to his mistress? I think not. Yet they stand in open judgment of you for
defying their conventions."

Marcus was completely fascinated by the way her blue eyes
glittered angrily in the darkness during her impassioned speech.
He rescued one of the tiny star orchids that had worked its way
loose from her plait. "I admit this experience is a new one for
me. I am not in the habit of having my honor defended twice
in one evening."

She met his gaze frankly. "I do not regret either instance, my
Lord. They may have convention behind which they can hide,
but you have dignity. It is worth far more."

He twirled the delicate flower in his fingers. "Is that another
bit of your father's wisdom?"

She snatched the flower from his hand. "As a matter of fact, yes it is. I even wore these flowers tonight because of my father's lesson on dignity."

Marcus looked at her expectantly. Thacea leaned back against the arbor. Her eyes took on a faraway look. Marcus watched in fascination as her expressive face softened into a sentimental daydream.

"When I dressed this evening in this wonderful gown," she shot him a tiny smile, "it made me remember one of the most pleasant events of my childhood. It was, in fact, one of the last private moments I had with my father before he died."

She paused, carefully choosing her words. She must be careful not to mention Raman to Marcus. "I was fourteen years old when my grandfather died, and my father returned to the palace as Sultan of Ardahan." She looked at Marcus and laughed. "You will not be surprised to learn I was more impressed by the elegant clothing than anything else."

"I imagine it was quite an adjustment after spending the first part of your life in the desert."

"My uncle had an extensive harem, of which my father greatly disapproved. Nevertheless, those women wore the most fascinating clothes. In the desert, we wore soft cotton tunics and pantaloons to ward off the heat and protect us from the sun and the wind. When we arrived at the palace, I was amazed at the colors and the rich silks and linens."

She paused. Raman had laughed at her enthusiasm. He preferred his comfortable desert clothing to the finery he was forced to wear about the palace.

"One afternoon, I managed to borrow one of my mother's tunics and carry it to my chamber. I was admiring the way I looked in the elegant fabric when . . ." She paused. Raman had come strolling in unannounced and caught her. "When one of the other children came into my chamber and began to tease me."

Marcus pictured her standing before her mirror playing dress-up in her mother's clothes. "I imagine you didn't enjoy teasing when you were a child."

She laughed. "No more than I enjoy it now. I was looking at myself rather dreamily in the mirror when my . . . friend said, 'You look silly in that, Thace. It's of no use. It wouldn't do you a bit of good in the desert.' "

She looked at Marcus sheepishly. "I was tremendously offended, of course. Even now I remember being fascinated with the way the soft silk moved against my skin."

Marcus stifled the urge to groan. He found the notion rather fascinating himself. "Did you kick him in the shin?"

"No, I was considerably more civilized in those days. I started an argument with him instead. 'I think it's beautiful,' I said, with all the haughtiness I could muster. There was a large bowl of orchids on my dressing table, and I picked one up and tucked it into my hair for added emphasis."

"Your young friend was unimpressed?"

"Considerably." Raman had laughed. "He told me I looked funny and that I was much more at home astride a horse than in the palace."

Marcus imagined that was probably true when she was a child, but he could understand why the comment had hurt. "That was cruel."

"He didn't mean to be cruel, but I was at an age when I was feeling particularly self-conscious. He made me furious. 'What do you know about it?' I demanded in my very best princess voice.

" 'I know you get moon-eyed whenever Yusef is around,' he taunted back."

She looked at Marcus closely. "That really was a horrid thing to say, Marcus. I was quite in love with Yusef—even if he was skinny and rather awkward at the time."

Marcus's eyes twinkled in the darkness. "So then you kicked him?"

"No," she said. "I do remember blushing, however. 'I don't either,' I said.

" 'Yes you do,' he argued. And then he threatened to tell

Yusef. You can imagine how I reacted to that. I threatened him within an inch of his life if he told."

She paused, laughing slightly. "I didn't thoroughly lose my temper until he laughed at me. I could not stand the smug expression on his face, so I reached behind me and picked up the bowl of orchids, intent on tossing the water on him."

"Behavior completely becoming a princess," Marcus said drily.

"The bowl proved to be heavier than I thought, however, and it slipped from my fingers, splashing water all down the front of my mother's beautiful silk tunic."

She paused, completely caught in the memory. Raman had run from the room crying that he would tell their father what she'd done. Thacea had looked at the ruined fabric in horror. She hadn't begun to cry until Raman had called out to her that he was on his way to find Yusef.

"I knew that my father would find out what had happened. I did my best to dry the silk, but the front of the tunic was badly stained. I spent one of the most agonizing afternoons of my life waiting for my father to come to my chamber to scold me."

She looked at Marcus. "I think in truth I was more concerned that Yusef might find out. I was never really afraid of my father.

"Nevertheless, when he knocked at my door, I nearly jumped through my skin. I remember thinking Baba looked much larger inside the confines of the palace than he did in the vast open canopy of the desert. Inside my chamber, he looked enormous.

"I must have looked petrified, because I remember he smiled at me and sat down on the end of my bed. I think he did that so he wouldn't look so tall.

" 'Hello, Ayat,' he said, and he reached over and ruffled his hand through my hair. 'You don't look very content this afternoon.'

"I asked him if he knew what had happened, and he nodded. His knowing eyes traveled to the ruined tunic where it lay draped across the end of my dressing table. 'Is that your mother's tunic?'

" 'Yes, Baba. I have ruined it,' I said.

" 'So I hear,' he answered. He assured me he did not believe it was such a terrible tragedy," she told Marcus.

"I imagine you were beginning to feel relieved."

"I was too busy being startled. I sniffled a good bit, if I remember, having spent the better part of the afternoon crying into my pillow. 'You don't?' I asked.

"He shook his head, indicating the tunic with a wave of his hand. 'They are of little use, these silken garments.' "

"Ah," Marcus said. "An eminently practical male view."

Thacea nodded. "I believe I managed a watery smile in return and accused him of sounding like . . . my friend. Baba nodded and said, 'No, it isn't the tunic that concerns me.' I shall never forget the long agonizing seconds while I waited for him to continue. I was certain he was going to say I'd disappointed him with my behavior. As you said, it was behavior not entirely becoming to my royal status."

Marcus raised an eyebrow in amusement. "I take it he was not overly concerned?"

She shook her head. "No. He sat there and studied me. I sat silently amid the cushions on my bed and waited for the inevitable lecture. Finally, he smiled at me. 'I'm more concerned,' he said, 'that another young man may be stealing my daughter's affections.' "

Thacea laughed at the memory. "I blushed to the roots of my hair. I was horrified that he knew about Yusef. He seemed not to notice, though."

"He noticed," Marcus said quietly. "No one could fail to notice when you blush. It's one of your most attractive qualities."

Thacea was pleased that the darkened arbor hid the incriminating pink flush in her cheeks. She ignored Marcus's comment and continued. "I asked him how he knew about Yusef, and he informed me he ruled Ardahan. It was his business to know everything."

"I see arrogance is a family trait."

"Something you should be able to relate to quite well, my Lord."

Marcus laughed. "Touché, my Lady."

Thacea nodded. "Thank you. Baba wanted to know, of course, if he knew Yusef."

"Of course," Marcus agreed.

" 'He's Baden's youngest son,' I said. Baden was one of my father's advisors," she explained.

"My father grunted something and reached out to remove the crumpled orchid from my hair. 'All the same,' he said, 'you will dine with me in my chambers tonight.'

"You can imagine how astonished I was. Since our return to the palace, the tense political situation had occupied my father's attention. My uncle resented surrendering power, and my mother had made a practice of isolating us as often as possible. It was unheard-of for a man of my father's position to spend an evening with only his daughter for company, and I remember thinking he must be angry about Yusef. Surely he wouldn't demand my presence in his chambers if he didn't intend to lecture me."

She studied the small orchid in her hand for several long seconds. Marcus finally prompted her to continue. "Did you agree?"

"Of course. I said, 'If that is what you wish, Baba,' and he nodded and rose to his feet. 'It is what I wish,' he told me.

"After he strode from the room, I spent the better part of the day torn between seeking revenge on my friend and planning how best to apologize to my father. I was stunned when Saban, my father's servant . . ." She paused at Marcus's confused look. "Saban was his valet of sorts," she explained.

Marcus nodded, and she went on. "I was stunned when Saban knocked at my door shortly before the dinner hour. I was worried that I was late and told him so.

" 'No, Princess,' he said. 'Your father does not expect you for another half hour.' "

Thacea's imitation of the servant's accent made him smile.

"Saban held a small padded chest in his arms. I remember how curious I was. I asked him what it contained.

" 'A gift from your father,' he said." She looked at Marcus. "You must remember, Saban was nearly a member of our family. It was unlike him to be so formal with me. I believe that's why I was so intimidated.

"I asked him what the gift was," she continued, "and he said, 'He asks that you wear it tonight.' And then he placed the chest on the floor and disappeared down the long corridor. I stared at the blue chest for several minutes before I mustered enough courage to open it.

"When I finally did, I gasped at the contents. Neatly folded inside was a white silk tunic, shot through with silver threads and delicate pearls. The fine fabric shimmered in the soft candlelight of my chamber. Seven tiny star orchids . . ." She paused and showed Marcus the flower in her hand. ". . . like this one, lay on top of the tunic. There was a folded vellum note, and I recognized Baba's seal immediately. I sat on the floor next to the chest and removed the note, carefully breaking the seal.

"It said:

Ayat,
    There will be many Yusefs to send you flowers. It is the desire of my heart to be the first.

Baba"

She paused and smiled at Marcus. "I cried, of course."

"Of course," he said with a slight smile.

"When I joined him for dinner, he spent the entire evening telling me he was proud of me, and that he loved me. He told me he had chosen those flowers just for me, and that I should never accept anything less than the very best from any man who wanted to win my favor. If Yusef was worthy of my attention, he would earn it. I would not have to earn his." She paused and looked at Marcus. "He gave me dignity."

Marcus removed the tiny flower from her fingers and tucked

it back into her plait. His eyes met hers and he ran one finger gently along the line of her jaw. "Your father was right. Yusef was a fool for having allowed you to slip away."

"There is the consummate Brandtwood charm I remember so well. My father used to say, 'Beware the merchant who seeks to empty your purse by filling your ego.'"

Marcus laughed. "This merchant wishes nothing more than a waltz from your Ladyship before the evening is over. I have not enjoyed the pleasure of dancing with you yet."

Thacea rose to her feet. "After the scandal I have already caused this evening, I cannot see the harm in one waltz, your Lordship."

Marcus followed her out of the arbor. They turned down the brick path back toward the ballroom. Neither of them noticed the Duke of Albrick standing in the shadows, watching them thoughtfully. Thacea would have been considerably more anxious had she known he'd overheard their conversation.

Eighteen

The remainder of the fortnight passed in relative calm. Thacea was generally able to set aside her worries and enjoy the freedom of life at Sedgewood. Caroline had indeed been pleased with the success of her ball, and had delighted in reading all of the London reports.

The weather soon turned cold again, but Thacea didn't let the bite in the air deter her from riding each morning. The day before they were scheduled to return to London, however, she awoke to the soft whisper of snow. She threw off the covers and walked to the window, staring in delight at the tiny snowflakes that clung in lacy patterns to the glass. Having spent the greater part of her life in the desert, she had never seen snow except from a distance. In Ardahan, the mountaintops had been white almost year-round. When she and George had lived in India, they'd been in a warm province, and the only snow she'd ever seen was the snow that peaked the Himalayas. She had never seen it up close, however, and she watched the tiny, sparkling flakes in fascination, wondering if it were really true that no two snowflakes were identical.

She stood at the window and curled her toes into the carpet, watching the white drifts deepen on Sedgewood's exquisitely manicured lawns. She realized a bit sadly that this was to be her last full day in the country. She looked resolutely at the clock, determined that she would not miss a moment of it.

It took her only a few minutes to dress in her green wool

habit. She found her fur-lined cloak and the matching gloves, and slipped her feet into her riding boots. They barely showed beneath the hem of her riding habit. They would give ample protection from the drifting snow. With an eager smile, she cracked open her door and peeked down the corridor. No one was moving about, so she slipped silently down the hall, tiptoeing down the long staircase and out the door.

Marcus was leaning against a tree, watching her make her way across the snow. He had been unable to sleep the night before, a problem that had grown considerably worse since his arrival at Sedgewood. He'd been standing at the window of his bedchamber when the snow had begun to fall. His thoughts had turned instantly to Thacea. He was certain she would be delighted with snow. As soon as the sun had risen enough to light the misted sky, he'd dressed and let himself out of the house, hoping the cold weather would clear his head. He was all too aware that they would return to London the following day. The issue of his relationship with Thacea was no more settled now than it had been before. In truth, it had grown considerably more complicated.

He no longer considered a casual affair with her an option. Yet he was unwilling to contemplate simply turning away. It was all very convoluted, and he was slowly, if reluctantly, coming to the realization that this was the one woman with whom he might contemplate a long-term relationship. He had nearly admitted as much to her the night of Caroline's ball. A woman who believed in his dignity was not one to be casually dismissed. The specter of her marriage to George Worthingham, however, loomed above them as an immutable obstacle. One with which Marcus was becoming exceedingly vexed.

For his part, it wouldn't particularly matter that she was married to the bastard, as long as Marcus knew they were married in name only. It wasn't as if he was suddenly intent on setting up house. He wanted Thacea as his companion—she need not be his wife. She had made it increasingly clear to him, however, that she would not come to him so long as she remained married to George. Marcus's only hope was to convince her to change her mind. It was a bleak option at best.

Now, in the cold air, he watched her making her way across the snow and he frowned. He was no closer to a solution now than he had been several hours before—only a good bit colder.

Thacea crunched through the snow in delight, absently catching the tiny flakes on her tongue. The cold, wet crystals stung her cheeks slightly. She wiped the moisture from her face, smiling at the intricate lacy patterns the snow left on her suede gloves. Her father told her a story once about children building things in the snow. She reached down and clasped a handful, fascinated with the way it clumped into shape between her fingers.

The soft *thud* on the back of her hooded cloak surprised her. She turned around to find Marcus standing behind her. Nothing in his expression suggested that he had thrown the soft snowball at her. Only the white flakes that still clung to his fingers gave him away. She smiled slowly. "Your Lordship. I didn't expect you to be out so early."

He shrugged, carefully watching the clump of snow she held in her hand. "I was unable to sleep." He indicated the white drifts with a sweep of his arm. "Is this the first time you've seen snow?"

She nodded, casually turning the snowball over in her hand. "Isn't it wonderful? I had no idea it was so beautiful when it fell."

Marcus walked toward her. "Fresh snow is indeed a delight— if rather cold. I wondered when I saw it this morning if this would be your first snowstorm."

Thacea laughed in delight. Her breath misted in the cold air. "It's quite marvelous, really. I've seen snow on mountain peaks, of course, but never up close."

"It is one of nature's miracles."

She moved a step closer. "And so much fun," she said, stuffing the clump of snow beneath his cravat and into his shirt. His eyes widened momentarily in shock. Thacea laughed, turning quickly to scoot away from his reach.

He looked at her, his eyes glittering in the morning light, and she momentarily forgot to run. "Behavior very becoming a princess," he said softly.

She took another step backward when he advanced toward her. "I was only paying you back for the one you threw at me. And don't deny it," she hastened to add as his expression turned dangerous. "I saw the snow on your fingers."

He stepped forward again. "I would point out I merely tossed a handful of snow at you to gain your attention. You, on the other hand, have taken the game a step further."

She retreated several more steps until her back bumped against a tree. "Now, Marcus," she said warningly, squealing when he suddenly lunged forward and grasped her around the waist with his strong hands.

He picked her up and held her feet off the ground. "There was something you wanted to say, your Ladyship?"

She giggled. "Marcus, put me down."

"With pleasure." He dropped her in a heavy drift of snow.

Thacea sputtered and sat up, white snowflakes clinging to her hair and her eyelashes. "I cannot believe you did that."

He grinned at her smugly. "I was merely repaying the compliment."

Thacea grabbed him about the ankle. Under normal circumstances, she would not have been able to budge him, but the snow had hardened beneath his feet. He lost his footing. He landed on his side next to her with a heavy *thud*. She laughed at his startled expression. "Now I believe we are even."

"Not quite." He grabbed her before she could react. Grasping her head in one of his large hands, he pushed her face playfully toward the snow. "Have you ever tasted fresh snow, my Lady?"

"Marcus stop this, at once. I . . . NO!" she shouted when he pushed her face briefly into the snow.

"Are you prepared to apologize?"

She was laughing too hard to answer. He pushed her back

into the cold snow once again. "I will not apologize," she laughed when he released the pressure on her head and allowed her to come up for air. He lowered her face into the snow once again. "All right! I'm sorry, I'm sorry!"

Marcus released her instantly and rolled her onto her back. He smiled down at her and wiped the flakes from her face with his gloved fingers. If she hadn't been laughing, he might have felt at least a twinge of guilt. "Are you all right?"

The heated look in his eyes made her suddenly forget all about being cold. She brushed a snowflake away from his lower lip. With a groan, he captured her hand in his, lowering his mouth to hers for a searing kiss.

Marcus's kiss was so hot, Thacea was certain the snow beneath them was melting. His lips moved over hers for several long seconds before he finally lifted his head, all traces of laughter gone from his eyes. He shut his eyes as he rested his forehead against hers. "You are driving me mad, my Lady," he whispered, his voice a warm, damp caress on her face.

She wiggled beneath his weight. "Marcus, this is our last day. Can we not simply . . ."

When she trailed off, he raised his forehead and opened his eyes. Their green fire scorched her. "Yes?"

She ran her tongue slowly over her lips. "Can we not simply enjoy it?"

Marcus levered himself away from her. He surged to his feet and offered her his hand. "I very much doubt it, my Lady," he said, pulling her up beside him. "But I will do my best to accommodate you."

Thacea smiled at him gratefully and they turned to walk through the snow.

High above them, in her husband's second-story bedchamber at Sedgewood, Lady Caroline Erridge watched them from the window. "Jace," she said softly over her shoulder, "come here a moment."

The Marquess groaned. He was sprawled on his back amidst

the tangled sheets. The heavy scent of their recent lovemaking still hung in the air. "Again?" he asked suggestively.

She shot him an exasperated look. "There is something I want you to see."

He grinned wickedly at his wife's figure, clearly visible beneath the thin lawn of her nightgown. "I have an ample view from the warmth of my bed."

She glared at him and he mumbled something beneath his breath about catching pneumonia before he tossed aside the covers and strolled naked to stand behind Caroline. He wrapped his arms around her from behind and pulled her back against him, nuzzling the side of her neck with his beard-stubbled chin. "What is so intriguing at the window, my love?"

She laughed and arched her neck to give him better access. "I want you to see why I think this party has been an enormous success."

Jace tilted his head and looked at Marcus and Thacea walking through the snow. He sighed. "That's rather sad, isn't it?"

She nodded. "In a manner, yes. I have a feeling, though, that everything is going to work out. They belong together."

Jace smiled at her knowingly. Caroline was nothing if not the eternal optimist. "What makes you so sure?"

"Because," she said, turning into his arms. "I have just seen Marcus Brandton playing in the snow. I now believe anything is possible."

Nineteen

In keeping with his promise, Marcus spent the rest of the day with Thacea, doing his best to ignore the reality that their time together was at an end. They walked through the snow-covered grounds until she finally admitted to him that her toes had grown cold and her fingers numb.

When they returned to the house, Marcus left her only long enough to change into dry clothes. He joined her in the library, where they spent the rest of the day in front of the fire.

They talked more that afternoon than they had since they'd first met. Thacea spoke freely of her childhood in Ardahan, telling him dozens of stories. He listened more to the musical sound of her voice, though, than to the actual words, and occasionally, a strained silence would fall between them, filled only by the relentless ticking of the clock. Finally, Marcus could stand it no more.

"Damn it!" he said, surging up from his chair and planting his hands on the mantel. "I cannot do this any longer."

Thacea drew a deep breath and looked at him in concern. "I . . . I do not know what you mean."

Marcus turned around abruptly, his eyes narrowing intently on her face. "You do know," he said, his voice deceptively quiet. "I cannot sit across from you and pretend that nothing at all is awry. I cannot look at you and know that there is unsettled business between us. I cannot listen to your voice, and wonder if I will hear it again after tomorrow."

She looked at him in consternation. "Marcus, I . . ."

"No! I cannot play this game of thrust and cut between us any longer. I have done all I can to accommodate you. I have deferred to your every desire. I have exercised every ounce of self-control I possess, and a good bit more I do not."

Thacea rose from the couch. "I do not know what to say."

He stared down at her. "Then do not say anything. Listen to me, instead. I have yielded to every demand. I have done what I could to prevent myself from forcing you to decide."

"That is true."

"But I cannot return to London with this matter unsettled." He grasped her shoulders. His voice turned slightly hoarse. "Have you any idea what this is doing to me?"

She shook her head, unable to tear her eyes away from his. He groaned and released her. "Sit down, please," he said quietly.

She looked at him in surprise. "Marcus, I . . ."

"Sit down. I cannot guarantee that I will continue to act the gentleman I am not if you insist on standing so close to me."

Thacea moved quickly back to the sofa, watching him warily. He drew several deep breaths, clearly struggling for control of his temper. Finally, he turned to face her. "I realize," he said, his level voice contradicting the tumult she saw in his eyes, "that I have said many things to you which you may have interpreted as insulting."

She shook her head, but he held up his hand to prevent her from speaking. "It was never my intent."

"I know," she said quietly.

"If, however," he continued on as if he hadn't heard her, "I have failed in any way to make my intentions clear, I want to do so now. While at first, I will admit, I did not think beyond the temporary nature of a romantic interlude between us, I have done all I could to make you aware of the change in my intent."

"Marcus . . ."

"No," he cut her off. "You cannot really believe, not any more, that what I offer you is nothing more than a secret liaison conducted behind drawn curtains and closed doors."

"There can be nothing else, Marcus."

His eyes flared. "But there can," he said quietly.

Thacea's eyes met his. She shook her head. Marcus walked forward and knelt on one knee beside her, grasping her chin in his hand. "Come away with me, Thacea," he said, his voice barely above a whisper.

She shook her head imperceptibly. "Marcus, I . . ."

He ignored the interruption and continued. "I will give you the world. We will travel anywhere you desire. I will take you places you have never been, and I will spend my life making you happy. I swear to you," his voice deepened and he moved his fingers along the curve of her jaw. "We will go somewhere far away and close the gates of paradise and I will never let anyone harm you ever again. No one, and I give you my word on this, Thacea, no one will be allowed to intrude on our happiness."

A tear spilled over the corner of her eye. She traced the hard plane of his face with her fingertips. Marcus closed his eyes at the featherlight caress. He alone held the key to her heart. All she wanted was before her. She had no choice but to turn her back on it. "Marcus, I cannot answer you."

He looked at her, his gaze intense. "Then don't," he persuaded. "Give me your problems. I will solve them all." He would move a mountain if she asked him to.

She shook her head as several more tears slid down her face. She longed as never before to tell him about Raman. To cry against his shoulder and surrender the anxiety and worry of the past. But Raman was her burden and hers alone. "I cannot, Marcus. You must understand."

He grasped her face in both his hands. "I cannot understand, Thacea. How can you ask it of me? Do you expect me to simply return to London and continue about my life as if nothing had happened?"

She shook her head and he continued on relentlessly. "How can I live day to day knowing you are with that insufferable bastard? My God! I have only to think of him touching you—

hurting you—to go mad! Yet you expect me to walk away never knowing if you are hurt or in need. I cannot do it, Thacea. You cannot ask it of me."

Marcus was breathing heavily, as if he'd just run a great distance, and Thacea stared into his eyes, her heart pounding so loudly, she was certain he would hear it. The tears were streaming down her face now. They spilled from her eyes, pouring over his long fingers. She was not entirely certain, but in that instant, she thought perhaps she heard the sound of her heart breaking. She was as certain of what she must do as she'd ever been in her life, however, and she sent up a silent prayer that Marcus would some day forgive her.

Thacea drew a deep breath and curled her fingers around his wrists, tugging his hands away from her face. Not trusting herself to meet his gaze, she rose to her feet and stepped away from him, walking slowly toward the door. When she reached it, she paused, her fingers on the knob, and looked back at him. In a voice so low, it was very nearly a whisper, she said, "Under the circumstances, your Lordship, I believe it will be best if I do not see you again. I regret any inconvenience I may have caused you."

Twenty

Marcus slammed the door of his library in his London town house and walked somewhat unsteadily to the beverage cart. It had been three days since his return to London, and he'd done what he could to remain either unconscious or numbingly inebriated. He poured a glass of brandy, cursing at the way the decanter wobbled unsteadily between his fingers. He tipped his head back, and emptied the contents of the glass in a long swallow before pouring himself another and weaving his way across the room to his chair by the fireplace. He sank down into the leather chair, the glass of brandy in one hand, the crystal decanter in the other.

He was vaguely aware of the persistent ache that had begun pounding in his head three days before. He swallowed another long drink of brandy, hoping he would soon lapse into unconsciousness once again. His memory nagged at him, though. He stared into the fire, replaying the scene that had possessed his thoughts since he'd left Sedgewood before dawn the day after the snowstorm.

After Thacea had left the library that afternoon, Marcus had been enraged. Her words echoed in his head over and over in a relentless cadence that made his temples throb persistently. They had not stopped since.

Marcus had disappeared for what remained of the day, not appearing at dinner that evening. The moment the sun crept above the horizon, he'd ordered his carriage and returned to

London. Brandtwood House had been ominously silent since his return. His servants walked about in fearful apprehension of his temper. Madelyne had retired to her chambers and refused to see him. Marcus had left instructions with his staff that he was not to be disturbed for any reason. As the days passed, his mood grew blacker. He had not shaved in days. He could not remember the last time he'd changed his clothes. He was relatively certain he hadn't eaten. And except for the brief exchange with his butler when he'd run out of brandy, he had not spoken to anyone since he'd issued his instructions upon his return.

Marcus swigged another glass of brandy and felt the room tilt. "Caused me any inconvenience, indeed," he muttered, his speech slurred. In a sudden burst of anger, he hurled his brandy glass at the fireplace. When he heard it shatter against the brick, he was amazed he had hit his target. He tipped back his head and swallowed another long drink of brandy from the decanter, ignoring the drops that trickled from the corner of his mouth and stained his cravat.

On the other side of London, Thacea stood at the window of George's town house and watched the sheeting rain. The weather was slightly warmer in London, and a steady rain had been falling since her return from Sedgewood. She'd been unable to stop crying since her conflict with Marcus, and after a tearful good-bye to Caroline, had returned to London to await George's arrival from Paris.

Fortunately, he had returned in good humor. George believed he was closer than ever to receiving his Paris appointment, and he'd been too busy celebrating his new status to pay much attention to her. She had sent him word through Molly that she was ill, and except for a brief visit to her chamber, he had ignored her completely since his return.

Despite Molly's best efforts, she had not been able to eat since her return to London. As the days passed, she grew more and more miserable. Her only consolation was that Raman was still safe, so far as she knew, and every day she prayed fervently for word from him. But nothing came. Just as nothing had come since she'd left Ardahan. She'd begun to believe she might have to endure her loneliness forever.

Thacea ran her fingers over the cool glass and tipped her forehead against the pane. The tears began streaming down her face once more, and she shivered, suddenly desperately cold. On the street below, a black lacquered carriage drove by. Her thoughts fled once again to Marcus.

She had tortured herself with thoughts of where he might be, or more specifically who he might be with. At every thought of him, her tears fell a bit faster. She had not felt so desolate since the day her parents had died, and she sank suddenly to the floor, crossing her arms on the window seat, lowering her face to sob against them. She stayed there until she was too exhausted to cry any longer, and then she slipped between the heavy quilts of her bed and fell into a fitful sleep.

"You have never seen two more miserable people in your life, Jonathan," Aiden Brickston said to the older man sitting across from him in an office at the British War Department.

Jonathan Fielding smiled at the Duke and idly tipped a white envelope on his palm. "I'm not so sure, Brick. I remember when a certain Lady Sarah Erridge had you rather stirred up at one time in your life."

Aiden smiled. "That is true enough, but this is different. The Earl of Brandtwood has virtually disappeared from sight since our return from Sedgewood. I understand he has cloistered himself in his library, and he is not accepting any visitors."

The older man nodded. "I checked for you on the whereabouts of George Worthingham. He has been arrogantly celebrating his pending Paris appointment since his return to London. There has been no sign of Lady Worthingham, however."

Aiden leaned back in his chair and thoughtfully stroked his

chin. "I would not trust the bastard not to have harmed her. That's why I am in such a hurry for this information." He indicated the envelope in Jonathan Fielding's hand. "Is that the report from your man?"

Fielding looked at Aiden carefully. "I have only just received it. It hasn't been reviewed."

Aiden shrugged. "I requested it for personal reasons, not as a matter of State. It shouldn't need to be reviewed."

"Willoghby has informed me it might be rather . . . sensitive."

"I expected as much."

"I would not wish to be connected with a scandal at the Foreign Office over their next Paris Emissary. I am far too old for this sort of thing." He handed Aiden the envelope.

"You will not regret it, Jonathan. I assure you." He looked at the envelope in his hand. "You have not forgotten my request for information about Raman ben Hamid?"

Jonathan shook his head. "The brother? No. We are still checking. All the official reports indicate he drowned in the accident with his parents."

"But no body was recovered."

"No body. I will let you know as soon as I have anything on that. In the interim, do not do anything half-witted, Brick."

Aiden accepted the envelope with a rakish smile. "You needn't worry. I've nothing to gain from this but the satisfaction of knowing that a bastard like George Worthingham won't be representing the crown." He tucked the envelope into his jacket pocket and rose to go, extending his hand. "It's been a pleasure as always, Jonathan."

Jonathan Fielding shook his hand firmly. "Give my regards to the Duchess."

"I will. You must come by and see us before too much longer. My children are beginning to whine for one of your stories."

The older man laughed. "Very well. I will check with your secretary and make plans for one evening next week." He pointed to Aiden's pocket, where he'd slipped the envelope. "I assume I will not be regretting having given you that information so soon."

Aiden shook his head and pulled on his greatcoat. "In fact, my wife will most likely be feeling enormously gratified toward you. You may even expect to eat your favorite meal when you call on us as a token of her appreciation."

Jonathan walked with him to the door. "If you are right about George Worthingham, Brick, I'll have all the satisfaction I need in knowing he's been stripped of his office."

"By the time I'm through with him, he'll be missing a good deal more than his Paris post." Aiden turned and strode down the long corridor, his coat swirling about the tops of his boots. He was anxious to read the contents of the report he'd requested, almost certain his suspicions were correct.

He stepped into his carriage in front of the War Department and rapped sharply on the box with his walking stick, signaling his driver to hurry their return to Albrick House. Inside the comfortable confines of his navy lacquered coach, he slit the seal on the white envelope and quickly scanned the contents. By the time they reached his town house, his blue eyes glittered with barely suppressed rage.

He mounted the stairs and handed his walking stick and his coat to his butler. "Ask my wife to join me immediately in the library," he ordered, pausing only briefly to look up from the report in his hand. He strode to the library and read the rest of the report, his lips settling into a tight line. With a sharp tug on the rope behind his desk, he summoned his secretary and began firing off rapid orders. Servants bustled in and out of the room, racing about in a harried frenzy.

He had just completed a note to Caroline Erridge and was handing it to his secretary for immediate delivery when Sarah came rushing into the library, an anxious expression on her face. "Aiden, is something wrong?"

Aiden was leaning against the front of his desk, his arms crossed over his chest. His secretary bowed to Sarah and hurried from the room. Aiden stretched around to his desk and scrawled an address on a white piece of vellum paper before he looked up at her. "Henry is waiting for you out front with the carriage. I want you to go by and fetch Caroline, and then go immediately to George Worthingham's town house. Here is the address." He extended the piece of paper to her.

She took it from him with a worried frown. "What is the matter? Is something wrong with Thacea?"

"I cannot be certain." She inhaled a sharp breath and started to speak. He laid a finger across her lips and said, "I do not have time to explain. I want you to go there immediately and exercise your best judgment. If she appears to be all right, simply wait for me there. If Worthingham acts even the least bit suspiciously, however, I want you and Caroline to leave there with her immediately. I will send four footmen with you with orders to use force if necessary. Do you understand?"

She nodded gravely. "Yes, of course."

He dropped a hard, brief kiss on her lips. "Go. I have already sent word to Caroline to expect you."

Sarah sped from the room and Aiden tucked the envelope back into his jacket pocket. He mentally ticked off the orders he had given his secretary until he was satisfied he had not forgotten anything. When he strode from the library, his butler was already waiting with his walking stick and greatcoat in hand. Aiden took them without breaking his stride. He hurried down the front stairs and stepped into his curricle, catching the reins his groom tossed him. The poor young man barely had time to step back onto his ledge at the rear before Aiden snapped the reins. Despite the cold afternoon, he set a rapid pace for Brandtwood House, hoping the frigid air would cool his temper.

When he reined in his horses in front of Marcus's town house, Jace Erridge was already waiting for him at the foot of the stairs. Aiden jumped from the curricle and threw the reins to the young groom. He looked at Jace grimly and mounted the stairs two at a time.

"What the hell's the meaning of this, Brick?"

Aiden rapped on the door. "I will explain everything when

we are inside. I may require your assistance to prevent Brandt-wood from murdering George Worthingham."

Jace raised an eyebrow and looked at Aiden in surprise, falling silent when the door swung open. The stony-faced butler looked at the two of them carefully and said, "His Lordship has left instructions he's not to be disturbed."

Aiden was not daunted. He shouldered his way past the butler. "He'll see us. Where is he?"

The butler looked harried. "I have my orders, gentlemen. He's not accepting any visitors."

Aiden glared at the butler. "Damn it! I want to know where he is right now or I'll tear the bloody house apart."

"Brick," Jace cut in smoothly, "the poor man's just doing his job." He turned and looked at the butler. "We will inform his Lordship you did all you could to prevent us from disturbing what I wager is his drunken sulk. I do imagine he will be considerably vexed, however, if you allow my friend to begin destroying his household."

The butler looked from Jace to Aiden and back again before he pointed rather weakly at the library door. "He's in the library."

Aiden muttered something beneath his breath as he pivoted to stride across the foyer. Jace walked close behind. When they reached the library door, Aiden rattled the knob and swore softly when he found it locked. He took a step back and kicked the door open, striding into the library with the subtlety of a hurricane wind. "Bloody hell," he grumbled, looking at Marcus, who was slumped down in his leather chair. "He's out cold."

Jace picked up one of three empty brandy decanters on the floor. He held it up for Aiden's inspection. "I imagine he would be if he's drunk all this. Hell, Brick, I don't think even you have ever been this drunk."

Aiden snorted and walked over to the chair, cracking Marcus's eyelids with his fingers. "I was this drunk over your sister, if I recall." He looked up at Jace. "He's alive anyway. He's just stone-cold drunk, and a good bit sicker."

Jace nodded. "What are we going to do with him?"

Aiden grabbed Marcus's limp hand and tugged him from the chair, lifting his large body onto his shoulder. He steadied himself carefully beneath the dead weight and turned to Jace. "We're going to sober him up."

Marcus awoke the instant his naked body landed in the tub of ice-cold water. He rattled off a colorful stream of expletives when his head surfaced, and did his best to focus on the two shadowy figures standing over him. Before his vision cleared, an enormous splash of cold water hit him square in the face. He swiped his arm over his eyes with a muttered curse. When he opened his eyes, Jace and Aiden snapped into focus. "What the bloody hell are you doing?"

Aiden bent beside him and shoved his head back into the cold water, holding it down for several long seconds. When he released his hold, Marcus surged forward and glared at him. "If I weren't so damned drunk I'd beat your bloody hide to a pulp for this." He was vaguely aware that his speech sounded somewhat slurred.

Jace tossed a bar of soap into the bathwater. "Wash! You smell like a pig."

Marcus swiped at the soap. He missed it the first time, and tried twice more before Aiden stuffed it into his hand. "What the hell are the two of you doing here? I left instructions . . ."

Aiden cut him off. "We're well aware of your instructions, Brandtwood, but while you have been drinking yourself to death for the past three days, I have been rather busy dredging up information on George Worthingham."

At the sound of George's name, Marcus felt his nerve endings begin to tingle with life. He scrubbed the bar of soap vigorously across his chest. He was aware for the first time that his valet was racing about the room laying out clean trousers and polished boots. "I will need a starched cravat," he called out to the man.

"A shirt will be a nice touch," Jace added.

Marcus felt as though his head was stuffed with cotton. He

plunged it back into the cold water and sloshed it about, cursing the incessant throbbing at his temples. He lifted his head, slinging the water out of his hair, and stared at Aiden. "What about the bastard?" he asked.

Aiden removed the white envelope from his jacket pocket. "I have a colleague at the War Department who is adept at asking the right questions of the right people."

Marcus stood up and accepted a towel from his valet. He did his best not to stagger when he stepped from the tub, but he was grateful for the support of Jace's shoulder all the same. He rubbed briskly at his skin. "What are you saying, Albrick?"

Aiden waited until Marcus had buttoned his trousers before he handed him the envelope. Marcus looked at him curiously and removed the report. He opened the white paper and stared at it for several seconds, momentarily unable to focus on the scrawled handwriting. The letters distorted briefly and then snapped into startling clarity. Marcus felt a tight knot of white-hot anger explode in his gut. He was suddenly stone sober.

He looked up from the paper. An ominous tremor raced through him. "I'm going to kill the dirty little son of a bitch!" he roared, slinging the report at Aiden and stalking toward the door.

Jace raised an eyebrow and accepted the rest of Marcus's clothes from his valet. "I imagine we'll finish dressing him en route."

Marcus strode down the hall while a blinding rage clawed at his insides. Oblivious to the fact that he wore nothing but his trousers, he ignored the startled looks of his staff and brushed past his butler with nothing more than a cursory nod. Jace and Aiden caught up with him by the time he reached the pavement in front of his house. Vaguely, Marcus realized that it was mid afternoon, but he was completely unaware of the shocked looks he was receiving from passersby. Members of the ton were unused to seeing the Earl of Brandtwood in a shocking state of undress standing in front of his town house in the middle of the day.

Aiden brushed past him and stepped into Jace's carriage. Jace pushed Marcus up the step and into the coach, pausing only long enough to give his driver George Worthingham's address. He swung inside the carriage and pulled the door shut even as it began to move. He settled on the padded bench across from Marcus and handed him his shirt. "Put this on."

Marcus accepted the shirt, and clenched his teeth. A tiny muscle had begun to twitch at the edge of his jaw. He bit out a low curse as he shrugged into the shirt. "I swear, I'm going to break every bone in that slimy little bastard's body." He shoved the buttons into place and snatched his cravat from Jace's hands with an angry jerk.

Aiden took Marcus's jacket and boots from Jace and handed him the report in return. He handed Marcus his stockings while Jace skimmed the report. "Brandtwood, I'm not going to let you murder the man."

Marcus glared at him as he jerked on his stockings. "You aren't going to damn well stop me!"

Jace's breath came out in a low hiss and he looked up from the report. "I may help him do it, Brick."

Aiden nodded and tossed Marcus one of his boots. "I didn't say I wasn't going to let you beat the hell out of him. I merely said you couldn't kill him."

Marcus jammed his foot into his right boot and reached for the left. "I'm going to do whatever I please to the bastard."

Aiden handed him his cuff links. "Your vocabulary is becoming a bit limited, Brandt." Marcus glared at him. Aiden leaned forward and fastened the cuff link, aware that Marcus's concentration was not up to the tedious task.

Marcus swore beneath his breath and turned his other sleeve for Aiden to fasten. "Why should you care if I slit his throat?"

"Brick's right," Jace said. "The little swine isn't worth hanging for. We'll let you beat the life out of him, and then we'll dump him on a ship and threaten to skin him alive if he sets foot on English soil again."

Marcus was breathing heavily, his anger completely overriding the pain in his head. Every muscle in his body was coiled into a focused knot of uncontrollable rage. "It's not good enough."

Aiden studied him. "You'll have ruined his career at the Foreign Office. He'll be stripped of his title and whatever lands he possesses. It's enough, Brandt."

"No." Marcus shook his head. His fingers flexed into a tight fist. "It isn't." He described in graphic detail how he wouldn't be satisfied until he emasculated George Worthingham.

Jace looked at Aiden thoughtfully. "That wouldn't be murder, Brick."

Aiden glared at him. "You aren't helping." He turned his attention back to Marcus. "Listen to me, Marcus. It's Thacea and her safety which should concern you, not George Worthingham. I received this information through War Department channels. If Worthingham heard so much as a hint of it through his contacts at the Foreign Office, there's no way of knowing what he might do."

Marcus was rubbing his unshaven chin in absent agitation when his heart leapt in sudden fear. "If he lays so much as a finger on her, I'll . . ."

Aiden held up his hand to interrupt. "Sarah and Caroline are with her now—as are four of my footmen. Sarah will know what to do if there appears to be any trouble."

Marcus's fingers clenched into the muscles of his thighs. "Bloody hell! How much further?"

Aiden tugged back the curtain to look out the window. "Only a few more minutes. I will have a promise from you before I allow you to set foot in George Worthingham's house, Brandt."

"I won't promise not to kill him," Marcus bit out.

"I accept responsibility for preventing that. No, I want your promise that you will marry Thacea this evening."

Jace looked at Aiden in surprise. "Good God! Is that possible?"

Aiden nodded. "Fielding has procured a license. It will be waiting at Brandtwood House when we return."

Marcus stared at him. "You want me to marry her tonight?"

Aiden leaned forward, his eyebrows knitting together in a frown. "You do want to marry her, don't you?"

Marcus swore. "Of course I want to marry her! I also want to do what I can to protect her reputation." At Jace's surprised glance, he waved a hand in dismissal. "Despite what either of you may think, I am entirely capable of doing the honorable thing."

Jace lifted an eyebrow. "I didn't think for an instant that you weren't."

"I simply do not know that she will want to endure the gossip of a sudden marriage."

Aiden shook his head. "Her physical protection is more important than her reputation, Brandt."

Marcus knew that. "Without question."

"Then I have your promise?"

Marcus was surprised when he felt the tight clamp that had squeezed at his heart for the past few weeks suddenly spring loose. He looked at Aiden and nodded as the carriage rolled to a stop in front of George Worthingham's town house. Marcus grabbed his jacket from Aiden and stepped from the carriage, jamming his arms into the sleeves. "You have it," he shouted, mounting the stairs two at a time and kicking open the front door.

The startled butler looked at Marcus in surprise, and blanched a bit beneath the predatory glare in his green eyes. Marcus towered over the man, vaguely aware that Jace and Aiden had entered the town house behind him. "Where the hell is Worthingham?" he roared.

The butler looked at Marcus nervously and shook his head. "He's not accepting callers this afternoon."

Marcus grabbed the butler's lapels and lifted him off the floor. "He is now," he growled. "Where is he?"

The butler evidently decided that the three men staring at him so ominously were considerably more daunting than his employer's instructions. "He's in his study," he squeaked.

Marcus dropped the butler unceremoniously and stalked across the foyer. He kicked open the door to the library, assuming correctly that George's study would be connected to the library on the main floor. He crossed the large room in ten strides and kicked open the door to the study. George Worthingham sat behind his desk with a voluptuous half-dressed blond woman seated on his lap.

At the sound of Marcus's angry roar, he looked up in startled disbelief. "What the hell do you think you're doing, Brandtwood?"

Marcus strode across the room. He was vaguely aware that Jace and Aiden were leaning casually on the door frame, evidently content to let him do as he wished to George Worthingham so long as he didn't kill the man. He pulled the startled blond from George's lap and thrust her away. His fingers curled into George's cravat. He lifted George from his chair, oblivious to the blond woman's hysterical screams. Marcus pulled back his fist, prepared to bury it in George's flushed face. His fingers were still looped through George's cravat, when he shook him once, glaring at him in stark fury. "You aren't even married to her, you son of a bitch!"

Twenty-one

Thacea looked at Caroline and Sarah in surprise. "Are you quite certain that's what he said?"

Sarah squeezed Thacea's hand reassuringly. She and Caroline had arrived at the town house nearly a half hour before. After they'd finally convinced the butler to announce their presence to Thacea, she'd received them in her bedchamber. Following her cryptic conversation with Aiden that morning, Sarah had been extremely concerned about Thacea's well-being. Other than the dark circles under her tear-reddened eyes, however, she appeared to be all right. Sarah and Caroline had set about explaining to Thacea that something was dreadfully wrong. While neither of them was entirely certain what had transpired, they were sure Aiden had intended to fetch Marcus and bring him to the house. "I wouldn't worry, Thacea," Sarah reassured her. "Aiden knows precisely what he's doing. He never does anything without thinking through the consequences."

At that moment, they heard the screams from downstairs and the loud, ominous crashing sound followed by a wave of commotion. The three women looked at each other in alarm and Thacea leapt to her feet. "Good Lord, he's trying to kill George."

She raced from the room, mindless of the fact that she still wore only her brocade dressing gown. Caroline and Sarah ran after her; more because they didn't want to miss the inevitable confrontation than because of their concern for George Worthingham.

Several more loud thumps and crashes sounded from the direction of the library. The incessant feminine screaming had risen to a fevered pitch. Thacea raced down the long staircase, her hair streaming behind her in scattered disarray. She crashed through the door of the library, intent on stopping Marcus before he did something rash.

When she reached the door of George's study, she skidded to a stop between Jace and Aiden and gasped at the sight of George's body flying through the air. He landed with a terrific crash on top of his desk, and barely had time to move before Marcus's fingers curled into his lapels and lifted him into the air. The woman was still screaming. Thacea watched in horror as Marcus slammed his fist into George's bloodied face. "Marcus!" she shouted, racing into the room.

George managed a well-aimed punch at Marcus's jaw, but only because Marcus was momentarily distracted by the sound of Thacea's voice and the sight of her clad only in her dressing gown. When George's fist connected with his face, Marcus uttered a loud expletive and growled at him, then sent him sailing across the room once again.

Thacea rushed forward to grab Marcus's arms, seeking to restrain his temper. Sarah and Caroline had reached the door of the study. Sarah cast Aiden a scathing look before rushing into the room. The blond woman continued to scream. George was shouting vile accusations at Marcus, and Marcus was growling at him in return. In the midst of the bedlam, Sarah picked up the woman's discarded gown and thrust it at her. "For God's sake," she shouted. "Put your clothes on and hush!"

Caroline was right behind her and she gave the woman a push in the direction of the door. "Better yet, put your clothes on and leave."

The woman ran from the room at the same instant that George rushed at Marcus from behind. Marcus spun and grabbed George's arm, twisting it until it cracked sickeningly. George collapsed with a howl of pain and stared at Thacea. "You bitch!" He screamed again when Marcus kicked him solidly in the ribs.

Thacea looked at Marcus and placed her small palm against his chest to restrain him. "Marcus, what is happening? What are you doing?"

Marcus swiped his sleeve across his sweat-dampened face and glared at George. "Tell her, Worthingham. You'd better do it now before I slit your damn throat."

Thacea looked at George. She hoped he was aware that all that stood between him and Marcus's wrath was her small frame. Marcus could move her out of the way in less than a heartbeat. "What is the meaning of this, George?"

He glared at her. "That monster you're so enamored of forced his way into my study and assaulted me."

Marcus took a menacing step forward. "Tell her the truth, damn it, or I will force it out of you."

George looked at her pleadingly. "It is all lies, my love."

Thacea was becoming increasingly agitated. The warm feel of Marcus's body, tightly coiled with barely leashed rage, hovering behind her, was making her anxious. She knew if she but stepped out of the way, Marcus would renew his assault on George. "What are you talking about?"

Jace handed Thacea the white envelope. "I believe this will shed some light on the circumstances," he said gently.

She looked at him, bemused, and cast a glance at Marcus's brooding features before she slowly withdrew the report. Her eyes widened in shock. "Oh my God."

Thacea's hand flew to her mouth. She stared at George in horror. Sarah walked to her side and pulled the report from her fingers. "This is an official War Department inquiry into the marriage of Lord George Worthingham and the Princess Thacea Kamal Hamid."

Caroline began to read the report over Sarah's shoulder. Thacea was still staring at George in shock. "According to this," Caroline said, "the marriage papers aren't legal documents. They were forged."

George looked at Thacea pleadingly. "I didn't know," he moaned. "I swear I didn't know."

Sarah turned the page. "It goes on to say that a large sum of money is transferred once a month to George Worthingham's private account by the current Sultan of Ardahan."

Caroline gasped and pointed to a place lower on the page. "And here's a sworn statement from the man who conducted the ceremony saying that Lord Worthingham and the Sultan paid him to impersonate a clergyman."

Thacea was having trouble breathing. She turned to stare at Marcus. He momentarily forced aside his anger and enfolded her in his arms, nearly crushing the breath from her lungs.

George had struggled to his feet. "It's all a lie, I tell you! You cannot believe any of this."

Thacea trembled against Marcus. He hugged her close. "Shut up, Worthingham," he snarled, "before I forget what I'm about and finish what I began."

Aiden left his post by the door. Carefully taking the report from Sarah, he folded it and slipped it back into his pocket. He turned his steely gaze on George, and suddenly kicked his feet out from under him so he collapsed to the floor with a loud howl of pain. Aiden planted his foot squarely in the center of George's chest. "I've a carriage waiting for you outside, Worthingham. It will take you to the docks at Dover, where you will board the ship of your choice and leave England."

George gasped. "You cannot get away with this. My contacts . . ."

"Have already been alerted," Aiden interjected smoothly, "that you fled the country in disgrace."

George howled. "I'll have your head for this, Albrick. You cannot do this to me!"

Aiden smiled at him smugly. "Oh, but I can. In fact, I already have."

Jace stared down at George. "We should make it clear as well, Worthingham, that if you return to England—ever—I will take personal pleasure in alerting Brandtwood of your presence."

George looked at Marcus, his eyes blazing in fury. "I will pay you back for this, Brandtwood. You cannot try to disgrace me and get off with it." He rolled away from the constraining pressure of Aiden's foot and struggled to his feet. "You can't possibly want that cold little bitch. No one should know that better than I."

Thacea was shaking almost uncontrollably. Marcus tightened his hold. "You have exhausted my patience, Worthingham."

Thacea turned her face from Marcus's lapel and met George's wild eyes. He hurled an angry curse and stared at her. "I will kill you for this, you slut. Do you hear me? I will kill you!"

"Get him out of here," Marcus growled, "or I swear, I will kill the son of a bitch." Jace shoved George, forcing him through the study door. George spat out vile accusations and threats until finally he was forced from the house and the front door slammed. An ominous silence filled the room.

Thacea was clutching frantically at Marcus's lapels. He was becoming desperate to comfort her. He had completely forgotten his anger at George Worthingham in light of his nearly overwhelming need to calm her. He stroked his hands along her back, holding her close against him. A violent shiver raced through her. Marcus lifted her in his arms. He glanced momentarily at Aiden as he carried Thacea toward the door of the study. "I will send your carriage back to you after your driver delivers us to Brandtwood House."

With a nod, Aiden stepped aside so Marcus could exit. Sarah slipped into the curve of his arm, wrapping her arms around his waist. He was not surprised to find she was crying. Caroline, too, looked distressed. She fled the room, mumbling something about finding her husband. Aiden tucked Sarah securely against him and tenderly wiped the tears from her face. "I'm sorry you had to witness that, love."

She shook her head. "Oh Aiden, it's so awful. How could he . . ." she gulped in a great gasp of air, ". . . do that?"

Aiden hugged her tight. His wife was forever the romantic, never willing to believe the world was not the pleasant place she imagined. "It is over now, sweetheart. You needn't be so worked up."

She tipped her head and managed to give him a watery smile. "You are quite wonderful, do you know that?"

"I am eminently pleased that you think so."

"You made the inquiry through Jonathan Fielding, didn't you?"

Aiden nodded. "There were bits and pieces of Thacea's story that concerned me. I knew her father, you know?" Sarah shook her head and he continued. "Yes, he worked with us briefly during the war. In any case, the entire situation seemed somewhat suspicious to me, so I asked Jonathan to make a few inquiries."

Sarah caressed the line of his jaw with her fingertips. "It had nothing whatsoever to do with the fact that Marcus and Thacea were so clearly in love?"

He looked at her in surprise. "Certainly not. It is you who harbors such notions, not I. I was merely concerned that a man of Worthingham's unscrupulous principles was on the verge of procuring a coveted Paris appointment. I did not think it in England's best interest for him to represent the crown."

Sarah sniffed, and wiped her eyes with the back of her hand. "Of course. It was for England," she said, putting deliberate emphasis on the words.

He laughed. "Despite your continuing efforts to turn me into a chivalrous hero, I am still the cynical man you married."

Sarah tipped her head onto his shoulder with a sigh. "Of course you are, Aiden. I never suspected any differently."

Inside the confines of the carriage, Marcus held Thacea against his chest and tugged back the curtains to let the light in. She was shaking violently from the shock. He was becoming seriously alarmed. "It is over now, Thacea. You are safe with me."

She clutched at his jacket, fighting a fresh bout of the shivers. "How could he, Marcus? How could he?"

He stroked her back, doing his best to give her comfort. "I do not know, love, but he will not hurt you again. I swear it."

Thacea struggled for breath. "I believed him, Marcus. I never doubted that he told me the truth."

"I know," he said quietly.

"I have been such a fool. I should have . . ."

"No!" His voice sounded like a pistol report in the confines of the carriage. He tenderly took her face in both of his hands. "No," he said more quietly, "I will not allow you to accept blame or responsibility for any part of this. Do you understand me?"

Her lip quavered slightly, but she nodded her head, reaching up to touch his unshaven face. "You look terrible," she said, her teeth chattering together.

"You are no prize yourself." He had not failed to notice the way her cheekbones were more prominent, nor the pallor of her skin. "When was the last time you ate properly?"

She buried her face against his shoulder once more. "Luncheon the day before we left Sedgewood. Oh, Marcus, I have been so unhappy."

Marcus pulled her back against his chest, wondering rather desperately what he could do to soothe her. He was seized by the insane notion that perhaps it would be best if she cried. As a general rule, he despised hysterics of any type, but he was not entirely certain he didn't want to weep himself. He rocked her against him. His own body shook slightly from the emotional turmoil of the last several hours. He whispered endearments to her, softly stroking his hands through her hair. Each time she trembled against him, he vowed silently that he was not yet finished with George Worthingham.

Finally, the carriage rolled to a stop in front of Brandtwood House and Marcus kissed her softly on the forehead. "We are home," he said quietly, and Thacea began to weep.

Twenty-two

Thacea wept through the better part of the next two hours. Despite his best efforts, Marcus found he was powerless to calm her, nor did he want to. Instead, he sat very still on the bed with his back propped against the headboard and cradled her in his lap. Only when he feared that she would truly make herself ill did he send for a bottle of laudanum.

Thacea swallowed the dosage more because he wanted her to than for any other reason. Marcus would surely believe she'd taken leave of her senses if she couldn't rein in her rampant emotions. Finally, the laudanum began to take effect, and its calming influence, coupled with her utter emotional exhaustion, lulled her into a deep, dreamless sleep.

Marcus sighed when he felt her fingers loosen on his lapels. He continued to hold her for several more minutes, just to be sure she was truly asleep. Finally, he shifted her gently to the bed and eased away from her, exhaling a long breath when she turned her face into the pillow and slept soundly on.

He smoothed a damp tendril of hair from her tear-stained face, fighting a surge of unaccustomed emotion. He forced himself to walk away from the bed, aware that there were at least a half dozen details he must attend to. He slipped into the corridor and cast a final worried glance at her sleeping form before he pulled the door shut with a soft *click*.

He nearly collided with Molly. She was standing outside Thacea's room, dabbing her eyes with a white handkerchief.

"Who the devil are you?" he asked, more from curiosity than interest.

She looked at him in surprise. "I'm Molly Hale, your Lordship. I'm the maid you sent to her Ladyship some back. Is her Ladyship going to be all right, your Lordship? I think I would likely die if anything happened to her."

Marcus was inclined to agree. He had a vague memory of Thacea telling him something about her maid and the young woman's penchant for chatter. As Molly prattled on, pausing only to dab at her eyes, he was beginning to think perhaps that had been the understatement of the century. "Molly," he cut in smoothly. "I believe her Ladyship will be fine. She is resting now, and I would like for you to sit by her bed until she awakens."

Molly sniffled into her handkerchief and nodded. "Oh, yes sir. I will, of course. His Grace is waiting for you in the library, and I know you have details to see to. I was so upset I . . ."

"You will of course alert me immediately if there is any change in her Ladyship's condition?"

Molly nodded, and Marcus opened the door to Thacea's room, waiting for Molly to slip inside. "Thank you. I'll be in the library if I am needed." Before Molly could launch into another stream of chatter, Marcus shut the door, exhaling a relieved breath.

He made his way quickly to the library, assuming correctly that Aiden was waiting for him there. "Brick," he said with a brief nod. "I do not have to tell you how deeply I appreciate what you have done."

Aiden shook his head. "It is entirely unnecessary." He removed a folded piece of paper from his jacket pocket and handed it to Marcus. "Here is your marriage license. I need only to add your date of birth to complete the record."

Marcus walked to his desk, reaching for his pen. He scrawled the information in the appropriate place and handed it back to Aiden. "What arrangements are left to be made?"

"None, really. The time is up to you. I have taken the liberty of notifying a friend of mine who is a member of the clergy.

You may, of course, choose someone else to conduct the ceremony if you like?"

Marcus shook his head with a rueful smile. "I do not have many friends among the clergy. It would be exceedingly difficult for me to produce one at this late date."

"All that is left then is for you to select the time and location. I see no reason why the ceremony cannot be performed here."

Marcus looked around the library with a frown. The carpet was still littered with empty brandy decanters and broken glass. Even if his servants tidied it, it would be impossible to completely rid the room of the smell of spilled brandy and stale cigar smoke. He shook his head, indicating the room with a sweep of his hand. "This is hardly the background I envisioned for my wedding."

Aiden looked at him in amusement. "That comment is almost sensitive, Brandtwood. I believe perhaps there is hope for you yet. Very well, I will be delighted to speak with my friend, Reverend Penride. I am certain he will allow us the use of his church."

"Excellent." Marcus looked at the clock on the mantel. It was after three o'clock. He imagined Thacea would sleep for several hours. "If eight o'clock is suitable for your friend, I believe that will be adequate."

"I do not think that will be a problem." He looked at Marcus carefully. "Do you think Thacea will be up to this?"

"She is resting now. You can well imagine the entire episode has been a tremendous shock. I believe she will be all right after she awakens."

"Is she going to agree to marry you, Brandt?"

Marcus looked at Aiden in surprise, feeling a bit alarmed for the first time. "Do you think she will not?"

"She has been through a horrendous ordeal. I'm not entirely certain she will be predisposed to the idea of marrying anyone so quickly."

Marcus felt something inside his stomach clench. "But she must. George Worthingham threatened her, for God's sake. How else will I protect her?"

Aiden nodded in agreement. "It is merely something I feel you should be prepared to handle. You are not some unfledged rakehell without a clear head on your shoulders. You will persuade her to do what is best."

Marcus's fingers tightened into a fist. "I'll do what I must."

"There is only one other thing I feel we should discuss, then," Aiden said.

Marcus raised an eyebrow inquisitively. "What is that?"

"In light of George Worthingham's threats, I think perhaps it would be best if you and Thacea remained here in London until we know for certain where he is settled. I have already received word that he left this afternoon on a ship bound for France, but until we have a certain fix on his destination, I would feel better if you remained close at hand."

"Not leave for a wedding trip, you mean?"

Aiden nodded. "At least not for the moment. We do not know how strong Worthingham's contacts are within the Foreign Office. In the interest of safety, it will be easier if we wait."

Marcus looked at him thoughtfully. "I will not live in fear of him."

"And there's no reason to. But his threats on Thacea's life are not to be taken lightly. I am only asking you to postpone your travels for a month—two at the most."

Marcus nodded. "I am in agreement."

Aiden slipped the license into his jacket pocket, and pulled out another piece of paper, extending it to Marcus. "Very good, then. I will see you at the church at eight o'clock. Here is the address."

"Eight o'clock. We will not be late."

Aiden turned and strode from the room. Marcus sat for several moments studying the tiny scrap of paper. How much everything had changed in the past twenty-four hours. Within a few hours, Thacea would belong to him as he'd always meant her to. At the thought, he was suddenly seized with a desire to clear away whatever obstacles remained in their path. He reached behind his desk and gave the bell cord a violent tug before settling into his chair and waiting for his secretary.

Madelyne smiled at Marcus and leaned over to kiss his cheek. They were seated in her room. He had just finished explaining to her, as delicately as possible, all that had transpired that day. It was shortly before seven o'clock, and Marcus had finally completed the business at hand. He had stopped by Madelyne's room on his way to shave and change for his wedding.

Madelyne had clearly been delighted with the news, and Marcus smiled at her, rising to his feet. "I see I have your approval on my pending nuptials." She nodded. "I will leave you to dress, then. We are expected at the church in just over an hour."

Marcus strode from the room and paused in front of Thacea's bedchamber. He had postponed this until the very last, telling himself he wanted her to rest as long as possible. He could not deny the tiny sliver of dread that had worked its way into his thoughts, however. He stood outside her door for several long minutes, drawing deep, calming breaths. Finally, he pushed open the door and entered the darkened stillness of her bedroom.

"How is she?" he asked Molly.

"She's resting very comfortably, your Lordship. Hasn't nearly stirred since you left this afternoon."

Marcus nodded. "Excellent. I understand all of her Ladyship's gowns have been transferred here?"

"That's right, your Lordship. His Grace had everything delivered this afternoon. He wasn't certain about . . ."

"I want you to go through everything. Save only the gowns her Ladyship had at Sedgewood and discard the rest. We will order a new wardrobe tomorrow." Molly's eyes widened. "And Molly?"

"Yes, your Lordship?"

"Select something suitable for her Ladyship to wear this evening and have it pressed."

"Yes, your Lordship. May I ask what the occasion will be?"

Marcus looked at her, the corner of his mouth tugging into a brief smile. "Her wedding."

Twenty-three

Marcus took a deep breath and walked to the side of Thacea's bed. He sat and watched her for several long seconds before he reached out to tenderly caress her face. She mumbled something in her sleep and batted his hand away. He smiled, relieved to know she had not lost her spirit. The temptation her lips presented proved to be too much for him, and Marcus leaned over and kissed her, coaxing her awake with his mouth.

Thacea was drifting somewhere between sleep and wakefulness. She sighed in pleasure at the rush of warmth flowing through her. It was like bathing in the sun-warmed waters of an oasis. The heat intensified. She decided it was actually more like standing beneath the sun itself. When she felt her limbs begin to tingle, and a nearly overwhelming warmth race through her blood, her eyes flew open. There was only one experience she knew of that gave her precisely that sensation.

Marcus sensed she was awake and lifted his head. "Hello," he whispered.

She frowned at him, momentarily disoriented. Then she remembered it all. She let her eyes drift shut. "Hello," she said miserably.

"How are you feeling?"

She shook her head against the pillow. "Miserable."

Marcus took her hand. "I believe the worst is over. You can take solace in that."

She opened her eyes to look at him, a tiny frown creasing

her brow. "I have nothing left, Marcus. Nothing at all. What am I going to do?"

"That is what I'd like to talk to you about."

She continued on as if she hadn't heard him. "I cannot return to Ardahan so long as my uncle sits on the throne. I cannot remain in England as the penniless scandalous woman George Worthingham . . ." she trailed off, unable to complete the sentence.

Marcus cupped her face in his strong hand. "I have given this matter a great deal of thought, and I would like you to listen to what I have to say."

She nodded miserably. Nothing Marcus could say could possibly make her feel any more desolate than she did now.

"Thacea," he continued, his voice warm and persuasive. "Aiden Brickston and I have discussed this at length, and we are in agreement that the very best solution is for you to become my wife."

She blinked. She could not have possibly heard him correctly. "Your wife?" she repeated.

He nodded. "I will give you the protection of my name and my fortune. You will not want for anything. If you like, I will even settle a substantial sum of money on you, by legal contract of course, before we are married." There. She should find it difficult to argue with that bit of logic.

Thacea looked at him, her eyes wide with shock. "Marcus, you cannot be serious."

He shrugged. "Why on earth not? Given the mutual attraction between us, I believe it to be an eminently satisfactory arrangement."

Thacea closed her eyes and laid back against the pillows. An eminently satisfactory arrangement. The man had just proposed marriage, for God's sake, and he'd made it sound as matter-of-fact as a business exchange. She had an urge to ask him if he'd like to check her references before he signed the contract. She opened her eyes to stare at him. "I cannot possibly make a decision of this magnitude now, Marcus. I need time to think.

After what I have been through today, I do not feel quite capable of reasoning through anything at the moment."

Marcus took a deep breath. "I have thought of that as well, and while I hate to rush you, I feel it will be best for both of us if we are married immediately. Tonight."

"Tonight! Have you gone mad? I cannot possibly marry you tonight."

"A special license has been procured. It is all absolutely legal."

She suddenly felt like she'd been tossed in the midst of a great swirling wind. She desperately wished she could find something solid to hold on to. He could not possibly be serious. Yet the look in his eyes told her he was deadly so. She stared at him for several long seconds. "Then my answer is no. I cannot do it."

"Thacea, you must listen to me. George threatened your life. That alone is cause for a certain amount of alarm. I cannot allow you to remain unprotected."

"I will arrange something else. The embassy will help me."

Marcus shook his head. "There will also be a considerable amount of gossip—some of which you will find to be quite cruel. What I offer you is the protection of my name. There will be very few who will dare cross me by insulting you, and I will deal with those who do. Surely you can see the logic in the situation."

"It isn't about logic, Marcus. It's about marriage. And frankly, having been married once, I must admit I am none too fond of the state."

The warm light in Marcus's eyes faded. His green gaze took on a new, guarded look. "I do not have time to discuss this with you, Thacea. We are expected at the church at eight o'clock. Either you dress and come with me willingly, or I will take you there by force if necessary."

He rose from the bed and she felt a tight knot of anger stirring about in her insides. "You will force me to marry you? And in light of that, I am expected to believe that marriage to you will be any less a prison than marriage to George? You could have any woman you want, Marcus. Are you truly willing to go to these lengths to make me your wife?"

He was halfway to the connecting door that led to his room when she shot out the accusation. He turned to her, an angry glint in his eyes. "When it comes to the issue of your safety, madam, you will be amazed to what lengths I am prepared to go. I will expect you to be ready within the hour."

He strode from the room, slamming the door behind him. Thacea lay back against the pillows with a heavy sigh. She already regretted her sharp words. It had been grossly unjust to compare Marcus to George in any way, but she had been hurt and threatened by his presumptive proposal. She shuddered at a lingering memory of the morning's events and admitted that Marcus was somewhat justified in arguing that her safety might be threatened. She had been more preoccupied with worry over Raman than with worry over herself, and she had not yet been able to sort through the ramifications of all that had been revealed in the report.

If George was indeed receiving money from her uncle, had he been lying to her about Raman's safety? She had not, after all, heard from her brother since her marriage to George. Was it possible that George had already alerted her uncle of Raman's whereabouts?

Thacea tossed back the covers with a depressed sigh and walked to the dressing table. The laudanum was having lingering effects. Her head felt stuffed with cotton wool. She sank down on the padded seat and stared at her reflection in the mirror. Her face was thinner than it had been even a week ago. She knew she'd lost several pounds in the few days since she'd returned from Sedgewood. She had been too miserable to eat since her return to London in the aftermath of her final argument with Marcus. She had spent a miserable three and a half days doing all she could to put him out of her mind. It was that realization that helped her decide.

She loved Marcus. She had known it before. She knew it now. Even if he gave her an indefinite period of time to make her decision, the outcome would be the same. She would not marry him because he offered her safety and security. She would marry him because she loved him.

There was still the problem of Raman to be reckoned with, but she decided she could certainly afford to wait until her head was a bit clearer. Her decision made, she looked around the unfamiliar room until she found the bell cord. She certainly hoped Marcus had arranged for her clothes to be brought to Brandtwood House. If not, he would have to be content to marry her in her brocade dressing gown.

She smiled when Molly came rushing into the room with the elegant white gown she'd worn at Sedgewood draped over her arm. "You're awake, ma'am! This is so terribly exciting. I was so worried about you after what happened this morning, and then when his Lordship told me to have your gown pressed, well I must say it was all I could do not to rush down to the stables and tell Jake. I wish you had a new white gown to wear tonight, but his Lordship told me to discard all your old gowns." Molly began helping Thacea with her dressing gown.

Finally, Thacea interrupted her. "Molly. I need you to run an errand for me. I can finish dressing myself, but this is very important."

Molly stopped her chatter and looked at Thacea expectantly. Thacea walked to the small secretaire and rummaged about in the drawers until she found pen and paper. Penning a short note to Sarah Brickston, she handed it to Molly and said, "The Duke of Albrick's house is three doors down, Molly. I want you to take one of the footmen and deliver this note to the Duchess. I need to borrow something from her this evening, so I will need you to wait for her answer."

Molly took the note and nodded. "Yes, ma'am. I'll go right away. Are you sure you will . . ."

"Molly. I have become quite dependent on your help, but I am relatively certain I can manage on my own. Hurry on. It is most important."

Molly raced from the room. Thacea sighed in relief at the

welcome silence. Her senses were still a bit dulled from the emotional tumult of the day, and while she generally enjoyed Molly's chatter, she was not particularly up to it.

She made quick work of her bath, toweling her hair dry until it gleamed in black waves down her back. She worked it into a thick plait, twisting it atop her head in the same fashion she'd seen Molly use. It didn't look nearly as professional, but she decided Marcus probably wouldn't notice. He'd be too busy frowning over the neckline of her gown.

Molly rushed into the room just as Thacea was pulling on her delicate striped stockings. She smiled when she saw the small parcel in the maid's hand. "Here it is, ma'am. I came as quickly as I could."

Thacea accepted the parcel. "Thank you, Molly. You are just in time." She cast a quick glance at the clock on the mantel and was relieved to see it was only half past the hour. She turned to Molly with a smile. "I believe I am ready. Why don't you go below stairs and enjoy your dinner. I need to speak to his Lordship before we leave this evening and I would like to do so in private."

Molly nodded. "I understand, ma'am. I'll see that your fire is lit and your bed's turned down for when you return this evening."

"Thank you. Have a good evening."

"Yes, ma'am," she said, muttering something beneath her breath as she left the room.

Thacea carefully unwrapped the parcel from Sarah Brickston. The contents, she decided, would suit her purposes quite nicely. She finished dressing, slipped on her white suede shoes, and drew a deep breath before crossing to the connecting door.

She knocked softly.

"Come," she heard Marcus's barked command. She opened the door a bit apprehensively, not entirely certain what to expect.

He stood in front of his dressing table, wearing only his trousers and boots. He had slathered his face, and was bent close to the mirror, shaving his three-day beard. When he saw her in the mirror, he looked at his valet. "Leave us." The command was a low order, and the valet placed the rest of Marcus's clothes on the enormous bed and slipped from the room.

Thacea walked nervously to the bed and toyed with Marcus's cravat. She was seized with a sudden urge to giggle. She wondered a little wildly how many brides sat on their groom's bed and watched him shave before the ceremony. Marcus's eyes met hers in the mirror. He swiped the razor along his jaw. "Did you want something?"

"Yes." She nodded. "I wanted to apologize for what I said. It was inexcusably rude."

Marcus lifted an eyebrow and swiped another clean stroke, slinging the lather from the blade into the basin. He was still smarting from her earlier remarks. He had no intention of making the matter easy for her. "Is that all?"

She shook her head. "No. I wanted to speak to you about the nature of our marriage."

"I am listening," he said, continuing to shave his beard.

Thacea looked at his strong, muscled back and inhaled a deep breath. Her stomach was tied up in knots, and she was unsure whether the conversation or his half-dressed appearance was contributing more to the phenomenon. "Marcus, do you love me?" She hadn't meant to be quite that blunt about it, but it was said now, and there was no sense in pretending she wasn't interested in the answer. She met his eyes in the mirror and waited.

His hand stilled momentarily in the process of shaving his chin. He should have anticipated the question. Thacea was a deeply sensual woman with a substantial number of romantic notions. He would have to choose his words rather carefully if he did not wish to risk another argument. "I will not lie to you, Thacea."

She nodded. "I know. That is why I asked."

He stroked the razor a final time on the side of his face, then reached for the white towel next to the basin. Wiping the last vestiges of lather from his chin, he turned to face her. She was seated on his bed, dressed in that absurdly low-cut white gown. He had a sudden notion to forego the wedding altogether. He mentally chided himself for his undisciplined thoughts and walked to the bed, shrugging into his shirt.

"It is a difficult question," he said, slowly doing up the buttons. "I admire you immensely for your courage and your integrity." He finished buttoning his shirt and accepted his cravat from her. "I care for you a great deal, and I want you physically as I have never wanted another woman in my life."

He had looped the cravat through his collar and was tying the intricate knot. "But this notion of love that women have is a strange thing. As my wife, you will want for nothing. I will take care of you and protect you, and because we are . . ." he paused, searching for the right word, ". . . friends, because I trust you, I believe we will get on well together."

Thacea met his gaze. He was struggling with his cuff links and she leaned forward to fasten them for him. "But you do not love me."

He extended his other sleeve to her. "No," he said bluntly. "What I offer you will have to be enough."

She had a most ridiculous urge to begin crying again. She pushed it aside with some effort. It wasn't as if he'd said anything other than what she'd expected. "I am glad we understand each other, Marcus. I would not want either of us to enter into this marriage with false expectations."

He frowned at her blunt statement, uncertain what he had expected. She handed him his silver waistcoat. He pulled it on, doing up the buttons as he struggled with an unreasonable burst of temper. "I imagine it is best," he said tightly.

She nodded. "Certainly the most logical approach."

Marcus opened his mouth as if to speak, but then thought better of it. He reached for his jacket. "We had best leave for the church, or we will be late." He paused as he slipped his arms into his black evening jacket. "Have I failed to mention how beautiful you are this evening?"

She looked at him in surprise. "I thought you hated this gown."

He shook his head and dropped a tender kiss on her lips. "I

do not hate the gown. I only hate the way other men are afforded such an ample view of your bosom. You will not wear it in public after tonight," he said matter-of-factly, motioning for her to precede him out the door.

She thought about arguing with him that she would wear whatever she chose to wear, but decided against it. Without knowing he had done so, Marcus had confessed he was jealous. It was most certainly a step in the right direction. He may not love her yet, but she had his trust. She knew Marcus did not give it easily. She could work with that.

The wedding was a simple, uncomplicated affair. Thacea was actually quite relieved. Only Madelyne and Peter, Jace and Caroline, and Aiden and Sarah were present. They dispensed with the vows in an almost nonemotional fashion that she found strangely detached. The only uncomfortable moment in the entire ceremony was when Marcus turned to slide his ring on her finger. She realized belatedly that she had forgotten to remove her wedding band.

She slipped it from her finger and looked anxiously at Marcus's frown. She pressed the ring into his palm. Despite the reverend's rather startled look, she asked him to wait. Stretching up on her tiptoes, she whispered to Marcus, "Read the inscription."

He looked at her curiously and turned the ring over in his palm, holding it to the light. It read:

To my Ayat with love, Baba. Spring, 1805

Marcus looked back at her with a slight smile and lifted her right hand, sliding the ring onto her finger. She then extended him her left hand, and he slid his ring home. Thacea told Reverend Penride to continue, and the rest of the brief ceremony passed without mishap.

They said their good-byes to Peter Drake and the other two couples, and then Madelyne, Marcus, and Thacea climbed back into his carriage and headed for Brandtwood House. Marcus seated himself next to her, and pulled her gloved hand into his own. His warm presence in the carriage was making her grow nervous as she became increasingly aware of the night that lay before them.

The ring of the horses' hooves on the pavement seemed to echo relentlessly in her ears as they drew closer to Marcus's town house. She had to take several deep breaths to calm her jangled nerves. She regretted it instantly. The spicy scent of his shaving lather was ridiculously apparent to her. Her fingers fluttered slightly within the firm grasp of his hand.

The carriage rolled to a stop. Marcus stepped down, helping Madelyne to alight before he extended his hand to Thacea. His eyes glittered dangerously in the darkness. Thacea swallowed a great gulp of the cold night air, trying desperately to restore some of her equilibrium. The door of Brandtwood House swung open and she wet her lips nervously and stepped inside, no longer a visitor, but now the Countess of Brandtwood.

Twenty-four

Thacea anxiously twisted the tie of her dressing gown and paced nervously back and forth in the quiet darkness of her room. After she and Marcus had returned with Madelyne, the three of them spent a strained hour in the library desperately trying to concentrate on the bottle of champagne. When Madelyne had retired to bed, leaving Thacea alone with Marcus, Thacea had nearly begged her to stay. The door of the library had clicked silently shut behind her, and Thacea felt a flutter of anxiety race up her spine.

"There is something I would like for you to see upstairs," Marcus had said. "If you will go now, I will join you in a moment."

She had looked at him, wondering a little frantically what she should do. His reassuring smile had done little for her taut nerves, however, so she'd merely nodded, fleeing the room and his heated look.

She had calmed considerably when she'd entered her bed-chamber and found a profusion of star orchids arranged in vases about the room. The tiny flowers filled her with hope. Marcus never missed an opportunity to verbally remind her how unemotional and practical he was. But there were well over a hundred blossoms of the exotic flowers in her bedchamber. It was not the act of an unemotional man.

Molly had been unnaturally quiet, barely speaking as she helped Thacea out of her gown and into a filmy nightdress and a white velvet dressing robe. Thacea did not recognize either garment, and imagined Marcus must have had them delivered that afternoon. Molly had left the room a few minutes later, and Thacea had begun to pace.

She looked at the clock, anxiously twisting the sash of her robe once more. Marcus was taking an inordinately long time. She was beginning to fear losing her nerve altogether. When he finally opened the connecting door and entered her chamber, she momentarily stopped breathing. He wore only a long black dressing robe. He looked so absurdly enormous framed in the doorway, her knees threatened to buckle.

Marcus did not miss her tiny intake of breath. He smiled to himself. Her hair fell about her shoulders in glossy black waves, and he realized quite suddenly that he'd never seen it loose before. At the thought of tangling his hands in the heavy tresses and bringing his mouth into contact with hers, his loins grew heavy with desire. He drew a deep breath, fighting for control.

The extended silence was making her nervous. She indicated the orchids with a sweep of her hand. "This was enormously thoughtful of you."

He walked into the room. "I am glad you are pleased."

"How ever did you find so many in one afternoon?" She was vaguely aware that she sounded idiotic rambling on about the flowers, but she seemed entirely incapable of doing anything about it.

"My secretary has had men scouring the city since late this afternoon."

She walked to the window, her fingers still coiled in the sash of her robe. "Marcus, there is something I would like to discuss with you."

He moved to stand behind her and placed his hands on her shoulders, gently rubbing at the taut muscles. The scent of her hair filled his nostrils.

"Something else?" he teased, impressed at the remarkably calm tone of his voice. "I thought we settled your concerns earlier this evening."

He bent his head to nuzzle the curve of her throat, and she shivered. "There is something you should know before we carry this very much further."

He nipped at her earlobe. "I am listening."

"I would not want you to feel I deceived you."

Marcus felt something twist in his gut. His heart began to pound in sudden anxiety. He clenched his teeth. He went absolutely still. "What is it, sweetheart?"

She hesitated. "I . . . there is some truth to what George told you. I fear you may find you are very disappointed with the whole business of things—so far as my part is concerned."

Marcus blinked, momentarily confused. "I'm afraid you'll have to be a bit more clear, love. I haven't the faintest idea what you are talking about."

Thacea felt the color rising in her face. He wasn't making this at all easy on her. "George told you this morning that I am . . ." she hesitated, almost too embarrassed to say the word. She swallowed a deep breath and told herself he'd know soon enough. "That I am cold," she said. "I'm afraid he was not lying about that."

A flood of relief rushed through him. Marcus turned her around to face him. "Do you mean to say that George believes you are unresponsive?"

She turned her face away, unable to meet his gaze. "He is right," she whispered, her voice so low he could barely hear it.

God help him, he started to laugh. Thacea's startled gaze met his and he laughed delightedly, hugging her against his chest. "You have forgotten, madam wife, that I have every reason to believe you are amazingly responsive. If you flared any hotter at my touch, we would undoubtedly burn the house down."

A flood of color swept over her skin. She buried her face against his lapel. "You have only kissed me, Marcus," she whispered. "That is different."

Marcus tipped her head back with his fingers, smiling gently. "I assure you, it is not different. Is that why you have been so tense all evening?"

She wet her lips nervously with her tongue. Marcus followed the tiny action and stifled a groan. She shook her head. "There is something else."

He raised an eyebrow. Was there to be no end to this? "Still?" he asked.

"I cannot bear children," she blurted out, watching him in concern.

Marcus shrugged. "As I do not particularly care for children, I do not see that as an obstacle. If anything, I am now free to have my wicked way with you without fear of consequences."

She stared at him in disbelief. "But Marcus, don't you want an heir?"

He shook his head. "Not particularly. I have any number of distant cousins who will be delighted to fill the role when the time comes. Now, are you through with your confessions?"

She nodded rather weakly. He smiled, lifting her in his arms and carrying her toward the connecting door. "Good! I am more than ready to explore a few concerns of my own."

He strode into his bedroom and kicked the door shut behind him, slowly lowering her feet to the thick-carpeted floor. Her body slid down the length of his. He released a ragged sigh, covering her lips with his own in a kiss that clearly conveyed his desire to her.

Thacea immediately parted her lips. Marcus took full advantage. He swept his tongue inside her mouth and plundered the moist interior in a sensual exploration. A curl of heat worked its way up from her toes. Marcus felt her melt against him. He groaned in reaction, deepening the kiss. Thacea tilted her head to give him better access.

She felt utterly vulnerable crushed against his chest. His kiss demanded nothing less than total surrender. When he tore his mouth from hers and moved his lips across her jaw to settle on the sensitive lobe of her ear, she whimpered in protest.

Marcus nipped the lobe with his teeth, wrenching a moan from her throat. Desire raged through him. Having wanted her so desperately for so long, he felt his control slipping away at an alarming rate. He knew he should slow down. He groaned when her fingers moved restlessly into his hair, and gave up the fight.

He moved his hand to the tie of her robe and tugged at it until the soft velvet fell open. Her breathing came in ragged gasps when he cupped the weight of her breast in his hand. Marcus flicked his thumb across the taut nipple. She clutched at his hair, silently demanding that he kiss her again.

He was only too happy to yield. He crushed his lips on hers once more. "My God," he whispered against her mouth, "how have I survived without you?"

She moaned restlessly and squirmed against him, seeking relief from the pressure that had begun to build in her lower body. "Please, Marcus. I cannot bear it."

Marcus murmured her name and swept her in his arms, carrying her quickly to the bed. He jerked back the covers with one hand, and laid her in the center of the bed. When her white velvet robe fell open, his green eyes flared at the sight of her body clearly visible beneath the filmy white nightgown and the decidedly scarlet garters she still wore with her stockings.

When he did not immediately follow her down onto the bed, Thacea forced her eyes open. She smiled softly at the stunned expression on his face. His heated look emboldened her. She stretched her arms above her head, watching with no little satisfaction as he sucked in a ragged breath. "You have always said you were greatly concerned with the color of my garters, my Lord," she whispered, amazed that she managed to be so blasé when her skin yearned for his touch. "Sarah Brickston was kind enough to lend me this pair. I hope they have met your expectations."

Marcus was having a great deal of difficulty breathing. He seemed entirely incapable of dragging his gaze from those sinfully tempting garters. "I will admit they are having a dramatic effect on me." His voice sounded hoarse even to his own ears. He wondered how on earth he was going to live through the night if he didn't soon do something about his inflamed need for her.

When he didn't move, Thacea pushed herself up so she knelt on the bed in front of him. The way he was staring at her was making her feel restless. She decided she would feel considerably more comfortable if his green eyes weren't searing her skin. On impulse, she slipped one hand inside the lapel of his robe so she could feel the pounding rhythm of his heart.

At the featherlight touch of her fingers, he sucked in a breath and closed his eyes, his arms crushing her to him. "My God." He gritted out, "Have you any notion of what you are doing to me?"

She looked at him in surprise. "Marcus, I . . ."

He slanted his mouth over hers before she finished the statement. His hands moved along her back to her shoulders, where he pushed her white velvet robe away, leaving her clad only in her filmy nightgown and stockings. She sighed in pleasure and leaned against him, opening her mouth for his kiss.

Marcus dropped it to the floor with a soft plop. He inhaled a great breath, reveling in the scent of her hair. Her breasts were pressed against him. He could feel the turgid peaks of her nipples through the fabric of his dressing gown. His heart was slamming painfully against his chest. He felt a streak of white-hot desire flash through his hardened body when her small hands tugged at the knot at his waist.

Thacea made a tiny frustrated sound in the back of her throat and wrenched her mouth from his so she could turn her full attention to the task of loosing his robe. He chuckled softly and toppled her back onto the bed, jerking the knot free with an efficient flick of his wrist. When his robe fell open, Thacea saw the extent of his need for her. She felt the breath catch in the back of her throat. Her hand fluttered nervously to her heart, but try as she might, she was unable to divert her gaze.

He shrugged out of the robe to stretch out beside her. He summoned every vestige of control he had, calling on hidden reservoirs to calm his senses enough to wait for her. "Are you afraid of me, sweetheart?"

Thacea shook her head and managed to meet his gaze. At the molten look he gave her, she gasped. "No," she whispered.

It was unconvincing at best. "Good," he said, propping himself up on an elbow to watch her. He lifted his free hand and ran his index finger along the rounded swell of her breast. When he touched the sensitized nipple, she shuddered, her eyes drifting shut in pleasure. "Because I am afraid of you," he said.

Thacea's eyes popped open. She stared at him. "What?"

He bent his head and kissed the curve of her breast through the soft fabric of her nightgown. She clutched absently at his hair. He smiled, moving his head lower.

When he pulled the taut nipple between his teeth and sucked gently, she gasped. "Marcus."

He continued the exquisite pressure until she squirmed beneath him, watching as the wet fabric of her nightgown stretched taut over her swollen breasts. "That is precisely why I am afraid of you. You excite me so unbearably with the way you respond to me, I am not at all sure I will be able to exercise any level of control."

Thacea stared at him. He could not be serious. She saw the tiny beads of perspiration on his lip. She noticed the grim set of his jaw. Experimentally, she touched the hard muscles of his chest and watched his reaction in avid fascination. His muscles clenched taut, as if he'd been scorched. She tried it again, running the tips of her fingers along the corded line of his shoulder. He shuddered in reaction.

Thacea lifted her gaze once more and saw that his eyes were clenched shut and his teeth were clamped tightly together. His breathing was labored, as if he'd just run a very great distance, and Thacea suddenly felt amazingly powerful. She had not spent the greater part of her adolescent years among the ladies in her uncle's harem without hearing quite a number of things about the way things were supposed to be between a man and a woman.

But with George, certain things about her had never seemed

to function quite properly. She had always viewed the act of making love as something degrading. Seeing how Marcus's body reacted even to her barest caress affected her so deeply, she nearly wanted to cry.

And with the knowledge that she affected him so intensely came another, more thrilling realization. She could give Marcus pleasure. As much as he gave her.

Her fingers were moving over his skin in the barest whisper of a caress. Marcus finally trapped her hand against his heart, unable to bear the sweet torment any longer. He opened his eyes and met her gaze. "I cannot take much more of this, Thacea."

She smiled a secret smile and kissed the center of his chest, her dark hair falling around him. "You will not have to, my Lord."

She scraped her teeth over one of his flat male nipples. He groaned, clenching his hands in her hair. "I am not made of steel, love."

She moved her hand lower and trailed a featherlight touch over the hard muscles of his abdomen. "I am not so certain, my Lord."

Marcus's mouth went dry when she dipped her finger into his navel. He clenched his teeth until it became painful. He had vowed he would not frighten her. He had vowed he would control his raging desire until Thacea learned what pleasure she would know in his arms. But he was clinging to his control by the merest thread. The feel of her lips against his heated flesh threatened to snatch even that away. He tugged on her hair. "Kiss me." His voice sounded raw.

Thacea moved along the length of him and nipped softly at his lower lip with her teeth. He released his breath in a low hiss. She smiled, gliding her lips over his at the same instant she moved her hand lower to cradle the hardened evidence of his desire.

When Marcus felt her fingers close around him, he clenched his hands in her hair and ground her lips against his in an aching kiss. Holding her fast against him, he rolled her to her back, coming down on top of her. Her soft fingers were slowly moving along the length of him. He gasped against her mouth when she circled the sensitive tip with the pad of her thumb. "Thacea, you must . . ." his voice faded into a ragged sigh when she gently squeezed the end of his shaft.

She laved his lower lip with her tongue, as she ran her fingers along the length of him until she reached the base. He swelled against her hand. She scraped the tip of her fingernail along the velvet heat of his skin.

Marcus lost what remained of his fragile control. His blood roared in his ears. He could no longer think of anything beyond pumping himself inside of her over and over again until he found release. He grabbed two fistfuls of her nightgown and tugged it over her hips, wedging his leg between her soft thighs. "I'm sorry," he murmured against her heated flesh. "I'm sorry. I cannot wait any longer. I have to be inside of you."

Thacea still held his manhood in her small hand. "It is all right," she whispered, guiding him to her hot, wet passage.

He thought to die from pleasure. "My God," he whispered against her mouth. "You have bewitched me."

Thacea sucked at his tongue. Marcus embedded himself in her tight, wet sheath in a forceful stroke. The muscles of her body closed around him, and Marcus withdrew, only to drive even deeper into her snug passage.

Thacea watched the strained expression on his face in a haze of passion. The tight, full feeling of having him inside of her was unlike anything she had ever known. She lifted her knees to wrap them around his waist.

Marcus felt the smooth strength of her thighs through her stockings. He threw back his head. His entire body went suddenly rigid. The muscles in his face drew taut.

Thacea felt the wet heat as he emptied his seed deep into her with a hoarse shout. He collapsed against her, crushing her into the pillows. She clung to him, feeling wonderfully content and secure within the strong cradle of his arms.

Twenty-five

Marcus lay on top of Thacea, dragging in great breaths of air. He was vaguely aware that he must be crushing her with his weight, and equally aware that he was completely incapable of doing anything about it. His fingers moved absently in her hair. He stayed deep inside of her, waiting for the racing speed of his heart to slow. Finally, he summoned what remained of his strength and rolled to his back. Thacea followed him, curling against his side. He was absurdly pleased. "My God," he said, still a bit stunned.

Thacea's fingers absently caressed the hard plane of his chest. Lying close against her husband in the aftermath of lovemaking was a unique sensation for her. She found she truly enjoyed the comforting warmth of his muscled body. His legs were twined with hers, and she moved the arch of her stocking-clad foot along the strong line of his calf. "You are very eloquent this evening, my Lord," she whispered.

"You have robbed me of more than my eloquence, madam wife."

Thacea pushed up on an elbow and looked at him in concern. "What do you mean?"

Marcus studied her for several long seconds, his hand moved in leisurely possession along the line of her hip. Her deep blue eyes were filled with worry. She had unwittingly tightened her fingers in the mat of hair on his chest. He suspected she was completely unaware of the telling action. Silently, he damned

George Worthingham to hell. "I am speaking of my discipline, madam. Your beauty," he paused and lifted her hands to gently kiss each of her fingers, "and the magic of your touch, have caused me to go mad with my desire for you. Do not think I am unaware that I rushed on without you like a charging bull."

She watched him closely. "Are you shocked?"

He pulled her closer against him. "No, indeed. I never doubted a woman of great passion lay beneath the surface. I am delighted she has exceeded my expectations."

Thacea smiled softly and laid her head against his chest once more. "I must admit, Marcus, I was unprepared for how pleasurable the experience would be."

His hand halted its casual caress along her spine. "I assure you that you will find it even more so in the future."

She looked at him again. "More so? I do not think you should expect so much of me, my Lord. I have heard a great deal, of course, about the nature of . . ." she paused, an embarrassed flush staining her cheeks, ". . . of making love." Marcus grinned at her wickedly. She summoned her courage and went on. "And there is no doubt that you are considerably," she looked at him pointedly, "if not vastly more experienced than I."

He lifted her fingers to his mouth once more so he could nibble at her sensitive fingertips. "That is undoubtedly true. And at the risk of sounding grossly arrogant, may I add it is to my great delight that I alone shall have the privilege of fulfilling your curiosity."

Thacea felt a sudden stab of jealousy as she considered how many other women he had lain in bed with and cajoled with his casual humor. She glared at him. "You are right in saying, my Lord, that you are grossly arrogant."

He pulled her head down for a brief kiss. "Are you jealous, my love?"

She looked at him honestly. "Of every woman you have ever touched, my Lord."

The teasing glint left his eyes. "I cannot change who I am," he said quietly.

"Nor would I want you to. It does not mean, however, that I am pleased with the notion that other women have lain in this bed with you."

"I chose to give only one my name, Thacea. Does that mean nothing to you?"

She ignored the question and continued to watch him. "My jealousy aside, Marcus, I meant what I said about the danger of your expectations."

"You think them dangerous?"

"I do. You will doubtless be disappointed."

Marcus rolled her to her back. He propped himself on an elbow and leaned over her. "I see I shall have to do a much better job of it next time, or you shall remain quite convinced you will not receive any pleasure from the experience."

She shook her head, while he ran his finger along the line of one scarlet garter where it still held her stocking firmly in place. "I found it pleasurable, Marcus. More so than I ever . . ." The statement faded into a soft moan when Marcus untied the garter and slowly slid it free.

He smiled at her. "I knew you would moan in precisely that way when I did that. Shall I try it with the other one?" he asked, his voice a seductive whisper.

His hand was caressing the inside of her thigh. She shifted beneath the scalding heat of his touch. "I do not think—"

"I do not want you to," he interrupted, tugging gently at the knot of her garter.

His strong fingers brushed against her most secret place as he pulled on the silken garter. She gasped, her hips rising instinctively at the raw pleasure.

He tugged the garter free. She rewarded him with another moan. Her face had become flushed. He brushed his fingers over the dark curls at the apex of her thighs, fascinated by the way she rotated her hips against the pressure of his hand. He withdrew his hand slowly from between her thighs and leaned over her. "Not this time, madam. This time I will not allow you to drive me mad with your touch."

"Marcus . . ."

"Nor will I succumb to the fire that roars in my blood when you say my name in precisely that fashion."

He dropped a heated kiss on the peak of her breast and she gasped. His fingers were sliding her elegant stockings along the curves of her legs. "And while I am hardened almost unbearably at the thought of burying myself in your warmth, I will not do so until you ask me." He paused and rasped his tongue on the taut peak of her breast. "And ask me nicely," he added, finally pulling the nipple between his teeth in answer to at least one of her silent demands.

"Marcus, please. I cannot bear this!" Thacea's voice was a high, keening cry. Marcus raised his head from between her thighs and watched in pleasure as she neared her first, delicious climax in his arms. Her face was flushed with passion. Her hair lay in damp tendrils on her cheeks. Her eyes were clenched shut. Her hands twisted restlessly in his hair.

"Yes you can, my love. You are almost there, aren't you?"

Thacea had only a vague idea where "there" was, but she was entirely certain she would die if she didn't soon reach it. "Marcus, I . . . oh!" He flicked the pad of his thumb over the ultrasensitive nubbin of flesh that controlled her desire. She bucked against his hand.

"Do you like that, love?" he asked, his voice a dark seductive promise.

"Yes," she whispered.

"And this," he asked, replacing his thumb with his mouth, "Do you like this as well?" He kissed her with searing intimacy and suddenly, Thacea felt the twisting heat that had spread through her limbs grind into an exquisitely tight, torturous knot beneath the fire of his lips.

Marcus raised his head once more. "That's it, love. You are so beautiful."

She moved her head back and forth on the pillow, clutching at his hair. Her breathing was coming in ragged gasps. She felt the knot tighten and expand. He kissed her once more, simultaneously sliding a finger into her tight warmth. At the intimate touch, Thacea exploded into a thousand tiny fragments and screamed his name.

Marcus knew in that instant he'd never seen anything so magnificently beautiful in his life. He surged over her and plunged into her shuddering heat even as the tremors of her climax were beginning to subside. His own release was upon him almost instantly. He uttered her name in a hoarse whisper and spilled his seed.

Exhausted and deliciously sated, he clutched her to him and rolled to his back until she lay sprawled across his stomach, one of her shapely thighs wedged between both of his. In peaceful contentment, he ran his fingers through the heavy waves of her black hair. She stirred against him and he groaned. "You cannot possibly want more," he teased.

Thacea buried her face against his shoulder, feeling embarrassingly emotional and overwrought. She had no doubt that he would not appreciate a tearful outburst. She bit down on her lower lip to prevent it from trembling. The sheer force of their passion had left her feeling vulnerable. Marcus's ready retreat into casual banter had shattered the intimate moment completely. Thacea wanted to cry at its loss. She clung to him instead.

Marcus sensed her delicate mood and rubbed his hand along the graceful curve of her spine. "You are all right?"

It was more a statement than a question, and Thacea nodded. "I am safe," she whispered. It was the only security she had, and for now, it was enough. Almost.

Marcus rolled over in the midst of a rather erotic dream and splayed his hand on the cool sheets. She was gone. His eyes popped open. He squinted in the morning sunlight. When he determined she was not only gone from his bed, but from his room as well, he tossed the covers aside with a low growl and strode for the connecting door.

He found her seated on her bed, wrapped comfortably in her velvet robe. A great bunch of the delicate star orchids lay in her lap. She was toying with them absently as she stared out the window. When she heard him enter, she looked up in surprise. "My Lord. I was not aware you had awakened." Marcus was completely naked. Thacea did her best to concentrate on the fierce expression on his face rather than the stark evidence of his growing desire. "Are you angry?" she asked.

Marcus mumbled something beneath his breath. "I have discovered I do not like the feeling of waking up in my bed and finding that my wife has deserted me."

Thacea shifted uncomfortably beneath his penetrating glare. "I was restless. I did not wish to disturb your sleep."

Marcus sat on the side of the bed facing her. He picked up one of the flowers, twirling it between his long fingers. "You are not feeling well, are you?"

Surprise registered in her blue eyes. "I feel fine."

He shook his head. "You forget, my Lady, I am not some green-backed young man unfamiliar with the way of the feminine mind." He studied her carefully, his eyes sobering. "Tell me what is wrong, Thacea. I will fix it."

She managed a weak smile at that. "Such arrogance, Marcus."

He shrugged. He had vowed before he would move a mountain if she asked him to. Nothing had changed. "Only confidence, love." He paused and tapped the wilted flower on her nose. "Now, tell me what is bothering you."

Thacea fought a fresh burst of tears. She had awakened early in the morning feeling almost overwhelmingly depressed. Sometime deep in the night, she had decided not to tell Marcus about Raman. In just a little over four months, her brother would be old enough to take the throne from her uncle. She had no way of knowing what George had already told her uncle, and no way of stopping what he would tell him in the future. As long as George remained alive, he was a continuing threat to Raman's life. She had decided it would serve no purpose to drag Marcus into the problem by revealing the secret.

In the wake of that decision, however, she had been filled with an unnatural surge of homesickness and loneliness. Since her marriage to George, she had been isolated and alone. It had seemed a tolerable existence while she waited for Raman to come of age. Once she was free of George's threats and her own fear, she had always intended to return to Ardahan.

But now, everything was different. She was married to Marcus. While he had made it quite clear he did not love her, she could not deny that she loved him. Marcus affected her so deeply. She felt bound to him in a way she almost feared. When she had awakened that morning, his arm had been tucked possessively around her waist. She'd felt perilously close to tears at the memories of all that had happened to her.

He was seated on the edge of her bed now, studying her with concerned green eyes. She looked at him, a fresh surge of tears welling up in her eyes. With a slightly strangled sound, she threw herself against his chest and began to sob. "Oh, Marcus. What am I going to do?"

Surprised, Marcus lifted his arms and hugged her to him, tangling one hand in her soft hair. "Do not cry, sweet. You are overwrought is all. It is no wonder after what you have been through." Her shoulders were shaking with great, uncontrolled sobs. He rocked her against his chest, desperately seeking to calm her.

Thacea clung to him, not even caring that he must think her an idiot for her emotional outburst. "My entire life has been turned bottom to top," she said between broken sobs.

"I know. This has all been terribly difficult for you. I have perhaps pushed you too hard. In time you will see it was for the best, though."

His hand was stroking her back reassuringly. She clutched at his shoulders, still unable to stop sobbing. "I cannot even go home, Marcus. I always had the hope of going home."

She was hardly making sense now. He kissed her head, whispering endearments in her ear. It disturbed him considerably that she did not consider her life with him in any terms of permanence. "You are home," he insisted softly.

She shook her head, gulping in breaths between her sobs. "I am so alone. I have lost everything now."

"You have gained me. Surely that counts for something."

Thacea heard the slightly bitter note in his voice and leaned back so she could see his face. "Oh, Marcus, it counts a great deal. At the moment, it is all that keeps me breathing."

He misinterpreted her meaning. "I have vowed to you that you are safe from George's threats. He will not harm you." No one would ever harm her again. He would see to it.

"It is not George who upsets me, Marcus. I have no doubt you will protect me."

"Then why are you crying?"

She sniffed against him. "Because it isn't George I fear. It's myself."

He watched her as she wiped away her tears with her hands. It disturbed him to see her so upset. Reaching up, he took her face between his hands. "Will I ever understand you?" he asked quietly.

She looked at him in surprise. "I am not so very complex, my Lord. In fact, I am quite transparent." She smoothed the worried frown from his forehead with her finger. "You see, while you have told me quite clearly that you do not and cannot love me, I have made the mistake of falling in love with you. And now I am completely trapped by the knowledge and I . . ."

"Wait!" His voice sounded like a pistol report. "What did you say?"

"I am completely trapped?"

"Before that."

"I have made the mistake?"

He smiled against her hair. "In the middle," he said gently.

She drew a deep breath. "I have fallen in love with you?"

He tipped back her head with his fingers, fighting an inexplicable surge of elation. The woman was making him daft. Countless women had told him they loved him. It usually incensed him. But now, his fingers were a bit unsteady, and there was an unsettled feeling in his gut. "Is that true?"

She looked at him worriedly. "I know it is a great nuisance to you, Marcus. You have made your feelings on the matter quite clear to me. I'm sure you would have much preferred that I kept it to myself."

He stared at her. "Is it true?" he asked again.

"Yes. I have known it for weeks. Since Caroline Erridge's house party, actually."

Marcus gave an exultant shout and toppled her back on the bed. "Say it again," he demanded.

She looked at him in surprise. "Marcus, you are ruining my orchids."

"I will buy you a thousand more. Say it again."

"I love you," she said.

He smiled at her. "I shall never grow weary of hearing it." His lips covered hers in a ravenous kiss and Thacea sighed, allowing him to calm her fears and replace them with a passion that nearly made her forget he didn't love her in return.

When Marcus finally left her bed that day, it was well after luncheon. Thacea watched him as he placed the finishing touches on his cravat. He looked exceedingly handsome in his fawn-colored trousers and burgundy waistcoat. His white shirt made his shoulders look broader than usual. He must have sensed her scrutiny. His eyes met hers in the mirror. "You are awake," he said quietly.

She nodded. "I am amazingly tired, my Lord."

Marcus strolled to the side of the bed. "I do not find it at all amazing. And you may feel free to pay me such compliments any time you wish."

"You will become terribly conceited if I do." Tossing back the covers, she swung her legs to the carpeted floor. Marcus watched with an appreciative eye as she reached for her velvet robe and slipped it on, pulling the knot tight at her waist. "Are you going out?" she asked.

He nodded and turned toward his bedroom. "I am meeting with Aiden Brickston on several important matters," he called over his shoulder, crossing through the connecting door.

Thacea hesitated only briefly before she walked to her small trunk and pushed back the lid. There was a small parcel on top, neatly wrapped in brown paper. She picked it up, walking quickly toward Marcus's room. "Is everything all right?"

He looked up from the task of pulling on his boots. "Yes. I simply want to ensure that no details have been overlooked. I do not wish to take any unnecessary risks."

She hurried forward to help him with his other boot, laying the small parcel on the bed next to him. She knelt beside him and slid the boot into place, using the hem of her velvet robe to polish its already mirrored sheen.

Marcus watched her in surprise and allowed her to guide his foot into the boot. "I do not expect you to wait on me," he said quietly. "I have a valet for that."

She looked up at him. "It is not considered an act of servitude, my Lord." She sat back on her heels and studied him carefully. "In Ardahan, gentlemen find it very difficult to keep boots clean. The sand and the wind destroy the polish. A pasha shows his love for his favorite wife by providing her with an opulent wardrobe, giving her the very finest chambers in his harem, by caring for her family if they are in need, and by tending to her personal needs. One of the ways a wife demonstrates her love for her husband is by keeping his boots polished. When he is seen in public, everyone knows he has the favor of his wife. My father used to say, 'A woman's love for her husband is clearest in the reflection of his boots.' "

Marcus felt his heart warm. He pulled her to her feet to stand between his legs, resting his strong hands on her narrow waist.

"I'm certain my valet would be delighted to know you would like to take over the task of champagne-polishing my footwear."

She poked him in the chest. "I am nearly convinced not to give you your present now that you have offended me with that remark."

He nuzzled his lips in the fragrant valley between her breasts. "Madam wife, I am not entirely certain I can live through another one of your presents."

Thacea laughed and sank down on his lap, reaching for the parcel. "That is the perfect answer, and you are forgiven," she said, handing him the gift. "This is for you."

He raised an eyebrow. "What is it?"

She looked at him curiously. "Do not be addlepated, Marcus. I am not going to tell you what it is before you open it. It is something I bought before Caroline's house party. The occasion never arose to give it to you before, so now you may consider it a wedding present." She handed him the parcel and waited expectantly.

Marcus looked at the parcel warily. Carefully he tore back the brown paper, revealing a small wooden lion. It was intricately carved in dark brown walnut. The details were so exquisitely cast, it appeared almost alive. He turned the beautiful object over in his hand, admiring the skill it had taken to render it. When he looked at its face, two tiny emerald eyes glittered at him. He looked at Thacea. "Heart of a Lion?" he asked, correctly remembering the name she had given him on the green.

She nodded. "It reminded me of you."

"I shall cherish it always. Thank you."

She slipped from his lap. "Now, I will not be accused of making you late, my Lord." Thacea reached for his cuff links on the small table by his bed and slid them into place in his cuffs in a gesture that had now become customary. "What time is Aiden expecting you?"

Marcus looked at the clock on the mantel. "I have a few

minutes, yet. Will you come to the library with me before I leave?"

She looked at him in surprise. "I am not dressed."

He shrugged. "I assure you my servants will not be shocked." He thought with a wry smile that they had seen a good many undressed women running about his household, but thought better than to tell he so. "I have something I'd like to give you."

"You do not need to give me anything, Marcus. I told you, I bought the lion several weeks ago, and I . . ."

He laid a finger across her lips and rose to his feet, reaching for his charcoal-grey whipcord jacket. "I have actually had this for some time. It had slipped my memory until just now." He shrugged into his jacket and straightened his waistcoat with a sharp tug on the points. "Are you coming?"

She nodded, and accepted his outstretched hand. They walked in a leisurely manner along the corridor and down the long staircase. Thacea decided it was a strange, if nice, feeling being married to Marcus. He had been right in saying his servants would not be shocked at her state of undress. She did not receive so much as a second glance from any of the footmen in the foyer. Marcus swung open the door of the library and allowed her to precede him into the large, welcoming room. "Come over," he said, walking toward his desk. "I have locked it in my safe."

Thacea followed him, looking at him in surprise. "What can you possibly have purchased that needs to be locked in your safe?"

Marcus swung open the picture on his wall, revealing the metal safe. "Something you once told me was of infinite value." He removed a tiny key from a hidden drawer in his desk. Placing it in the lock of the safe, he twisted it, and the door swung open. He removed an object wrapped in heavy black velvet and handed it to her.

She looked at him curiously. "I do not recall ever telling you that."

He snapped the picture back into place. "Open the cloth. It will no doubt refresh your memory."

Thacea folded back the black velvet and gasped in delight at the sight of the gold, jewel-encrusted dagger. "My father's dagger! However did you . . ." She looked up at him suddenly. "You gave me the thousand pounds, didn't you?"

"At the time, I was merely protecting your financial interests. I would have been unable to find a buyer to give you its worth with such short notice. I intended to hold it until my secretary found the appropriate buyer, and then I would forward the rest of the money to you."

"But you never told me."

He shrugged. "I did not think you would accept the thousand pounds if you knew they came from me."

She looked at the dagger lovingly, and traced her fingers over the intricately carved handle. Marcus watched the tiny action and could not help but think of how she caressed him in just such a way. He mumbled something to himself and shifted his weight uncomfortably. "Later," he said, more for his own benefit than for hers. "I kept it because I knew it was important to you."

Thacea felt a tiny bubble of happiness spring into her heart. Marcus was very much closer to loving her than he imagined. She threw her arms around his neck, kissing him soundly on the mouth. "Nothing could have pleased me more," she said, ending the kiss and burying her face against his chest. "Thank you."

"It is not every husband who gives his wife a weapon as a wedding present."

Thacea tipped her head back to look at him. "But no bride could be happier with her gift than I am. You cannot know how much this means to me."

Marcus decided to give up the fight against kissing her. Her sweetly curved mouth, and the soft scent of her hair, were too much of a temptation. He was well aware that the passion between them would probably cause the kiss to soon soar out of control, but he imagined Aiden Brickston would forgive him for being late, in light of the circumstances. He bent his head and kissed her lightly, softly, savoring the taste of her mouth.

Thacea sighed and leaned into him, amazed that she could desire him again so soon. At her tiny surrender, Marcus groaned and deepened the kiss. His fingers moved to the knot of her velvet dressing gown. Thacea felt his hardened flesh swell against the fabric of his breeches. She rubbed against him, unwittingly seeking to deepen the caress. When Marcus's hand moved inside her robe to cup the sensitive fullness of her breast, she gasped and sucked his tongue into her mouth.

At that instant, the door to the library flew open and Marcus's butler stepped inside. Marcus was dimly aware of the intrusion and started to lift his head to scowl at the butler. But Thacea seemed completely oblivious to the entire matter. When her small hands threaded through his hair, holding his head closer to her own, he decided he didn't much care what his butler saw or didn't see. . . . Until he heard him announce, "Her Ladyship, the Dowager Countess of Brandtwood, Lord Foxley, Lord Carlyn, and Sir David Lynch."

Twenty-six

"Hello, Harriet." Marcus lifted his head, noting with arrogant pleasure that Thacea's eyes still seemed to be a bit out of focus. He calmly tugged her robe into place and reknotted the tie at her waist.

"There, you see," Harriet Brandton said. "I told you he had married her. Now each of you owes me one hundred pounds."

Thacea had to blink several times before the full severity of the situation reached her. When she finally realized that their intimate embrace had been interrupted by Marcus's mother, of all people, she dropped her head on his rock-hard shoulder with a groan. He chuckled, and continued to hold her close against him, seeming entirely undisturbed by the enormously embarrassing circumstances. Thacea made a mental note to chastise him on the matter later—if she didn't first die of mortification.

Marcus schooled his features into a cynical smile. "Am I to understand, Harriet, that you've placed a wager with each of these three gentlemen on my recent nuptials?"

Harriet shifted uncomfortably beneath his cool tone, but the three men seemed not to notice the tense overtones in the room.

Sir David Lynch stepped forward. Marcus knew him as one of his mother's many young suitors. He had always detested the young idiot, and his estimation of him had just plummeted severely. "That's right, Brandtwood," Sir David said. "The news is all over London by now, chap. I couldn't hardly credit it."

"He told me about it this morning at the club," Lord Foxley interjected. "I was the one who suggested we ask the Countess."

"Were you?" Marcus said blandly.

Lord Carlyn nodded. "He did at that. We all went directly to her Ladyship's town house where she wagered each of us one hundred pounds the rumor was true."

Marcus looked at his mother. Her face had paled slightly. She was no stranger to recognizing his moods. She clearly understood the silent message behind his menacing stare. "Very considerate of you, Harriet. I'm surprised you had such faith in my willingness to marry the lady."

Harriet raised her chin slightly. "Do not be trite, Brandt. I have heard what has been going on in this house. As soon as I heard what had happened, I had no doubt you had done something so foolish."

Thacea had been standing with her back to the other four occupants of the room with her face buried against Marcus's shoulder. Harriet's waspish comment snapped her resolve to remain silent. When she felt Marcus stiffen at his mother's harsh words, she spun around in the circle of his arms. "Well, your Ladyship, now you clearly know your suspicions were correct. I would ask that you collect your wager and kindly leave my house."

My God! The woman looks like a carnival act, Thacea thought, trying not to stare at Harriet Brandton. She wore an enormous amount of powders and rouges. Her lips and eyes were painted in garish colors. Her flowing pink gown looked almost tawdry on a woman her age. Her hair was an unnatural yellow color, and the black poodle she held in one arm only contributed to her startling appearance. Molly had told Thacea a great deal about Harriet Brandton, but nothing had prepared her for the woman's appalling appearance, and even more appalling lack of good manners.

Harriet stared at Thacea baldly before she swung her gaze back to Marcus. *"Her* house? Have you lost complete control, Brandt?"

Marcus smiled a tight, dangerous smile. He placed his hand

on Thacea's shoulder. "Not at all, Harriet. It is all part of the usual contract. My wife is now the Countess of Brandtwood."

Thacea did not miss the pleading look Sir David shot in Harriet's direction. Harriet continued to ignore everyone but Marcus. "I cannot believe you have done this. You realize you are the laughingstock of London."

Marcus leaned more comfortably against his desk and regarded Harriet with an upraised eyebrow. "Is that so?"

"Yes. That you have married this scandal-ridden woman who clearly tricked you out of your money." Harriet paused and looked scornfully at Thacea. "And that she is from some entirely uncivilized country somewhere in Africa or Asia, or wherever it may be, has made you the joke of the ton. And," she continued, looking at him pointedly, "do not think the stories of her deportment at the Ridgefield house party have escaped my attention."

Thacea felt a cold knot of anger begin to simmer in her belly. Marcus's fingers flexed on her shoulder, silently asking her to hold her tongue. As much as she longed to give Harriet Brandton a well-deserved tongue-lashing, she desired more to ease the uncomfortable scene for Marcus.

Marcus felt Thacea's tension. His gaze narrowed menacingly on his mother. "I have heard enough of this. Though I hardly feel your observations deserve rebuttal, in deference to my wife, I will give it to you. I have not been tricked out of anything—particularly not money. Her Ladyship married me against her own objections—a notion I would think you'd find vastly amusing and certainly to her credit. As for her lineage, I would think you would be delighted to learn I have married a member of the royal household of an important British ally on the Black Sea. And so far as your comment about deportment," he swept a meaningful glance over the other three men in the room, "I shouldn't think you would concern yourself with that."

Harriet's lips thinned into an unpleasant line. She stroked the head of the black poodle. "I see you are your usual unpleasant self, Brandt."

"I do not appreciate being disturbed while I am, in a sense, on my honeymoon. As it happens, however, I am already late for a meeting with the Duke of Albrick." He levered himself away from the desk and gave Thacea an affectionate slap on the behind. She turned startled eyes to his. He winked at her, clearly enjoying the scene. "I will leave our guests to you, darling. I'm certain you'll know how to handle them."

Before Thacea could comment, Marcus swept from the room without so much as a backward glance at any of them. She stared at the closed door for several stunned seconds before she turned back to face Harriet. With Marcus gone, his mother's self-confidence seemed to have returned in full force. Thacea didn't miss the dramatic way she sank down onto the long sofa. She waited while one of her three gentlemen friends fetched her a cup of tea. Then she looked at Thacea, a condescending smile on her lips. "In England, my dear, *ladies* dress before receiving their guests."

Thacea squared her shoulders and tugged the tie of her velvet dressing gown a bit tighter. She refused to let the harridan intimidate her in any way. She met Harriet's gaze. *"Ladies* also do not barge uninvited into other people's libraries."

Harriet sucked in a breath. "I have always been welcome in Brandt's home. Would you deny me that?"

"As his wife, I'll do as I please." She looked briefly at the three men and noticed that Sir David was beginning to look particularly peaked. "If you will excuse me, however, I will dress and join you again shortly."

"By all means, dear." Harriet took a sip of her tea.

Thacea bit back a retort and walked as calmly from the library as possible. She barely resisted the urge to slam the door behind her before stomping up the stairs to her room.

Molly was waiting inside, a worried expression on her face. "Is it true what they say, ma'am? Is her Ladyship really downstairs?"

"Yes. She's downstairs. I want my blue silk gown, Molly." She crossed to the dressing table and picked up one of her bone-handled brushes.

Molly cast her a worried look and hurried to the wardrobe, to fetch the pale blue gown. "I see she's not wasting any time making sure her position is still secure."

Thacea was pulling the brush through her hair when she paused to look at Molly. "What do you mean?"

"Well, his Lordship gives her money—quite a bit I hear—and with his marrying you and all, I imagine she wants to make sure she's still going to get it."

Thacea thoughtfully began brushing her hair again. "Why should she think I'd have any control over that?"

Molly shrugged and shook the wrinkles out of the dress. "It depends on how much you'll be wanting to spend. You may not want his Lordship sending so much to his mother."

Thacea put down the brush and walked to the bathing closet. As she expected, there was already hot water in the tub. Marcus would not have overlooked such a detail in the daily operation of his household. She stepped into the warm water and twisted her hair into a knot on top of her head. "Do you really think that's why she's here?"

Molly followed her into the bathing closet and knelt by the tub to hand her the soap. "Did she have a gentleman with her?"

Thacea began scrubbing her skin with the lilac-scented soap. "Yes. Three, as a matter of fact."

"Then that's certainly why she's here. Everyone knows her Ladyship is . . . very generous to the young gentlemen who call on her regularly."

"Your description didn't hardly do her justice." She lowered her voice to a conspiratorial whisper. "She's wearing the most awful dress in a candy-colored pink."

Molly shrieked. "Is her hair still yellow?"

Thacea nodded. "And she's carrying around that nasty little black poodle you told me about. I wasn't prepared for her to look so . . . well, so . . ."

"Ridiculous?" Molly added helpfully.

"Pathetic," Thacea concluded. "If she wasn't such a mean-spirited hoyden, I'd almost feel sorry for her." She rose from the tub and accepted a towel from Molly. "And now Marcus has left me here to entertain her."

Molly laughed delightedly and followed Thacea into her bed-chamber. "Perhaps it's his Lordship's way of letting you know he'll let you make the decisions about his mother. I'm sure her three gentlemen friends are here to find out if their finances are about to be rutted."

Thacea sat at her dressing table and watched in the mirror while Molly plaited her hair. "I've disliked that woman ever since Peter Drake first told me the story of how he met her." She waited, thoughtfully tapping her finger on the top of her dressing table. When Molly finished arranging her hair in an intricate plait, she rose and stepped into the blue silk gown.

"It's a beautiful gown, ma'am. One of the finest you have."

Thacea looked back at the mirror, distracted by her thoughts. "Yes. Yes it is."

"His Lordship left instructions to have a whole new wardrobe done up for you, your Ladyship. Do you want me to send for Madame Drussard?"

Thacea's eyes narrowed speculatively. "Yes, do that. Send her a note and let her know his Lordship will make it well worth her trouble if she comes as soon as possible. Make sure she's shown into the library immediately."

Molly handed her the blue slippers that matched the gown. "Won't you be entertaining his Lordship's mother?"

"Yes I will," Thacea said, slipping on the shoes.

Thacea forced herself to walk slowly down the hall, despite the rather pressing need she had to confront Harriet Brandton. She deliberately paused and spoke with one of the chamber-maids, gave instructions to the butler regarding Madame Drus-sard's impending arrival, and stopped to rearrange a bowl of flowers in the foyer before she walked back into the library.

Harriet was still seated on the sofa holding court for her three young swains. Thacea glided into the room and nodded casually at Harriet before settling herself into the large leather chair. "Now, I must apologize if I seemed somewhat inhospitable earlier. You will understand of course that you took me completely by surprise."

Harriet nodded, her smile not quite reaching here eyes. "Of course. I regret any discomfort we may have caused you, but as it was after twelve o'clock, I naturally assumed you would be up to receiving callers."

Thacea poured herself a cup of tea. "That would be quite understandable if one weren't so aware of Marcus's . . ." she paused carefully, ". . . rather extraordinary stamina." She took a cup of tea and watched Sir David's uncomfortable expression over the rim of her cup. "But all is well now. I am delighted to have the chance to meet you. I have heard a great deal about you."

Harriet's eyes narrowed. "Have you?"

Thacea nodded and settled back in her chair, setting her cup down on the small table. "Yes indeed. And I'm very grateful you decided to simply arrive here this afternoon. You have saved me the trouble of calling on you."

"You would have called on me?"

Thacea looked at her in surprise. "Well, of course. I will be making some changes, you know, and I wanted to meet you before I made any final decisions." Thacea watched with immense satisfaction as all the color drained from Sir David's face and into Harriet Brandton's.

Twenty-seven

"Damn it, Brick!" Marcus slammed his palm down on the desk. "This situation is intolerable. How could they have lost track of him?"

Aiden leaned back in his chair. They were seated in his study in Albrick House, and he raked a hand through his hair in a habit of agitation. Jace had reported to him only that morning that his contacts had lost track of George Worthingham after he left Dover. Their only hope of finding him now was a chance sighting by one of their men in another port. "It's unfortunate, I'll grant you, but I wouldn't worry over it unduly, Brandt. Worthingham is hardly the sort of chap one credits with either the courage or potential to devise anything truly dangerous. He was on the wrong side of the hedge when the brains were handed out, I'd say. I know he cast about some rather disturbing threats, but I do not think you should be alarmed."

"And what am I to do in the interim? I cannot simply hide my wife away and wait for the slimy little bastard to show his face."

"And neither would I," Aiden said, taking a long draw on his pipe. "I think you should make every effort to be seen in public. Attend the theater, accept a few invitations."

Marcus looked at him wryly. He very much doubted Aiden Brickston would understand that the kind of invitations he received were not the usual sort of entertainments where a man arrived with his new bride on his arm. "I am not entirely certain that is a wise course of action."

Aiden looked at him knowingly and handed him a heavy piece of vellum paper. "This is an invitation to join Sarah and me at the Theater tomorrow evening in our private box. The new Rossini opera is opening. Sarah has been begging me to take her."

Marcus looked at it dubiously. "Are you certain you wish to do this?"

"In the event that you haven't noticed, my wife rather enjoys creating a scene. She is still desperately seeking a measure by which she can best Caroline's ball at Sedgewood. It will give her no small pleasure to know that the eyes of the ton are on our box all evening. Jace and Caroline will be there, as well. Sarah also tells me you have a younger sister you have not yet introduced to Society. She was the young lady at your wedding, I believe."

Marcus looked up in surprise. "That is correct. Madelyne has not been well."

"If she is feeling well enough to attend, she is welcome too, of course."

Marcus tapped the invitation thoughtfully on his knee. It would be good, he knew, for him to be seen with Thacea amid respectable company. She would doubtless suffer a bit of gossip as a result of his reputation. The unpleasant scene with Harriet had proven that. Openings at the Theater were generally very well attended. He imagined a good number of the ton would be anxious to see his new bride. The Duke's closed box would make protection very much easier than an open ballroom. He nodded slowly. "All right. I will relay your invitation to Thacea. I'm certain she'll be delighted to attend. It's exceedingly generous of you."

Aiden shrugged. "As for your other problem, do not concern yourself unduly with Worthingham's disappearance. We'll have our eyes open, and I think you will find you can effectively write him off your list of worries."

Marcus rose to his feet and extended his hand to Aiden.

"You've been an enormous help to me, Brick. I cannot thank you enough."

Aiden stood and shook his hand. "I'm delighted things have worked out so well for you. I don't have to tell you my thoughts regarding the life you had been living."

"I am all too aware. You'd be amazed at the change in my perspective, however."

"Less amazed than you might think. Now, I imagine your wife is waiting for you and you've considerably better things to do than hang about my house all afternoon."

"As the nature of my wedding was rather rushed," he said, shooting Aiden an amused look, "I have yet to purchase a ring for my bride."

Aiden laughed. "After that little scene you nearly created at the wedding over the old one, I hope you purchase a large, obnoxiously expensive one."

"The very biggest one I can find."

By the time Marcus arrived home, Brandtwood House had been thrown into bedlam. He strode up the front stairs and froze on the doorstep at the veritable army of seamstresses in his foyer. There were trunks of fabric strewn in every direction, the footmen were running about in utter confusion. Several large paintings he was certain he'd never seen before leaned against the walls while an artist was busily working on another. There was an enormous porcelain vase of indeterminable make on the table. His solicitors were speaking in an extremely agitated fashion with Colonel Samuelson. And his mother's incredibly annoying poodle was running about barking its high-pitched, equally annoying bark. He scowled and shouldered his way through the confusion, intent on finding his wife. He crashed open the library door and stopped, completely forgetting his momentary annoyance when he saw Thacea standing on a low ottoman, her arms raised high above her head, wearing nothing whatsoever while Madame Drussard argued with her over the propriety of a piece of red silk Thacea had evidently requested for a nightdress. He shut the library door, lest his wife find herself exposed to the rather large crowd in his foyer, and leaned back against it casually. "May I say, my love, that this activity would probably be much more appropriate in your boudoir."

Thacea looked at him in surprise, then stepped down quickly and reached for her robe. "I did not expect you home so soon, my Lord."

He raised an eyebrow and walked to her side. "Evidently not." He stayed her hand as she moved to don her robe. "Do not bother on my account. I rather prefer you in dishabille."

She cast him a chiding look as she slipped her arms into the robe. "I truly am sorry, Marcus. I intended to have everything in order by the time you arrived."

His attention was directed once again to the scene in his foyer. "What the devil is going on out there?"

"Your mother," she said pointedly, "has decided to stay for a visit."

His eyes darkened. "What the bloody hell for?"

"Now, Marcus, do not get upset." She looked briefly at Madame Drussard. "I believe you have enough to begin with, Madame, I will complete the order early next week."

The French dressmaker looked at her in consternation. "Of course, Madame. We can begin on ze gowns you have ordered today, but do you not wish his Lordship to see zem first?"

Marcus shook his head and took the scrap of red silk from Madame Drussard's hand. "If all of her Ladyship's taste is as extraordinary as this, I do not need to see them. Make certain you include the robe and garters to match this, Madame."

Madame Drussard evidently knew better than to quibble over the details of what promised to be an enormous order, and took the scrap of silk back from Marcus. "Of course, your Lordship. We will do what we can to complete her Ladyship's order right away."

Marcus nodded briefly and waited until Madame Drussard had hurried from the room before he turned his gaze back to

Thacea. "Now, would you kindly explain to me what the devil you've done to my house?"

She tugged the tie of her robe into a tight knot. *"Our* house," she said. "If one more person reminds me today that this is your house, and I'm to follow your orders, I think I shall scream."

He raised an eyebrow. "Is that what this is about? Are you angry with me about Harriet's scene this morning?"

"Do not think I am so muddleheaded as not to know what she's about, Marcus."

"Then perhaps you'd like to enlighten me. I seemed to have entirely missed the point."

Thacea glared at him. "If she believes she can come in here with her young friends in tow and make me believe she has greater precedence than I in this house, she is sadly mistaken. I may perhaps concede that Madelyne is more important in your household, but not her."

Marcus stared at her. "What on earth are you talking about?"

Thacea appeared not to have heard him. "That woman is here for no other reason than to demonstrate to me that she controls you."

His eyes glinted dangerously. "No one controls me," he said quietly.

"Precisely my point. You care a great deal for Madelyne. You have even said you care for me. But as to your mother, I will not have her disrupting the order or the peace of my household for her petty games and devious plans."

"So you very logically invited her to stay here when she has a perfectly functional, ridiculously opulent town house of her own, for which I pay dearly, I might add, on the other side of London."

"I did not invite her to stay here."

"Then why the bloody hell did you let her?"

"Because I have no intention of becoming a victim to her wicked gossip. Are you aware what she would have said had I not allowed her to stay in the house?"

Marcus shrugged. "I have never concerned myself with gossip before."

"In most cases, neither have I. I will not, however, give her the satisfaction of having the upper hand. I guarantee you, she will not be staying long."

Marcus poured himself a glass of brandy, then settled into his chair. "She had better not. As a rule, I do not like to be around the woman any longer than is absolutely necessary."

"Then do not worry yourself with it."

He grabbed her hand, tugging her down onto his lap. "If she isn't staying long, why is she moving in all her earthly belongings?"

Thacea absently toyed with his cravat. "It is really not so bad as it appears. Most of the mess in the foyer is Madame Drussard's entourage."

"And why," he said, looking at her suspiciously, "were you having your fittings in the library?"

"Because the footmen are running about upstairs carrying in your mother's trunks and personal items. You didn't miss that rather hideously ugly vase she insisted on having, did you?"

He shook his head. "Unfortunately, no. Neither did I fail to notice the artist."

"She's his patron."

Marcus frowned and took a sip of his brandy, his hand running leisurely along the curve of Thacea's hip. "That means *I* am his patron. He isn't even any good."

She laughed and slapped ineffectually at his hand when it slipped inside her robe to caress her stomach. "In any case, I did not wish to have my fittings in my room while there was all that activity upstairs. It seemed very much easier to have them here in the privacy of the library."

"With the door unlocked?"

"Colonel Samuelson was outside. He would not have allowed anyone to enter but you."

He shook his head. "And what are my solicitors doing here?"

"Oh, that."

"Yes, that."

"I asked Colonel Samuelson to set about nullifying the contract you signed yesterday."

Marcus blinked, momentarily forgetting that he had bestowed a rather enormous sum of money on her in the hour preceding his wedding. "What?"

"The contract. I would never have accepted such a large sum of money from you, Marcus. My only excuse is that I wasn't thinking very clearly. Anyway, I have asked Colonel Samuelson to set about nullifying it, and he is arguing the matter with your solicitors."

His hand stilled in its intimate exploration. "I do not want it nullified."

"Well, I do." She looked at him carefully and lifted her hand to trace her fingers over the strong curve of his chin. "I do not ever want to be accused of having married you for your money. That disturbed me considerably."

He looked at her in surprise. "I made you a promise, Thacea. I have every intention of upholding my end of the bargain."

"And you have. You signed the contract. But I never promised to accept the money, and I have no intention of doing so."

He bent his head to nuzzle her neck. "We have a good many years to argue about this, I suppose."

She squirmed against him when he nipped her earlobe with his teeth. "There is to be no argument about it." She was well aware her voice sounded breathless and unconvincing, but Marcus's hands and lips were distracting her.

"Then perhaps you will accept something else from me," he said, his hot breath tickling her ear.

"I do not want anything else from you, Marcus." She moaned and tipped her head back when his tongue touched the sensitive whorl of her ear.

"Nothing?" he asked, moving against her deliberately.

She turned her head to kiss him. "Only this," she whispered, laying her lips against his. *And your heart,* she added silently.

The kiss went on for several long seconds before Marcus raised his head. "I really do have something for you, love."

"I know," she whispered, snuggling closer against him.

He laughed delightedly and slipped his fingers into the pocket of his waistcoat to pull out the enormous diamond ring he'd purchased earlier that day. He slid one hand along the length of her left arm until he reached her fingers. Lifting them gently to his lips, he kissed each one, then placed the ring onto her third finger, where it nestled beside her wedding band. "That too, love, but tell me if you like this first."

Thacea looked at the ring in surprise, then back at Marcus. "Oh, Marcus." Thacea blinked several times, her lower lip trembled ever so slightly. *"Oh, Marcus!"* She threw her arms around his neck and hugged him fiercely.

Pleasantly surprised by her effusive reaction, he hugged her close to his heart. "I take that to mean you approve of my selection."

"Yes! I approve even more that you thought of it." She leaned back and looked at him. "You are doing a very poor job of convincing me you have no feelings, my Lord."

He grinned at her wickedly. "I have any number of feelings, madam wife. At the moment, I have an intense feeling that I would very much like to ravish you here on the library carpet."

She blushed. "Don't you think that would be a bit risky after what happened this morning."

He nuzzled his face against her throat. "It's all the more exciting when you take risks, my Lady. Besides, my secretary is exceedingly well trained. If you left instructions that you were not to be disturbed, I can assure you, you won't be."

She smiled at him and tugged loose the knot of his cravat. "Then pray, my lord husband, I see no reason at all to tarry."

Marcus groaned and slanted his lips over hers in a kiss full of seductive promise.

Twenty-eight

It was not until late that night, when Thacea lay securely in the cradle of Marcus's arms in the quiet darkness of his bedroom, that she relented to the pent-up tension of the day and released a heavy sigh.

"That sounded dramatic," Marcus said quietly.

"I thought you were asleep," she accused.

"Nearly." He rolled to his side and propped his head on his elbow, studying her in the flickering glow of the firelight. He was indeed very pleasantly exhausted. Thacea had proven to be completely uninhibited in bed. He found, to his continuing delight, that she was not at all missish about lovemaking. She owed her "expertise" to her rather extensive curiosity during the time she'd spent among the women of her uncle's harem. He delighted in the knowledge that she felt entirely comfortable questioning him about any number of matters. He considered it one of his more enjoyable husbandly duties to satisfy her inquisitive nature.

"You are disturbed about dinner, aren't you?" It surprised him that he was already so accustomed to her moods.

She nodded, her fingers moving absently on his chest. "It was a horrid affair."

"Any evening with Harriet is a horrid affair. I would have gladly told you so before you invited her to stay in my—*our* house."

She rewarded him with a smile for remembering her insistence about the ownership of Brandtwood House. "I cannot believe she was so cruel to Madelyne. I spent nearly two hours with her this evening trying to soothe her."

Marcus traced a finger along the curve of Thacea's nose. "I made it quite clear to Harriet that Madelyne is a member of this household. I will not tolerate a reoccurrence of that."

She raised troubled eyes to his. "She was no kinder to you, Marcus."

He lifted one shoulder in casual disregard and leaned back against the pillows, linking his hands beneath his head. "Harriet's barbs have long since lost their ability to affect me."

"But they did once," she said quietly.

"I suppose. Any young boy would find that environment difficult. I accepted it in time, however, and realize now it really had nothing at all to do with me personally."

That's rather unemotional, Thacea thought. She moved her hand along Marcus's chest, aware that a dull ache had settled in her heart. He had been such an amazingly lonely little boy. It was no wonder at all he'd grown into a lonely man. She snuggled closer to him, seeking to give him warmth. Marcus misinterpreted her small action and hugged her close. "You have only to say the word, love, and I will tell her to leave."

She shook her head. "I do not want her to leave, Marcus."

He stroked his hand along the curve of her spine. "I will not have you upset."

"You'll *have* me any way I will allow you."

He rolled her to her back suddenly and loomed over her. "Wicked woman. I have made you quite wanton, you know. Tell me again about your inability to respond."

"Do you regret it?" she asked, linking her hands at the nape of his neck.

"Not by any wager," he said, bending his head and capturing her lips once more.

When Marcus awoke in the morning, he inhaled a great breath of lilac-scented air. Thacea was snuggled against him, the soft, rounded curve of her bottom nestled against the hard cradle of his thighs. Her back was to him. The top of her head lay on the pillow just beneath his chin. One of her knees was drawn up, and her other leg extended the length of his. Her shapely little foot fitted against the muscular curve of his calf. She shifted slightly in her sleep and unwittingly knocked his rib cage with her elbow. He groaned softly, tightening his hold on her waist.

Marcus lay still for several long minutes, savoring the new-found feeling of waking up with his wife in his bed. It wasn't the first time by any means that he'd awakened with a woman curled up next to him. It was, however, the first time he hadn't felt the need to immediately extricate himself from the predicament. Usually, mornings in bed with women brought about a great number of complications, not the least of which were un-wanted declarations of love and undying devotion. But Thacea had told him a half dozen times during the night that she loved him, and each time his heart had soared.

The intensity of his reaction had stunned him. Making her happy, seeing to her safety and comfort, had suddenly become the most important things in the world to him. God help him, if she ever stopped loving him, he thought perhaps he would die. The notion made him slightly uncomfortable, for he was slightly loath to give her that much power over him, but in truth, he could not deny it. He hugged her close, deciding there was but one way to ensure she was really his.

She moved her soft bottom against his groin once more. He needed no further invitation. Slowly, careful not to awaken her, he slid one hand along the length of her strong, smooth thigh. She sighed in her sleep, bringing a smile to his lips. Thacea always turned into his touch like a flower turned to the sun. It pleased him enormously.

He continued the tender exploration until his hand reached the fullness of her breast. Gently, he cupped the weight of it in his palm, rubbing his thumb against the soft brown nipple. It hardened almost immediately, and Thacea sighed again, moving slightly with the rhythm of his hand. He felt his desire harden.

Marcus shifted just enough to free his other hand, and he slid it along the flat plane of her stomach, down the line of her thigh. Her legs parted unconsciously. He kissed the nape of her neck, sliding his hand between the silken warmth of her thighs. When he felt her moist heat, he groaned, a surge of desire causing his hardened shaft to swell against the curve of her buttocks.

Thacea awoke to the sudden realization that she was being ravaged by her husband. "Marcus." Her voice was little more than a breathless sigh.

He chuckled in her ear and nipped her earlobe with his teeth. "I should hope so. Otherwise I shall have to abandon my current very pleasurable pursuit to call out the strange man in my bed."

She moaned when his fingers moved intimately against her wet heat, and she reached down to heighten the pressure of his hand. "You make me wild when you do that."

"I like you wild," he said, flicking his thumb over her most sensitive spot. "I like the way your body heats up for me." He rubbed his thumb in a slow, exquisitely torturous circle. She gasped his name, moaning softly. "I especially like the noises you make in the back of your throat when I touch you," he said, sliding one finger inside her. "Do you like that, love?" he asked when she moaned again.

"Yes. Oh, Marcus, yes!"

He ran his tongue along the whorl of her ear, his other hand still slowly caressing the hardened peak of her nipple. "This too, hmm?" he said, rolling the sensitized bud between his thumb and forefinger.

"Yes," she said, her voice a throaty moan.

Marcus's fingers were sliding in and out of her, and she pressed her bottom back against the hard length of him, seeking release from the delicious torment. "Not yet, love," he whispered. "Not until you are ready to scream for me."

She tipped her head back against his shoulder and pressed fiercely at his hand. "I am ready now, Marcus," her voice caught on his name when she felt his desire surge against her. "I cannot stand any more of this."

He sucked on her earlobe. "Then raise your breast for me. I want to suckle the peak, and it is not high enough."

She hesitated only briefly and Marcus removed his fingers from her womanly desire. She cried out and pressed her breast up with her other hand. He obliged her and sank his fingers deep inside her once more, levering himself down to take her upthrust nipple into his mouth. He sucked on it, laving the turgid peak with his tongue until he felt the taut muscles of her body begin to clench around his fingers. With a deep growl, he pushed her down on the bed and surged into her. She rotated her soft bottom against his groin, seeking release. When he gave it to her, she did indeed scream for him.

To her credit, he shouted her name when he exploded.

She lay beneath him, pulling in great gulps of air. Her response to Marcus's body amazed her. On the one hand, she resented the level of experience that made him such a skilled lover, but her body burned for him. He had only to touch her—to *look* at her with those jungle-green eyes and she was ready for him. She sighed, and enjoyed the feel of his pounding heart close to her ear. He was no less affected than she, it seemed.

Marcus rolled to his back. "You will undoubtedly be the death of me, madam wife."

She giggled and turned her face on the pillow to look at him. "A most appropriate way for you to die, don't you think?"

He shot her a sultry look. "If I had the energy, I'd make you pay for that remark."

She pushed herself up to her knees, not caring at all that he was afforded an ample view of her naked body, and poked him in the chest. "You would not," she said. "You are mostly bluster, my Lord, and don't think I do not know it."

He was clearly disgruntled. He mumbled something, reaching out a hand to touch her. She slapped at it. "There will be no more of that. I've a great many things to do today, and I do not have time to while away the morning in bed with you."

He raised an eyebrow. "I can think of few more satisfying pursuits."

She smiled at him and swung her legs to the floor. "Perhaps, but," she frowned over her shoulder when he reached over and pinched her bottom. "All right, *certainly,* but I am no more amenable, you lecher. I meant what I said. I've got things to do."

Marcus leaned back against the pillows. "So have I. John assures me I am immensely derelict in my correspondence."

She pulled her robe on and frowned at him. "Too much time spent in more pleasurable pursuits, no doubt."

"No doubt," he agreed, tossing aside the covers. He squinted at the clock on the mantel. "And where the devil is my valet? It's after nine-thirty."

Thacea had reached the connecting door between their chambers. "Mr. Langford," she said.

He looked at her in confusion. "Who the hell is Mr. Langford?"

"Your valet. His name is Mr. Langford. It would be a very nice gesture on your part if you remembered it in the future."

He scowled at her. "Damnation, woman. I haven't the least intention of throwing my entire household into disorder."

She smiled at him. "I have. And you'd very well better get used to it. Mr. Langford is not here this morning because I gave him explicit instructions to wait until you called him." She blushed. "I did not want to be disturbed until we were ready," she said softly, slipping through the connecting door.

Marcus stared after her, uncertain whether he would rather turn the impudent wench over his knee for her proprietary manner, or ravage her once more for her comment. He strode toward the door of his room, intent on finding his damned valet. He was expected at the War Department in Aiden Brickston's office in less than a half hour. Either course of action would have to wait until later.

Thacea shut the connecting door and sighed in the stillness of her bedchamber. Following the disastrous evening they'd spent with Harriet, Thacea had made several decisions about what she must do. In the clear light of morning, they seemed daunting. She crossed to her secretaire and sank down in the small chair, staring disconsolately out the window. Perhaps she was going about the entire thing completely wrong.

Was it wise to make so many changes in Marcus's life so early in their marriage? Her instincts told her she stood no chance of winning his heart if she allowed him to settle into a comfortable routine. If she simply fit in to his previous life, with no disruptions, and no obstacles, she would earn his good-natured approval, but not his love. She treasured the latter far more than the former.

Her eyes lingered briefly on her father's dagger and she thought of Raman a little desperately, her spirits falling another notch. It was all such a dreadful mess. Her parents had trusted her to keep Raman safe. The knowledge that he was completely out of her hands now was vastly upsetting to her and she ran her finger along the blade of the dagger. A sudden image of her father's laughing eyes popped into her head. She felt the sting of tears.

"Baba, what am I to do?" Several large tears spilled over and plopped onto the desk. She swiped at her eyes in frustration, realizing it was doing her little good to sit about and mope. She could no longer protect Raman, but she could protect Marcus. It was an equally important task.

Thacea managed to ignore most of Molly's idle chatter while she dressed, and carefully thought of what she would tell Madelyne this morning. The girl had been enormously upset by Harriet's behavior the previous evening. Thacea had done her best to soothe her, but somewhere between Madelyne's tears and her own comforting words, a thread of resentment had worked its way into Thacea's heart.

Marcus cared deeply for Madelyne. It was plainly obvious even to the most casual observer. That Madelyne had still not broken her silence seemed of little concern to him, as if he were entirely content to simply keep her within the confines of his home and care for her forever. But Thacea was not. Had she believed Madelyne was truly ill, her feelings might not have been so strong, but her compassion was rapidly being pushed aside by a growing resentment of the knowledge that Madelyne held Marcus's heart while Thacea did not.

When she was dressed in a day gown of green velvet, she turned from the mirror and looked it Molly. "Thank you, Molly. You have not forgotten that his Lordship and I are expected in the Albrick box at the Theater this evening?"

"Oh no, ma'am. I plan to press your gown this afternoon. I am hoping, though, that one of your new ones will arrive in time."

Thacea nodded absently and walked toward the door. "Yes, that would be nice. Make sure I have a gown ready in time, however. His Lordship wants to leave promptly at eight o'clock, and I do not wish to make him late."

Molly nodded and scooped up Thacea's robe from the chair. "I will, ma'am. If there's nothing else, I was asked to inform you that Lady Brandton would like to see you in her chambers as soon as you are dressed."

Thacea froze, her fingers on the knob. "I beg your pardon?"

Molly looked at her warily. "I don't know anything about it, ma'am. Betsy, that's her Ladyship's maid, told me I was to inform you that Lady Brandton wanted to see you in her chambers first thing this morning."

Thacea looked at Molly coolly. "I was unaware that her Ladyship was in the habit of rising so early in the morning."

"She's not. Not usually, anyway. But Betsy said she's rather in a state today."

Thacea gritted her teeth and jerked the door open. "You may tell her Ladyship that I will be unavailable to give her an audience until after luncheon. When I have an available minute, I will receive her in my drawing room."

Molly nodded. "Yes, ma'am."

"And Molly?"

"Yes, ma'am?"

"In this household, you are lady's maid to the mistress of the house. The next time Betsy gives you an order, be certain she hasn't forgotten that."

Molly looked enormously pleased. "Yes, ma'am."

Thacea swept from the room and slammed the door, her hands balling into fists at her sides. *How dare that hoyden summon me to her room.* When she reached the bottom of the stairs, she turned toward the drawing room and nearly collided with Colonel Samuelson.

"Your Ladyship! I'm dreadfully sorry. I should watch where I'm going instead of burying my nose in these letters," he said, waving the sheaf of papers in his hands.

Thacea forced a smile to her lips. She genuinely liked Colonel Samuelson. She was especially appreciative of his loyalty to Marcus. She saw no good reason to vent her frustration on him. "I imagine that would be quite a bit easier if my husband weren't so recalcitrant in fulfilling his duty."

The Colonel smiled. "He is not usually as derelict as he has been of late. May I say, my Lady, that you are having a most pleasant effect on him."

Thacea laughed slightly. "You may say things like that anytime you wish, Colonel."

He inclined his head in a slight bow. "And before I forget what I'm about, your Ladyship, you have a visitor in your drawing room."

Thacea frowned. "I was not expecting any callers today, Colonel."

He looked slightly abashed. "I'm sorry, my Lady, I took the liberty of seating the Marchioness of Ridgefield in your drawing room. I assumed . . ."

Thacea held up her hand with a sigh of relief. "That is another matter entirely. Lady Erridge is hardly a visitor. Thank you for seeing to her comfort."

He looked vastly relieved. "I have sent in a pot of coffee, my Lady. Will you be needing anything else?"

She shook her head, "No, Colonel. That will be all."

Thacea turned toward the drawing room, hastening her step. She was delighted at the unexpected pleasure of Caroline's visit. It would be a pleasant diversion in a day that was souring nearly from the start. She reached the drawing room and pushed open the door, stepping hastily inside. "Caroline! What a delight to see you."

Caroline leapt from the sofa and hurried across the room to embrace Thacea. "Are you certain I'm not intruding? Jace said it would be horribly rude of me to call on you so early. Especially on the second day of your honeymoon."

Thacea walked with Caroline back to the sofa, sinking down into the cushions. "Nearly anyone else would be intruding, Caroline. You, on the other hand, are a welcome reprieve." Caroline lifted her eyebrows in surprise and Thacea laughed. "Good heavens, not a reprieve from *that*. I certainly do not need a reprieve from that."

"I didn't think so. Marcus is rather legendary, you know. Not that I'm the least bit interested," she hastened to add, "but you have become quite the talk of the ton."

Thacea looked at her warily. "The gossip did travel quickly, didn't it?"

Caroline shrugged. "The ton has always found Marcus fascinating. They've gossiped about his parties and his exploits for years. Something so completely startling as his wedding is bound to turn heads."

Thacea reached for the heavy silver coffeepot, pouring out a cup for Caroline. "It disturbs me that people are so quick to assume the worst of Marcus. It's dreadfully unfair, you know."

Caroline raised her eyebrows and accepted her cup from Thacea. "That is most certainly the statement of a woman in love."

Thacea flushed and poured out her own cup, adding two spoonfuls of sugar. "Is it so painfully obvious?"

"So much so, you will undoubtedly be the buzz of every breakfast table in London after you join us at the Theater this evening. You are coming aren't you?"

Thacea nodded and dumped another spoonful of sugar into her cup. "Marcus especially wants to attend."

Caroline took a sip of her coffee. "Why especially?"

"I am unsure," Thacea said, thoughtfully adding a fourth spoonful of sugar to her coffee. "His moods are unreadable lately."

"Only lately?"

Thacea looked at her in surprise. "Despite what you might think, Caroline, I find Marcus relatively easy to understand most of the time."

Caroline swallowed another sip of her coffee. "You really do have a terrible case, don't you?"

"The worst."

"Then why," Caroline asked pointedly, "are you so upset today?"

Thacea dumped another spoonful of sugar in her coffee and stirred it. "Why would you think that?"

Caroline shot a knowing look at Thacea's coffee cup. "Because I've just seen you put your fifth spoonful of sugar into that coffee."

Thacea made a sound that was more of a sob than a laugh and dropped the cup to the table with a loud clatter. The syrupy brew splashed over the rim, and she scooped up a napkin from the tray and began dabbing at it more frantically than was necessary. "I don't know what is wrong with me today, Caroline. I've no reason whatsoever to be upset."

And then, to her absolute horror, she burst into tears. Caroline placed her cup on the table in alarm and hugged Thacea close, waiting patiently for her tears to subside. Only after Thacea had completely spent her tears did she manage to confide in Caroline her anger at Marcus's mother, her growing resentment of Madelyne and her lingering loneliness over her parents' death. It was only with the greatest deal of difficulty that she managed to avoid confessing her mounting anxiety over Raman. Finally, she pulled back from Caroline's comforting embrace and dabbed her eyes with one of the napkins, blowing her nose indelicately. "I'm sorry, Caroline. I'm certain you didn't expect any of this when you called on me this morning."

Caroline poured two fresh cups of coffee, handing one to Thacea. "Actually, it is exactly what I expected." Thacea looked at her in surprise and Caroline continued, "It was not so long ago that I was a young bride, far from home with few friends and no family." She squeezed Thacea's hand sympathetically. "You have been through a terrible ordeal. It is not at all surprising that you are feeling out of sorts. I am rather surprised you aren't completely done in."

Thacea waved her sodden handkerchief with a brief smile. "I'd say I'm a good bit done in at least."

Caroline laughed and took a sip of her coffee. "Now that we've gotten this out of the way, tell me how everything else is going. I understand you have Madame Drussard in a dither."

Thacea dabbed her eyes with the handkerchief, wiping away the lingering tears. She recounted the events of the previous day, ending with the story of Madame Drussard and the red silk nightdress.

At some point during the morning, Colonel Samuelson sent in a tray of sandwiches, and luncheon came and went with hardly a notice. In fact, Thacea had nearly forgotten her worries altogether when the door swung open and Harriet Brandton stormed into the drawing room wearing an obscenely ruffled gown of canary yellow, flanked by her three gentlemen friends and her yipping black poodle.

Twenty-nine

"How dare you!" Harriet stormed, advancing into the room like a ship in full sail. "How dare you send me that trite little message. I did not *ask* for an audience. I demanded one. And in the future, you would be wise to pay better heed."

Thacea set her empty cup down on the table with careful precision and slowly rose to her feet. "Lady Brandton," she said, ignoring Harriet's outburst, "may I introduce my friend, Lady Caroline Erridge?"

Caroline looked at Harriet in amusement. "It is a pleasure to meet you, Lady Brandton."

Harriet shot her a scathing look and turned her hostile gaze back to Thacea. "I have had all of this I will tolerate. I am the Dowager Countess of Brandtwood. As such, I have the right to expect certain privileges. How dare you treat me as an intruder in my son's home."

"It is my home," Thacea said firmly. "And I have made it quite clear you are welcome to stay as long as you wish."

Harriet sneered at her. "I do not want to stay, you stupid chit. Surely you must know why I am here."

Thacea felt her anger beginning to simmer into a low boil. "I assume you are here to ensure that your monthly allowance from the Brandtwood treasury will not be altered." She noticed with no little satisfaction that Sir David coughed nervously.

"Allowance! It is not an allowance. That money is my due. And Brandt will not simply cut the sum on your whim. You

cannot be so foolish as to believe you actually have any sway with him."

Thacea squared her shoulders. "Sway or not, he will honor my wishes in this, I assure you."

Harriet advanced another step, her face turning purple with rage. The poodle was running about her legs in an agitated fashion. Thacea did not miss the horrified expression on Sir David's face. Harriet's eyes narrowed. "You little slut!" she screamed. "You tricked him into marrying you, didn't you? What is it? Are you pregnant with his child? I pity you if you are. The babe will doubtless be as mean as he is."

Thacea's hands balled into fists. She met Harriet's angry stare with one of her own. "I will not honor that with an answer."

Harriet's lip turned into an ugly smile. "It must certainly be true, then. There is no other reason why he would have married you. You know, the two of you are the laughingstock of Society."

Thacea took several deep breaths and glared at Harriet. "I would not shriek too loudly about laughingstocks, Harriet. I do not parade about with a flock of young fops at my beck and call." She turned her angry gaze on the men standing behind Harriet. "How much does she have to pay you for your services?"

Sir David visibly blanched. Harriet let out a shriek of anger. The black poodle began barking. Harriet had to scream to be heard over the din. "You bitch! You conniving little bitch! You dare speak to me that way when you have married a walking disgrace? Brandt is shunned by Society because of his flagrant debauchery and behavior. He is nothing more than a filthy, profligate beast who is no doubt exercising his considerable experience with some overpainted doxy right now!"

Something inside of Thacea snapped. Before she fully realized what she was doing, she slapped Harriet across the face. Harriet's jaw dropped open. She stared at Thacea, momentarily stunned into silence. Thacea felt a wave of anger shoot through her. The poodle was barking so loudly she could hardly think straight, and for the moment, she was too angry to bother. "Do not ever," she shouted above the sound of the poodle, "say anything like that about my husband again. You are a mean-spirited, black-hearted, ignorant, overaged trollop, and I want you to take your mean comments, and your mean friends," she scooped up the yipping poodle, thrusting it at Harriet, "and your mean dog and *get out of my house!*"

Even the poodle seemed stunned by Thacea's outburst. He suddenly stopped barking, plummeting the room into an ominous silence. Harriet narrowed her gaze on Thacea and all but spit out, "Do not think I will fail to report this to Brandt."

Thacea was about to retort that she didn't particularly care whether she did so or not when his voice sounded from the doorway. "There is no need for that, Harriet. I have witnessed the entire scene from a very comfortable distance."

Thacea looked at him in horror, then rushed from the room with a muffled sob, too afraid to meet his eyes. She had no doubt she would find recrimination in their green depths.

She did not stop running until she reached the door of Madelyne's room. Her anger at Harriet was still racing through her in a rush of adrenaline. As she was quite certain Marcus would be furious with her over what she'd just done, she decided on impulse to finish the task she'd started. With a tiny curse, she threw open the door of Madelyne's room, not bothering to knock.

Madelyne looked up in surprise at the outburst. Her smile faded at the sight of Thacea's angry expression. She set down her needlework and rose to her feet, watching warily as Thacea stalked into the room.

"Sit down, Madelyne. I have something to say."

Madelyne promptly dropped back into her seat. Thacea paced about the room in agitation. "Marcus has been very good to you, Madelyne. You cannot deny that."

Madelyne shook her head.

"And in exchange for his kindness and concern, you have given him nothing in return. You continue to keep your silence, despite his efforts to cajole you out of it. You seem to have no intention of ever making your way in Society. Which leaves me to believe you desire nothing more out of life than to prey on Marcus's kind nature for the rest of your days."

She looked at Madelyne. The girl was looking at her in absolute shock. "Well, I won't have it! Too many people have used Marcus for their own gain for too long, and I won't have it. If you are nothing more than another in a long line of Marcus's family that sees no more worth in him than his control of the purse strings, then I want you out of this house!"

Madelyne had begun to cry, her eyes wide with shock. Thacea steeled herself not to relent. "I will not tolerate this any longer. Either you are well enough to end this ridiculous charade, or you are so ill that you belong in an institution. The choice is yours."

Madelyne buried her face in her hands and shook her head. "Very well," Thacea said, "I will ask Colonel Samuelson to make arrangements for your departure immediately."

She turned to leave and her fingers were on the knob when she stopped short at the sound of Madelyne's voice. "No, please, Thacea. You mustn't believe that of me."

Thacea turned around slowly and stared at Madelyne. "What else am I to believe?"

Madelyne sniffed and looked at her through watery eyes. "It is nothing like that, I swear it. I have only been so afraid."

Thacea advanced a few steps into the room. She would be unwise to back down until she got most of the story from Madelyne. Fear was an emotion she understood too well to remain entirely impassive, however. "You should have trusted Marcus enough to know he would not turn you out," she said quietly.

Madelyne shook her head. "It wasn't that. I was afraid of what might happen if he tried to introduce me into Society."

Thacea raised her eyebrows and walked back to Madelyne's side, sinking down into the chair across from her. "I want to hear the entire story, Madelyne. From the beginning. I will not allow Marcus to be hurt by this."

Madelyne nodded, clearly doing her best to stop crying. "When Mamma died, she sent me to London to find Marcus."

"I know that."

"I had nothing. No money, nothing to sell, nothing of value. I didn't know what to do."

Thacea imagined London would be a very frightening place for a young girl who'd spent most of her life in the country. "Go on," she said quietly.

"I used the last bit of money we had and bought a ticket on the coach for London. It was an awful trip. The coach was overcrowded, and there was a sick baby aboard who cried most of the way." She paused and shuddered a bit. "There was a very unpleasant man aboard too, and he kept saying things to me and trying to touch me. By the time we reached Bedford, I was terrified."

Madelyne wiped away a stray tear and sniffled. "We stopped at an inn for dinner, and I met Lord Martin Danbury. He was older, closer to Papa's age, and he seemed very nice. He asked me several questions and I . . . I told him about the trip, and the man in the carriage, and that I was on my way to London to find Marcus."

Thacea was beginning to have a grave suspicion about the direction of this story, and a new fear was developing that she would have to talk Marcus out of murdering Martin Danbury. "He was very sympathetic, I'm sure," she said cynically.

"He seemed so kind and understanding, I didn't even stop to think about the possible consequences of accepting when he offered me a ride in his carriage." She paused, her fingers twisting in the fabric of her skirt in an anxious fashion. "The remainder of the trip passed without mishap. It was not until we reached London that he . . ."

Madelyne's voice trailed off. Thacea squeezed her hand reassuringly. "You must tell me the rest, Madelyne."

She sniffed again, visibly trying to regain her composure. "He took me to a . . . a place where men purchase the favors of women. My father had described such a place to me once, and I recognized it immediately. I didn't become really terrified, though, until I heard him discussing how much of a price I would bring from a gentleman seeking the pleasures of an untouched girl." Madelyne's eyes filled with tears again and she looked at Thacea. "They were going to . . . to sell me, and then blackmail Marcus by threatening to expose me as his sister."

Thacea lost whatever shards remained of her anger and hugged Madelyne to her. "I was so terrified," Madelyne sobbed. "I didn't know what to do. So I ran into the street and kept running until I finally collapsed. It was raining that night, and I must have caught cold. I do not remember how I arrived at the workhouse. Only that Colonel Samuelson came to see me and he and Marcus brought me here."

Thacea stroked Madelyne's hair while she sobbed against her shoulder. When the girl finally seemed to calm a bit, she set her away and looked into her eyes. "Why didn't you tell us this before, Madelyne?"

She sniffed. "At first, I was afraid if I were well too soon, Marcus might turn me out." She didn't miss the glint in Thacea's eyes, and she shook her head. "Only at first. I was afraid he would resent me because of Papa."

Thacea waited for her to continue. Madelyne wiped her eyes with her handkerchief. "Then, when it became clear that he wanted to introduce me into Society, I was afraid. It was very likely that we would see Lord Danbury at some turn or another, and that he would still try to blackmail Marcus with what he knew about me. Then Peter Drake entered the picture and the entire thing has become a horrible mess."

She threw herself back into Thacea's arms. "I am so sorry, Thacea. I am so dreadfully sorry. I was so frightened, and I didn't know what else to do."

Thacea drew a deep breath and held Madelyne against her. "You have caused us a great deal of worry, Madelyne."

She nodded her head miserably. "I know."

"I believe you can begin to make amends now if you go and tell Marcus what you have told me."

Madelyne raised her head and looked at Thacea. "Do you think he will be angry?"

"He cares for you deeply, Madelyne. If you hold that close to your heart, I think it will make the telling very much easier."

Madelyne wiped at her eyes one more time and rose to her feet. "Will you come with me?"

Thacea shook her head sadly. "No. I believe you need to tell him alone. Besides, I have to begin moving my gowns." She pushed herself out of her chair and left Madelyne staring after her.

The short walk down the corridor seemed a mile long. When she finally reached her room, she was relieved to find Molly was nowhere about. She shut the door behind her and sank down in front of the fire with an exhausted sob. As soon as she finished crying, she would direct her attention to the wardrobe.

Thirty

Marcus exhaled a long, relieved sigh and mounted the stairs to his bedchamber, silently berating himself. He had behaved like an ass. Somewhere between the amused pride he'd felt when he had stood in the doorway of Thacea's drawing room and watched her tongue-whip his mother, and the nearly overwhelming flow of gratitude and warmth his talk with Madelyne had elicited, he had finally admitted the truth to himself. He was in love with his stubborn-to-the-soul, eccentric, high-spirited wife.

Having made the admission, he was amazed at the almost instantaneous relief he felt in his heart. He had fought the knowledge too long, loathed the thought of anyone, especially a woman, having that level of power over him. But he knew his heart was safe in her gentle hands, and with the dawning realization, his spirit soared.

Things suddenly seemed a great deal more settled to him. He no longer felt the driving need to set himself apart, holding the world at arm's length. Instead, Thacea had freed him from the shackles of fear. He longed for nothing more than to gather her close to his heart and tell her all the things welling up inside him.

He reached the top of the hall and turned toward her room, a carefree smile on his lips. He stopped to pluck a rose from a large bowl of flowers and grin at the young chambermaid busily polishing the hall table. "I'm sorry. Your name seems to have slipped my mind. What is it?"

The young woman looked up at him in surprise. Marcus

nearly laughed at the astonished look she gave him. He had not directly addressed a servant in his household for longer than he cared to remember. He'd probably scared her to death. She dropped a low curtsy and looked at him warily. "It's Mary Beth, your Lordship."

He nodded. "So it is. Mary Beth. As you are the only Mary Beth I know, you wouldn't think I would have so much difficulty remembering it, would you? Are you married?" he asked suddenly.

She evidently didn't have the slightest notion how to answer that, so she merely stared at him and nodded. He smiled. "Excellent. Your husband is obviously a very fortunate man. Anyway, I shall make every effort to remember your name in the future, I assure you."

Mary Beth curtsied again and looked at the rose in his hand. A bit nervously, she pulled another one from the bowl and handed it to him. "This one is nicer, your Lordship. Unless you particularly want that one."

Marcus made a great show of comparing the two roses before he handed her the one he'd originally pulled from the arrangement. "No. You are right. It is certainly the nicer rose. Do you happen to know if the Countess is in her chamber, Mary Beth?" he asked, casually twirling the stem of the rose between his fingers.

She nodded. "Her Ladyship entered her room nearly an hour ago, your Lordship. I haven't seen her come out."

Marcus raised his eyebrows. "Good God! You haven't been polishing this table all that time, have you?"

Mary Beth looked at him worriedly. "I know it seems a very long time, your Lordship, but . . ."

He held up his hand. "That's absurd. It certainly looks clean enough to me." She stared at him. He reached down and took the polishing rag from her hand, tucking it into her apron pocket. "Go find your husband, Mary Beth, and tell him I said you are to enjoy the rest of the afternoon."

"But, your Lordship, the table . . ."

"There are a great many things in life considerably more important than the thickness of polish on my hall tables. If anyone asks about the table, send them to me."

Mary Beth looked at him in astonishment. He strode purposefully toward Thacea's room. He knocked once on the door and waited until he heard her muffled reply. He opened the door and entered, finding her seated on the bed, her gowns strewn from one end of the chamber to the other.

Marcus leaned casually back against the door. "Are you having more trouble than usual deciding what to wear this evening, love?"

Thacea raised miserable eyes to his. He saw the telltale signs of her recent flood of tears. He had been right. He had been an ass. She shook her head and sniffed. "I am sorry this is taking me so long, Marcus. I should have finished by now."

Marcus advanced into the room, aware he was about to receive another lecture on Ardani marital customs. "Finished what?"

"Moving the gowns I'm going to keep down the hall."

He raised an eyebrow. "Won't it be very much more convenient to have your gowns here in your room?"

"This isn't my room anymore."

He nodded and sat down on the side of the bed. "I see."

She continued as if she hadn't heard him. "According to Ardani custom, when a wife shames her husband, she is moved from her chambers and banished to the concubine area of the harem."

"Ardani men keep wives and concubines?"

She looked at him in surprise. "Of course, Marcus. Why on earth would a man need more than five wives?"

He nodded gravely. He was having a devil of a time keeping his smile. "Why indeed?"

She wiped her sleeve across her eyes and continued to toy with the delicate fabric of a white silk dressing gown. "Anyway, I am aware that things are somewhat different between us. I mean, I am your only wife, after all."

"That is so."

"But nevertheless," she went on, ignoring his interruption, "I have still shamed you."

He leaned back on his hand and watched her closely. "I seem to have missed that part. You'd better explain it to me."

"You saw what happened with your mother."

He nodded, an amused glint sparkling in his eyes. "Yes."

She sniffed. "I should never have done that. Especially not in front of guests."

"They were her guests. Except Caroline, of course, and I think she rather enjoyed the entire episode."

"A wife should never insult her husband's mother. A man can have many wives, but he only has one mother."

Marcus couldn't bear it any longer. He started to laugh. "Suppose, however," he said, his eye twinkling with amusement, "that a man much prefers the company of his wife to the company of his mother?"

She looked at him in surprise. "That is for him to decide. Not his wife."

He nodded thoughtfully and tapped her chin with the rose. "Is that why you allowed my mother to stay in the house?"

She nodded miserably and accepted the rose. "Where did you get this?"

"Mary Beth gave it to me."

"Who on earth is Mary Beth?"

"One of the chambermaids. I suppose that's as close as I come to concubines." He lowered his face close to hers. "Are you jealous?"

Thacea shook her head. "No."

"Damn," he said, leaning back on the bed.

She looked at him curiously. "You are acting very strange, Marcus."

"I suppose I am at that."

"Are you angry with me?"

"Lord, no!"

"Then why are you acting so odd?"

He looked at the clock on the mantel. "Have you any idea

how late the hour is, sweet? If we don't get you ready, we will be late for the Theater."

She raised her eyebrows. "You still want me to accompany you?"

"Of course," he said, rising from the bed and striding toward the bathing closet. "I imagine you will want a bath," he called over his shoulder.

"Molly already had the water sent up," she said. She heard him testing the water with his fingers. She studied the rose. He was in quite the strangest mood, and she wasn't at all sure what to make of it. "Marcus?"

He walked out of the bathing closet drying his hand with a towel. "Yes, my Lady?"

"Did you speak with Madelyne?"

He reached the side of the bed where he pulled her to her feet. Her gowns pooled around them in a profusion of color. "Yes." He turned her around and began deftly undoing the buttons of her gown. "There are no words to express my gratitude for what you have done. I believe she will truly recover from the experience now."

His soft voice fanned across the sensitive skin of her nape. She shivered as his fingers brushed her spine. "What are you going to do about Lord Danbury?"

Marcus slid the last button free and pushed the gown from her shoulders. It puddled at her feet in a soft *whoosh*. "I'd very much like to call the bastard out and murder him," he said quietly. "But for the sake of Madelyne's reputation, I think it best to let well enough alone. I do not believe Danbury will dare cross me, and he'll pay the consequences if he does."

She nodded, barely noticing that Marcus had slid her chemise from her shoulders and was kneeling in front of her, lifting each of her feet to remove her stockings and shoes. "I was angry that Madelyne had not confided in you earlier," she said cautiously.

"She told me."

Thacea steadied her balance by placing one hand in his dark

hair. "She should have trusted you, Marcus. After all you have done for her, she should have trusted you."

He slid one stocking down the length of her leg. "She had much to lose, love. In light of the circumstances, and particularly in light of my reputation, she was reasonably frightened I might turn her out."

Thacea shook her head while he turned his attention to the other stocking. "You wouldn't have. She should have known that about you."

He removed the stocking and regarded her frankly. "The point is important to you, isn't it?"

She nodded. "You care for Madelyne a great deal. It was unjust of her not to trust you."

Marcus rose to his feet and smoothed a stray tendril of her hair off her forehead. "My father ran away with Madelyne's mother when I was barely ten years old," he said quietly. "I received one letter from him after he left."

Thacea looked at him in surprise. "I thought you never heard from him again."

"I never told anyone about the letter. I was twelve or thirteen by then. Madelyne was barely out of diapers. He told me in great detail what a beautiful child she was, and how much she looked like I had looked when I was her age." He sighed. "In the letter he begged me to consider Madelyne my sister and he promised he would do whatever he could to bring us together."

"You never heard from him again?" she asked quietly.

"No. In reflection, I believe he posted the letter because even then he feared for his health. I was only sixteen when my father died, and if his health had begun failing early, it was reasonable to assume he would want me to take care of Madelyne and her mother with the Brandtwood fortune."

"But you never knew where to reach them."

"He did not give me the address in the letter. I made several efforts to find them, but each time I came up empty-handed. I believe he left instructions with Madelyne's mother to contact me after his death and she refused to do so."

"So when Colonel Samuelson told you about Madelyne, you already knew."

"It would not have mattered. The resemblance is too striking for me to have doubted her story."

Thacea looked at him carefully. "Had she never spoken again, you would have kept her here forever, wouldn't you, Marcus?"

"I always believed Madelyne must be an extraordinarily special child for my father to have sacrificed all that he did for her."

Thacea felt the tears sting the back of her eyes at the simple statement. Behind the completely dispassionate explanation lay the desperate reasoning of a boy cast aside by his father on behalf of another child. "I should not have interfered in that either, Marcus," she said miserably. "It was between you and Madelyne, and I had no right to threaten to send her away."

Marcus finished undressing her and scooped her up in his arms. "On the contrary, darling. You love Madelyne. That gives you every right."

Thacea looked at him in surprise. "Marcus, what are you doing?"

"Giving you your bath," he replied, setting her on her feet inside the steamy bathing closet. He paused long enough to shed his jacket and roll back his sleeves before he picked her up once again and slowly lowered her into the hot water.

"Molly will be here soon. You needn't do this."

He knelt on one knee by the sunken tub and began pulling the pins from her hair. "I told Molly I would see to your needs this evening. She is spending her afternoon with Jake."

Thacea stared at him. "You really are acting very odd. Are you certain you are feeling all right?"

He threaded his fingers through her hair. "I cannot remember the last time I felt quite so well as I do this evening."

Thacea closed her eyes at the wonderful feel of his strong hands in her hair. The tension in her shoulders began to give way to her emotional exhaustion and the melting combination of Marcus's firm ministrations and the hot, scented bath. She barely realized he had finished washing her hair until she felt him wrap it gently in a towel. She tipped her head back against the tub and listened to Marcus quietly rustling about in her bedchamber. When he slipped into the water beside her and pulled her into the cradle of his arms, she sighed, pillowing her head on his chest.

There was nothing sensual in his touch. She melted against him, drawing comfort from the heat of his big body next to hers in the water. She had no idea how long Marcus held her, gently running the soap over her skin. And when he finally lifted her to her feet and rinsed her skin with cool, clean water, she swayed against him, her bones feeling like wax.

He kissed her softly and wrapped her in her velvet robe, arranging the lapels just so across her breasts. Thacea opened her eyes to meet his gaze. His eyes were limpid pools of green velvet, watching her so warmly, she felt a shiver run all the way to her toes. "Marcus, I . . ."

He covered her lips with his fingers and picked her up into his arms, carrying her back to her chamber. When he set her down on the small chair in front of her dressing table, her eyes met his in the mirror.

He held her gaze for several long seconds before tearing his eyes away and walking toward the hearth. "Are you cold, love?" he asked quietly, his voice sounding a bit odd.

Thacea noticed for the first time that he was still undressed from the bath he'd shared with her. Streams of water ran down his body, and she thought about telling him she wasn't a bit cold. "A little," she said instead.

He tossed two logs on the fire, then turned toward the connecting door that led to his room. "Do not move from that spot," he said softly. "I am going to fetch my robe."

Thacea stared at the door after he disappeared, wondering if her overwrought emotions were giving her hallucinations. Marcus's behavior had escalated beyond odd and was now bordering on bizarre. When he reappeared in the doorway clad in his black dressing gown, she followed his progress toward her with anxious eyes.

Marcus watched the changing emotions in her expressive eyes and damned himself. She was unused to this level of tenderness from him, or this level of attention, for that matter. Her wariness was clear in the dark stormy blue of her eyes. He smiled reassuringly and reached for one of her bone-handled brushes, gently unwrapping the towel from her hair. She stayed his hand. "Marcus, you are not going to brush my hair."

He looked at her closely. "Why ever not?"

"Well, you never . . . that is to say I . . . I don't know why not," she finished a little desperately. "It just seems out of place."

He dropped to one knee beside her and laid the brush down on her dressing table. Cradling her face in both his hands, he kissed her softly. "On the morning after my wedding," he said, lifting his head, "my bride told me a husband shows his love for his favorite wife by providing her with an opulent wardrobe, giving her the very finest chambers in his harem, by caring for her family if they are in need, and by tending to her personal needs." He paused. "Have I remembered it all correctly?"

She nodded. "Yes."

"Thus far, I have done my best to give you a wardrobe that will be the envy of London, you occupy the only room in the house that connects to mine, I have done what I could for your family by returning your treasured possession to you and by giving you my name." He stopped and looked at her meaningfully. "And now, I am seeking to tend to your personal needs."

Thacea felt her lower lip tremble and she stared at him. "Marcus, are you saying that you . . ."

He smiled at her softly. "I do not know that I can find a clearer way of telling my wife I love her," he said quietly.

Thacea threw her arms around his neck and launched herself at him with such force he toppled back onto the soft Aubusson carpet. He held her close to his chest and laughed. "I take this to mean, madam wife, that you are pleased with the notion."

She looked at him closely. "You are not teasing me, are you, Marcus? I couldn't bear it if you were."

He closed his eyes for a moment in silent anguish. When she

had asked him the night of their wedding if he loved her, he'd been painfully blunt. Completely wrong, but blunt. He was not surprised she was having difficulty believing him. He opened his eyes again and stared into hers. "I have never been more serious in my life, love. It may have taken me a very long time to realize it, but I do love you."

The tears gathered in her eyes. She buried her face against his neck. "Oh, Marcus."

He hugged her close. "I will admit I had planned a rather more appropriate setting than the floor of your bedroom for such a momentous pronouncement."

She lifted her head and swiped an arm across her eyes in the now familiar gesture he had come to adore. "There could not have been a better setting. I love you so much, Marcus. That is the only reason I so completely lost my temper today."

"I must confess, I cannot remember the last time I enjoyed myself more than I did this afternoon when I saw you berating my mother in the drawing room."

She looked at him in surprise. "I made a complete idiot out of myself."

He arched his neck up and kissed her lightly. "Ah, but you did it on my behalf. That is a perfect excuse."

She kissed him more thoroughly, sighing in pleasure when his tongue explored the full curve of her lips in a leisurely fashion. "Marcus, if you continue on this course of action, we will be late for the Theater."

He growled and rolled her to her back. "I think Sarah will forgive our tardiness."

When his hand tugged at the tie of her robe she giggled. "Marcus, there is a very comfortable bed only a few feet away."

He looked at her, his vivid green eyes suddenly serious. "I have waited a lifetime for you, darling. I cannot wait any longer."

Thacea decided that a plush Aubusson carpet was a rather enjoyable place to make love after all.

Thirty-one

Thacea rolled over in bed and inhaled a deep contented breath, releasing it on the barest whisper of a sigh. The sun had just made its way over the horizon, and the soft darkness of Marcus's bedroom was giving way to a warm orange glow. She opened her eyes and found him staring at her. "Good morning," she whispered.

"Good morning. I love you."

She smiled sleepily and snuggled closer to him. "It is no less pleasant to hear in the light of day, my Lord."

He kissed her softly. "Do you think I will get the same reaction if I try it later in the afternoon?"

She nodded. The crisp hairs on his chest tickled her face. "Most likely."

"Then I shall certainly make a note to do so."

She tipped her head back to look at him. "Do not be ridiculous, Marcus. We cannot spend the entire day locked in your bedroom."

He kissed her forehead. "I was thinking more along the lines of forever."

Thacea laughed and hugged him. "Your practical nature has always attracted me."

"Only my practicality?" he asked, a teasing note in his voice.

She smiled and ran her palm down the length of his chest, pausing when she reached his abdomen. "Among other things," she conceded.

He captured her hand, bringing it to his lips. "Then I see no reason whatsoever not to spend the rest of the day exploring in more detail what it is you most admire about my 'other things.' "

"After what happened at the Theater last night, I'm sure no one would be surprised."

Marcus paused. They had indeed been late for the Theater, not arriving until the start of the second act. Their tardiness had earned little more from the other inhabitants of the box, however, than an amused grin from Sarah. It had taken nearly twenty minutes before Thacea had relaxed enough to recognize what was happening throughout the rest of the Theater.

Upon their arrival, they had instantly become the focus of attention. Marcus had not been unduly surprised. He had known an enormous amount of gossip had surrounded their wedding and the subsequent goings-on at Brandtwood House. News of his mother's eviction had no doubt reached every drawing room and salon in London by late that afternoon. It had merely added fuel to the rapidly spreading fire of rumor the ton was already enjoying about his venture into the marital state.

He had been about London far too long not to know what the rumors were. There were doubtless those who believed Thacea had forced him to marry her, while a good many others were inclined to argue he must have forced her, as no sensible woman would have had him. As had been his practice all his life, he had dismissed the entire matter as beneath his attention. It had not occurred to him, however, how deeply the scrutiny would affect Thacea.

Until they had reached the Theater that night, he had not realized that she hadn't set foot from Brandtwood House since their marriage and the difficult circumstances surrounding it. Except for her visit with Caroline, she had foregone contact with Society. Marcus had simply not considered the fact that Thacea had no knowledge of the level of speculation surrounding George's disappearance, nor the insinuating innuendos regarding her immediate subsequent marriage. Her background as a diplomatic wife, and particularly in light of the seclusion George had enforced on her, would not have adequately prepared her for the inevitable.

When they settled in the box, he had immediately been aware of the unnatural hush over the Theater. He had become seriously worried about what her reaction might be for the first time since they'd left the house. Carefully, he had draped his arm across the back of her chair in a casual gesture of possessiveness that clearly stated his territorial intention to protect her. Thacea had looked at him in surprise, whispering beneath her breath that such a public show of affection was unheard-of. Marcus had not relented.

Nearly twenty minutes of the anxious buzzing amid the occupants of the Theater had passed before Thacea began to realize what was happening. Caroline was looking at her worriedly. Marcus tightened his grip on the back of her chair. Slowly, she had turned her eyes from the opera on stage and scanned the rest of the audience. An audible gasp had sounded. Fans began to flutter furiously in vain attempts to hide speculative eyes and cynical glances. Thacea's eyes had traveled from one box to the next, her gaze resting only briefly on the more blatantly curious occupants. When she had finally completed her inspection of the Theater, her eyes had met Marcus's.

He had been watching her intently as she surveyed the crowd. He had not realized he had forgotten to breathe until her amused gaze had collided with his. Her lips had tugged into the faintest hint of a smile as she leaned forward, placing her hand on his thigh. She had been aware, he knew, that every eye in the Theater, save perhaps those of the performers, was focused on them. "My Lord," she had said, her voice barely above a whisper. "It seems we are the cause of much curiosity this evening."

Marcus had nodded, carefully gauging her mood. "So we are."

"Do you think they are wondering why I married you?"

He had lifted an eyebrow and regarded her frankly. "A good number of them are, yes. It is odd enough for them to see me in the company of someone as respected as the Duke of Albrick, but the fact that I am here with my wife," his voice had lowered another notch, "and that I am so obviously enamored of her is nearly more shock than they can withstand."

Something had sparked in her eyes. "I imagine a good number of your former lovers are here."

He hadn't missed the slightly waspish tone in her heated comment. "I have only ever loved one, darling."

At the warm promise in his voice, her eyes had softened a bit. "In the desert," she had whispered, "a man must always be careful to clearly mark the boundaries of his territory. Raiders and bandits are common, and a man can only defend what is clearly his."

"Are you feeling a bit primitive this evening, love?"

She had nodded. To his complete surprise, she leaned forward and passionately kissed him in full view of the entire Theater. He couldn't clearly remember whether he'd simply imagined it, or if the singing on the stage had suddenly stopped. Thacea had finally ended the kiss and settled back into the curve of his arm, seemingly oblivious to the sudden roar of conversation that erupted in the crowded Theater.

At the memory, Marcus ran his hand along the graceful curve of his wife's hip. "You did behave rather shamelessly, love. I am certain we are the focus of every breakfast table and lovers' tryst in London by now."

Thacea sighed. "Do you mind horribly much, Marcus?"

"Not in the least! And may I say that you are welcome to démarche your territorial claims in that manner any time you choose."

Thacea kissed him lingeringly on his warm mouth. "I suppose," she said, turning her face back against his chest, "I should apologize to Sarah."

A deep chuckle rumbled in Marcus's chest. "I believe Sarah was delighted to have played hostess to such a scandalous display."

Thacea absently twirled her fingers in the hair on his chest. "Even so, I would not wish to . . ."

A sudden sharp knock at the door interrupted her statement. Marcus lifted his head from the pillow and frowned. "Damn!" he said quietly.

The knock sounded with more insistence. He scowled again. "This had better be important."

Thacea expected him to walk to the door. She dove under the sheets in mortification when he called, "Enter!"

"Marcus!" she squeaked.

He looked at her and smiled as his valet walked toward the bed. He did, however, tug the sheets up to her neck, unwilling to push the notions of propriety too far. Thacea could not help but notice that his valet was unconcerned by her presence in Marcus's bed and wondered a little jealously how many other women he'd seen in just this spot.

"What do you want?" Marcus asked shortly.

"Mr. Langford," Thacea whispered in his ear insistently. "His name is Mr. Langford." When Marcus didn't respond, she pinched him. He pinched her back.

Mr. Langford had reached Marcus's side of the bed and he handed him a small parcel. "I am sorry to disturb you, your Lordship, but this arrived just a few moments ago. Your instructions were very clear on the matter."

Marcus picked up the parcel and looked at it closely, his eyes narrowing. "Yes, so they were."

The valet inclined his head in a show of deference and turned to leave. "And, Langford," Marcus called out, earning a startled glance from the man who had just heard his employer use his name for the first time in twenty years.

"Yes, your Lordship?"

"Lock the door on your way out."

Thacea would have sworn a smile twitched at the corner of the valet's mouth. She groaned in embarrassment when the door clicked shut behind him. "Marcus, how could you?"

He looked at her innocently. "I thought you wanted me to call him by his name."

"I cannot believe you asked him to lock the door."

"I was merely stating my territorial claims, love."

Thacea glared at him. He kissed her softly on the forehead before he sat up in bed and swung his feet to the floor. She heard him pull back the paper on the small parcel and she scrambled to her knees to look over his shoulder. She pressed against his back and watched as he unwrapped the tiny package. "What is it?" she asked.

"I am unsure. I hope it is something that will give us some indication of Worthingham's whereabouts. I have a rather crushing desire to leave London and go on a very long, very intensive honeymoon." He paused and looked at her meaningfully before returning his attention to the parcel. "And I am vastly irritated that George Worthingham is presently depriving me of the pleasure. I . . ." Marcus's voice trailed off and his hand stilled on the parcel.

Thacea could not see what it contained before he pushed the paper back into place. "What is it, Marcus?"

"Darling, where is the gown you wore last night?" he asked quietly.

"My gown? What has my gown to do with anything?"

"Is it in your wardrobe?" he asked.

"Yes. Molly hung it last night before I joined you here. Marcus, what . . ."

"Would you fetch it for me, please?"

His voice was strangely quiet, and Thacea looked at him anxiously. "Is something wrong, Marcus?"

"Just fetch the gown, love. Please."

She scooted from the bed and scooped up his discarded shirt, slipping it on as she walked quickly across the carpet to her room. Inside, she pulled open the wardrobe and located the pale blue gown she'd worn to the Theater. She pulled it down and sped back to Marcus's room, an anxious frown marring her forehead. "Here it is."

He slowly pulled back the paper on the parcel and removed a scrap of fabric that perfectly matched the fabric of the gown. Thacea frowned at it. "What is it, Marcus?" He ignored her and slowly turned the gown over in his hands until he found a place where the hem had been cut. The scrap in his hand fitted perfectly into the hole in the gown. Thacea gasped. Someone had been close enough to her the previous evening to cut the hem of her gown and she'd never even known it. Her hands flew to her mouth and she stared at the ruined gown in horror.

Marcus raised his eyes to hers, torn between a deep, consuming rage and gut-wrenching fear. How could he have allowed this to happen? She'd never left his side the previous evening. That this had been perpetrated beneath his cautious, watchful gaze caused a curl of fear to work its way down to his toes. "Is it possible," he said quietly, "that the gown was cut before you dressed yesterday evening?"

She shook her head. "Don't you remember? It arrived from Madame Drussard's yesterday afternoon. Molly had just finished pressing it when you finally let her in the room to do my hair."

He nodded. "What about after? Could it have been cut last night?"

"Molly always locks my door on the way out, per your instructions. No one could have entered my chamber without a key."

He looked at her closely. "Then it must have happened while we were out. I want you to think very carefully, love. This is urgently important. Do you remember seeing anyone, anything that you recall as being at all suspicious or out of place?"

She shook her head, a shiver running up her spine. Marcus placed the gown on the bed beside him and pulled her into the V of his thighs, holding her close against him. "Damn it! I should never have allowed this to happen."

His voice was rife with self-recrimination and she threaded her fingers through his hair. "It is not your fault, Marcus."

"You were with me all evening. How could I have allowed this to occur beneath my very nose?"

Something he said triggered Thacea's memory and she shook her head slightly. "No! No, I was not with you all evening. Don't you remember? When we prepared to leave, there was a mixup with the carriage queue. You had to go and find Nathan and have him bring the carriage 'round."

Marcus did remember. The crush in front of the Theater had been worse than usual. He and Aiden had left Sarah, Caroline, and Thacea with Jace while they'd gone in search of their carriages. "But you were with Jace."

She nodded. "I know, but the crowd was so heavy." She gasped suddenly. "Marcus, the man! I completely forgot."

His eyes narrowed. "What man?"

She looked at him. "He was dark, eastern-looking. I wouldn't have noticed him at all except that someone bumped against me and I dropped my reticule. He was standing nearby and he retrieved it for me from the pavement. I thought he looked at me rather oddly, but Nathan was already driving 'round with the carriage, and when I looked again, he had vanished."

Marcus nodded and rose to his feet, hugging her against him. "I need to go out for a while, darling. I will double the protection at the house, but all the same, I would ask that you stay in today."

She nodded against his chest. "I am afraid, Marcus."

"I know, and I am sorry. I swear to you, though, we are doing all we can."

She nodded miserably. "I know."

"Would you like me to send word to Sarah and Caroline and see if they will call on you today?"

She shook her head. "I think I will spend the day with Madelyne. I have yet to apologize to her for my behavior yesterday."

Marcus set her slightly away from him and looked at her closely. "I will not allow anything to happen to you. You do believe me."

"I trust you, Marcus. I love you."

He kissed her long and hard before he walked her to the connecting passage that separated their rooms. "Why don't you go back to bed for a while, love? If you have Molly bring you up some heated milk, perhaps you can sleep a while longer."

"I would not be able to sleep." She tugged a bit nervously at the hem of his shirt, where it reached her thighs. "Please be quick about it, Marcus. I will not feel safe again until you return."

Her words echoed over and over again in his head in cadence to the sharp clatter of his horses' hooves on the pavement. He had ordered his phaeton, knowing he could travel through the early morning traffic in London a good bit faster than he would be able to in his carriage.

After he had shut the door that connected his room with Thacea's, he'd called his valet and made quick work of dressing. He had penned a brief note to Aiden Brickston and sent it ahead, arriving at Albrick House only a few minutes later.

"Good morning, your Lordship," the butler said, taking Marcus's greatcoat. "His Grace is waiting for you in the library."

Marcus nodded shortly and strode through the great foyer, pausing only briefly while a footman swung open the door of the library.

"Brandt!" Aiden called. "What the devil has happened?"

Marcus walked quickly across the room and handed the scrap of fabric to Aiden, acknowledging Jace's presence with a brief nod. "This," he said. "It was delivered to me this morning. It is a piece of fabric from the hem of the gown Thacea wore last night to the Theater."

Jace's breath came out in a low hiss. "Good God!"

Aiden looked at it thoughtfully. "Are you certain it was cut last night? Not before, or after?"

Marcus nodded. "I am certain. The only thing Thacea remembers as being out of sorts was a man who retrieved her reticule for her while we were looking for the carriages."

Jace nodded thoughtfully. "Yes, I remember that chap. He was an odd-looking fellow. Very dark."

"That is what Thacea remembers as well."

Aiden sat down behind his desk. "Sit down, Brandt. I have something I hope may shed some light on the situation."

Marcus sat down abruptly and stared at Aiden. "Have you found Worthingham?"

Aiden handed him a piece of paper. "I received this only a few hours ago. It's from Frederick Arnheim. He's my most reliable source."

Marcus took the piece of paper and studied it carefully. "George is in Prussia! What the hell for?"

Jace looked at Aiden in surprise. "It is rather odd, Brick."

Aiden nodded. "Frederick gives a relatively detailed accounting of George's whereabouts. Evidently, a colleague of his from India is ambassador there. According to Arnheim, George is in Thuringia mourning the death of his beloved wife."

Marcus stared at Aiden. "Surely he knows he'll be caught in a lie like that."

"Eventually, but I suspect he hopes to procure passage to Ardahan prior to his day of reckoning. He was no doubt too low on funds to reach the Black Sea after his precipitous departure from London."

Marcus tapped the paper against his knee in agitation. "Then why is he threatening Thacea? *How* is he threatening her? You said yourself he does not have the financial foundation to conduct such an intrigue."

Jace said, "That is so. But there can be no doubt, particularly after what happened last night, that she is at least being followed, if not threatened."

Aiden nodded in agreement. "That is true. Right now, however, I think it will be best if we simply bide our time. I am not convinced George is behind this," he said, waving the tiny scrap of fabric.

Marcus looked at him in surprise. "Who else would it be?"

"I have a number of theories on that. Nothing solid, however.

Just give me another few days, Brandt, and I think everything will become much clearer."

Marcus slammed his palm on the desk. "Damn it, Brick! This is not a game of hunt and snare. Thacea's life may be in danger. You cannot expect me to simply sit about and wait for Worthingham's next move."

Aiden shook his head. "I don't. On the other hand, if we move now, we will only succeed in trapping George once again. If there is a broader issue, as I suspect there is, it will have escaped our notice, and he'll be ready to strike again when we are least suspecting it." He paused. "No. I would rather wait a few more days and maintain our guard for hope of capturing the larger prize. In the interim, Arnheim will not allow Worthingham to slip through his fingers."

Marcus drew several deep breaths to calm his temper. He had never before experienced this gut-twisting anxiety, and the waiting was nearly driving him mad. "I do not like this," he said quietly.

Aiden looked at him closely. "I am certain you don't. In truth, neither do I, but surely you can see reason, Brandt."

He paused, carefully turning the problem over in his head. Aiden was right, of course, that if they closed the net on George now, his fellow conspirators would not suffer the consequences. It would be unwise to act too quickly when a few more days could end the matter entirely. He nodded slowly. "All right. I will wait for seventy-two more hours. If we do not know anything by then, I am taking my wife and leaving London." He paused. "Forever, if necessary. I will not be a prisoner in my own home. Especially not to the likes of George Worthingham."

Marcus rose from his chair and turned to leave, giving Aiden a final look. "Be quick about the matter, Brick," he said, repeating Thacea's words from earlier that morning. "I will not feel safe until it is resolved."

Thirty-two

The tension in Brandtwood House mounted over the next three days. After his meeting with Aiden and Jace, Marcus was somber and preoccupied a good bit of the time. Thacea did her best to lighten his mood, but he only seemed unreserved and completely at his ease when they made love.

Her own anxiety was beginning to build with each passing day. The longer she remained cooped up inside Brandtwood House, the more frayed her nerves were. She had spent as much time as possible with Madelyne, getting to know the girl all over again as she began to fully recover from the shock and fear of her early days in London. Peter Drake called on Madelyne regularly, and Thacea was beginning to suspect that Marcus would soon have to deal with Peter when he offered for Madelyne's hand.

Peter had been a great comfort to her during the anxious days that passed. He had remained in place at George's town house, sorting through his personal effects for some clue to his whereabouts and the broader implications of his contacts in London and abroad. He would occasionally bring her small items from the house he thought she might find interesting, but her growing anxiety, coupled with her now constant fear for Raman's safety, soon diminished even the simplest measure of Peter's warm concern.

As for Marcus, he was nearly out of his mind with worry. The thought that Thacea might suddenly be snatched from him had added a new dimension to his fear, and he would lay awake at night, holding her close to his heart with something akin to desperation. Without realizing he had done so, he had become dependent on her presence for his life's breath. As the days slipped by, he became nearly frantic in his need to expunge the pending threat. His natural inclination was to suffocate her with his protection, never letting her out of sight, and the impossibility of it made him all the more irritable. He was sitting in his library brooding over the matter one afternoon when he was disturbed by Peter Drake. "Drake! I should have thought you would be upstairs paying suit to my sister."

Peter looked at him gravely and lowered himself into the chair across from Marcus. "I would much rather, I assure you."

"What is wrong, Peter?" He was struck by a sudden thought and he leaned forward abruptly. "Thacea. Is she . . ."

Peter held up his hand. "Calm down, Brandt. She is fine so far as I know. It is a personal matter I wish to discuss with you."

Marcus sagged back in his chair in relief. "If you have come to offer for my sister you can go to hell, Drake."

Peter looked at him wryly. "Thank you for the compliment. But no, that is not my reason for coming here. Not today at any rate."

Marcus studied him warily. "What is the matter, Peter?"

Peter leaned forward, a heavy sheaf of papers in his hand. "I have been systematically searching through George Worthingham's possessions for some indication of what he may be about."

Marcus nodded, suddenly alert. "Have you found something?"

Peter sighed, his fingers tightening on the sheaf of papers. "As your friend, I am honor-bound to give you this. I would give half of what I own to spare you from it, though."

A trickle of dread worked it's way up Marcus's spine and he took the heavy sheaf from Peter. "What is it?"

Peter rose from his chair and picked up a decanter of brandy, carrying it back to the table next to Marcus. "I will leave you to that discovery." He waved the bottle briefly before he set it down. "This is all I know to do for you now."

Peter turned and left the room. Marcus stared in silent dread at the sheaf of papers. That they contained his fate, he had no doubt. He barely resisted the urge to toss them into the fire without surveying the contents. He was filled with a sudden, almost overwhelming, desire to find Thacea and sink himself deep into her warmth, begging her to reassure him and soothe the fear that had now become a consuming fire within him.

But instead, he opened the sheaf of papers and began to read.

Thacea was on her way down the staircase when she heard Marcus's enraged shout followed by the distinct sound of shattering glass. She jumped in alarm and hurried down the polished staircase, racing for the library door. She nearly collided with Peter Drake on her way. "Peter! What has happened? What is wrong with Marcus?"

He looked at her angrily, his fingers biting into the skin of her upper arms. "How the bloody hell could you?" he shouted, his eyes glittering with rage. "You heartless little shrew, how could you have done this to him?"

Thacea looked at him in shock. "Peter, what are you talking about?" She looked worriedly at the door when another loud crash sounded from inside the library. "Get out of my way, Peter," she said, pushing past him.

Peter did not release his hold on her upper arm. "He will very likely kill you if you go in there. I am not uncertain that you deserve it."

Her jaw dropped open. She looked at him in shock. "Unhand me, Peter. I am going inside."

He dropped her arm with a brief disgusted curse. "I have done my duty by warning you. I will not interfere."

Thacea barely heard the last comment as she swung open the library door and stared at Marcus. He was standing in the center of the room, his back to the door. His shoulders were rising and falling with the force of his angry breaths. Scattered about on the floor were hundreds of pieces of paper. The splintering sounds had evidently come from the two liquor decanters he had hurled into the fireplace. He held the third loosely in his fingers and lifted it to his lips for a long swallow.

Thacea softly shut the door behind her. "Marcus?" she said quietly.

He spun around and stared at her, his green eyes narrowing to dangerous slits. "Madam wife!" he said cynically. "Have you come to survey the rest of my ruin?"

She looked at him anxiously. "Marcus, what has happened?"

He laughed a short, humorless laugh. "I have only just learned the level of your betrayal, Madam."

"My betrayal?"

Marcus kicked at the papers on the floor sending them scattering about in a flutter. "Drake has just done me the very great service of showing me your correspondence with your Ardani lover. Very touching stuff, my love."

She looked at him in shock. "My lover? Marcus, what are you talking about?"

He swallowed another long swig of the liquor, before he met her gaze again. "George must have intercepted your letters before you posted them. They are all here. You cannot lie to me."

Thacea looked at the white papers in confusion, suddenly recognizing her own handwriting. She stooped to the floor and picked up a handful. "My letters to Raman! George never posted them." Marcus uttered a fluent stream of obscenities and she looked at him anxiously. "Oh, Marcus, you thought . . ."

He cut her off. "I thought nothing. I have seen them with my own eyes and drawn my own conclusions."

Thacea rose to her feet, the letters still clutched in her hand. "No, Marcus. It isn't . . ."

"Tell me one thing," he went on relentlessly, "was I merely another part of the plot?"

She shook her head frantically. "Marcus, you don't understand. You must listen to me."

"I am through listening," he roared. "Have you forgotten who I am? Any member of the ton will tell you I will not hesitate to wring your pretty little neck for this. I am the ruthless, 'Wicked Earl.' "

She shook her head. "Marcus, stop! Let me explain."

He took a menacing step toward her. "There is nothing to explain," he said coldly. "You used Worthingham in an attempt to get your lover safely out of Ardahan. It is all in your letters."

"No!"

"And when the attempt failed, you turned to me in his stead. I had more money, and considerably more prestige. It was only a matter of time before you were able to conspire a means by which the two of you could be together."

"Marcus, no!" she cried, her voice a strangled sob. "You don't understand."

His laugh was so cold it sent shivers down her spine. "No," he said quietly. "I most certainly do not understand." He paused and swallowed another long drink of liquor, leveling his gaze on her. His eyes were chips of green ice within the haggard plane of his face. "I do not understand how I could have been so asinine as to have trusted you. I do not understand how I could have allowed you to play me for a fool."

"Marcus . . ."

"And," he went on relentlessly, "I cannot understand how I could have been so damned hot for your delicious little body that I believed every one of your lies."

Thacea shook her head and stared at him. "Stop this, Marcus. It isn't what you think at all. You must let me explain."

Something primitive flared in the depths of his eyes and she watched as the corner of his mouth turned into a cynical, bitter smile. "You cannot explain, madam, because I can no longer stand the sight of you. Get out." The command was lethally quiet.

"Marcus . . ."

"Get out!" he roared, and she turned and fled the library, running past Peter, through the wide foyer and out the front door of Brandtwood House, never once considering the consequences until a carriage door flew open, and a gentleman grabbed her from behind and tossed her inside. Before she thought to scream, a dark, wet cloth covered her face and she lapsed into unconsciousness.

Thirty-three

Marcus lounged back in his chair and watched blearily as the last of the white letters disintegrated into ash and the dismal day gave way to evening. After Thacea had fled from the library, he had locked the door and attempted to forget his deep sense of betrayal with the aid of a well-aged bottle of brandy. When the spirits had failed him, he'd begun reading and burning each of the letters in turn. The more he read, the deeper his resentment grew. In the long, soul-wrenching letters, Thacea had poured out her heart to this young man. She shared with him intimate details about her life Marcus had never been privy to. She recounted tales of her childhood, which she had spent, at least in part, with this young man at her side. And as Marcus read on, he hated him more passionately for possessing Thacea's heart when he did not.

He had been surprised when he came to the letters that talked about his own relationship with Thacea. She spoke of him always in a manner that confused Marcus, making him desperately want to believe that she no longer loved her Ardani friend. But the evidence was too damning, and he had tossed the last letter onto the flames and watched it flare briefly before crumpling beneath the heat of the fire.

Marcus did not even realize it had grown dark outside until he heard the key turn in the door of the library and Madelyne walked in. He glared at her. "Leave me be, Madelyne."

She glared back. "No. Peter has told me what happened. You

have been in here long enough." She paused, wrinkling her nose at the strong smell of liquor in the room. "And you've had more than enough to drink."

He frowned. "Drake had no right to tell you anything. I'll beat his bloody hide for that."

Madelyne stooped and picked up Marcus's jacket where he'd dropped it on the floor. "No you won't, and you will shut up and listen to me."

He looked at her in surprise. "Who the bloody hell do you think you are?"

"I am your sister," she snapped, sitting down in the chair across from him. "And despite your rather considerable efforts to be so disagreeable, I care for you."

Marcus uttered an ugly obscenity and sank back against his chair. "Then leave me in peace, Madelyne."

She shook her head. "I won't. I want you to listen very carefully to what I have to say, Marcus, because at the rate you are going, your very life may depend on it."

He glared at her. "Don't be overdramatic."

She picked up the empty bottle of brandy and plunked it on the table between them. "I am not. Peter told me about the letters. He also told me about your reaction."

"Did he tell you Thacea has been merely using me like some lapdog so hot for her favors that I would agree to bring her lover safely to England?" He smiled bitterly at her stunned expression. "If you are shocked, imagine how I must have felt."

Madelyne glared at him. "Marcus, you do not really believe that?"

He swept a hand in the direction of the fireplace. "I have just burned the evidence of it."

"Did Thacea not tell you there was a reasonable explanation?"

He laughed shortly. "She tried to, yes. It was another lie."

"Are you certain?"

"Of course I'm certain," he snapped.

"Do you not owe her more than that?"

Marcus stared at her. "What the hell do you mean?"

"She had heard a great many things about you as well, Marcus. She was never so quick to credit them as true."

"Those were nothing more than trite societal rumors with little or no foundation in reality."

Madelyne waved her hand in disgust. "Was she not the woman who created a scene at Caroline Erridge's ball when your reputation was attacked? Was she not the same woman who defended your honor to the Dowager Countess? Consider what she has done for you, Marcus. You are a reasonable man."

He stared at her. "You do not understand. You didn't see the letters."

She shook her head. "I do not have to see them. She has showed you at every turn in the lane that she loves you, Marcus. Despite whatever evidence there may have been, you should have trusted her." Madelyne placed her small hand on Marcus's knee. "Do you not believe she would have trusted you in return?"

"It is not the same!"

"Isn't it? You expected everything from her, Marcus, and she gave it to you. Nothing made her angrier than the thought that the people around you were using you toward their own gain. Her heart truly beat with yours, and now you would throw away your last, best chance for happiness because of a stack of papers extruded from the desk of a man you would have happily murdered less than a fortnight ago! If you do it, you will get precisely what you deserve."

Marcus stared at her, a tiny shaft of doubt working its way into his muddled senses. She could not possibly be right. There couldn't be an explanation for all those letters. Could there? Certain questionable phrases he had read began to work their way into his memory. He knew, God but he knew, what an amazingly passionate woman Thacea was. But the letters were not florid love letters filled with the showy words of one lover to another. Could it be that she had not deceived him after all?

Had he listened to her explanation, might it have resolved the contradictions he had seen within the pages of those letters?

His eyes settled suddenly on a stray envelope where it rested on the floor and he scooped it up, staring at her delicate, feminine script on the front. With some difficulty, his eyes focused on the name: RAMAN BEN HAMID. His heart thudded sickeningly and he looked at Madelyne, his eyes filled with anxiety. "Where is she?" he asked quietly.

"She is gone," Madelyne said.

Marcus suddenly felt violently ill. He struggled visibly for control, his face draining of color. "Did she go to Caroline, or Sarah perhaps?"

"I don't know," Madelyne said. "She ran from the house after you shouted her down this afternoon. No one has seen her since. Unless you have gone completely daft, you will clean yourself up and go in search of her immediately. Frankly, if I were she, I might very well refuse to take you back." Madelyne got up and left him alone in the library.

Marcus's hand tightened on the envelope until it crumpled beneath his fingers. "I will beg her if I have to," he said quietly. He levered himself out of his chair with some effort and walked toward the door with a growing sense of urgency. She should not have rushed from the house in such a rash fashion, particularly not when he suspected Worthingham had been behind her strange encounter at the Theater. If someone were watching her, it would have been too easy to . . . He squelched the thought with determination. She had most certainly gone to Caroline's. If she had been upset, it was the first place she would have turned. He would wash and change quickly and then make his way to Caroline Erridge's town house, where he would do whatever necessary to win her back. Madelyne was right, he had been a fool.

He was halfway to the door when it crashed open, nearly falling off its hinges, and quite the largest man he'd ever seen burst into the library, flanked by a young man of about eighteen and two more giants of equal proportion Marcus decided he had most certainly had too much to drink.

All four of the strangers were in an almost shocking state of undress, their loose-fitting pantaloons and tunics reminiscent of the white riding clothes Thacea had worn at Sedgewood. They wore yellow leather boots, tied below the knee with red suede strips. Tucked into the top of each boot was a gold-handled dagger. The three giants were bare-chested. Their tunics lay open to their waists, and Marcus saw several ominous-looking firearms tucked beneath the folds of the tunics into the waistbands of their pantaloons. The young man stepped forward and glared at Marcus, his stormy blue eyes glinting in the firelight. "I am Raman ben Hamid, Supreme Sultan of Ardahan. What the bloody hell have you done with my sister?"

Marcus was torn between a sudden desire to embrace the young man, and a now pressing urgency to find Thacea and beg her forgiveness. He stared at Raman a full twenty seconds before he realized Aiden and Jace had walked into the room. Aiden jiggled the library door where it hung precariously on one hinge and grinned. "I see you two have met. Friendly chap, isn't he, Brandt?"

Marcus looked at Aiden in astonishment. "My God! What is going on?"

Aiden advanced into the room, carefully weaving his way between the three giants. "This is Raman ben Hamid. He is Thacea's brother. Until recently, he has been in hiding from his uncle."

Marcus's head began to whirl and he started to regret the rather enormous amount of brandy he had consumed. "Why the devil haven't I heard of this before?"

Raman regarded him insolently. "My uncle believed I died in the accident with my parents. I have been in the desert with my nomadic relatives for four years. No one was supposed to know I was still alive."

Marcus felt the first traces of rage begin to race through his bloodstream. He took a menacing step toward Raman, ignoring the answering steps from the three giants. The pieces of the puzzle were beginning to fall into place. "You arrogant little swine! Do you have any idea what your sister has suffered to keep your secret?"

Jace stepped forward and placed a restraining hand on Marcus's arm. "Calm down, Brandt. His Royal Highness disappeared into the desert before Thacea was married. Until three weeks ago, he believed her to be safe, if unhappy, within the confines of his uncle's palace."

Raman nodded. "It was not until I received a communication from the British War Department that I knew my sister had been abducted to England in a plot conceived by my uncle."

Marcus took a deep breath and stared at Aiden. "You are behind this," he said.

Aiden nodded. "I knew Raman's father. He was our Black Sea contact during the campaign against Napoleon. When I heard Thacea talking about her life in Ardahan at Sedgewood, my suspicions were piqued when she never mentioned her brother's name. I had heard, as had the rest of the world, that he was killed in the accident. Something did not ring true to me, however, and I asked my contact at the War Department to look into the matter. When we found Raman, we explained to him what had happened. Britain owed his family a great debt for their part in the war, and as way of repayment, we promptly ensured he had the strength to seize the throne he rightly holds."

Raman glared at Marcus. "Now that you have your explanation, I want to know what you have done with my sister!"

Marcus looked expectantly at Jace. "She is with Caroline," he said quietly.

Jace shook his head. "No. I met Aiden here. I have not seen her since we left the Theater last night."

"Oh my God!" Marcus said, sinking down into the leather chair. "Oh my God!"

"What's wrong, Brandt?" Aiden asked, his voice sharp.

"We quarreled earlier this afternoon," Marcus said tonelessly. "When she left the house, I assumed she would go to Caroline or Sarah." He raised his head and looked at Aiden, his green eyes strangely haunted. "She is gone."

"Damn it!" Raman turned on his heel and delivered a stream of orders to his three giants in rapid-fire Ardani. They hurried from the room and he looked back at Marcus, his eyes a focused blaze of anger. "I know where she is, but we will have to hurry. We must reach Dover before morning or it will be too late."

Marcus looked at him in surprise. "Dover! What the bloody hell makes you think she's in Dover?"

Raman made a small, aggravated gesture with his hand. "I have had her followed since I first received notice from England."

"What!" Aiden's voice sounded like a pistol report.

Raman looked at him closely. "The English are not the only ones with well-developed intelligence. I immediately sent a communiqué to London contacting my man here and telling him to keep careful watch on Thacea until I could come fetch her. I suspected my uncle would try something like this."

"The man at the Theater!" Jace said. "He was yours."

"Yes," Raman said. "I had instructed him to remain in the background unless he sensed Thacea's life was in danger. I feared that my uncle would abduct her once again and use her to force me to surrender the throne. Benzan told me about the incident with Thacea's gown. I am not surprised that my uncle would stoop to such measures to terrorize her. He's always been a coward."

Marcus was beginning to feel panicked. "You believe your uncle's men are holding her in Dover?"

Raman nodded. "I met with Benzan when I arrived in London. He told me my uncle's men have a ship waiting in port at Dover. If they abducted her this afternoon, that is where they have taken her. They are waiting until morning to embark."

Marcus dragged a hand through his hair, aware of a sick feeling in the pit of his stomach. "What makes you think they have not sailed already?"

Raman smiled. "An Ardani never leaves port at night. It is unwise."

Marcus exhaled a deep breath. "Is that another of your father's proverbs?" he asked quietly.

Raman shrugged and looked at him in amusement. "I see my sister has been spinning my father's fanciful cobwebs for you. No, it hasn't anything to do with sage advice. Ardahan is a desert country. We do not have sophisticated navigational equipment on our ships. It is too difficult to steer the proper course in the dark."

The three giant men that protected Raman had set about procuring horses for their ride to Dover. Jace and Aiden had left Brandtwood House to make arrangements of their own, and finally, three-quarters of an hour later, the seven men rendezvoused at the edge of London and set a harried pace for Dover.

It was a moonless night, and Marcus spent the long hours of the ride fighting a growing sense of fear that threatened to overwhelm him completely. He refused to consider that Raman might be wrong and Thacea would not be in Dover. But any other number of considerations worked their way into his mind, and he rode on relentlessly, his heart beating in cadence to the galloping drive of his horse.

And somewhere on that dark, harrowing ride, he finally relinquished all that remained of his bitterness and hurt and clung with an almost desperate urgency to hope. He vowed in the silence of the night that he would never again be a victim of his past transgression. That he would never again let his fears and his disappointments rule his actions and govern his heart. Thacea had loved him, and by doing so, she had set him free from a lifetime of scandal and pain. Only when he won her back would he be completely whole.

Thacea sat in the bottom of the creaking ship and fought a fresh surge of tears. When she had awakened and found her hands bound behind her back, and the dirty burlap gag forced into her mouth, she had feared that George had managed to abduct her. But presently, sounds and smells became familiar. The pungent odor of eastern tobacco had carried on the sea air, and she recognized the great kegs of wine that lined the cabin as a favorite among Ardani men. As best she could determine, the ship was not moving, and she had struggled for a while with the cords that bound her hands, before giving up the effort in vain. In the darkened cabin, something scuttled across her shoe and she recognized the squeaks of ships' rats in the corners of the cabin.

She suppressed a violent shudder and strained her ears, trying to catch snatches of the conversation she heard above. When she heard her uncle's name, she gasped, finally aware of the implications of her plight. If her uncle abducted her and carried her back to Ardahan, she would not survive the experience.

Her heart turned suddenly to Marcus and she thought sadly of the scene in the library. The pain in his eyes had haunted her even in her unconscious state, and she was gripped with a sudden rush of fear. If she did not return to him, he would never know the truth. He would very likely go to his grave believing that Raman had been her lover, and that she'd run to him when she left Brandtwood House. She twisted frantically at the knots on her wrists, ignoring the sharp twinge of pain when the rope cut her skin.

The rats were scuttling about her feet, and she had a sudden memory of something her father had told her. Taking a deep breath, she scooted around on the floor until she found the spigot on one of the kegs of the sweet Ardani wine. Ardani wine, she knew, had an inordinately high sugar content, making it easier to store in extremely high temperatures. She pushed up against the keg and twisted the spigot, letting the sticky, warm wine pour over her wrists and hands before she shut it off once more.

It took every ounce of will she possessed, but she scooted herself around and worked her way toward the sound of the gnawing, squeaking rats. Finally, she felt them sniffing at her fingers and closed her eyes, feeling suddenly sick when they began chewing on the wine-soaked ropes. Her father had been right. The smell of her skin had prevented them from gnawing at her fingers, but the sweet wine and the jute rope had proved too great a temptation.

Marcus stared at the ship and felt something between a wild surge of relief and a rush of anger race through his body. His natural inclination was to simply race on board, doing away with everyone and anyone in his path until he found Thacea. Aiden constrained him with a hand on his shoulder. "We cannot risk her safety, Brandt."

Marcus nodded and studied him carefully. "I want this over with quickly."

Raman laughed and rode forward. "I do not travel with these three hulking brutes all for show, you know. They are exceedingly well trained as my bodyguards. And if my report from Benzan is correct, we should have no great difficulty taking his men."

Aiden nodded and looked at the docked ship. "All right. There are two planks. I suggest Jace, Raman, and I board aft and Marcus and our three giant friends board at the stern. They are probably holding her in one of the cabins. Marcus can begin searching the ship while we hold them at bay."

Raman relayed the orders in Ardani and the three men nodded in understanding. "Remember," Aiden continued, "our objective is to get Thacea off the ship safely. We do not want to cause an international incident." He looked meaningfully at Raman. "What you do to your uncle's men is your affair. On behalf of England, I am only here for Lady Brandton."

Raman nodded shortly and issued another stream of orders to his three bodyguards. In unison, the three let out a bloodcurdling cry and galloped their mounts toward the ship. "Damn," Aiden said beneath his breath, charging after Raman. "There is nothing like having the element of surprise on your side."

* * *

Thacea heard the scream and went absolutely still, listening intently. When the noise erupted above her, she knew she had not been wrong, and she began to frantically tug at the ropes. She didn't doubt for a minute that Marcus was up there attempting some idiotic act of heroism, and if he didn't die in the attempt, she might very well kill him herself.

The sound of clashing swords and pistol shots pierced the night air and she tugged on the ropes with all her strength, her heart soaring when she heard Marcus's deep voice call her name. She felt the ropes give way slightly as she pulled at them, and despite the warm trickle of blood where they'd cut her skin, she redoubled her efforts.

There was a great deal of shouting above deck, and she smelled the pungent odor of gunpowder that clogged the still night air. Marcus's voice had grown closer, and she was certain she heard his footsteps above her head. She realized she must be in a trap beneath one of the cabins, and she was beginning to feel slightly panicked lest he not find her. With a final tug, she yanked her hands free of the ropes and clutched at the gag in her mouth. Spitting away the dirty burlap, she screamed his name and began frantically pulling at the ties around her ankles.

As suddenly as the knots gave way, he was there, pulling her against his heart in an almost desperate manner, holding her to him as if his life depended on it. "My God!" he breathed into her hair. "My God! Are you all right?"

Thacea clung to him. "Yes. Yes. Marcus, it was not what you thought, I swear it."

He heard the tiny exclamation despite the muffling sound of her sobs, and drew a deep breath filled with self-recrimination. There would be time for apologies later however, as the conflict still raged above them. He heard Aiden's voice calling out several short orders and he lifted Thacea in his arms and walked toward the door. She was clinging to his shirt, sobbing almost uncontrollably, and he held her to him, whispering soft, comforting words in her ear. He walked up the rotting stairs and forced open the hidden door that led to the captain's cabin. If Thacea had not called out to him, he would have missed the door in his hasty search of the cabin.

There were several more gunshots from above deck, followed by a repeat of the bloodcurdling scream Raman's three giants had issued earlier, which in turn was followed by a sudden cessation of activity that was deafening in its intensity.

Marcus looked down at Thacea and smiled, walking purposefully toward the upper deck. When he emerged with her in his arms, Aiden and Jace stood looking warily at the rather large piles of bodies that littered the deck. Raman was standing with his back to the sea, flanked by his three bodyguards. Aiden saw Marcus first and let out an audible sigh of relief.

Raman turned his head, his white teeth glinting in the darkness, and strode across the deck to where Marcus stood, still holding Thacea. Marcus felt a sudden fear claw at him as he remembered Raman's words about taking Thacea back to Ardahan with him. He vowed silently that no matter what it cost him, he would not force her to stay. He was not beyond begging, however.

Raman walked over and touched his sister's shoulder. She looked up at him with a strangled exclamation and twisted free of Marcus's arms, flinging herself against Raman. "You are safe! Oh, Raman. You are safe!"

Marcus tried to ignore the dull ache in his heart as he watched Raman gather his sister close. "I am," the young man said quietly. "Due in large part to you. You must believe I had no way of knowing what you suffered on my behalf."

Thacea shook her head, her hands roaming restlessly over his shoulders and arms, assuring herself he was truly well. "It doesn't matter, Raman. None of it matters."

Raman sighed and rocked her against his chest. "I will never be able to repay the debt I owe you."

She sniffed, her tears flowing freely. "There is no debt. I did what I did because I love you. You do not owe me anything for that."

"Nevertheless," he said quietly. "I know I have been a bit tardy about it, but I have come to take you home, darling."

Thacea stepped back and looked at him in surprise. Raman smiled. "I sit on the throne of Ardahan now. It is my wish that you return home with me."

Thacea looked back at Marcus, her eyes meeting his in the pale glow. He was watching her closely, the pained look in his green eyes visible even in the darkness. She knew because she loved him—knew because she herself had suffered when she'd believed Madelyne alone held his heart—that he was suffering untold agonies. In the space of those few seconds, Marcus's eyes pleaded with her. She was free to go with Raman, she knew. Marcus would not force her to stay in England.

Make whatever choice you will, he seemed to be saying, *but God help me, I will beg you if I have to.* In the silence, she heard him as clearly as if he had spoken the words. Marcus evidently still did not understand there was no choice for her. There never would be again. She would spend the next sixty years or so making him sure of it. She smiled at him briefly and turned back to Raman, raising up on her toes to softly kiss his cheek.

Marcus was watching her, his stomach nearly turned inside out. Only a few seconds had passed since his gaze had met hers, but in that short space of time, he'd felt his world crash in around him. Something akin to physical pain shot through him when she kissed her brother. *My God! I have lost her!* The words were roaring in his head, but no sooner had he accepted their truth than she kissed her brother's other cheek and stepped away, lacing her fingers into Marcus's. He nearly fainted.

"Oh, Raman," she said quietly. "I *am* home."

Thirty-four

Marcus rolled over in bed, a sudden fear gripping him. When his arm landed across his wife's waist, he sighed in relief and pulled her close against him. It had not been a dream. She had returned to Brandtwood House with him. Her brother Raman was sleeping in one of the guest bedrooms, with his three bulky friends on the carpet, but at the moment Marcus didn't at all care about any of it. What mattered most was that she was here, safe in his arms, close to his heart. He felt Thacea's soft fingers trace a lazy pattern on his arm and he smiled. "I thought you would be asleep by now," he said.

She shook her head and turned over to look at him. It had been nearly three o'clock in the morning by the time they'd returned to Brandtwood House and all the explanations had been made. Marcus had suggested they stay in an inn at Dover as the hour was so late, but Thacea had insisted on returning home with him. He had been more than happy to accommodate her, anxious to have her within the security of his home once more. He had promised himself on the ride back that as soon as she felt up to the journey, he would take her to his estate at Brandton Woods, where they would chart out their honeymoon.

"I was only thinking, Marcus," she said quietly.

He reached up and brushed her hair away from her forehead, kissing her lightly. "About what?"

"Do you know why I came to see you in the library this afternoon?"

Marcus closed his eyes briefly at the anguished memory. "I know that I will never be through apologizing for my behavior and begging for your forgiveness. I should have trusted you, my love. I should never have doubted you. That I nearly lost you will haunt me for the rest of my days."

She covered his lips with her fingers. "It is an old quarrel, Marcus. I am done with it. Had I confided in you about Raman earlier, it would have been avoided."

He shrugged. "You were afraid. It was understandable."

She nodded. "You were afraid too. It was also understandable."

Marcus sighed and rubbed his hand lovingly along the curve of her rib cage. Dear God, but he loved this woman. "So why did you come to the library this afternoon?"

She smiled it him. "It was something Peter gave me yesterday. I had not taken the time to read it until this morning."

"Not another of Drake's revelations," he groaned.

Thacea giggled. "Marcus, do you remember when you told me you didn't like children?"

He looked at her in surprise. "On our wedding night?"

She nodded.

"Yes," he said carefully.

"Is that really true?"

He shrugged. "I have never given the matter much thought. As it is not an issue between us, it is not particularly important."

She looked at him. "But would you like to have a baby? If we could, I mean?"

A sudden picture of her carrying his child, holding the babe to her breast to suckle surged into his mind and he felt his heartbeat quicken. Yes, he would like it very much. He would like it very much indeed. But the fact that Thacea could not bear children did not make him love her any less. It was that he sought to convey. "It is a hypothetical question, love. I have already said I will not be heartbroken if we do not have children. You are all I need."

She traced a pattern on his chest. "But would you like to have a baby?" she insisted.

At the moment, he could deny her nothing. "If it were possible, then yes, I admit I find the notion of having you bear my children almost breathtaking in its effect on me. But you are not to worry about it. Nothing else is of importance as long as I have you with me. Do you understand?"

She smiled it him. "Oh, I'm not worried about it. I'm not worried at all."

He looked at her curiously. "What are you trying to say, love?"

Thacea snuggled close against him and kissed his chest. "Only that one of the things Peter brought me from George's desk was his physician's report. He had to have one, you know, to satisfy the Foreign Office's requirements."

Marcus held his breath in wary anticipation. "You read the report yesterday?" he asked, schooling his voice carefully.

"Um-hmm." She tipped her head back to smile at him, tears glistening in her eyes. "Oh, Marcus, it wasn't I that could not bear children. George was impotent! He lied about that, too."

Marcus smiled, an unexpected surge of joy shooting through him. He had never done anything, he knew, to deserve what he had been given, but he would spend the rest of his days making himself worthy of the gift. He rolled over, trapping her beneath the weight of his chest, and smiled at her. "Are you telling me you believe we will have children after all?"

She nodded. "I see absolutely no reason why not, and while it's far too soon to know anything," she said quietly, "my monthly is late."

Marcus grinned. "Then as your husband, I recommend we get started on this project immediately."

She linked her hands behind his neck and smiled back. "As your wife, my Lord, I would say we are already well past an excellent start."

Marcus kissed her and finally lifted his head, his eyes suddenly intense, all traces of humor gone from their green depths.

"I will never get enough of you, Thacea. I am bound to you so long as I shall live."

She shook her head and kissed his chin. "No, Marcus. Neither of us is bound. All I ever wanted was to set you free."

Dear friends,

Every book, it seems, is a story in a story. SCANDAL'S CAPTIVE is no different. I first noticed Marcus Brandton in the pages of THE PROMISE—my first historical romance. He was standing at a ball, where the ever friendly Caroline Erridge warned her friends away from him. That fascinated me. Why did she react so strongly? At the time, I had no idea.

Then, as romantic heroes are want to do, he appeared again in the pages of A MATTER OF HONOR. This time, he forced himself on to the railway station platform as Josiah Brickston's godfather. For the life of me, I couldn't figure out what brought on the transformation. I didn't want to like him. I TRIED not to like him. But he was an insistent sort, even before he started talking on paper.

I was in the midst of a great personal crisis when I wrote this book, and I suppose it shows in the person of Marcus Brandton. He struck me as a desolate sort, friendless, embittered, alone. This book is about his salvation—his transformation from the mean-spirited man in THE PROMISE to the benevolent godfather in A MATTER OF HONOR.

He gave me fits, I'll admit. But he made me stronger in the process. I'd be interested to hear your opinion. You can reach me at 101 E. Holly Ave., Ste. 3, Sterling, VA 20164. Email neesa@fls.infi.net, or visit my website at http://www.shirenet.com/nhart

Best wishes,

Mandalyn Kaye,
aka Neesa Hart

P.S. If you enjoyed this book, I hope you will also look for SCOTTISH MAGIC, an anthology I participated in with Elizabeth Ann Michaels, Stobie Piel and Hannah Howell; and for PRICELESS, my recent historical romance from Ballantine Books.